NOV 20 2015

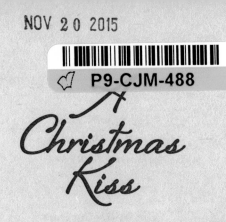

P9-CJM-488

A Christmas Kiss

NAPA COUNTY LIBRARY
580 COOMBS STREET
NAPA, CA 94559

Also by Deborah Fletcher Mello

The Sweetest Thing
Craving Temptation
Playing With Fire

Also by Regina Hart

Trinity Falls
Harmony Cabins
Wishing Lake
Mystic Park

Published by Dafina Books

A Christmas Kiss

CELESTE O. NORFLEET
REGINA HART
DEBORAH FLETCHER MELLO

Dafina
BOOKS

Kensington Publishing Corp.

http://www.kensingtonbooks.com

To the extent that the image or images on the cover of this book depict a person or persons, such person or persons are merely models, and are not intended to portray any character or characters featured in the book.

DAFINA BOOKS are published by

Kensington Publishing Corp.
119 West 40th Street
New York, NY 10018

Copyright © 2015 by Kensington Publishing Corp.
"Sealed With a Kiss" copyright © 2015 by Celeste O. Norfleet
"Mistletoe Lane" copyright © 2015 by Regina Hart
"His Christmas Gifts" copyright © 2015 by Deborah Fletcher Mello

All rights reserved. No part of this book may be reproduced in any form or by any means without the prior written consent of the Publisher, excepting brief quotes used in reviews.

If you purchased this book without a cover, you should be aware that this book is stolen property. It was reported as "unsold and destroyed" to the Publisher and neither the Author nor the Publisher has received any payment for this "stripped book."

All Kensington Titles, Imprints, and Distributed Lines are available at special quantity discounts for bulk purchases for sales promotions, premiums, fund-raising, and educational or institutional use. Special book excerpts or customized printings can also be created to fit specific needs. For details, write or phone the office of the Kensington special sales manager: Kensington Publishing Corp., 119 West 40th Street, New York, NY 10018, attn: Special Sales Department, Phone: 1-800-221-2647.

Dafina and the Dafina logo Reg. U.S. Pat. & TM Off.

ISBN-13: 978-1-4967-0050-6
ISBN-10: 1-4967-0050-3
First Kensington Mass Market Edition: October 2015

eISBN-13: 978-1-4967-0051-3
eISBN-10: 1-4967-0051-1
First Kensington Electronic Edition: October 2015

10 9 8 7 6 5 4 3 2 1

Printed in the United States of America

Contents

Sealed With a Kiss   1
CELESTE O. NORFLEET

Mistletoe Lane   115
REGINA HART

His Christmas Gifts   229
DEBORAH FLETCHER MELLO

Sealed With a Kiss

❧❧❧❧❧

CELESTE O. NORFLEET

Chapter 1

~ VISIT STILES BED & BREAKFAST
THIS HOLIDAY SEASON ~

RELAX IN COMFORT AND TREAT YOUR SENSES TO THE SOUNDS OF HOLIDAY MUSIC, THE WARM, WELCOMING GLOW FROM THE FIREPLACE, AND THE SIGHTS AND SMELLS OF THE HOLIDAY SEASON. SIP OUR SPECIAL HOLIDAY CIDER, HOT SPICED TEAS OR OUR FAMOUS HOMEMADE LEMONADE. AS YOU UNWIND, ENJOY A STRESS-FREE HOLIDAY SEASON BEGINNING WITH THE FESTIVAL OF LIGHTS JAMBOREE, AND THEN STAY FOR A WEEKLONG HOLIDAY CELEBRATION ENDING WITH HAYDEN'S ANNUAL HOLIDAY PARADE— FEATURING A SPECIAL SURPRISE GRAND MARSHAL.

Carmen Stiles stopped typing and read the copy she'd just written. Yes, it made sense. Yes, it was accurate, but it didn't take a literary maven to know it was horrible. She grimaced, then glanced over at the time displayed on the monitor. The short holiday blurb for the local newspaper that was supposed to be due earlier that day was turning into a major mental undertaking.

For the last few hours she'd been repeating the cycle of writing, editing, rewriting, re-editing and getting nowhere. What should have taken fifteen minutes at most, had taken all afternoon. At this rate, she'd be sitting in front of the computer the rest of the evening.

Frustrated, she turned her attention to incoming emails. After reading through and replying when needed, she checked the bed-and-breakfast's website and then confirmed the last three New Year's holiday reservations. Then, having run out of valid excuses, she went back to the blurb, knowing that Thomas Ford, the head of the town's council, would be asking for it any minute.

She sighed. She didn't often procrastinate, particularly when it came to the family-owned bed-and-breakfast. But since it was only a few days before Christmas and they'd been sold out for the last six weeks, it seemed pointless to invite guests to stay when there were no rooms available. Still, her mother had promised the town council a blurb, so . . .

She sat up straight, tried to be more attentive, and read the copy again. It sounded even worse than before. She slouched. "Ugh. Even I wouldn't want to stay here after reading this," she grumbled as she leaned her elbow on the front counter and her chin in the palm of her hand. She looked around the open foyer for inspiration.

As with the rest of the Stiles Bed and Breakfast, the foyer was elaborately decorated for the holiday season—Christmas trees, candle glowing lanterns, twinkling lights, evergreen, fresh poinsettia plants, berry and fur holiday wreaths, nutcrackers and an array of holiday favorites. They even had a sprig of fresh mistletoe, which she avoided standing under like the plague. So one would think writing a short holiday blurb would be a breeze. But it wasn't, at least not for her.

Her shoulders slumped. The holiday season always made her anxious. She knew how important it was to the family business, and she'd tried her hardest to make everything so perfect this year. She wanted to make her mother and father proud. But today, like the last few days, had been nearly impossible. Earlier, the microwave broke, then a guest bumped into the twelve-foot Christmas tree and knocked it over, breaking some of her favorite glass ornaments, the Christmas lights hanging from the back of the house fell down, and the attic roof started leaking again. And that was all just this morning. So, if one more thing happened . . .

Just then an email from Thomas Ford popped up. The subject title was, *HOLIDAY BLURB NEEDED ASAP!!* She didn't bother opening it.

"That's it, I give up." Carmen pressed and held the delete button for the sixth time that evening. Why her mother insisted on making gingerbread cookies this late in the evening instead of writing this was beyond her. She looked at the blank screen and shook her head woefully.

Just then she saw her mother walk by humming a classic holiday tune and carrying a huge bouquet of white flowers. Carmen smiled in cunning delight. "Mom . . ." she began sweetly.

"Yes, honey," Marion Stiles said as she continued to the marble table in the center of the open foyer. She placed the bouquet down beside the antique vase already in the center of the table. "I just love monochromatic flowers in winter floral displays. Chrysanthemums, hydrangea, paperwhites, orchids, and just the perfect touch of green with eucalyptus and fur sprigs right from the Christmas tree. "They're beautiful, don't you think?" Marion said.

"Yes, they're beautiful. So, Mom, I need you to write the blurb for the newspaper, okay."

"Carmen, you were supposed to take care of that hours ago."

"I know, but writing it seems kind of pointless since we're completely booked up until after the New Year anyway."

Marion fanned out the flowers on the table. "The blurb should be about the bed-and-breakfast, but also it should bring people to Hayden. So write about Hayden's quaint small-town ambiance, the friendly residents, and how our family bed-and-breakfast is the perfect holiday setting. And yes, even though we're fully booked, you know how people love to stop by just to enjoy our holiday decorations and the amazing waterfront view of the town. Plus . . ."

"See, you're so much better at writing this, so I think you should be the one to . . ."

"Carmen, this is your hometown and Christmas in Hayden, Georgia, is beyond amazing, you know that. Inspiration is all around you with the festival of lights celebrations, the ice sculptures and gingerbread house contests, the giant Christmas tree-lighting ceremony in the center of town, the spectacular holiday parade and . . ."

An email notification popped up on the computer screen and, knowing her mother was only just starting one of her long holiday pep talks, Carmen opened and read the email. "Hmmm, this can't be right," she muttered to herself. She stared at the computer screen and shook her head. "Why would he cancel his reservation? Mom, have you heard anything about this?" she asked.

"About what, honey?" Marion asked as she picked up a large white hydrangea blossom, trimmed the lower leaves, and then stuck it in the water-soaked Oasis floral foam in the bottom of the holiday vase.

"I just got an email from Senator Alistair Harrison. He cancelled his reservation. He's the town's grand marshal for the holiday parade. As a matter of fact, I expected him to have checked in by now. So why would he cancel? Do you know if he's staying someplace else in town?"

"He canceled because he's not the grand marshal anymore," Marion said while trimming the leaves from another bloom.

"What? When did this happen?" Carmen asked as she walked over to stand beside her mother at the table. She picked up a stripped bloom and arranged it in the vase. "I thought everybody was excited to have him as grand marshal this year. Why would they make a change this late? The parade is in a few days."

Marion handed Carmen another large bloom to stick into the oasis. "Alistair was the council's second choice. He understood when we told him. And, to tell you the truth, I think he was happily relieved. You know his daughter and son-in-law just had another child and he really wanted to be with them this holiday season."

"Fine so who is the town council's first choice?"

"Dean Everett."

Carmen stopped and looked at her mother. "Dean Everett."

"Yes, he's agreed to be the grand marshal this year. He'll be great. He was always my first choice."

"Oh God, no. Mom, please tell me this is another one of your really, really bad jokes."

"Of course it's not a joke. Dean Everett is finally coming home for the holidays," Marion said proudly.

"Dean? Why him of all people? Whose idea was it?"

"Mine. I've suggested him every year, but he always declines because of his schedule. And well, there were still a few naysayers, but I changed their minds. He's coming and I, for one, am thrilled. And he's also agreed to come to stay with us here rather than in town."

Carmen put the flower down, then walked away shaking her head. "No. No. No. He can't stay here. That's impossible. We're booked."

"You know very well the town council has a room on hold for the parade's grand marshal. It's tradition."

"No, tradition or not, he still can't stay here."

"Carmen Marie Stiles, I have never known you to get this upset over anything, especially not a guest," Marion said, placing a long-stemmed flower into the vase.

"You don't understand."

"You're right. I don't understand. Since this place was founded by your great-great-grandfather over a hundred years ago, the Stiles Family Bed and Breakfast has always opened its doors to any and everybody, and that includes Dean Everett."

Carmen knew the history of the Stiles residence better than anyone. It was ingrained into her heart as far back as she could remember. A member of the Stiles family had always owned this place, and always would, and she knew it.

"Honestly, I don't understand. You haven't seen Dean since the day he graduated from high school. I thought you'd be happy he was coming home for the holidays, delighted even. It's been ten years."

"Mom, why would you think anyone in the town would be delighted he's coming back? You know everybody in this town hated Dean."

"Oh, don't exaggerate, Carmen. Nobody hated Dean."

"Fine, they despised and ostracized him nonstop. Most of the town labeled him a menace, a troublemaker, and likely to be in jail by the age of nineteen, remember? It was almost a public holiday when he left town. Thomas Ford did everything he could to get rid of him. He even started a petition to have him kicked out of school. The day Dean left town, he threw a party."

"You know as well as I nobody took that petition seriously, especially not Dean. And as for the party, Tom threw it for his daughter, Rachel, who was graduating high school with Dean."

"Yeah, right, that's what he told everybody else, but Rachel told me differently. And you know Dad hated him. That's why he was always so hard on him."

"Carmen, your father didn't hate Dean. As a matter of fact, he really liked and admired him."

"What? No, Dad never liked me hanging around Dean."

Marion nodded. "True, but the reason he seemed hard on Dean was because he knew how much you liked him. He didn't want Dean turning you away from here, from the family business."

"That makes no sense."

"It did to your father. Dean made no bones about wanting to leave Hayden. And even though you were just a grade behind him, your father was afraid you'd run away and go with him when he left."

Carmen shuddered. She didn't respond. That's exactly what was supposed to happen. The day Dean left town, he had asked her to go with him and she'd agreed, but then she couldn't. "Mom, you're on the town council. Why didn't you tell me he had been invited?"

"I've been inviting him to come back for years. But he always declined because of a scheduling conflict. But this year he said there might be an opening in his schedule. That's why we had the posters read, 'a special guest.' Dean's assistant just confirmed this morning."

Carmen shook her head, exasperated.

"Carmen, he's your friend," Marion insisted.

"Correction, he *was* my friend," she emphasized, "and that was a very long time ago." She went back to helping her mother with the flowers. "I haven't heard from him in years."

"And whose fault is that?" Carmen didn't respond. She had deliberately avoided Dean for years. "Well, be that as it may," Marion continued, "Dean is coming home and I, for one, will be happy to see him again. He was always a nice young man, and you know he's done very well for himself. CEO and president of his own very successful software company is a remarkable achievement. And now I saw he's selling his company to one of the top ten Fortune 500 companies. If that happens he's going to be worth some outrageously obscene amount of money. Imagine that."

Carman looked at her mother. "And how do you know this?"

"I read the Internet," Marion said smugly.

"Yeah, apparently, and that's what I'm afraid of."

Marion laughed then smiled slyly. "You know, Dean is also gorgeous and sexy. So you know those gold-digging women are going to be all over him."

"Sexy? Mom!" Carmen said, surprised by her mother's bold assertion.

"What? I told you, I read the Internet. I'm connected to social media and I have lots of friends there. Dean is one of them. He's gorgeous, rich, and, as some well-informed websites put it, he's sexy as hell."

"Mom, I am not having this conversation with you."

Marion shrugged off. "The whole world is crushing on him and, if I remember correctly, you had a bit of a crush on him too, didn't you?"

"No."

"No?" Marion repeated, then looked at her daughter, knowing better.

"Don't start, Mom."

"Start what?"

"I'm serious, no meddling," Carmen warned, giving her mother a stern expression meant to remind her of the last time she'd meddled in Carmen's personal life.

"What? When have I ever intentionally interfered in your personal life?"

Carmen stopped what she was doing and just stared at her mother. "You are kidding me, right? How can you even ask that question? You signed me up to an online dating site, without my knowledge. I still get emails from that craziness. Then we went out to dinner, which turned out to be a speed-dating event, and then there's the ad you put in the newspaper a few months ago."

Marion opened her mouth to defend herself and then closed it instantly. "Fine, but for the record, the

newspaper ad was for the Valentine's special and I
needed a grand prize and you were it," Marion said.

"Whatever, just no interfering," Carmen clarified.

"Of course not, I wouldn't think of it," Marion agreed.

"Good. Thank you." Carmen took a deep relieved
breath. "Also, the news says that Dean is merging his
company, not selling it."

Marion nodded. "You're right, that's exactly what
the news says."

"And you know the only reason the town council
really wants him here is because they say he's looking
to move his new company headquarters to the East
Coast," Carmen said. "They need him and his company
here."

"How do you know that?" her mother asked.

"I read the Internet too," she said as she picked up
a few more blooms and tucked them into the vase as
the moment between them fell silent. She began to
think about Dean and what her mother had said.
There was no denying it. She'd seem pictures of Dean
over the years. She was right about everything. "All
right, fine," she suddenly relented out of the blue. Her
mother looked up at her, obviously wondering about
her sudden outburst. "I give in, he is gorgeous."

Marion smiled. "And . . . ?"

Carmen shook her head and sighed. "I can't believe
I'm talking about this with my mother."

"And . . . ?" Marion insisted.

"Fine. He's also sexy as hell," Carmen added, repeating her mother's earlier words. An instant later, they
looked at each other and giggled like schoolgirls. Then
her curiosity got the best of her. "Okay. So, when does
the big event happen? When is Dean actually getting
here, the day of the parade?" Carmen asked.

Marion looked up and smiled warmly. "Dean, you're here, right on time. Welcome back home," Marion said happily.

Carmen froze. There was no way her mother's bad joking skills were this convincing. She watched in astonishment as her mother walked around her, looking toward the front door.

"Hello, Mrs. Stiles. It's good to be home. You look amazing, as always," he said.

Chapter 2

Dean Everett had been on the phone for the last thirty miles. Before that he'd flown across the country, spending most of his time in videoconference with his attorneys and assistants. The sale of his company was going well and was nearly complete. As a result, key members of his inner team had been fielding phone calls and questions nonstop from entrepreneurs, financial managers, investors, acquisitions specialists, and financiers. Apparently everybody wanted to know about his next startup adventure and if he was really moving the new satellite headquarters to the East Coast.

Being successful had a way of drawing people in from every direction. Being extremely successful, selling a multimillion-dollar, number-one-rated African American tech company to a huge corporation, and getting an insane cash payout with mind-boggling stock options, had a way of making them want to ride your coattails to the next moneymaking venture no matter what or where.

His cell rang. He checked the car's caller ID connection. Seeing it was one of his assistants, he answered. "Yeah?"

"Dean, it's Kellie. I emailed you a copy of the processing forms you wanted and included the notes from the good-faith employee allocation contracts you reviewed last week. Do you still have the blueprints and architect renderings with you?"

He glanced at the black plastic architect's tube on the seat beside him. "Actually I have the Texas ones, but they'll do for now."

"Do you want me to send you the recent ones?"

"No, I'll use these for now. The structure won't change."

"Okay. I'll forward the changes they made and the site plan notes from the Realtor. Is there anything else you needed this evening?"

"No, I'll go over everything this evening and check in with you tomorrow."

"Okay, have a good night," Kellie said.

"Thanks, you too."

He smiled to himself as he ended the phone call and then exited the highway. His next big adventure had nothing to do with the computer world. It was personal, and getting yet another request from his hometown to participate in the annual holiday parade fit into his plans perfectly.

Fifteen minutes later, he passed the sign welcoming him to the small town of Hayden, Georgia. Not surprisingly, it was the same sign he remembered seeing when he first came here fifteen years ago. Just thirty-five miles south of Savannah, Hayden was perched right on the water with stunning views from every direction. It was an idyllic location with small-town appeal, perfect weather, and down-home Southern charm unequal to most small towns in the area.

It had a rich and varied history that had been established just after the Revolutionary War. Then it had slipped into poverty during the next war. From then on, it experienced decades of prosperity, hardship, affluence, poverty—continuously finding itself in constant vacillating flux.

Years ago, it had been surrounded by working farms, small factories, and a large manufacturing plant that employed most of the residents, but not anymore. With the plant moved overseas and the factories closed, the town might have fallen into destitution. But it hadn't. Instead, Hayden had survived and looked to be in the process of going through a recovery phase. Though it was ripe with growth possibility, its success was still debatable.

Dean drove down Main Street, checking out the sights. The varied structures looked more like colorful monopoly pieces than storefronts. A number of new shops, boutiques, cafés, and restaurants had replaced the ones he'd once known. There were changes everywhere. Nothing seemed familiar anymore. But, no matter how many changes were made, Hayden would always be the same for him—a small town steeped in historic beauty, forever on the verge of something new.

To his surprise, several people smiled and waved as he drove by. He nodded and returned the gesture, even though he didn't recognize them. But he knew it was the small-town way, welcoming and friendly. Unless of course you were a thirteen-year-old kid from Detroit with a few anger issues.

He stopped at a traffic light and looked around, noticing several other storefronts empty or for rent. Then he remembered his time there. No matter how much time had passed, he'd never forget this place. This had been his home after his parents divorced.

He'd come to visit his grandparents for four weeks one summer, and then had been made to stay for the next five years because neither parent wanted him.

For a long time after that, he'd equated his time in Hayden to a prison sentence complete with wardens and guards. The day he left was like being paroled. He was finally free. It was the best day of his life and the worst. His one regret was leaving Carmen behind. But he'd had no choice. She had left him first.

Thinking about her always made him pensive. What he'd lost with her was special. Although he had tried to find it with other women, no one had ever really come close. He'd loved her then and he loved her now. Coming back, he wasn't sure what to expect. They hadn't exactly ended well, but then their beginning hadn't exactly been conventional either.

He chuckled to himself, remembering how they'd met. Climbing out onto that attic roof that day had been pure insanity, but it had begun a friendship that was the best thing that had ever happened to him. As the light changed and he drove off, his cell phone rang and the electronic voice announced the caller, Jared Carr. He pressed the button on the steering wheel and answered. "Yo, what's up?"

"Hey, welcome back. I just heard you're in Hayden."

Dean smiled. Hearing his old friend's voice after hours on the road was a welcome surprise. They hadn't seen each other in several months because of their demanding work schedules. Yet they still kept in touch as much as possible. They had been best friends, frat brothers, and roommates in college, and they had kept their friendship strong over the years since. Jared had become a major public relations and crisis management professional whose clients were mainly in the political realm.

"Now how did you hear that? I just got here a few minutes ago. I'm driving through town right now."

"You know how small towns are—everybody knows everything instantly. If you sneeze in Savannah, someone in Hayden says gesundheit."

Dean chuckled. Jared had always made him laugh. "Ah yes, of course, the small-town added bonus, gotta love that."

"And you know, in my business, I hear everything. Especially when a celebrated computer mogul visits the area while in the process of merging his company, making a wad of cash, and possibly searching for a new site."

"That's not what's going on and you know it. No one can know that I'm actually selling the company. The stocks would go crazy and my employees' livelihood would be in jeopardy. The only one here who knows is Marion Stiles."

"Speaking of which, how's the sale going?" Jared asked.

"So far, so good. My attorneys are doing their part. Everything should be done by Christmas Eve, so I get to take a short break for the first time in years."

"When's the official announcement?"

"Monday morning."

"Well, enjoy it while you can. I have a feeling it's not going to last too long."

"Yeah, I know. That's why I'm trying to keep a low profile. And it helps that I have a great team already in place."

"Smart. Plus, hanging out in a no-name town in the middle of nowhere was a good idea. You know word is you're about to usher in another Silicon Valley East and everyone wants to know where."

"I don't know where they get these news bites from."
Dean chuckled again. "So, tell me, what's going on
with you?"

"I'm on my way to D.C. There's a situation that
needs my attention. I'll be back the end of the week.
You know we have to celebrate this thing big time. It's
a major accomplishment. It's not every day you sell a
multimillion-dollar company for some insane amount
of money. We have to get the crew together."

"Definitely. A celebration sounds good, but we're
gonna have to wait on that until after the final announcement. I'm keeping everything under wraps
for now."

"Understood. So where are you staying in Hayden?"

"The Stiles, it's a small bed-and-breakfast just outside
of town. Three floors, eight full bedrooms, incredible
views, and small lake in back. It's perfect for a little soli-
tude. I used to work there when I was a teenager."

"Oh yeah, I remember you telling me about that
place when we were in college. Maybe I'll stop by there
one day. But, are you sure you don't want to crash at
my place in Savannah? It's only a few miles away, five
bedrooms, six bathrooms, heated pool, Jacuzzi, game
room, full kitchen, basketball court, and five minutes
from a serious golf course."

Dean laughed. "Come on, man, don't tempt me.
You know I have unfinished business to take care of."

"Grand marshal, yeah, I heard," Jared said, chuckling.

"Of course you did."

"I'm surprised you agreed to do it. If I remember
correctly, you had some interesting stories about that
sweet little town when we were in school."

"True, but I have my reasons."

"Yeah, I'm sure you do. So, I'll catch up with you later."

"All right, sounds good. Take care." Dean ended the call just as he passed through the familiar iron and stone archway. It was adorned on either side with the now massive azalea, hydrangea, and peony bushes he had helped plant long ago. He followed the canopy of snarled, tangled branches dripping with Spanish moss from century-old oak trees until he eased around the last bend that led to the majestic Stiles Bed and Breakfast.

Sitting atop a small mound of perfectly manicured grass and adorned with beautiful white Christmas lights, the massive four-story Victorian-style structure was breathtaking. It was white with hunter-green shutters, stained-glass windows, gingerbread trim, and classic accents. It had a wraparound porch with ornate railings that extended around three sides of the building. The front porch was lined with handmade rocking chairs and large potted plants filled with colorful flowers. Not surprisingly, the entire front was completely covered with festive holiday decorations.

Dean parked his car in the small lot on the side of the building, then looked around briefly. Although he knew it was the same structure, a lot had changed with renovations and remolding. He headed up the front steps and looked around at the magnificent view. It was good to be back. As soon as he opened the screen door and stepped inside, he stopped. The sights, sounds, and smells of the holiday season were all around him. He was home.

He walked farther into the foyer and saw two women laughing and talking at a table in the center of the space. One was Mrs. Stiles, the owner of the bed-and-breakfast. The other woman stopped him instantly. Seeing them, seeing her, filled him with elation. Even though her back was turned, he knew it was Carmen.

He smiled. Her laughter was infectious and he instantly realized how much he missed the sound of her voice.

He watched her lean across the table and grab a flower. There was no doubt, she had definitely filled out in all the right places. Her dark hair was a lot longer. It was swept up in a ponytail that hung straight down the center of her back. She wore a red knit sweater that hugged her slender body perfectly and the sweet sway of her hips in the trim skirt was damn near hypnotic. She had always had a certain style that was sweet and innocent, but now it was much more seductive.

A moment later, Mrs. Stiles noticed him standing there. She smiled and welcomed him. Dean watched as she walked over to greet him. She was still a striking woman with ageless beauty and perfect features. As they hugged, he turned his full attention to Carmen. Her back was still to him, but then she turned around. She took his breath away.

Years ago, she had been his best friend. He smiled. No, that wasn't quite right. She had been his only friend. They'd met shortly after he arrived in Hayden. He had been thirteen years old and he'd had no idea what was really going to happen to him when he came to town. Then, when his parents left and he didn't, he'd known he was stuck there.

He'd felt betrayed by too busy, too selfish, too distracted-to-raise-him workaholics, constantly bickering about their divorce. They'd dropped him off and never looked back. After that, he hadn't trusted anybody, not even his grandparents, because they'd known all along he was staying.

A short while later, he'd started getting into trouble. Then he'd met Carmen and everything changed. He wasn't as angry anymore. He told her everything, his hopes, his fears and his dreams. He trusted her. Yes, he still got into trouble, but she was always there to believe in him. She had saved him so many times without even knowing it. He loved her then and, as they got older, his feelings of love had deepened.

For the last ten years they had been apart—he on the West Coast and she on the East. Over the years, he had tried numerous times to contact her, but he'd never heard back. She refused to speak to him. Now she had no choice. She had to communicate with him; he intended to make sure of that.

Chapter 3

Carmen felt her heart jolt. She looked down and watched her hands tremble nervously. "No, this can't be happening," she whispered to herself as she placed the flower she'd been holding back on the table. But his voice, rich and soulful, was unmistakable. It was as deep and smooth as she remembered. Melted chocolate on a hot summer day, and now it was more mature, sexy, and sultry. Her stomach quivered and her insides sparked. The burning ember she'd been holding on to all these years had ignited once again.

"Oh, you are such a flatterer," Marion joked.

Carmen turned slowly, seeing Dean Everett standing in the foyer smiling. He had already swallowed her mother up in a huge warmhearted hug, but his eyes were unwaveringly focused on her.

They stared at each other. She felt paralyzed as the sight of him stole what was left of the breath she'd been holding. He looked good, but then again, he always looked good—tall, dark, perfectly muscular, and too damn handsome. He had the same beguiling, half-crooked, captivating smile, and the same mischievous glint in his soft brown eyes. He was a bad boy all grown up and by the reaction of her body, he was still every bit as dangerous to her heart as before.

He had always been the one. They had chosen each other when they were young. The first time she'd seen him, she had been sitting out on the roof of the attic watching the sunset. He had been with his grandparents at the annual barbecue get-together her father had always thrown at the beginning of every summer.

"Hey, you up there, you gonna jump off?" he'd yelled up.

She'd looked down, surprised anyone even noticed she was sitting four stories up on the attic roof. She'd shaken her head.

He'd smiled. "I'm just asking 'cause I don't want you falling down on my head when you decide to jump."

"Your head is safe. I'm not jumping," she'd shouted down, surprised by her boldness. She was always shy around people, but for some reason, maybe because she was sitting on top of the roof, she felt bold and empowered.

"So what are you doing up there?" he'd asked.

"Looking at the view," she'd said.

He'd turned, seeing a mass of trees behind him. "What view?"

"You can't see it from there."

He'd nodded and walked away. A few minutes later, to her surprise, he'd crawled through the attic window and that had been the beginning of their friendship. She'd known right then there was something special about him. None of her other friends would ever dare climb out on the roof of the bed-and-breakfast attic. After that, through junior high and high school, they had been inseparable.

Their last Christmas together was ten years ago. They'd sat out on the roof late that night and promised to stay together and then they'd sealed their friendship with a kiss. Of course she had been in love with him long before then.

Her heart had claimed him, and no amount of online dating, computer dating, speed dating, or her mother's incessant matchmaking was going to change that. No man ever compared to Dean, and she knew none ever would.

"Hello, Carmen," he said.

She didn't speak. She just nodded, silently fearful that if she tried to open her mouth she'd either scream her head off or run and kiss him senseless. Thankfully her mother had continued talking to him as she turned back to the flowers.

She could have blamed her sudden muteness on being tongue-tied by seeing him again, but that wasn't it. Suddenly it was ten years earlier and they were right here in this foyer again. He was professing his love for her and she was turning and walking away. She'd never forgotten how she'd felt—empty and alone. But she'd had to let him go because she'd known he would never be happy there. She hadn't spoken to him since.

Now he was big news, and all of the sudden the small town of Hayden was proud and honored to be his hometown. They proudly boasted that they were his roots and he'd gotten his computer savvy from living in the tech-forward town. And now that he was about to be extremely wealthy and possibly invest in a new community, the small town of Hayden wanted to make sure they stood first in line for his attention.

Of course, every city, town, borough, and hole in the ground wanted a piece of him. Hooking him meant hooking his company, and that meant jobs, money, publicity, and prestige. What town wouldn't want that? So why did Hayden's council all of a sudden want him here? The answer was obvious. Who wouldn't want him?

"We're all so thrilled you could come home this year. And you know you're just in time for the festival of lights," Marion said. "Unfortunately you missed the holiday craft fair, the gingerbread house contest, the children's choir sing-along, the vintage car festival, and of course the Christmas-tree-lighting ceremony in the town square. It was glorious, but that's okay. You're just in time for the ice-sculpting event featuring scenes from Dickens's *A Christmas Carol.* Plus the sensational Night of Lights celebrations and of course the spectacular holiday parade on Christmas Day."

"Mom, Mom, he knows all that already," Carmen said.

Marion smiled. "Yes, of course you do. After all, this is home," she said as she reached up and gently touched the side of his cheek. "It's so good to have you back home with us where you belong."

Dean looked around the open foyer and smiled. "You're right, this was always home for me. I hung around here more than at my grandparents' house. And, there's no way I'd miss the rest of the Hayden Christmas festivities," he said, then glanced at Carmen, who was now back to working on the floral arrangement. "So, Mrs. Stiles, I have a . . ."

"Oh, none of this Mrs. Stiles formality. It's Marion."

He nodded. "Marion, I have a small favor."

"Sure, what can I do for you?" Marion asked eagerly.

"I've been on the road most of the day. Please tell me you have some of your famous Christmas gingerbread cookies in the kitchen."

Marion smiled. "Of course I do. I made a fresh batch earlier this evening, just for you. And I also made some gingerbread biscotti and planned your favorite meal for dinner tonight, so I hope you're hungry," Marion said, smiling as Carmen's head popped up.

"I'm starved," he said, looking right at Carmen.

"Well, I guess I'd better get you checked in. Carmen, why don't you show Dean around? There have been a lot of changes in the last ten years. I'll grab those cookies and get dinner started."

"Mom, actually, I think I'd better . . ." Carmen began, then paused and smiled, grateful for the fortuitous interruption. The front desk phone's ring had perfect timing. ". . . answer the phone," she said, but was quickly interrupted by her mother rushing past her.

"No, no, no, I'll take care of the phone. It's probably for me anyway. I'm expecting a call. You stay, talk to Dean and catch up." Marion hurried to the office and closed the door behind her. Something she'd absolutely never done before.

Chapter 4

The sound of the door solidly closing meant they were very much alone. Carmen glanced around the open area, then toward the front door. She mentally ran through a gamut of exit strategies. She could pretend to faint, fake a dire emergency, or just run out the room, but all were the coward's way out and none of them remotely plausible. Besides, being rude to a guest was unthinkable, though Dean Everett wasn't just any guest. She groaned inwardly. This was not going to be pretty.

The air around them seemed to crackle with electrified energy. Like a magnet pulling against its nature, she resisted the need to go to him. It was obvious the connection between them was still there, at least for her. She quickly turned her back and continued with the floral display to keep her hands busy. Of course ignoring him wouldn't work for long, but she needed just a few more seconds to calm her nerves, gather her thoughts and try her best not to still want him so badly.

"Thank you," he said.

"For what?" she asked turning to him. He smiled,

beautiful, straight, pearl-white teeth and sexy, sensuous lips. Her stomach flipped and her insides nearly melted.

"For not running out of here when you saw me. For staying to talk," he said softly. His voice was calm and soothing. She looked at him and frowned, embarrassed and annoyed that he could still read her so well.

"That's not what I was going to do," she lied feebly.

The sly, knowing smirk on his face showed he didn't believe her. "Yeah, of course it was," he said.

"I'm not that same timid little teenager anymore, Dean."

"You were never timid, not with me."

He was right. She had never been shy and timid around him. For some reason, being with him always made her feel brave and fearless. Maybe it was because he was so confident. But she looked at him and held her tongue. "Ten years is a long time and I'm all grown up now," she defended proudly.

"Yes, I can certainly see that." His eyes slowly drifted down her body and his smile broadened. Bold and brazen, he made no pretense about what he was doing.

In equal audacity, and to prove she was still just as bold and brazen, she reciprocated, gazing down his hard body and openly enjoying everything she saw. When she raised her eyes, he was staring at her again.

"It's good to see you again, Carmen. It's been a while," he said as he watched her pick up a flower and stick it into the vase. He walked over to the table and stood beside her. "How've you been?"

"Good," she said quickly, then moved to the opposite side of the table in the pretense of checking the arrangement from that angle. She picked up some greenery and inserted them one-by-one into the foam.

Dean nodded and continued to watch her as she worked. Seeing her now brought back wonderful memories from their time together. "I missed you. I tried to contact you over the years, but you never . . ."

"Dean, I know you have to be here. I get that. Like any other prominent businessman you accepted the town council's invitation to be the grand marshal. You're here professionally, so I suggest we keep this strictly professional. We're not going back to the good old days. You're a guest here, that's all."

"Are you sure that's all?" he asked.

"Yes," she said definitively.

He nodded and smiled. "Okay, if that's what you want." He looked around the foyer, then into the large living room and conservatory as he rounded the table to move closer to her again. "The place looks terrific. I see a lot of changes since I left. But like you said, ten years is a long time."

She nodded and eased away again, continuing to check the arrangement from all sides specifically those as far away from him as possible.

"I was sorry to hear your father had passed away. He was a good man—didn't like me much, but he was a good man."

Carmen nodded silently a second time. She remembered he had sent a huge bouquet of flowers when her father died. She was tempted to smile with his last remark, but held tight to her professionalism. He was right. By all appearances, her father hadn't liked him much. He had been one of those who'd thought Dean was trouble and he hadn't wanted his daughter anywhere near him.

"Carmen, the last time you and I were in this room . . ." he began.

"Well, it looks like my mother is going to be a while, so I guess I should check you in," she interrupted him and then walked over to the front counter and looked at the computer. "I'm sure you're tired from your long trip."

Dean followed and stood opposite the desk. "So, that's it? You're not going to talk to me or even look at me for the next few days?"

She looked up at him with a professionally trained smile plastered on her face. "Of course I'm going to talk to you. You're a guest of Stiles Bed and Breakfast, and we're delighted to have you staying with us."

He shook his head. "Why are you being like this?"

She grabbed a key. "The town council always reserves the grand suite for the parade's grand marshal, so that's where you'll be staying. I hope it's okay."

He nodded. "I'm sure it will be fine."

"Do you have any bags?"

"They're in the car. I'll bring them in later."

"Okay, here's your key. Enjoy your stay. I'm sure you remember where to find the grand suite."

He looked around and slowly shook his head. "Actually, I don't. Would you show me the way?"

Knowing he was lying, she opened her mouth to protest, then closed it and swallowed hard. Then she smiled tightly. "Sure. Follow me."

"Always my pleasure."

She nodded curtly, then headed to the small elevator. Then, on second thought, she walked past it to take the stairs to the third floor. The last thing she wanted was to be enclosed in a tiny space with Dean.

Her four-inch heels and knee-length fitted skirt weren't exactly climb-the-steps-wear, but she'd have to deal with it. Then she heard Dean clear his throat behind her. She turned to see him standing by the elevator. "Is the elevator working?" he asked.

She smiled again. "Yes, of course."

He pressed the button and the elevator doors

opened instantly. He stepped aside and held the doors to allow her to enter first. She walked in, then stood in front of the floor panel. As soon as he stepped in, she pressed the button to the third floor. The doors closed.

"We really need to talk," he said, standing way too close.

"No, we really don't."

"Your mother told me you had moved back here to Hayden permanently," he said, just over her shoulder. "I was glad to hear it. You were right—this was always where you belonged."

Carmen closed her eyes, knowing she definitely had to have another chat with her mother about sharing her personal life.

"There's so much I want you to know."

"There are a lot of changes in town. I'm sure you're going to be impressed when you see them," she began, cutting him off. Then she continued talking about the weather and all the plans the town had for the festival and parade. She knew he already knew about the festivities, but she wasn't ready to hear what he was going to say.

As soon as the elevator doors opened, she hurried down the corridor to the grand suite at the end of the hall.

Dean followed and she knew he was watching every move she made, but she couldn't think about that right now. She just needed to get him to his room and put as much distance between them as possible. She opened the door to the suite and held out the key for him to take. But instead of taking it, he stopped and stood right in front of her.

"God, it's so good to see you," he whispered. "You look even better than I imagined."

"Imagined?" she repeated. "You imagined me?"

He nodded slowly. "Oh yes, so many times, so many very inappropriate times. It's been so long, too long. I missed you." He reached up and stroked her face tenderly.

She looked up into his soft brown eyes. She knew exactly what he was thinking. She shook her head. What she saw in his eyes made her heart skip a beat. "I need to go," she said quietly, more for her own benefit than his.

She felt the tiny ignited spark in the pit of her stomach begin to flare, and every part of her body seemed to tingle at his touch. Her thoughts were spinning. She'd woken up this morning to an ordinary day and now everything had changed. Her world was turning upside down. She knew she'd never be able to get far enough away from her feelings for him. "Dean."

Then impulsively she reached up, wrapped her arms around his neck, and kissed him. It surprised him and shocked the hell out of her. She hadn't planned it. She just did it. Then she felt his body react and she melted into his arms. Strong and powerful, they encircled her holding her tight.

Her lips parted, his tongue entered, and the delectable kiss stepped up to mind-blowing insanity, sending tingles to every nerve in her body. She moaned and yearned for more. She pressed closer backing him against the doorframe. Raw and urgent, she reeled in blissful abandonment.

Right now there was no right or wrong; there was only what she wanted and she wanted to taste all of him. A guttural groan rumbled from his throat sparking him to surge deeper. The sensation was pure ecstasy.

This wasn't a couple of teenagers like years ago when they'd kissed. This was something very different, something more real than she'd imagined. The simple act of longing and desire was amped up to fierce hunger and intense passion. The need to be with him right now was beyond overpowering.

If she didn't stop now . . .

Suddenly the kiss broke with a yearning plea. "Come inside with me," he rasped huskily.

In shock, she shook her head to stave her lustful inner desires. She wanted him, but she knew she couldn't do this. Breathless, she backed off, shaking her head and staring at him. "Oh my God, Dean," she gasped, "I can't believe I just did that. I shouldn't have . . . I never . . . I'm sorry."

His usual charming smile had faded to stone-cold sincerity. His eyes seemed to pierce right into her soul. "I'm not."

"No, this was a mistake. It was wrong and reckless, and I can't . . ." she said then looked up at him and stopped midsentence.

She watched as he shook his head and slowly licked his lips as if to still taste her. If his intention was to entice, it was working. Her heart pounded like a jack-hammer gone wild. She felt him stroke the side of her face; then he tipped her chin up. She could see in his eyes he hadn't had enough. She closed her eyes, willing the moment to have never happened. But it did. She'd started this and she had no intention of his finishing it. "Um, I need to go."

"Carmen, open your eyes," he said pointedly.

No! she screamed in her own thoughts, but remained silent to him.

"Open them," he repeated, more demanding.

She did. "Dean . . . I . . . we . . ." she began again. He stepped closer. She placed her hands on the solid firmness of his chest to hold him in place. But it didn't matter. He wrapped his arms around her and pulled her close. Her lips parted in a silent gasp. An instant later, her world exploded a second time as he leaned in and took her thoughts away.

If the first kiss was the promise of madness, this was the fulfillment of pure unadulterated insanity. But there was no escaping even if she wanted to. Her body melted into him as he pressed her back against the open door. Nothing had prepared her for this. There was no control, no sanity, only the dizzying sensation of being captive by his hard body and kissed senseless and loving every minute of it.

Her thoughts whirled in excited delirium. But she knew this wasn't supposed to be happening. She wasn't supposed to feel this way. One kiss and she was melting into a puddle of desire. The sensation was mind-boggling. The room spun in every direction. She moaned, savoring the out-of-control passion. Need and desire mingled as want and longing took her to places she only dared imagine.

She felt his hand ease down her back and cup her rear, grasping hard. Her legs weakened as her thigh rose up of its own volition. She felt his hard erection pressing against her. Her body reacted in readiness for more.

Blinded by desire, she was lost in the heat of the moment. Her hips pushed hard, grinding into him. Her hands held tight to his neck, biting hard into his shirt. She wanted it off.

She ached to touch his naked body. She dropped her hand and squeezed between their bodies, grasping the long, hard silhouette throbbing against his pants. He ripped the kiss away and buried his face in her neck. She moaned too loudly. This was going to happen right here in the third-floor corridor. The realization was like a cold shower. No. This couldn't happen.

No matter how much she wanted to be with him, deep inside she knew she couldn't do this. So, with all her strength, she pushed and pulled back. Breathless, panting, with her thoughts completely muddled, she shook her head. This couldn't happen again.

A bell sounded down the corridor. Carmen turned seeing a couple getting into the elevator. Since she knew the couple was staying just two doors down the hall, she knew they had to have witnessed the kiss and everything else. Mortified, she turned away quickly hoping they hadn't recognized her. She'd never in her life done anything like this before. She didn't even know what to do next.

"Carmen," Dean began, his voice still husky and raw.

"Dean, you should stay at one of the hotels in town."

"Not a chance. I came here for you."

"No."

"Yes."

They stood a few seconds, each firm in their resolve.

"Here's your key."

"Thank you," he said.

She hurried to the elevator and jabbed the button. It was taking too long. She considered taking the stairs, but didn't trust that her legs wouldn't give out. Then the bell rang again and the doors opened. As soon as she got on, she turned, seeing Dean was still watching her from down the hall. The look on his face made her want to run down the hall and jump into his arms. Then the doors closed. An instant later, she was back in the lobby. Her mother was at the front counter talking with a guest.

She smiled briefly, maintained the last bits of her composure, and hurried past them to the kitchen. She grabbed a bottle of water, drank quickly, and began pacing. She needed to calm down, but she couldn't. She still couldn't believe she'd kissed him, then she'd kissed him back when he'd kissed her. What was she thinking? That's just it, she wasn't. Her professionalism and discipline had gone right out the window with her self-control. "Idiot. Foolish. Stupid. Reckless."

A few minutes later, her mother hurried through the swinging doors. "Carmen, what's wrong? What happened? Are you okay?"

"No, I'm far from okay. I just did the dumbest thing."

"Honey, what happened? Did you and Dean argue?"

She inhaled deep taking a long ragged breath. "I wish," she scoffed, taking another big gulp of water. "No, we didn't have an argument."

Marion looked at her. "Then what's wrong? You look shell-shocked, like you're about to explode."

Carmen took a deep breath and shook her head. "I checked Dean in and showed him to his suite and then I kissed him."

"And . . . ?" Marion said, still concerned.

Carmen sighed. "Mom, I kissed Dean. He's a guest and I kissed him. I can't believe I did that. I grabbed him and I kissed him. Then, on top of that, I'm sure another guest witnessed the whole thing."

"So?" Marion said simply.

"So?" Carmen repeated, completely appalled. "You don't understand. It wasn't just a quick kiss."

"Oh," Marion said, trying not to smile.

"I just need to get out of here before he comes back downstairs," she said, looking around nervously. She stared at the swinging doors as if Dean would be bursting through the kitchen door at any minute.

"Honey, honey, calm down. Relax. You know as well

as I, Dean is more than just a guest here, right. Right?" Marion asked and waited for an answer. Carmen reluctantly nodded. "You and Dean have known each other for what, over fifteen years? You've had feelings for each other since the very beginning. Your father and I always knew that. Maybe you both need to just take some time and sort through what's always been going on between you."

Carmen shook her head. "Mom, with everything going on right now, I don't want to have this talk."

"Honey, listen to me, I know you've been working really hard lately and this Christmas has been nuts to say the very least, but we'll get through this. We always do, you know that. You're stressed, so why don't you take a break? Go read a book, get your nails done, or do some retail therapy. Better yet, take the shopping list. I have a feeling tomorrow's breakfast is going to be very crowded."

Carmen looked around again and then slowly nodded. Getting some air was exactly what she needed to do to clear her head. "Yeah, good idea," she said, grabbing the shopping list from the refrigerator. Just then the bell on the front counter rang. They both turned.

"I'll get that," Marion said.

"No, I'll take care of whoever it is on the way out." She grabbed her jacket and purse and headed to the foyer. Marion followed.

As soon as Carmen got there, she saw Thomas Ford, head of the town council, standing at the foyer table and smiling. She groaned inwardly. She knew he was probably there to complain that the blurb was late. "Hello, Mr. Ford," she said.

"Good evening, Carmen," Thomas said, overly giddy.

"Hello, Tom," Marion said, walking up.

Thomas walked over and kissed Marion's cheek. "Hello, Marion. Wow, ladies, this place looks amazing. We should hold the holiday festival right here in the foyer," he added excitedly, then laughed at his attempt at humor. "And this winter white flower display is first rate, very lovely indeed."

Carmen looked at her mother. Marion smiled. "Why, thank you, Tom. We're very proud of our holiday decorations this year. Our guests are really enjoying them."

"Good. Good. So . . ."

"Thomas, the blurb isn't quite ready yet," Carmen said. "It's my fault. I'll have it for you as soon as I . . ."

"Oh, don't worry about that. I know you're busy with everything going on for the holidays," he said, looking around and into the conservatory. "Just get it to me by Wednesday morning. That should be fine."

"Sure," Carmen said, surprised by his relaxed demeanor.

"So"—he slapped his hands together happily—"I just heard the good news, our guest of honor has arrived." He looked around smiling. "Where is he?"

"Yes, Dean is here. I believe he's upstairs in his suite," Marion said.

"Excellent. Excellent. Well, I think I'll just run up and check on him to make sure everything's going well so far. Gotta take exceptional care of our special guest. I assume he's in the grand suite as usual," he said happily.

"Yes, but . . ."

"Hello, Mr. Ford."

They all turned and saw Dean walking down the last few steps. Thomas Ford rushed over immediately. "Ah, here he is now. Dean, our favorite Hayden resident, has returned. I'm so glad to see you. Welcome home, son." He grabbed Dean in a massive awkward hug and handshake, shocking everyone. "Good to see you made it home safely. How was your trip? Oh, and how's the business? I hear there's some exciting news on the horizon. I can't tell you how pleased we are you could take time out of your very busy schedule to participate in this year's holiday program. One of many, we're hoping." He laughed again.

Marion looked at her daughter. Carmen frowned. The obvious reversal of opinion had nearly given her whiplash. Thomas Ford was the one who'd really disliked Dean years ago and treated him like dirt. Now he was gushing all over him like he was the king of the world.

"No problem. It's good to be home. I have some business here I need to take care of, so it was perfect timing," Dean said, then he saw Carmen putting on her jacket. He walked over to help. "Are you going out?" he asked.

"Yes, I need to make a quick run," she said.

"How about some company?" he offered.

Carmen was just about to decline when Thomas spoke up.

"Um, actually, Dean, son, I wanted a quick chat with you. I thought we could iron out a few scheduling details for the next few days. And there are a few people who are looking forward to meeting you. I asked them to stop by. I hope you don't mind," Thomas said quickly.

Dean nodded reluctantly. "No problem."

"Well, why don't you two talk in the conservatory? It's quieter and I don't believe anyone's in there right now. I'll bring in some hot tea and Christmas cookies," Marion said.

Thomas nodded happily. "That would be wonderful, Marion. Thank you." He turned to Dean. "After you, son."

Carmen smiled as she left. She knew the beginning of their conversation was going to be awkward for Thomas. As Dean's biggest critic years ago, he had blamed Dean for just about everything that had gone wrong in the town. He had always been so sure Dean was trouble. And now that Dean was a respected businessman with enough money to buy the entire town, he had to make amends.

Carmen got into her car and pulled out just as several more members of the town council and a few other prominent Hayden residents arrived. She presumed they were the ones here to meet Dean. She shook her head. She knew Thomas's quick chat would probably last most of the evening and she had no intention of being around for it. She quickly drove off.

Chapter 5

Fifteen minutes later Carmen arrived at the gym. It was packed. Choosing to forgo her usual yoga and Pilates workout, Carmen elected instead to take an extreme-power aerobic workout and a spin class. Both were designed to de-stress and were exactly what she needed after the last few crazy, nerve-wracking days.

An hour and a half later, she walked out of the gym weak and exhausted. Heading to her car, she stopped, hearing her name called. She turned and saw a friendly face. "Hey," she said, smiling weakly.

"Hey, yourself. What's up with you? You look like crap."

"Thanks."

Jessie Singleton, a five-foot-ten-inch ex-model turned artist and recently returned resident like herself, owned a small art gallery in town. They had gone to high school together and lost touch over the years, but then, as they both moved and settled back into Hayden, they'd grown close.

"Don't mention it." Jessie smirked. "So what are you doing here? There's no yoga class scheduled this late."

"I took an extreme-power aerobic workout and a spin class."

"You took both classes, back to back?" Jessie asked, chuckling.

Carmen nodded. "I figured it's like riding a bike. How bad could it be?"

"Famous last words," Jessie said. "It must have been one of those days."

"You have no idea."

"You okay?"

Carmen nodded slowly. "Barely," she rasped.

"Why in the world would you . . . ? Oh, that's right. I heard. Dean Everett is back in town. I assume he's staying at the B and B," she said.

Carmen nodded. "Yeah, for the next three days."

"Well, you know everyone's already talking about the two of you together under the same roof again."

"What? He just got here."

"This is Hayden, remember?"

Carmen shook her head. Years ago, there had always been talk about her and Dean. Everyone assumed they'd be married and have a dozen kids by now. "Well, they can stop talking. Nothing's changed. He's just passing through just like before."

"If you say so. All right, I need details. How is he?"

"The same—smart, funny, drop-dead gorgeous, and sexy as hell," she said, quoting her mother again.

"Sounds nice."

"No, not nice."

"Well, at least you two can finally finish this."

"Finish what?" Carmen asked.

"The slow dance you've been doing since we were in high school. I was there too, remember. Shakespeare would have loved you two."

"I have no idea what you're talking about."

"Oh please, I could write a book about you two. Star-crossed lovers featuring Carmen and Dean—he's a poor teenager dumped here to live with his grand-parents who just happen to work for your wealthy father. Then he leaves to make his fortune and comes back years later to win back his true love. And then . . ." she said, looking at Carmen to finish.

"And nothing. Like I said, I have no idea what you're talking about."

"Yeah, I'm sure you don't." Jessie chuckled as she veered off to go to her car. "We still on for tomorrow afternoon?"

"Yeah, I'll be there."

"Okay, see you later. Oh, and by the way, try the kick-boxing class next time—works better, way more aggression."

Carmen smiled and nodded. "Thanks. I will. See you."

After leaving the gym, Carmen stopped at a market and a specialty food store and picked up a few more breakfast essentials. Driving back almost three hours later, she felt like herself again—strong, confident. She was back in control. She pulled into the driveway and saw that Tom Ford's car was thankfully gone, but a car she didn't recognize was there. Late-model, obviously expensive—she assumed it was Dean's.

She took a deep breath before getting out of the car. "Okay, I can do this," she affirmed confidently. She was ready to face Dean, Thomas, the blurb, and any other craziness coming her way. She grabbed the grocery bags and headed up the steps to the front door. It wasn't too late, but she knew her mother was already in bed since she got up extra early to prepare breakfast.

As soon as she opened the door and stepped inside, she saw the night clerk sitting at the desk smiling. They greeted each other and chatted for a few minutes, and then Carmen stopped in the conservatory to talk to a few guests still up socializing.

Carmen greeted them and casually looked around, noticing that Dean was nowhere in sight. She considered that maybe he'd gone into town with Thomas. The guests told her about their day and she suggested a few other places nearby they might want to visit. Afterwards, she continued to the kitchen. Her mother was sitting at the island counter working on the laptop. "Hey, I'm back. What are you doing still up?" Carmen asked, placing the bags on the counter.

Marion looked up and frowned. "You look worse than you did when you left here."

Carmen sighed heavily. "Yeah, I know, but I feel much better."

"Good, I guess that's something. And I just finished the blurb for Tom," Marion said, pressing the enter key. "Send and done."

"Thanks, Mom."

"We're all prepped for tomorrow's breakfast, and I was just about to check the attic roof and go to bed."

"No, don't worry about the roof. I'll check it."

"Okay, so what do you have there?" Marion asked.

"I stopped and picked up a few things from the market while I was out." She pulled out containers of strawberries and blueberries and a jar of lemon curd.

Marion stood and walked over. "Oh, that's perfect. I was just thinking about making homemade strawberry jam and blueberry scones. They'll go perfectly with the French toast casserole I'm making for tomorrow's breakfast."

"Mmm, that sounds delicious," Carmen said as she continued pulling groceries from the bags and putting them away in the refrigerator and pantry. "So, how was your dinner with Dean this evening?" she asked casually, trying not to sound too curious.

Marion chuckled. "Oh, it was wonderful. We talked and laughed about old times. He's still the same, funny and charming and very insightful when it comes to my daughter. He was disappointed when you didn't come back and join us for dinner."

Carmen looked at her mother and sat down. "Really?"

"Yes, really," Marion said, sitting down beside her.

"I didn't see him when I came in. Is he still here?"

"Of course. Where else would he be?"

"In town, maybe."

"No, I don't think he went out. He's probably in his suite working. He mentioned he had a few things to take care of this evening," Marion said. Carmen nodded. "Honey, you know you're gonna have to talk with him eventually. He is a guest and a friend."

"I know he's a guest."

Marion shrugged and looked around. "Well, I'm going to call it a night. Five o'clock comes earlier and earlier these days, and I do need my beauty sleep." She stood and kissed her daughter's forehead. "Get some rest, sleep well. Good night."

"Good night, Mom."

Marion left and Carmen got up and made a cup of tea. She sat at the counter and opened the laptop her mother had been using. Curiously, she typed in Dean's name. His company information came up along with his bio and well over two million other sites connected to him.

The first was of course about the merger of his computer software company. Then how it developed, what it was, and its net worth. She was stunned. She'd had no idea. She'd known he was wealthy, but she hadn't known he was this wealthy. She sipped her tea and continued reading through the many websites as one led to another and another. An hour later, totally distracted, she was still reading.

"Hey."

Startled, she jumped and spun around seeing Dean standing in the open doorway. "Hi," she said awkwardly, then quickly closed the laptop.

"May I come in?" he asked.

"Guests don't usually come into the kitchen."

"I'm not just a guest here," he said.

She nodded. "Yeah, sure, come on in."

He walked over to the counter and stood beside her. "I didn't know you were down here. I just came to grab something to drink."

She stood instantly. "Sure. What can I get you?"

"Carmen, relax. You don't have to wait on me. This isn't my first time being here. I know where everything is."

"I know, but . . ." she began, then watched as he added water to the teakettle, grabbed a mug, spoon, and teabag from the cabinet and drawer. "I guess you have been here a couple of times."

He smiled. "I'd say more than just a couple."

She nodded. "So, are you enjoying your stay here so far?"

"No, not really. The bed is too hard, the pillow too soft, there's a broken window, the fireplace is spewing black smoke into the room, the shower only jets out cold water, and there's a giant puddle in the middle of the floor."

"What?" she said quickly, stunned by his outrageous account. This was the last thing she needed to hear today. Standing, she quickly grabbed her cell phone from her purse to call the handyman. Then she stopped and turned to him realizing this couldn't all be true.

Dean was smiling and chuckling. She glared at him. "That wasn't funny," she said, sitting back down.

"Sure, it was," he said.

"No, it wasn't," she stressed, refusing to smile. But as much as she didn't want to, she did. "Really, not after the day I had today."

"What happened today?" he asked, making his cup of tea and refilling hers. They sat side by side at the counter, and she told him about her day and then the last few days. He shook his head, feeling her frustration. "And, to top it off, I show up."

"Yes, to top it off, you show up." She looked at him and remembered the kiss. Epic was an understatement. She licked her lips. "It's late. I need to go to bed."

"Mind if I join you?" he joked. Her jaw dropped; then she saw him smile. "You don't have to leave on my account."

"Actually, I was just on my way to check the attic when you came in." She quickly placed the laptop in the cabinet drawer and grabbed her mug.

"Carmen. Stop."

"I need to go. Like I said, it's late."

"Please, don't run again. I was hoping we could talk."

She stopped and nodded, knowing this was coming at some point. "Yes, you're right. We do need to talk." She sighed heavily and sat back down. "Uh, about what happened earlier, the kiss. I'm very sorry. It was unprofessional. I was wrong and I never should have . . ."

"Correction," he interrupted. "The kiss was perfect. You running away, not so perfect."

"This isn't funny, Dean. I messed up."

"What happened to the fun-loving Carmen I knew?"

She looked at him then shook her head. "She's gone. She grew up and learned she had responsibilities."

"That's a shame."

"Is that all you wanted to talk about?" she asked.

"You're not socially active."

"What?"

"Online," he clarified. "You don't have any social network footprints."

"Is that a question or a statement?"

He thought for a second, then answered. "Question."

"The Stiles Bed and Breakfast has a website and a social media page on most of the main sites."

"Yes, but not you personally."

"No, I'm way too busy to play on the computer."

"Come on, nobody's that busy. You need to relax and let your hair down. Have some fun, at least for the holidays."

She shook her head. "No, I don't think so. I have a real business to run."

"Are you implying that I don't?" he asked.

She frowned instantly. "No, no, that's not what I meant," she explained quickly. "Of course your business is real. Everybody knows it's very real. I just meant I don't have a lot of extra time on my hands."

He chuckled. "Carmen, relax, I'm just messing with you," he said, then watched her calm down. "Pity, you should try my games. You'd enjoy them."

"No time and, like I said, I have a business to run."

"Your mother has time," he said.

She turned to him, shocked. "What?" she said. He nodded. "No, the game system is connected to the television in the game room. She doesn't go in there, let alone play the games."

"I sent her a laptop and specially designed computer software. She's beta testing a new product for me. She's on my team. Actually, she's pretty good at slaying zombies and aliens."

Carmen had had no idea her mother played his

computer games. She smiled and chuckled at the
thought of her mother battling monsters and aliens.

"Now that's what I wanted to hear, your laugh. It's
been a long time and it's still music to my ears."

"Cut the crap, Dean," Carmen said quickly. "Remember, I know you."

"Apparently not well enough."

"Spoiler alert, I'm not that dewy-eyed teenager waiting for her first kiss from you anymore."

"Of that I am truly delighted. I remember our
first kiss very well. It was promising. But our last kiss
was . . ."

She shook her head. "Why are you here?" she asked.

Dean saw the fire in her eyes. He knew she'd always
had charm and innocence. That hadn't changed, but
now she had a feisty, spirited side of her too. She spoke
her mind, and he found that very attractive. "Haven't
you heard? I'm the grand marshal for the Hayden Holiday Parade."

She shook her head again. "Why are you really here,
Dean? I heard you declined numerous times over the
years. But this time you said yes. And you could have
stayed anywhere else in town."

He shook his head. "No, I couldn't have. You know
that. I told you I'd be back."

Her heart slammed hard. He was right. He had said
he'd be back—for her. But that was years ago and
he hadn't come back, until today. But none of that
mattered. It was all in the past. They stared at each
other; then she looked away. She knew what she was
feeling and saw it reflected in his eyes. She wanted him
and he wanted her. The kiss they'd shared earlier had
been merely an enticing prelude. Another kiss was

coming and she wasn't sure she could walk away this time.

"Breakfast is from six o'clock in the morning until ten. If you have any dietary restrictions, please let the front desk know and we'll adjust our menu to accommodate your needs. There are cookies, fruit, coffee, and tea available all day. Have a good night." She turned to walk out.

"It's a shame the Carmen I knew grew up. I miss her."

"I don't. She was weak and distracted."

"She was a lot stronger than you think."

Carmen paused, hearing what he said, and then she walked out. Tears began to fill her eyes, but she refused to cry. Crying was for the weak and she wasn't that person anymore. She had obligations and responsibilities. She needed to stay on track, and wanting Dean wasn't staying focused. He'd leave in a few days and she'd be crushed and broken-hearted and back to where she'd been when he left ten years ago.

Chapter 6

Dean watched Carmen leave. He smiled. She was right. She wasn't the dewy-eyed teenager he knew a long time ago. She was a woman and everything about her made him want her even more.

He picked up his tea to head back to his room. Then he remembered Carmen saying that she was going to check the attic. He continued up to the top floor, seeing the door was cracked. He walked over and peered inside. He saw the window open and Carmen sitting on the ledge looking out. He tilted his head and sighed. Her angelic face and flawless cinnamon complexion were just as radiant and beguiling as he had remembered. He'd always known she was a stunning beauty. Her long, curly lashes still framed the most exquisitely almond-shaped eyes imaginable and her full luscious lips staggered his imagination.

He knocked softly.

She turned. "Dean."

"Before you ask, yes, I am following you, but for good reason. You said there was a leak up here and I wanted to know if you needed any help."

"No," she said, glancing over to the bucket in the center of the room, "it's fine. The leak stopped."

He looked around. "Wow, this place is really organized."

She watched as he walked around the large open area. Neatly stacked boxes with labels were piled on wooden shelves along the sidewalls, furniture, rolled rugs, lamps, mirrors, pictures and chairs were neatly and orderly arranged in front. "I had a weekend free," she said.

"Looks like you had a few free weekends," he said, then turned to her sitting on the cushioned window seat. The window was open and she was leaning back against the side. "Thinking about jumping? Again?" he asked.

She shook her head and decided not to smile. "No."

"Are you sure? The reason I ask is I might go out walking later on tonight and I wouldn't want you to . . ."

"No, I promise I won't be jumping."

"So," he said, walking to the open window, "are you looking at the view or at the stars?"

"The stars. There's a meteor shower tonight."

His face brightened instantly. "Really, which one?"

"The Ursid."

He leaned out looking up at the sky. "Where, at Ursa Minor?"

"Yes. Just look toward Polaris, the North Star. It's supposed to peak tonight, but I haven't seen anything yet."

"You got me so hooked on watching meteor showers." He chuckled, searching the sky. "As a matter of fact, I actually considered being an astrophysicist for a while."

"Really? I didn't know that."

"Not a lot of people do. Mind if I hang around and watch the shower with you?"

She hesitated a few seconds before answering. "No, of course not. Pull up a cushion."

He sat down across from her. They both looked up at the sky. "Actually, I know where there's a better view of Polaris."

"Where?"

"My suite."

She looked at him warily. "You don't give up easily."

"Obviously," he said truthfully.

The unabashed, matter-of-fact way he responded made her chuckle, but then she stopped instantly. "Don't do that."

"Do what?" he asked.

"Make me laugh," she said.

"Why not? You have a great laugh and you need to laugh more. It's contagious."

"That's what my mom says."

"I know. I agree with her."

She frowned. "Since when have you two gotten so close?"

"We've kept in touch over the years, mainly when I was asking about you. But I guess it was really right after your father passed. She needed someone to talk to."

"She could have talked to me."

"You were busy in New York. Then, when you came back here to live, you were busy running this place. You stepped in for your father seamlessly. She's very proud of you," he said, gazing at her. She looked at him, then quickly looked back at the stars. "Your mother is a wise woman."

"My mother starring as Yoda, I don't think so."

"I do. She helped me a lot."

"Really how?"

"Sometimes it's easier to talk to someone not in the business. She has a great perspective on life. She reminds me a lot of you."

They sat in silence. Each lost in thoughts, memories, and long-ago dreams. His last comment was what her father had always said. But she'd never seen it. "You know, Thomas Ford and the council are gonna try and get you to move your company here. That's why they're being so nice to you all of a sudden."

"Really, all of a sudden? What, you mean they weren't nice to me before?" he joked. She smirked, then stifled a smile that almost crept free. He grinned. "Wow, was that almost an actual smile I just saw?"

"No, definitely not," she insisted, knowing he'd know she was lying. She looked at him, feeling a twinge of regret for being so rude and abrupt with him earlier. She stood and walked away. "I guess I was a bit harsh with you downstairs."

He got up and stood right behind her. He touched her shoulder and turned her around to face him. "That would be an understatement," he said, smiling.

"I'm sorry," she said softly. He took her hand and held it tenderly. Her heart slammed into her chest as he leaned in. Then, instead of kissing her like she thought he would, he just barely brushed his lips to her cheek as he just held her close.

"I know," he whispered. She swallowed hard and looked down at his hand. "Carmen," he said, tipping her chin up to look at him. "Don't shut me out again, please. You have no idea how hard it was walking away from you."

"You have no idea how hard it was knowing I let you go."

"But you did. And you never looked back. We promised each other we'd travel the world together. It would just be the two of us. No parents, no grandparents, no college. Remember that?"

She nodded slowly.

"You and me forever," he said, shaking his head regretfully. "It was a dream come true because I was so in love with you. But I was a fool."

She looked up at him quickly. Sadness covered her face. She opened her mouth to speak, but didn't.

"I believed you. But I learned my lesson. No one has ever gotten to my heart again."

"Dean, we were kids. We couldn't have done any of that. We had no money, no means to travel, how would we . . . ?"

"I was willing to try and you never even gave me the chance. I wanted you with me, and you pushed me away."

"Your grandmother told me that you got a full-ride scholarship. I knew you were going to turn it down. I couldn't let that happen."

"So you made the decision for me."

She nodded. "I had to. I knew you wouldn't."

"Growing up, you were like a sister to me. I always saw you like that, my best friend. But then after a while things changed. We changed. I knew what you were feeling for me, 'cause I was feeling the same thing. But I knew I was no good for you. They were all right about me."

"No, they weren't. They didn't know you. I did."

He smiled. "Yeah, you did, too well. Thank you."

"For what?"

"For pushing me away. For making me leave. It gave me the motivation I needed to want to succeed and to show you and everyone here that I could be more."

"I never meant to hurt you. My actions were never

meant to leave such pain on your heart. I only wanted to save you from . . ."

He looked up at her frowning. "Save me from what?"

"From me, from being here in Hayden. I knew how much you hated it."

He shook his head. "I spent so much time trying to figure out what I did wrong, why you just pushed me away."

"Psychology 101."

"Yeah. I got that eventually."

She laughed.

"Do you remember the last time we were up here?"

Her laughter ended. There was no way she would ever forget. That memory had been seared in her mind and heart forever. It was the first time they'd made love. "Yes."

"Do you remember what I told you, what I asked you?"

"That was a long time ago, Dean."

"I meant it. I still do," he said, moving closer. The sliver of space between them vanished. "Nothing's changed."

Everything about this moment warned her to turn and walk away, but she felt herself cemented in place. The instant he pulled her into his arms, she knew it was too late. Instinctively, she raised her arms around his neck. The kiss came in raw, urgent need.

Lips parted, tongues delved, as he kissed her with deep, hungry passion. She reciprocated with equal intensity. Her insides trembled with desire. She'd had one taste and now she wanted as much of him as she could get.

Suddenly she felt the wall at her back. His lips ripped from her mouth and dropped to her neck. Hearing his lustful groan excited her more. Right here, right now, was all she could think about. The last slivers of reality perched on the edge, but she refused to see it.

Pressed so close, she felt the hardness of his erection throbbing against her stomach. Her body sent a flood of passion to welcome him. His hand slipped between their connected bodies and grasped her breasts, massaging them until her nipples hardened. She moaned as she reached down and cupped his penis through his pants. Feeling him, touching him, stroking him, sent another wave of ravenous need through her body.

Breathlessness turned to panting, then turned to mindless desperation. Her body quaked. She licked her swollen lips to moisten them enough to speak. "Dean," she muttered.

"I know. Not here, not again," he said, nodding.

She stilled, as her hands dropped to her sides. He leaned his face into the sway of her shoulder, cupping the back of her neck to kiss her one last time—on her neck, her ear, her cheek, and finally, with the softest touch, her lips.

"Can we at least be friends again?" he asked.

"Yes, we can be friends. Friends is how we started." She looked up into his hopeful eyes. Her stomach tumbled and her insides felt as if they had melted away. She stepped away, quickly putting distance between them. "It's getting late, friend, and I have to get up early," she said, slipping her hand from his.

"What about the Ursid shower?"

"I'll see it next year. Enjoy."

"How about a friendly good-night kiss?" he joked.

She smirked, then turned to leave. "Good night, Dean."

He watched her leave. He saw the smile in her eyes. That was a start. Seeing her earlier, how she was acting, cold and grim, broke his heart. She had never been like that before, at least not with him. The soft, shy, cheerful teenager had turned into a humorless stiff, surrounding her feelings with a brick wall and wearing armor around her frozen heart. But he saw hope in her eyes.

She had healed him years ago, and he knew he had to be there for her now.

Chapter 7

It took what seemed like hours to get to sleep. Then after a troubling, restless night of dreams, Carmen finally fell asleep and woke up stiff, achy, and tired from her spin class and the power workout. But the punishment her body had taken the day before at the gym was nothing compared to what her heart was going through now. She could feel herself teetering on the edge of loving him again. But in truth, she knew she'd never really stopped. And the dreams she had didn't help.

They were erotic and steeped with passion and desire. Every dream started with a sweet and sexy kiss; then it exploded. Intense and powerful, raw and sensuous, each kiss drove her closer and closer to the edge. Then she'd wake up breathless and wanting more.

She'd had enough psychology classes in college to know that her subconscious wanted what she refused to allow her conscious to even think about. But, just like years ago, her mind had to overrule her heart. Dean was a distraction she didn't need right now. She had a business to run, a mother to take care of, and other guests who needed her attention.

She still couldn't believe she'd kissed him, and had

she not left the attic last night when she did, who knew what might have happened. She closed her eyes, took a deep breath, and released it slowly. She just needed to be patient. A few more days and all this would be over. The countdown was on.

She knew he'd leave right after the parade. After all, he had a business to run and she knew there was no way he'd even consider bringing his new company here to Hayden after everything the town had put him through years ago. Under his calm, composed demeanor with Thomas Ford yesterday, she'd known there had to be more. And a couple of smiling faces, a few welcome homes and well wishes weren't going to change that.

She rolled over and looked out the window. It was still dark outside, so she decided to stay in bed for a while longer. She smiled and snuggled beneath the covers, then closed her eyes, thinking about the day ahead. Hopefully it would be better than the day before. An instant later, her thoughts centered on Dean again. She eventually drifted off, remembering years ago when they'd hung out in the attic.

It had been their private refuge. There, surrounded by decades of Stiles family pictures, mementos, old furniture, clothes, books, and heaven knows what else, they'd had their first kiss. She was thirteen and he was fourteen. It was awkward and clumsy, but it was real and it felt amazing. She thought she had experienced nirvana. Since then, they had kissed many times with more passion and feeling than she'd ever imagined possible. Being with Dean had been her dream come true. But that was a long time ago, when they were young.

She sighed and slowly opened her eyes, leaving the past behind. She took a deep breath, stretched, and rolled over to see the clock again. She sat up instantly. She must have nodded off because it was forty minutes later. She jumped up, grabbed a quick shower, dressed, and hurried downstairs to help her mother prepare breakfast.

As soon as she got to the dining room, she saw the table was prepared and the side-buffet was already set up with drinks, fruits, cereals, mini pastries, condiments, and a muffin and scone breadbasket. Everything looked scrumptious. Then, smelling something delicious, she followed the mouthwatering aroma to the kitchen.

Her plan was simple for this morning. All she had to do was stay in the kitchen and get through the morning. She'd be out all afternoon and working tonight. She'd avoid seeing Dean all day and she wouldn't have to deal with what happened last night.

Hearing the oven buzzer go off, she pushed open the kitchen door and grabbed her apron, expecting her mother to be at the stove as usual. "Morning, Mom," she said, not paying attention and tying the apron round her waist. "Mmm, everything smells incredible. So, what can I do to help?"

"Hey, good morning," Dean said, turning the buzzer off and opening the oven door. "How'd you sleep?"

The sight of him stopped her cold. Dean was there, dressed in a black T-shirt and jeans that hugged his rear end to perfection. "Whoa, what are you doing? You're not supposed to be in here—you're a guest."

He chuckled, placing the tray of scones on the trivets on top of the counter. "Yeah, I suppose I am, officially. Do me a favor and check the strawberry jam on the stove."

Carmen turned, seeing the bright red bubbling mixture in the pot. She went over, picked up the wooden spoon, and began stirring. Then she added the rest of the berries and lowered the flame. The brisk boil slowed to a gentle simmer. "Seriously, Dean, what are you doing in here? Where's my mother?"

He dropped the oven mitts beside the tray of hot scones. "She had to make a quick run. Apparently one of your guests asked the front desk for some muesli this morning. And since you weren't up yet, I volunteered to keep an eye on the kitchen while she was gone. She told me the muesli was a special mix that only she knew how to make. So, here I am helping out until she gets back."

Carmen groaned inwardly—first, dreams of Dean all night, then coming down late, and now this. Obviously it was going to be another one of those days. "Okay, fine, thank you for helping out, but I'm here now. You can go."

Just then, the second oven timer rang. "I'll get it," they both said, then bumped into each other as they reached for the oven mitts. He relented and turned the buzzer off while she got the large baking dish out of the oven. She placed it on the stove, then removed the oven mitts. She cut off the strawberry mixture and turned to him. "Dean, thank you very much for your help, but I'm here now. Everything's under control. So, enjoy your breakfast and have a great day."

He nodded reluctantly. "You too." He removed his apron and turned to leave. Carmen watched him go. Then, not paying attention, she grabbed the baking dish to move the French toast casserole. A split second later, she shrieked, dropped the dish back down, and jumped back. She had burned her hand.

Dean instantly turned to help. He grabbed her, rushed her over to the sink, and ran cold water on her hand. She pulled away. "No, hold your hand still," he instructed firmly.

She immediately tensed as he stood right behind her, his body intimately pressed against hers. She held still and let him hold her hand in the stream of cold water. After a few seconds, the hot, stinging pain cooled and subsided. But another aching burn began elsewhere. Her legs felt weak and her body swayed back against him. She could feel the hardness of his body as his arm slipped around her waist. Her stomach dropped in free-fall like the first dip on a mile-high roller coaster.

"How's that?" he asked gently.

Her thoughts muddled and hazed. She knew he had spoken. She just had no idea what he'd said. All she could register were his perfect lips so close to her neck and the dreams from the night before.

"Is that better?" he asked again.

She nodded this time. Her mouth was too dry to speak.

"Good. Do you have any aloe vera?" he asked.

"No, I'm okay," she said, taking a deep breath. "It was just a quick burn. I should have been paying attention. I just grabbed the tray without thinking."

He grabbed a paper towel, dried her hand, and looked at the small red burn at the side of her palm. "I think you might need an herbal salve or some antibacterial ointment."

"Dean, I'll be fine. I've burned myself before and this is really no big deal." She turned to him, expecting he'd step back, but he didn't.

He looked at her hand and smiled, shaking his head. "Still as stubborn as ever." Her stomach jumped. Neither spoke for a few seconds. They seemed transfixed by the moment as the spark of intimacy hovered all around them. Then he leaned in just inches from her lips and stopped. The pause was seductive and tantalizingly sensual. As if caught up in the suspension of reality, she fought against the intimacy of the moment. "When are you going to relax?" he asked as he kissed her cheek, then eased down to her neck and shoulder.

She gasped and her heart slammed hard. In breathless anticipation, she licked her lips and shook her head slowly. "Dean. We can't do this again."

"We can do whatever we want. The question is, Carmen, what do you want?"

The answer was simple. She wanted him. Her heart knew it, her body knew it, but there was no way she was going to give in knowing that she'd be opening herself up to pain and heartache again. No, she intended to hold firm to her decision to keep as much distance between them as possible.

The decision was made. She was going to be strong. She blurted out her answer. "Nothing's changed, Dean. I know my responsibilities and what I want doesn't matter."

He shook his head. "No, you're wrong. Of course it matters. It always mattered."

His smile vanished instantly as he pulled her into his arms. In the blink of an eye, his mouth captured hers. The kiss rocked her to her core. They were still kissing when they heard someone clear their throat.

Carmen jumped back instantly. She was mortified to look over and see her mother standing in the doorway grinning. "Mom," she said, still breathless. "You're back."

"Good morning, honey. Yes, I am."

"Good morning again," Dean said. "Everything's taken care of—scones, muffins, jam, and the casserole is out of the oven."

"Excellent. Thank you, Dean," Marion said.

Carmen rolled her eyes.

"Any more bags in the car?" he asked as he walked over to take the grocery bag from her.

"No, I just have the one bag here, but there are a few cases of water bottles in the trunk of the car if you don't mind grabbing them," Marion added.

"Sure, no problem. I'll put them in the pantry," he said, then walked out the back door.

Carmen relaxed as soon as he walked out. She turned, put on the oven mitts, and then grabbed the baking dish. "I'll take this out to the dining room. The guests should be arriving for breakfast soon."

Marion smiled knowingly. She was still smiling when Carmen came back into the kitchen. Carmen grabbed the muffins and scones, then took them out to the dining room. When she came back in, after taking much longer than necessary, she looked around the kitchen.

"He's already gone," Marion said.

"Who's gone?" Carmen asked needlessly.

"Dean. You grabbed the scones and muffins and left so quickly I assumed you didn't want to be here when he returned."

"I wasn't avoiding him. I just wanted to put the bread out while they were still warm," Carmen said.

Marion nodded, only half believing her as she poured the last of the homemade strawberry jam into a serving dish. Carmen came over and waited until her mother was done. She picked up the dish, then paused. "What you saw earlier between me and Dean wasn't what you think."

"I didn't say a word," Marion said, putting the pan in the sink as she smiled to herself.

"It's complicated."

"It was a kiss," Marion corrected.

"No, it was . . ." Carmen attempted to continue.

"A kiss," she repeated.

"A weakness," Carmen said. "It won't happen again."

"Carmen, don't say that. Passion and love are not weaknesses. And the kiss I saw, the kind that curls toes and makes your heart soar and your stomach tumble, is a gift. I just want you to be happy, and if Dean makes you happy, then I'm over the moon for you both."

"Mom, I don't need Dean in my life to be happy."

"Honey, everyone needs someone. I had your father and we were very happy. I just want that for you too," Marion said. "I don't want the hotel to be all you have in your life."

"I'm fine. This is my responsibility now. I understand that and it'll be enough."

"No, it's not, and it shouldn't be either."

"Mom, it's about family. I can't walk away. I won't."

"You can do whatever you want to do."

She shook her head. "That's what Dean just said."

Marion nodded. "He's right."

Carmen opened her mouth to respond, but closed it when she heard voices out in the dining room. They looked up at the clock. It was five minutes after six. "Looks like it's time for breakfast to begin."

Marion nodded and picked up the two large coffee carafes. "Showtime. I'll be out front."

Carmen nodded. A few minutes later, the morning breakfast routine was in full swing. She stayed busy, keeping the kitchen in constant motion by filling and refilling the breakfast trays while her mother was the perfect hostess. It was a job she relished and Carmen didn't particularly care to do.

Guests, town residents, and visitors all came to enjoy

the holiday breakfast at the Stiles. On most mornings, there was barely enough room. Sunday brunch was always packed, but today it was so crowded they opened up the conservatory, the sitting room, and the porch to extra seating and dining. Word was out that Dean Everett was staying there, and everyone wanted to meet him.

When Dean finally came back down to breakfast, it was like a celebrity had arrived. Carmen knew the instant he was downstairs. She could hear the excited chatter in the kitchen. She stepped out into the dining room briefly and watched as he totally wowed everyone with his usual self-confident swagger. Dressed in a suit and tie, he looked magnificent. He was an instant hit. Completely surrounded and constantly interrupted with conversation and introductions, he could barely eat.

While talking with one of the council members, he, by chance, glanced up and saw her standing in the kitchen doorway. His smile widened and the charming glint in his eyes seemed to actually sparkle. Carmen shook her head and smirked. He had mesmerized her years ago. The moment she'd seen him, she'd fallen in love. Now it looked like the small town of Hayden had finally caught up. An instant later, he winked. She chuckled and turned, seeing Thomas Ford watching them and smiling triumphantly.

She quickly grabbed a few dishes and went back into the kitchen. It was time to start cleaning up. Thirty minutes later, with the kitchen in great shape, Carmen stepped out front again. Her mother was gathering the last of the serving trays from the side buffet. Carmen grabbed the coffee carafes and followed her mother back into the kitchen.

"Man, they really love him out there," Marion said, amused.

"Yeah, I know. I saw. Hard to believe these are the same people who called him trouble years ago."

Marion laughed. "I know. They're eating crow with breakfast now. We should just put it on the menu tomorrow," she said, then chuckled at her own joke.

"Well, the good thing is that it's ten-fifteen and breakfast is officially over."

"Not quite."

"What do you mean, not quite?"

"Well, most of the in-house guests are out for the day, but quite a few Hayden residents are still out in the conservatory. I don't think they're leaving anytime soon."

"What? What about the big meet and greet Dean has to do this afternoon at the town hall?"

"They're here, at least most of them. I wouldn't be surprised if it was canceled, but I doubt it. Thomas is looking forward to giving Dean a walking tour of the town."

Carmen looked up at the clock, shaking her head. "I'm supposed to meet Jessie at the gallery in an hour."

"You go. I'll finish up here."

"Mom, I can't leave you to finish all this."

"What 'all this'? You've already done everything. Sadie and Claire are upstairs cleaning the rooms. So, if I need help, I'll grab one of the ladies. You go have fun."

"Okay, I'll be at the galley most of the afternoon. Call me if you need anything."

"Go. Enjoy your day. Tell Jessie I said hello."

Carmen nodded. She went to her bedroom, showered, changed, and headed out to town. On the way she saw

Dean still talking with Thomas in the conservatory. With him busy with the council all day, she knew she wouldn't see him until evening. That meant she had the rest of the day to relax. But she knew she wouldn't. He was back in her heart, and there was nothing she could do about that.

Chapter 8

Once Carmen walked into the art gallery, she felt a sense of calm. She glanced around at the beautiful paintings, prints and sculptures around her. This was exactly what she needed—the perfect distraction. Here, she didn't have to worry about seeing Dean, talking to Dean, and most importantly, kissing Dean. Here, she could relax in peace and enjoy the afternoon with a good friend.

Jessie's assistants were helping customers when she walked in. But one spared a quick second to point to the rear of the shop, knowing she was there to see Jessie. Carmen waved, nodded, and headed to the back rooms. "Jess," she called. She knew the area well—she'd helped Jessie pick the location and move in.

"Yeah, I'm in the art studio."

Carmen walked through the corridor and found her friend leaning against the far wall looking at a large impressionist painting on the opposite end. Carmen walked over and leaned back beside her. Jessie tilted her head. Carmen did the same. "What do you think? And be honest," Jessie said.

"Wow, I love it. It's beautiful. The colors are serene,

but still vibrant and alive. And then the faint silhouette of the two people moving apart is kind of heartrending. It's sad, but also encouraging and tender, maybe because of the colors. Hmm . . . who's the artist?" she asked.

"I am."

Carmen turned to her friend. "You, really? You're painting again?" she said. Jessie nodded. "Jess, that's wonderful." Carmen hugged her friend, knowing how much she loved painting and how she'd had to give it up years ago. "I'm so happy for you, and this piece is absolutely perfect."

"I'm glad you like it."

"I love it. It's comforting and kind of sad with the two figures coming apart."

"Or are they coming together?" Jessie said.

Carmen looked at her, then back at the painting, now seeing it completely differently. "I don't know. Which is it?"

Jessie smiled and shook her head. "Art is always in the eye of the beholder. Maybe you'll see it differently another time. Come on, let's get to work."

Carmen and Jessie spent the next hour talking, laughing, and going through catalogues of paintings and artwork for the bed-and-breakfast. Since the building had been renovated and a lot of the rooms remolded, Carmen and Marion had decided to change and update some of the older artwork on the walls to more contemporary pieces.

Carmen, with Jessie's help, chose several paintings and prints, and then they went online to continue the search. But she didn't see anything else she liked. "I have an idea. Why don't I commission you to paint something for us?"

Jess shook her head. "I'm not ready for that yet. I'm still

too, uh . . ." She paused, taking a deep breath ". . . busy working here."

Carmen took her friend's hand. "I know. I understand. Take your time." Jessie nodded as Carmen continued. "So how have you been with everything, I mean since your husband's death?"

"I'm doing okay," Jessie said bravely, evasive as always. "I have good days and bad days." She shrugged. "I miss him."

"I know. And I'm here for you anytime you want to talk or scream or yell or cry, day or night. It doesn't matter."

Jessie nodded silently. "Thanks. Okay, enough about me and my world. So what do you think?"

"About this piece?" Carmen asked, looking back at the painting on the screen. "Nah, I don't think so. It's too dark."

"No, what do you think about Dean? Is he coming back to stay or what?" Jessie asked.

"No, of course not. Why would he?"

"Um, I could think of one reason—you."

Carmen shook her head. "No, he left before and he'll leave again. He once said he was just passing through. That's just how it is. We both know that. I stay and he goes."

"Yeah, but that was before. You were teenagers. Now you're two consenting adults with a lot of history and . . ."

"I kissed him," Carmen said, blurting out her confession quickly. "Twice, maybe more. I don't even remember now. And then he kissed me back."

Jessie shrugged. "You've kissed him before, haven't you?"

"Yeah, but not like this."

"What do you mean?"

"I mean this was a toe-curling, knees-weakening, mind-boggling kind of kiss. The kind you barely walk away from."

Jessie nodded. "Oh, that kind of kiss. Now this is getting interesting. And when were you going to tell me about this?" Jessie asked. "Never mind, I want to hear all the down and dirty details. How was it?"

Carmen closed her eyes dreamily and moaned. "It was insanely sensual, indescribably sexy, and a huge mistake."

"What? What do you mean a mistake?"

"It took one kiss and I'm right back where I was before. I can't go through that heartbreak again," she said, then sighed heavily. "Then last night when we were up in the attic looking at the stars, he and I . . ."

"Oh my God, you did it."

"Did what?" Carmen asked.

"You and Dean made love last night—finally."

"No. Not finally. We didn't go that far last night. We came very close though. But the attic is where he proposed to me years ago, so we . . ."

"Whoa, back up. You never told me any of this before."

"Because it didn't matter. I was engaged for all of one night. He asked the question, I said yes, hoping he'd stay here with me in Hayden. The next morning I was so happy. Then he started talking about us leaving after his graduation ceremony."

"So that's when he backed out?" Jessie asked.

"No, I did. I told him I couldn't marry him and he should just leave."

"What, why?"

"You know I couldn't just walk away from this place. Hayden is my home, and I knew I had responsibilities. I asked him to stay here with me before then, but he refused. He had to go. I understood. Not everyone is cut out for small-town life."

"So he left and that was it," Jessie surmised.

Carmen nodded. "Basically, but now ten years later he's back and I can feel it starting all over again. I swear, when he and I are together, I just lose all sense of judgment and I can't get enough of him. Yesterday I took him to his suite. I grabbed him and kissed him. Can you believe it? Just like that. And then this morning I was so busy watching his rear end that I grabbed a hot pan and burned my hand. And what happened next? I wound up kissing him again. How does this even keep happening?"

"You still want him and he still wants you—that's how it keeps happening," Jessie said. "I remember the two of you when we were younger. From the very beginning, it was like you were made for each other. Maybe it's fate."

"There's no such thing as fate," Carmen proclaimed.

"Fine. So how did you leave it with him?"

"He wants us to be friends again."

"Can you do that? Can you just be his friend?"

"Yes, but that's it. Just friends. I can't get emotionally involved with him again."

"I don't think you have much choice."

"I don't know what to do. Tell me what to do. How can I be his friend? A friend is invited to a friend's wedding and they're happy when they have their first child. How do I do that and the entire time wish I was the woman at his side? How do I not want him?"

"Sweetie," Jessie said, taking her hand and squeezing gently, "you never stopped. So my advice is, until that day with the wedding and the children with someone else, have some fun for a change. You're friends, so do the friends-with-benefits thing. Toss him down on the nearest bed or flat surface, or up against the wall, rip all of his clothes off, ride him until dawn, and enjoy every mouthwatering minute of him."

Carmen's jaw dropped. "What? No! No!" The shock on Carmen's face was priceless. Jessie started laughing. Carmen joined in. "I can't do that," she said.

"Okay, then make sweet, passionate love to him and then hold on to those cherished memories and never let go."

Carmen knew Jessie was talking about her own life. She reached out. They hugged until she heard her cell phone ring. She pulled it out and answered. "Hello."

"Carmen?"

"Yes, speaking."

"Hi, Carmen, this is Thomas Ford."

She frowned instantly. There was no way possible Thomas Ford would be calling her. She hadn't even known he had her phone number.

"Hello, Carmen, are you there?"

"Yes. What can I do for you, Mr. Ford?"

"First, you can call me Thomas. It's about time, don't you think? And second, I need a favor."

"A favor," she repeated.

"Yes, an emergency just came up and I'm in a bind. I was wondering if you could give Dean Everett a tour of the town."

"What?"

"I remember how close you were years ago and I thought you'd be the perfect one to show him around Hayden."

"Mr. Ford . . ."

"Thomas," he quickly corrected.

"Thomas, Dean already knows Hayden. He grew up here. I'm sure you of all people remember that well enough."

"Ah, but we've changed, new buildings, new streets, and a whole new attitude and outlook. Your bed-and-breakfast is part of the revitalization of Hayden, and who better to reintroduce Dean to the town than you? And I hoped you'd be willing to pitch in and help the town make a good impression. Having Dean return to Hayden and bring his new company here would be a tremendous boost to the town and in fact to all our businesses. Don't you agree?"

"Uh, yes, I guess, but I don't see how I can help. Beside, I'm right in the middle of . . ."

"Ah, now don't be modest, I know you'll do us proud."

"Unfortunately, I'm right in the middle of . . ."

"Excellent, I'll point him in your direction. Thanks again."

"But . . ." The call ended. "Wait . . ."

Jessie looked at Carmen. "Everything okay?" she asked.

"No, that was officially the strangest phone call I have ever gotten."

"What do you mean strange? How?"

"I think I just got hoodwinked."

"Hoodwinked, by who?"

"Salesman extraordinaire Thomas Ford, and you'll never guess what he wants me to do."

Jessie smiled. "Bet I can. He wants you to use your feminine wiles with Dean to get him to bring his company here. How am I doing?"

Carmen nodded. "Close enough, and he also wants me to give Dean a tour of the town. He said that he's pointing him in my direction. What does that even mean?"

"It means Dean is on his way here right now."

"No, that's impossible. How could he know where I am?"

"We live in a small town, remember. If you said hello to one person on your way here, then everybody knows where you are by now, or he could have just asked your mother."

An assistant's knock on the open door interrupted them. "Excuse me, Jessie. Sorry to interrupt. Paulette Jones just called, she wants you to call her back when you get a chance."

"Okay, thanks, I'll take care of it," Jessie said. Her assistant left and she turned back to Carmen. "So, what are you going to do?"

"Simple," Carmen said, grabbing her cell phone and purse, then standing to leave. "Stay as far from Dean as possible. He's supposed to check out Christmas Day, so I'll just not be around."

"You know that doesn't work in a small town."

"It will this time," she said, leaving the studio and walking down the corridor to the front gallery. "Look at me, I'm a mess. My heart is jumping, my nerves are on edge and I'm out of breath just thinking about seeing him."

Jessie smiled. "Oh my God, wait a minute." She grabbed Carmen's arm to stop her. "I was wrong. It's not fate. It's love. You still love him."

Carmen, with her mouth open in shock, looked at her friend. She shook her head as Jessie nodded. "No, no, I can't still love him. I did ten years ago, but not now."

"Of course you can. You do. Carmen, you and Dean have always had something special. Ten years can't erase that."

"That was a long time ago. We're different people now."

"Do you think that matters to love?" Jessie asked.

Carmen shook her head, turned, and started walking again. "What are you doing? Where are you going?"

"I'm getting out of here."

"You know Dean is probably on his way."

"Exactly, and if Thomas knows where I am, I'm leaving before they get here."

"But you just said you were back to being friends."

"I did. But I'm still leaving."

"Coward."

"Exactly. I'll see you tonight." Just as she got to the front gallery, she stopped cold.

Dean left the town hall building shortly after three o'clock. He'd just spent an hour and a half having Thomas and a number of local business owners tell him everything he already knew about Hayden. He was exhausted, and had every intention of heading back to his suite to get some work done.

He had been up for hours. Shortly after dawn, a marathon of phone calls, text messages, and emails had begun and they'd continued the rest of the morning. But that didn't matter since he hadn't gotten much sleep anyway. And the sleep he did get was laced with dreams of Carmen. Kissing her again and being with her in the attic the night before had him twisted in knots. And, in truth, he wouldn't have it any other way. Even now, the thought of her brought a smile to his face. Just then, a car horn blew and a man waved. Dean didn't recognize him but he waved anyway.

Thomas walked up beside him and also waved at the passing driver. "That was Bill Keys—he's new to the town. I brought him in myself. He owns the local newspaper. He wants to do a full-page feature article on you for the Christmas edition. I told him we'd think about it, but I think a better way to go would be to . . ."

Thomas kept talking as Dean looked up and down the street. There were people everywhere. And just as Thomas had professed over and over again, Hayden had certainly changed in ten years. All of a sudden, the sleepy little town he'd thought was so small and backwards was coming into its own. He considered going for a walk to check it out, but that would have to wait for another time. He had work to do.

Even though everything was going well with his company's sale, there was still work to be done and he knew he had messages and emails that needed his attention.

". . . don't you agree?" Thomas said, looking at him to reply.

Dean had no idea what Thomas had just said. Thankfully, just then his cell phone rang. He excused himself and took the call. He spoke a few minutes with his assistant, then ended the call and turned back to Thomas, who'd been very obviously eavesdropping on his conversation.

"Thomas, I'm going to have to cut this short. I have some calls I need to make."

"Oh, that's a shame. Carmen will be disappointed."

"Carmen?"

"Yes." He pointed across the street. "She's right over there in the art gallery. I know she's looking forward to giving you a tour of the new Hayden. She's waiting for you right now. We'd planned it earlier. But if you don't have time, I understand. It's just that Carmen is expecting you."

Dean nodded. "Fine."

"Excellent, excellent, I'm sure we'll see you at tonight's ice-sculpting event. It's going to be really cool," he said, chuckling hard, laughing at his awkward attempt at levity.

They shook hands; then Dean walked across the street, clearly pleased for the first time since earlier this morning. He knew Thomas was trying to use him to move his company to Hayden. A blind man could see that. Poker obviously wasn't his game, but even with all that, there was no way he was going to pass up seeing Carmen again.

As soon as he walked into the art gallery, a salesperson walked up to him, smiling. "Hi, how can I help you?"

"I'm looking for Carmen Stiles. Is she here?"

"Sure. I'll get her."

Dean nodded as the sales assistant walked away. He started looking around the gallery. Then, barely a second later, he heard his name and turned to see Carmen and a familiar face. He smiled. "Hi."

"Dean. You're here," Carmen muttered.

He nodded and walked over to them. "Yes, I'm here."

"I mean I didn't expect you so soon."

"Thomas said you were in here waiting for me."

She opened her mouth to continue speaking, but nothing came out. Her mind went blank. Everything Jessie had just said reverberated in her head and sunk into her heart a soon as she saw him. She knew then Jessie was right. Ten years didn't matter to her heart. She still loved Dean, even if he only wanted to be friends.

"Hi, Dean. I don't know if you remember me, I'm Jessie Singleton. We went to high school together. Welcome back to Hayden," she said, extending her hand to shake.

"Hi, Jessie. Yes, of course I remember you. It's good to see you again. How've you been?"

"Good, working hard. You know how that goes."

He smiled. "I gather this is your gallery?"

Jessie looked around nodding proudly. "It is."

He glanced around briefly. "You have some really nice pieces here. I remember you from high school. You painted, right? Are any of these yours?"

"No, I'm afraid not. But maybe one day," Jessie said.

He nodded. "I look forward to seeing them. So, Carmen, I hear you're supposed to show me around the town."

"That's right. You guys had better get started—there's a lot to see," Jessie said, ushering Carmen to the front door.

Carmen glared at her friend as Dean opened it and they walked out. Her last sight of Jessie was the very amused grin plastered on her face.

Chapter 9

As soon as Carmen stepped outside, she stopped and turned to Dean. "Let me guess, this tour of the town was your idea, right?"

Dean grinned. "No, not at all. Actually, I was under the impression from Thomas that it was your idea. He said you were waiting for me at the gallery."

She looked at him, then realized the truth. Not only had she been hoodwinked, she'd also been set up. "Thomas," she said knowingly. "He must be getting desperate. Why don't you just put him out of his misery and tell him you're not bringing your company here to Hayden?"

"Why would I tell him that?" Dean asked.

"Because it's true. You're not staying."

"Actually, I think I'm gonna have to."

"What?" she said, stunned. He smiled. She looked at him, not sure if he was joking with her or not. Then she resolved that he had to be joking. She knew he hated small towns like Hayden. Still, the possibility of him staying, no matter how improbable, made her unintentionally smile.

"What? Is that another smile I see? You're getting there."

"Okay, okay, let's get this tour started. What do you want to see first?"

"Surprise me."

She looked down the street then started walking. He followed, walking by her side. Several residents waved and greeted them while others stopped her to chat, and also to be introduced to Dean. She watched as he was his usual gregarious self—laughing, joking, charming to everyone they met. She shook her head in amazement as they continued walking.

"Well, everything is pretty much like before, but we do have a few new shops, boutiques and restaurants. "The bookstore, bakery, café, cell phone center, and of course Jessie's art gallery are recently new to the town. Plus we're hoping to attract a few more large franchise chain stores."

"Your friend Jessie was a model, wasn't she?" he asked.

Carmen nodded. "Yes, but she quit a few years ago."

"Why?"

"She had a personal tragedy. Her husband died suddenly."

"I'm sorry."

Carmen nodded. "It was quick and unexpected. She was away on a modeling gig and got the call. She moved back here a little over a year ago."

"Right around the time you moved back too," he said. She nodded again. "Your mother told me you once lived in New York City."

"Yes, I did. After you left Hayden I went to college there a year later. Then I got a job and stayed for a few years. When Dad got sick I moved back here to Hayden."

"Do you miss the big city?"

"New York, not really. Hayden will always be my home."

"It took me a while, but I can see why," he said.

"Really? That's surprising. You hated being here when you were younger," she said.

"Yes, I did, for a long time."

"So what changed?"

"Me. I changed. I was looking for something out there that was here all along."

"In Hayden?" she asked.

"In you."

She turned to him. "What do you mean, in me?"

"You, everything about you. Your love for this town and the people here. I never understood it until I left. It's all a part of you. Hayden is your family, your roots, and your history. I never had that growing up. You know how my parents were. They worked and traveled nonstop, anything not to be in the same house together. I used to always think it was about me, that I was the cause. It took me a while to realize I wasn't."

"What made you realize that?" she asked.

"Well, they each have new families now and they're exactly the same way. My mother is still obsessed with shopping and appearances, and my father is focused on working and money. They were my models for family life and relationships. Then, when I moved here, I got a glimpse of a real family dynamic through your eyes, and I didn't appreciate it until I left."

"But what about your grandparents?"

He smiled as if enjoying a private memory. "They are family. But I was too angry about being dumped here to appreciate them. I rebelled, as you well know."

She chuckled. "Yeah, I remember a lot of rebelling."

"The good old days."

"All I know is family. I learned that at an early age. The Stiles have lived here for generations. My ancestors started the bed-and-breakfast as a flophouse over a century ago. It was for people and families who weren't allowed to stay in other hotels and boarding houses because of their skin color. They were welcomed at the Stiles, and its popularity grew from that."

"So you're telling me, in all the generations, no members of the Stiles family have ever left Hayden?"

She smiled. "No, of course not. My dad left, my grandfather left, and I left. I went to college and then lived in New York for a while. It's just that even when we go away we always find our way back. This is and always will be my home."

Dean looked around. "So, what's going on over there?" he asked, seeing several foreclosed and for-sale signs in storefront windows. They crossed the street and stood in front of the vacant stores.

"Like with most of the nation before 2010, the failed economy hit us hard. Being a small town, it was much worse. Hayden suffered. It was a struggle for a while. A lot of people gave up, moved on, and a lot of businesses failed and closed down. But recently things have changed. The town is starting to come back to life. People are moving back and bringing new ideas."

"What kind of ideas?"

"Well, for one, the town has begun to model itself after the 1920s Harlem Renaissance in New York. It's reinventing itself as a charming cultural haven and a tourist and creative mecca.

"The town's main streets are intentionally lined with antique shops, small boutiques, and quaint art and craft studios. We have a small theatre for live performances and music shows just around the corner. But

Hayden's main attractions are the celebrated festivals and events throughout the year. The wine, craft, art, jazz, and antiques festivals are extremely popular events.

"Thousands come from all over the country. And now we're hoping to tap into the international market. This town has layers of history, and every building is artistically distinct. We're building on that," she said.

"You sound very proud of Hayden."

"I am. We've come a long way and there's a lot of promise for more growth here. And as you can see, the huge holiday festival this time of year draws a tremendous amount of visitors to the town. They come in droves. By Christmas Eve, the streets will be teeming with people."

He looked around, seeing all the new faces and feeling the tremendous joyful energy of the holiday celebrations all around him. "So where do you fit into all of this?"

"I run the bed-and-breakfast. People stay there."

"And you like being an innkeeper?" he asked.

She nodded and smiled. "Yes, very much. Some days are admittedly a bit trying, but overall, I love being there."

He nodded. "Yeah, I can see that now. This is nice, us talking and walking around town like this."

"This isn't the first time we hung out in town, Dean. We used to hang out here all the time."

"I don't remember that," he said.

"Sure, you do. Remember, we used to hang out at the amusement arcade around the corner?"

"Oh yeah, that's right. I remember," he said excitedly. "Come one, let's go. I'll play you at the video racing game." He hurried around the corner. She followed. He stopped, looking around. "Where is it? It used to be around here, right?" he said, still looking around.

"Yes, it used to be there," Carmen said, pointing to an empty building on the corner across the street.

"It's gone. What happened to it?"

"At-home video systems kind of eclipsed the corner amusement arcades. Everybody plays at home now with gamers all over the world. It's called progress."

He didn't respond. He knew he was part of that progress. His computer software helped get gaming systems into private homes.

They kept walking, coming to the end of the block. They turned the corner, then headed back down Main Street. "And so . . ." she said, then stopped. "Here we have the local newspaper. It's new. It's called the *Hayden Chronicle.* They print three times a week usually with local news." Carmen looked around. "And I guess that ends the tour."

Dean saw that they were back in front of Jessie's gallery. "This was nice."

"It was nice, talking and reminiscing."

"Thank you for the tour. I gotta tell you, this was definitely a welcome relief."

"What do you mean?"

He smiled. "Walking the streets and listening to Thomas drone on about the new and improved Hayden didn't exactly make my top ten list of things to do."

She laughed. "You're very welcome."

He smiled lovingly. "I love to hear your laughter."

They stared at each other a few seconds until someone blew a car horn and waved. They both waved back. "Well, I have some holiday shopping to do. So I guess I'll see you later."

"Actually, that's perfect. I have a few things I'd like to pick up as well. Mind if I tag along?"

"You're going to anyway, aren't you?"

He smiled. "Of course I am. But how about we grab something to eat first?"

"Sounds good."

"I'll drive. I know a great place to eat. Come on, let's go."

The great place, just outside of Savannah, was right on the water and absolutely perfect. The food was delicious, the atmosphere was charming, and the people were warm and welcoming. After dessert, they sat out on the terrace and enjoyed the sunset as the day ended. "How in the world did you find this place? I had no idea it was even here. It's wonderful."

"A friend of mine lives in Savannah and he came here a lot. When he found out the owner was having financial trouble, he suggested we buy it. The alternative was a developer who wanted to tear it down and build a franchise restaurant."

"So the two of you bought it and you now own a restaurant?"

"We're more like silent partners."

Surprised by his admission, she looked around admiringly. "I'm glad you bought it. It's beautiful just as it is."

"I agree."

On the drive back, they laughed and talked, listened to music and reminisced. When they got back to town, they went shopping. Forty-five minutes later, with several bags in tow, they walked past the jewelry store. He stopped and looked in the window. She went back and stood beside him as he eyed an array of bracelets then necklaces and finally rings.

The last thing Carmen wanted to do was walk into a jewelry store with Dean. As small-town gossip goes, everyone would know they were in there together even before they stopped at the first counter. She could just hear the rumors flying. She walked away. He very reluctantly followed. "Well, that's it for my shopping list. I'm done."

"Not me. I have one more present to buy and I'm kind of stumped. What do you want for Christmas, Carmen?"

She knew what she wanted. She wanted him. But wanting and having were two different things. "I have everything I need," she said.

"Need and want are two different things. Come on, if you could have anything, what would it be?"

"I know what I want. And I know I can't have it."

"Tell me. I promise I can make it happen."

She smiled. "Thank you for dinner. I had a wonderful time."

"Me too. And thanks for the tour. It was enlightening."

"You know Thomas has been trying to get a large company to move here for years. You're on his list. As a matter of fact, you're probably number one on his list now."

"You think so?"

"Yes, of course. He wants you to bring your company here to help restore the town."

"Really?"

She nodded. "If you bring your company here, then other companies are bound to follow. The Christmas parade is the day after tomorrow. Everybody knows you're leaving afterwards. So, he's gonna really turn up the pressure."

"Probably."

"What are you gonna do?"

"Nothing," he said.

"Nothing?"

"Nothing," he repeated.

"You're just going to let him grovel and beg?" she said. He smiled and chuckled. "That's cruel, Dean, even for you. Look, I know the man was a jerk to you back in the day and he probably deserves everything that's coming to him. And I'm sure he feels like a fool for everything, especially that stupid petition. But right now he's just trying to help the town and the people here. I know, just like before, you're just passing through, but he doesn't."

"Well, I can't say I'm not enjoying this. I am. Watching Thomas grovel is entertaining. The man was a bully to me. He had me handcuffed and arrested twice for no reason, and of course there was the petition to get me kicked out of school and void my scholarships. I can't wait to see his face when he hears the announcement. All of his groveling would have been for nothing."

Carmen froze. The last fragment of hope that he'd stay was gone with just a few words. She could feel her heart sink into the lowest pit of despair. It was already done. "The announcement?" she questioned. "So what was all this, the perfect payback?"

He looked at her. "I didn't say that."

"Dean, I know you better than you think you know me."

He scoffed in disbelief. "I doubt that," he said. "I know you."

"Okay, did you know this? Last night in the attic, when we were kissing and you thought I wanted to stop . . ." she began. He nodded attentively. She leaned in closer to his ear. "Well, I was going to suggest we go back to my bedroom and make love."

His jaw dropped in shock. "But why didn't you . . . ?" he began, then stopped, seeing her expression.

She smiled. It felt good catching him off guard for once. Even if it was the truth and he thought she was joking. "It's getting late and I need to get back."

"You're not staying for the ice sculpting tonight?"

"Mom will be here. I have setup duty. Tomorrow's Christmas Eve, a big day."

"I can help you," he suggested.

She chuckled. "No, you have to be here. It's all part of grand marshal duty. And if you're not here, Thomas will probably send out the Marines and Special Forces to come get you."

"No doubt."

He placed her shopping bags into the trunk of her car as she got in. "Thanks again for this evening."

"You sure I can't persuade you to stay here tonight?"

"Sorry. You can tell me about it later."

"I will, promise."

"See you tomorrow."

"Actually, I'll be away most of the day tomorrow. I need to fly out and take care of some business. I'll be back tomorrow evening for the Night of Lights."

"Okay. Have a safe trip. See you when you get back."

She drove off and headed back to the bed-and-breakfast. It was getting harder and harder to say good-bye to Dean. But in two days she knew she'd have to say it again—this time probably forever.

The thought gripped her heart. Tears began to rim her eyes, but she refused to let them fall. Just seeing Dean again was the best Christmas gift she could ever imagine. There was no need to wish for more. If she could, one more night with him would be it, but that hadn't happened and now it never would.

She knew she needed to resolve in her heart that he

was, as always, just passing through and she would always remain true to her family responsibilities. She loved him and her heart was breaking all over again. A lone tear finally fell because she knew there was nothing she could do about it. She had to let him go again.

Chapter 10

Christmas Eve breakfast was packed as usual. Carmen, Marion, and their two employees worked as a perfectly organized team, each performing her allocated duties with ordered haste and meticulous focus. Afterwards, amid the continuous mid-morning flow of guests checking out and checking in, Carmen maintained her usual cheerful demeanor as she looked for Dean each time the front door opened.

As a seasoned innkeeper, she happily gave each departing guest a Stiles Bed and Breakfast commemorative ornament and welcomed the new guests to her home with holiday cookies and beverages of their choice. As they arrived, she placed the previously wrapped gifts she'd purchased for them beneath the tree. As was customary, all guests would have a special gift to open on Christmas Day.

By late afternoon, all the bed-and-breakfast rooms were completely full again. The joy of the holiday season was that there were always new faces to welcome. But there was still one face Carmen had missed seeing all day. Dean hadn't returned, at least she hadn't seen him. She knew he had to be in Hayden to kick off the Night of Lights celebration tonight, but she had hoped he might come back early and stop to see her.

As the hours passed slowly, the day crawled slower and slower. Christmas Eve usually dragged, at least for children. Likewise, she impatiently waited for her special arrival. But still he didn't come. By early evening, the kitchen was prepped and everything was ready for the big Christmas Day breakfast the next morning. Since it was a special day, their breakfast reflected it with a huge menu. Most of the items had been previously started and some had even been brought in special.

As the sun set, so did Carmen's joyful mood. Everyone had gone into town for the Night of Lights celebration, but Carmen stayed. Both Marion and Jessie had asked her to go, but she'd chosen to stay. Someone had to remain behind to prepare the Christmas Eve cookies and drink selection for the guests when the event was over. Plus, she knew that even if Dean was there, they couldn't be together because of everything else going on. Hopefully she'd see him when he returned.

"I got back as soon as I could," Marion said, rushing in. "You missed one of the best shows ever. Dean was the perfect host. He was funny and charming, and everybody loved him."

Her heart instantly stilled. "I'm sure they did."

Marion looked around the dining room at the various cookies, fruits, snacks and drinks available for their guests. "Oh, Carmen, everything looks wonderful."

"Thanks."

Just then, the guests began arriving back from town.

Everyone talked incessantly about the Night of Lights' street-side luminaries and released sky lanterns. Carmen stayed and listened, happily delighted by their excitement. Of course she'd seen the event many times before, but hearing their exuberant enthusiasm made it feel new again.

She waited downstairs in hopes that Dean would return soon, but he didn't. After a while, she gave up and headed to her room. She knew she wouldn't be getting any sleep any time soon. She walked over to the French doors, opened them, and stepped out onto her balcony. Usually a crisp December breeze greeted her, but tonight the weather was unseasonably warm. She stared out across to Hayden in the far distance as she sat down.

For the first time in a long time, she didn't find peaceful serenity in the town's lights. She looked up at the stars. With her balcony facing south, she knew her bedroom faced away from Ursa Minor and the long-gone Ursid shower. Still, she searched the heavens. But her answers weren't out there and she knew it.

She thought about all the nights she had wished for Dean to come back to her and now he was here. He had gotten into her head and into her heart. She knew after the first kiss that she was still in love with him. Jessie was right, she thought as the image of her ripping his clothes off popped into her head. When he left this time, she wanted a memory to last her a lifetime.

Then, without a second thought, she stood up and walked to the grand suite. She hesitated a brief second. Excited, nervous, and thrilled, she felt her heart pound as if she were a teenager waiting for the popular guy in school to notice her. "This is ridiculous," she muttered to herself. "I'm a grown woman—I can do this. I can ask him to make love to me." She knocked on the door before her rational self came to its senses.

The brief wait seemed to take forever. After a few seconds, it was obvious he wasn't there. She hurried back to her room. What was she thinking? A few minutes later, she heard a soft quiet knock on her bedroom door. It was just loud enough to get her attention. She knew who it was even before she stood up. It was their special signal. She knocked her reply, then opened the door and saw Dean, casually dressed, standing there. His sexy smile was irresistible.

He reached out his hand. She took it and in silence he pulled her close and whispered in her ear. "Get dressed and meet me." Then he turned and walked away.

She gasped, ready to speak, but he was already gone. He didn't have to tell her where to meet him. Seeing him barefoot, she already knew. She quickly dressed in shorts and a top and hurried up to the attic. As soon as she walked in, she saw the far window open. No one ever opened that window except for him or her. It was the one place on the roof of the attic where the slant was level enough to sit out without fear of falling off. It was also the place they'd met years ago.

"Dean." She walked over and looked out. He was already out there sitting on the roof. "Hey," she said.

"Come on out. Careful," he said.

"You know our insurance rates are going to go through the roof if you slip and fall off."

"We've been out here a hundred times."

"We were kids," she said. Then she saw the blanket and small basket beside him. "So what is all this?" she asked.

"A celebration," he said, reaching his hand to help her out onto the roof.

Barefoot as well, she stepped out and sat next to him on the blanket he'd laid out. As soon as she was settled, he opened the picnic basket and took out two glasses and a bottle of champagne. He filled the glasses and gave one to her. "I guess everything went well today," she said.

He smiled. "I'll tell you all about that later." He raised his glass. "Right now we're celebrating. To you," he said.

She nodded and touched her glass to his. They sipped the champagne; then she nervously looked up at the sky. Millions of stars shined down on them. "Orion, Taurus, Gemini. Wow, I forgot how beautiful this view can be this time of year."

"I didn't," he said, looking directly at her instead of at the sky.

Seeing him staring at her made her blush. "You're supposed to be looking at the view, not at me."

"I'm looking at the only view that will ever matter."

She handed him her glass. If she was going to do this, she needed to do it now. "Dean, I have a question to ask you."

"Yes," he answered.

"You don't even know what the question is yet."

"It doesn't matter. The answer will always be, yes."

"This is my home and I can't leave. I don't want to leave. I have a responsibility and I know you do too. You're leaving tomorrow, so I was wondering, since this is our last night together, if we could . . ."

"I would have stayed for you," he said, interrupting her.

"What?"

"Before."

She nodded, realizing he was talking about years ago when they were younger. "I know, but you would have hated yourself and then one day you would have looked at me and hated me. This place that I love so much would have suffocated you. I couldn't let that happen."

"So you told me you didn't love me, so I'd be mad enough to leave you."

"You needed to go."

He shook his head. "No, I needed to be with you."

She shook her head. "None of that matters anymore."

"You know, for a long time I actually believed you. I was so mad at you, at myself, at everything. All that time we were together—I thought you had betrayed me just like my parents did."

"I'm sorry. I needed you to believe me and go."

"Carmen."

"I know we can't go back to the past. I understand that. I have a job that's important to me here. People depend on me. My family depends on me. Mom doesn't own this place, Dean. I do. My father left it to me to keep it in the bloodline. That's how it's done. I always knew that. That's how it's always been done in the Stiles family. So this isn't about wanting you to stay. I know you can't and . . ."

"Carmen," he interrupted.

"No, wait. I need to say this. You have your company. And it's major and I know that. It's just as important to you. I can't compete with that, and I'd never even try or even ask you to choose. You're leaving, and I just want us to be together for one night. To last a lifetime, that's all I need," she finally blurted out.

"Carmen," he said, cupping her face, "I'm staying."

She looked at him puzzled. "What?"

"I love you. I always have and I always will. I'm

staying here in Hayden. I have to. This is where my life is, with you."

"Dean, I . . ." The kiss came instantly. He wrapped his arm firmly around her waist to keep her from falling, then pulled her close. The kiss was hard and long, taking her breath away. It was intense and fierce and more powerful than she could ever imagine. She parted her lips and his tongue slipped into her mouth and hers into his. She savored the sensuous feel of their connection. Her mind soared to dizzying heights. Then suddenly she broke the kiss and looked at him. "You're staying, right?"

He nodded. She smiled and kissed him over and over again. This time, it was slow and passionate. Then, as the kiss lingered, she snuggled closer into his embrace.

"Look at that," he said, pointing across the water. She turned. In the far distance, just beyond the town, they saw two sky lanterns, brightly lit, gently float up into the night. She laughed. He joined in. "I feel like my heart is soaring just like the lanterns." They watched them climb higher and higher until they eventually disappeared into the night sky. "Marry me."

"Dean."

"Will you marry me?" he asked.

She smiled sadly. "No"

"What?"

"Dean, you know I want to say yes, I do, but I can't. How can I? I know you're leaving as soon as this is over. You have a business out there and you're right in the middle of a merger. You can't just walk away from that."

"Let me worry about that. Just say yes."

She shook her head. "No, I can't. You leave and I stay. Nothing's changed."

"Carmen, say yes and trust me."

She thought about the one night they were engaged

ten years ago. It was the best few hours of her life. She smiled and nodded slowly knowing this would be their last time together. "Yes."

He kissed her, then wrapped his arm around her as they laid back on the roof in silence. She curled into him and cuddled close as he held her tight and stroked her back. "This is a perfect memory. Thank you," she whispered.

"They're many more to come."

"That would be nice," she said, knowing it was possible.

"I think we should stay up here all night. I always wanted to make love to you out here beneath the stars."

She sat up and looked at him. "Really? On the roof?"

"Yeah, call it a fantasy. You, me, naked, making love up here on the roof beneath the stars on a night like tonight."

"That sounds tempting, albeit a bit challenging."

"Aren't you up for a challenge?" he teased.

She looked around, then at the ground four stories down. "Actually, I have a better idea. Come with me," she said, taking his hand. He grabbed the champagne and basket, and they climbed back inside.

A few minutes later, Dean opened the door to his suite. He smiled and stepped aside. Carmen walked in and looked around as if she'd never seen the room before. As always, it was perfectly neat. The only signs that someone was staying there were the large architect's open tube, some unrolled blueprints, the laptop computer, and the papers on the office desk in the alcove.

"Carmen."

She turned around, right into his embrace. Without a word, passion erupted instantly as their mouths fused. His hands went right to her breasts, which were covered only by the thin cotton T-shirt. Her nipples, already pebbled from the rooftop kiss, hardened instantly. He tweaked each one as he deepened the kiss. She moaned, writhing against the torturous, tantalizing pain that felt so damn good.

She grabbed at his jeans, unbuttoned them, and pulled at his zipper, getting it only halfway down. Impatiently, she began unfastening the buttons on his shirt, ripping the last two off. Then she pulled it away from his shoulders to see his strong, hard chest. She touched him and smiled. It was much firmer and broader than she remembered. It was a man's chest, a man's body. Breathless, she looked up at him. "This was a long time coming. Make love to me, Dean."

There was no response necessary.

In staggering speed they were all over each other. Frantic and desperate, hands and tongues grabbed, stroked, massaged, tweaked, pressed, licked, tasted, suckled in frenzied release. Both topless, they moved to the bed. He sat down and pulled her, still standing, between his legs. His hands rested on her hips. He looked up and down her body, then slowly unzipped her shorts and pulled them free.

She stood in just scant panties. He licked his lips, sending a shiver of delight through her body. He opened his mouth and pulled her close. The first time he licked her nipple, her body tensed. She watched in awe, amazed by his ravenous appetite. He was slow and seductive, licking, tasting, nibbling, and sucking his fill.

Then he reached back and squeezed her buttocks while he suckled both breasts side by side, over and over again. The sensation was mind-blowing. Her toes curled and her insides quivered as she nearly fainted. His torturous tongue licked and teased the rest of her body front and back until her legs wobbled. His mouth and hands were everywhere.

She gasped and moaned as her head rocked back from the blinding pleasure of him. Then his hand slipped between her legs, finding her swollen pleasure. He massaged her. She could feel herself coming as her nails bit into his shoulders. One finger, two fingers, three, went deep into her as the maniacal massage continued. The searing heat of his actions pushed her too close to the edge. Then she was over. She climaxed hard and long, then weakened, fell against him. He grabbed her and eased her down on the bed. Then he stood, removed his jeans, and grabbed a condom from his pocket.

In an instant, he covered himself and stood over her. Her breath caught at seeing him, long, thick, and hard. She smiled in nervous anticipation. She bent her knees and spread her legs, and he entered her slowly at first. Then he surged all the way, deep inside, filling her completely. She cried out in pleasurable pain.

"Are you okay?" he whispered.

"Better than okay," she said, breathless.

He pushed deeper in strong steady strokes. Slowly at first, then the frenzied fury of passion took him. He plunged into her and she met him with equal force. Her heart pounded as he raised her up and grabbed her rear, dictating the final pace. She thrust her hips up to meet him, each stroke hard, faster, deeper sending them closer and closer to the edge.

A muffled shriek escaped as she climaxed and spasm after spasm shot through her body. Then, seconds later, she felt him tense and a ferocious tremor surge through his body bringing a guttural groan from his throat. He held on to her and she held on to him.

With sweet, tender kissing, he eased over, pulling

her to his side. Breathless, she closed her eyes and lay against his chest. Hours later, the next time they made love, it was slow and unhurried and lasted a good long time. It was another one of Dean's fantasies.

Carmen woke up to pebbled nipples and something very hard poking into her back. "Hey," she muttered over her shoulder. "You're awake."

"Merry Christmas." He kissed her neck and continued stroking the curve of her body.

"Merry Christmas," she purred and snuggled back against him. "It's still dark. What time is it?"

Dean glanced over at the side table. "It's four-thirty."

"I need to get out of here," she said, then moved the covers back to get out of the bed. He quickly encircled her waist and pulled her back against his naked body. His penis poked her again. She smiled. "And put that away. You have a parade to do in a couple of hours."

"I have a better idea."

"Yeah, I bet you do."

"Do the parade with me," he said, kissing her neck and shoulder, then working his way down the side of her body.

"No way." She tried to scoot away, but he held her tight.

"Come on, it'll be fun. We can be grand marshals together. I'm sure Thomas will be delighted."

"Before or after his heart attack when you show up late?"

"Okay, okay, let's get in the shower. Kill two birds. And another one of my fantasies."

"How many fantasies do you have?"

"With you, the list is endless." He jumped up and grabbed her legs as she squealed and giggled. He picked her up, put her over his shoulder, and slapped her rear. She shrieked louder this time as he headed to the bathroom.

As soon as he got there, he set her down and turned on the shower faucets. Specially designed for the grand suite, the multiple jets immediately sprayed water. He stepped into the glass-enclosed shower and held his hand out for her to join him. "Come on. I want to see you wet."

"Let me guess, another fantasy."

He laughed. "Of course."

"We need a condom," she said, smiling.

He looked around the bathroom quickly. "I think I have one more in my briefcase. It's on the desk in the alcove."

"I'll get it." She nodded and hurried out. Naked, she walked over to the alcove. She opened his briefcase, looked in the top compartment pocket, and found a gold foil packet. "Got it."

"Hurry up! I'm getting lonely," he called out.

Smiling happily, she closed the case sending the rolled blueprints and papers flying everywhere. She quickly picked them up, barely seeing what was written on them. Then she stopped cold, reading the top of the blueprint and the architect renderings. "Texas site," she said.

Her heart collapsed. With this already done, she knew Hayden never stood a chance. "Payback." She put everything back on the table and quickly dressed.

"Hey, what's taking you so long?" he called out from the bathroom. He came out wet with a towel wrapped around his waist. He stopped, seeing her dressed and standing at the desk with the blueprints in her hands.

His jaw tightened in restraint. He knew exactly

what she thought. "Carmen, I know what this looks like, but . . ."

"What? What could this possibly look like, other than what it is? Your company is merging and moving to Texas. Hayden never had a chance and neither did I. All this was just a lie." She stormed away.

He rushed over and grabbed her arm before she got to the door. "Carmen, you've got it wrong."

"I know what just happened, I know what I just got. But I'm too much of a lady to say it."

"No, wait. Listen to me. I love you. This wasn't a lie."

"I guess I deserve payback too?" She shook her arm loose and glared at him. "Funny, the joke's on me. I love you and I don't know how to stop." She turned and walked out.

Chapter 11

Thankfully the excitement of Christmas Day took her instantly. She showered, dressed, and hurried down to get breakfast started as quickly as she could. The last thing she wanted was to run into Dean in the corridors.

Knowing that she had already prepped everything the night before, there really wasn't a lot to do except baking.

"Good morning," Marion said, already in the kitchen baking.

"Good morning, Mom. Merry Christmas," she said, kissing her mother's cheek.

"Merry Christmas, honey. Sleep well?" she asked as she always did each morning.

"Fine," Carmen lied, immediately busying herself with the morning chores. Since the Christmas morning breakfast had a fuller menu, there was more to do. In less than an hour, she set up the dining room, got breakfast ready, and prepared the last batch of cookies for the parade volunteers. The good thing was that very few town residents usually came to breakfast on

Christmas Day. That meant a lot less people, and that was fine with her.

After a while, she focused all her attention on getting the cookies packed up in the car while her mother took care of the breakfast guests. "Mom, I think I'm gonna get these down to the parade route. I'm sure some of the volunteers are already out there."

"Okay, but don't you want to wait to wish Dean a merry Christmas?"

"No," she said curtly.

Marion looked and her face frowned. "What happened?"

"We'll talk later. Merry Christmas, Mom. See you later."

"Merry Christmas, honey."

Dean stood, wet and half wrapped in a towel, staring at the closed door. He could have blocked the door, held her down, and made her listen, but he knew talking to Carmen right now would be futile. She'd never hear him. She was too angry. And he knew what it was like to be that angry and feel betrayed by someone who was supposed to love you.

He walked over to the desk and looked at the plans she found. Sure, he could see how they could be misconstrued if she didn't have all the information. But she'd never stopped to ask.

He shook his head and smirked, thinking this was the second time he had been engaged to the same woman for one single night. He had no idea how he was going to fix this. But he knew someone who could. He grabbed his cell phone and called his friend.

"Dean," Jared answered sleepily, "man, you had

better have a damn good reason for calling me this early in the morning. I just walked in the house."

"Jared, I have a job for you."

He laughed. "Since when do you get yourself jammed up?"

Dean sighed heavily. "Man . . . I don't know what to do."

"Start from the beginning," Jared said, sounding more alert. "Don't leave anything out. I want every detail."

Dean told him about Carmen, the morning, the night before, and the last few days. "I love her. I need her."

Jared chuckled. "Yeah, I can hear it in your voice."

"All this, everything I did, was for her. I owe her my life."

"Okay, so she's got the wrong information and there's no way you telling her will correct this."

"Yeah, pretty much. Plus I can't tell her about the impending sale. If I do, I'll jeopardize a lot of jobs and a lot of good people."

"Perhaps we can maneuver around that. Let me see what I can do."

"Thanks, man. I owe you. What do you need from me?"

"I'd say a bottle of Glenfiddich Roberts Reserve fifty-five or a Macallan twenty-six, but I'll settle for a nice twenty-five-year-old Chivas Regal Scotch and a Cuban."

"You got it. When will . . . ?"

"Social media should be trending by noon."

Dean smiled, shaking his head. Jared was a whiz at manipulating social media to move in any direction he pointed. As soon as they were on board, the national news cycles would follow within hours. All and all, he wasn't sure if his friend's particular skill set was a good thing or scary as hell. Either way, he knew right now it was saving his life. "You know, that's scary how you do that."

"Yeah, so I've heard. Now get off my phone so I can do my job. Oh, and don't forget my cigars."

"Merry Christmas."

"Right back at ya."

Dean ended the call, showered, and dressed. As soon as he gathered his paperwork, his room phone rang. He answered with the slightest hope that it was Carmen. But it wasn't. It was the front desk informing him that Thomas Ford was in the foyer waiting to escort him to the parade.

"Damn." He forgot all about the parade. Then it occurred to him that Carmen would be there. And suddenly he didn't mind. He headed down to breakfast and saw Marion in the dining room with Thomas. "Merry Christmas," he said.

"Merry Christmas," they said in unison.

Thomas stood quickly, slapped his hands together, and smiled brightly. "It's a beautiful day out there. Perfect for the parade. Shall we get started?"

"Thomas, let the man eat something first," Marion said.

"Oh, right, of course. By all means."

"Is Carmen around?" Dean asked.

"No, she's already in town setting up. You remember, we help supply the snacks for the parade volunteers."

He nodded. "Actually, I'm not too hungry. Let's get to that parade."

Thomas was so excited he nearly jumped into the air.

"Well, at least let me get you a cup of coffee and a little something to take with you," Marion said. "It's gonna be a long parade. Come on in the kitchen. Thomas, Dean will be right out."

As soon as Marion and Dean went into the kitchen, she turned to him. "What's going on with you and my daughter?"

Dean shook his head. "I proposed."

Marion's face instantly lit up to gleeful elation; then, seeing Dean's expression, it just as quickly turned to woeful trepidation. "What happened?"

"She saw some plans on my desk."

"What kind of plans?"

"The old Texas plans from before we sold the company. I liked what the architect did, so I pulled them out to scope out some property in the area here."

"And so it looks like you're moving the company to Texas instead of selling it," she surmised. He nodded. "So, just tell her the truth. You told me. "

"And you know I wasn't supposed to."

"But you did and now you need to tell Carmen."

He shook his head. "She's not listening to me right now."

"Fine, I'll tell her."

"No, I have to make this right."

There was a timid knock on the kitchen door; then Thomas stuck his head in smiling. "Ready to go?"

Three hours later, the parade was a huge sensation. According to Thomas's count, there were over ten thousand people in attendance—double the size from a year ago. He beamed the entire time. Carmen and Jessie handed out holiday cookies to all the parade volunteers and small kids gathered. "So, Grinch, what's up with you?"

Carmen shook her head. "I took your advice."

"Which advice?"

"With Dean."

Jessie grinned. "And?"

"It was horrible."

"What, he was bad in bed?"

"Oh, no, God, no, the man is amazing, but he's also a liar and a cheat."

"Meaning what? He's married?"

"No, although he proposed again last night."

"And you accepted, then dumped him. Seriously, what's with you two? I wish you'd just get married already. You clearly love each other, so what's the problem?"

"He told me he was staying."

"Great."

"I found out he's not. He's moving his company to Texas."

"Really? That's kinda strange."

"What do you mean?"

"He's trending. Didn't you see it?"

"See what? You know I don't do the social network thing."

"Woman, get an account," Jessie joked. "Anyway, it's all over the news in hashtag format. It's final. He sold his company for a crazy sum of money, plus stock options."

"And?"

"And, it looks like the previous rumors that he was merging his company and relocating were wrong. He's selling it, or rather he sold it."

"So, he doesn't have his company anymore."

"That's right."

"And he can stay here like he told me."

Jessie nodded.

"He didn't lie."

"No. But with the money he's coming into, he can

start a new company anywhere he wants, even here in Hayden."

Carmen shook her head. "Why didn't' he tell me?"

"Because I couldn't." Carmen and Jessie turned. Dean stood behind them.

"Merry Christmas and congratulations," Jessie said to Dean, then turned to Carmen before walking away. "See you tonight at Christmas dinner. Good luck."

"Why didn't you just tell me?"

"The deal needed to go through before it was made public. There's the problem with manipulations of stock. But since today is Christmas, the market is closed for the weekend, and the official announcement is Monday morning before the market opens, word leaked out prematurely. The deal is done. I signed off on it yesterday. My company has been officially sold."

"So you are staying in Hayden."

"Where else would I be? I've held my breath for years as a thousand random acts sent me all over this country, but it was love that brought me back here to you. How could I possibly leave here again? I love you."

"I love you, too," she said.

"So, looks like I'm out of a job. Know anybody hiring, maybe at the Stiles Bed and Breakfast?"

She grinned. "Yeah, I think maybe we can find you something to do there."

"Good."

"Now here's my fantasy," she said. "Will you marry me?"

He laughed. "Oh, sweetheart, definitely." He grabbed her up and spun her around, then set her back down. "And I have a little something for you." He pulled a small velvet box out of his pocket and opened it. There was a stunning single diamond stone set in the center of a double row of smaller diamonds.

"Oh, Dean, it's beautiful."

He took it out and placed it on her finger. "Merry Christmas. I love you forever."

"Merry Christmas. I love you forever, right back."

They kissed. "So what do you think about a wedding on the attic roof?" he asked.

She laughed. "No."

"How about the honeymoon?"

"No." She laughed again.

He pulled her into his embrace again. "I love to hear you laugh. How about anywhere you say as long as it's here in Hayden?" She nodded. They kissed again, knowing that this was the beginning of their life together, forever.

Mistletoe Lane

❧━◆━◆━◆━❧

REGINA HART

Chapter 1

"Picture this." June Cale made her pitch for the Kwanzaa presentation from the threadbare seat in front of her boss's desk at the Guiding Light Community Center. It was Monday morning, the second day of November. They were running out of time. "Saturday afternoon before Thanksgiving, our community room is set up like an auditorium. A makeshift stage is built in front of the room. Doctor Quincy Spates, professor of African American History at Trinity Falls University, stands on the stage. From a podium, he leads a free discussion on the seven values of Kwanzaa."

Benjamin Brooks, the center's new director and her boss of two months, lowered his coffee mug. As usual, his handsome sienna features were hard to read, emotionless. *The Iceman.* "How does a free presentation raise money for the center?"

"It's not a fund-raiser." June adjusted the project folder on her lap. "Doctor Spates's discussion is a community-engagement event. The goal of this event is to help strengthen our relationship with the community, which will—hopefully—make it easier to persuade them to support the center."

June considered her boss's conservative blue tie and the snow-white linen shirt that hugged his well-muscled shoulders. They both looked expensive—and out of place in the worn and faded office. Why had Benjamin Brooks really returned home to Trinity Falls?

Like his youngest brother, Vaughn, who was a professor of music at Trinity Falls University, Benjamin Brooks was a dangerously attractive man. His dark brown hair was cut neat and close. His square jaw was clean shaven. Piercing ebony eyes beneath thick dark eyebrows dominated his chiseled features. June's tripping pulse wasn't all due to nerves.

Yes, Ben Brooks is a good-looking man. But right now, I want to shake him silly.

"Has Quincy agreed to do the Kwanzaa presentation?" Benjamin wrapped his coffee mug between his hands. Was he trying to warm them? His office was like an ice box.

"I asked him to hold the date. But I need to confirm with him." June's nerves were tingling again. Benjamin was a lot less enthusiastic than she'd hoped.

"You're not giving him much time. Today's November second." Benjamin's gaze settled somewhere behind June. She assumed he was consulting the twelve-month calendar his predecessor had posted to the wall. "The Saturday before Thanksgiving is November twenty-first, less than three weeks away."

"If you approve of the idea, I'll invite him today." June waited for him to say the words.

June had approached Quincy when she'd started her position as deputy director and fund-raising manager in August. He'd agreed to hold the date. However, she hadn't wanted to confirm the event until her new boss had settled in after his September start date. With one center crisis after another, time had slipped away and the November date had rushed up on her.

"What else do you have?" Benjamin settled back on his gray cushioned chair. He seemed underwhelmed.

June regrouped. "Picture this. The community room transformed into a winter wonderland. Traditional Christmas dishes and desserts served in a winding buffet line while Christmas carols and secular pop songs provide music for a dinner dance." June saw it in her mind's eye. The image made her smile.

"Didn't a special community fund-raising committee just host a party for the center?" Again, Benjamin appeared less than impressed.

"That was in January. It was a twentieth anniversary party for the center." June had heard around town that the event had been an incredible success.

"We shouldn't host a fund-raising party in January, then another in December. That's overkill." Tension seemed to hover around Benjamin like a cloud. *Why?*

"Going forward, I think we should host a Christmas dinner dance. Then, the center's anniversary in January could be our annual online day of giving."

"What's that?"

"Giving Tuesdays and The Big Give are national examples of days of giving. We'll focus all our energies on one day, the center's birthday, and ask people to either make a donation online or mail a check. I'm working on a process for the project."

"It sounds like a good idea." Benjamin nodded as he sipped more coffee.

"Great. Then I'll move forward with the Christmas dinner dance." The anxious butterflies in her stomach settled down.

"I don't want to do a Christmas celebration." Benjamin

waved a hand, dismissing June's proposal. "Everyone's doing that."

"Who else is doing a Christmas fund-raiser?" June searched her mind but couldn't think of a single organization in Trinity Falls that was doing a similar event.

"Books and Bakery."

"Megan hosts a Christmas-themed store event similar to her Halloween party and story time. But it's not a fund-raiser." Megan McCloud was the owner of Books & Bakery. Her themed events were highly anticipated in the community.

"Close enough."

June couldn't disagree more. "Our event will be very different from Books and Bakery's."

Benjamin was shaking his head even before June finished speaking. "We should avoid events that are even remotely similar to long-established traditions like Books and Bakery's Christmas celebration."

June was almost speechless with disappointment. She tried a different approach. "One of the reasons I think a Christmas dance would be successful is that the January birthday party brought in a lot of money and increased attendance for our other events."

"Come up with something else, June." Benjamin's tone was flat with finality.

June took a moment to moderate her tone. Her gaze circled his office. It was Benjamin's ninth week on the job. Why was he making such slow progress toward moving all the way into his office? Shelf spaces and cabinet surfaces were bare. Faded patches on the walls revealed where his predecessor had hung framed photographs and plaques. When would Benjamin do the same? The only personal item in his office was a framed photograph of two young children. His son and daughter? They were beautiful.

She turned back to her new boss. "Do you have any suggestions?"

"I'm sure you'll think of something."

June was glad one of them thought so. "May I at least go forward with the Kwanzaa presentation? As you said, we need to give Dr. Spates time to prepare, provided he agrees to do the presentation."

Benjamin seemed to hesitate. "Sure, the presentation should be fine."

June stood to leave. Her gut burned with frustration. At the threshold of his modest office, she once again faced Benjamin. "We need a year-end event, something spectacular to engage the community. I spent a lot of time developing the proposal and budget for the Christmas dinner dance."

Benjamin leaned into his desk. "I appreciate your time and efforts. Perhaps some of your work could be applied to your new idea."

His message was loud and clear: her dinner dance was a nonstarter. *Come up with something else.* But did he have even one clue of what went into coming up with and executing these events?

"I'll see what I can do." June walked out of Benjamin's office.

Her heart wouldn't be engaged in any other idea, though. She'd wanted to raise money for the center but she also wanted to celebrate Christmas. Why was The Iceman being such a Scrooge?

Benjamin's cellular phone rang, interrupting his contemplation of the semi-empty refrigerator in his townhouse Monday evening. Welcoming the reprieve, he allowed the fridge's door to swing shut and fished his phone from the front pocket of his gray slacks. He recognized his ex-wife's telephone number on the identification screen. *Perfect.*

He counseled himself to keep calm as he accepted her call. "Hello, Aliyah."

"Ben, how are you?" She sounded hesitant. It had been almost a year since their marriage had ended, Christmas Eve's Eve. Still, in the seven months since their divorce had been finalized, neither of them had gotten used to the coldness of their new relationship.

"What is it, Aliyah?" He didn't want to chat or catch up. He wanted this call to be over, the sooner the better.

"When last did you hear from the children?" Aliyah's voice was tense.

"It's been a while." Benjamin had spoken with their nineteen-year-old son, Terence, and eighteen-year-old daughter, Zora, perhaps two weeks ago. He'd last seen them about three months ago when he and Aliyah had helped them move into the residence halls at The Ohio State University at the beginning of the school year: "Why?"

"They've stopped returning my calls."

"They aren't returning mine, either." When Benjamin did reach them, their conversations were frustratingly brief. He didn't know which was worse, their silence or the one-sided conversations with their monosyllabic responses. "They're upset about our divorce. They don't understand why we won't get back together."

"They know now," Aliyah reassured him.

"What do you mean?" Benjamin needed to sit down. He moved into the living room of his small, two-story townhouse.

His black leather recliner was one of the most uncomfortable pieces of furniture ever created. He'd bought his furniture—the black television stand, coffee table, and entertainment system, and the matching black leather sofa—to fill the room. Comfort hadn't been his first priority.

"I told them I'd had an affair." Aliyah's words were low with shame. "I didn't like what our breakup was doing to your relationship with them. It wasn't fair that they blamed you for our divorce."

"How did it go?" Benjamin sank deeper into the stiff recliner.

The discussion must have taken a lot of courage on Aliyah's part. Benjamin couldn't bring himself to express his gratitude for her confession, though. The wound her betrayal had caused was still too fresh. He couldn't get past it or the fact that, if Aliyah hadn't had an affair, they wouldn't need to tell their children about it. He wouldn't have had to leave his job. And he wouldn't have returned to his small hometown of Trinity Falls in northeast Ohio to start over.

"Telling them was difficult and ugly. And now they're not speaking to me." There were tears in Aliyah's voice.

"I'm sorry." Surprisingly, it was the truth. He was sorry their children were giving her the silent treatment. She'd been a faithless wife, but there was no denying she was a loving mother.

"So am I." Aliyah paused. "Thanksgiving is less than four weeks away. I thought they'd come home for school break."

"What makes you think they won't?" This would be the first Thanksgiving he'd spend without his family in nineteen years. Benjamin rubbed his chest to ease the weight crushing his heart.

"Well, for one thing, they're not returning my calls." Aliyah's words wobbled around a forced chuckle.

"They'll come around." It was time to get off the phone. He couldn't control his emotions much longer.

"What are you doing for Thanksgiving, Ben?"

Benjamin gritted his teeth. Why was she asking? What did she expect to hear? "I'll probably spend it with my brothers."

"I'd forgotten that Zach had moved back to Trinity Falls as well. Now all of the Brooks brothers are back in town."

Benjamin didn't find her observation amusing. He loved Trinity Falls, but he'd had a family and a life in Chicago—before the woman who'd promised to love and cherish him until "death do us part" had cheated on him. Repeatedly.

"I hope you and the kids enjoy Thanksgiving. I'll call." Benjamin pushed himself up from the recliner.

"Spend Thanksgiving with us." Aliyah's request rushed down the cell phone connection.

Benjamin froze. "You want us to be like a family again?" *She must be kidding.*

"I want the kids to spend Thanksgiving at home. I also want them to see us getting along."

Benjamin rubbed the back of his neck. "What about Larry?"

Larry Cox had been Aliyah's lover for almost two years. He'd also been Benjamin's boss at Hughes & Coal Corp., the Chicago-based financial investment company for which he'd worked for almost twenty years.

"Larry and I aren't seeing each other anymore." Aliyah's admission was surprising.

She'd waited until their divorce to break off her extramarital affair. What, if anything, should he read into that?

"I'll call you and the kids on Thanksgiving Day." He started to end the call.

"Ben, please. They're not speaking to me." Aliyah's voice broke. "I'm not too proud to ask for your help."

"There's nothing I can do for you. Terry and Zora

need time." Benjamin touched the screen to end the call.

Hopefully, time was all he needed as well to banish the bitterness and anger in his heart. June's pitch for the center's Christmas dinner dance came to his mind. Benjamin shook his head. How could he approve the event? He wasn't exactly in the Christmas mood.

June's cellular phone rang just as she entered her home Monday evening. She fished the device from her purse as she locked her door. The caller identification listed her son's name.

"Wow, two phone calls in one week." June kicked off her shoes, then crossed the entryway of her colonial home. "To what do I owe this bountiful pleasure?"

"Real funny, Mom." Noah's words held suppressed laughter. "How're you doing?"

June hung her emerald winter coat in the closet before walking to her family room. She collapsed onto the welcoming cushions of her foam-green love seat, a match to her sofa and armchair.

"About the same as I was when we spoke yesterday. How are you?" She turned up the volume on her Mom Hearing. She and Noah had always been close. But this evening, June sensed something more than that behind his attentiveness.

"Are you settling in okay in Trinity Falls?"

June's brows knitted at the concern she heard in her child's voice. *Why is he still worrying about me?* "Noah, I've told you I'm fine. This is your freshman year. You should be focusing on your classes."

Her heart swelled with pride that her son had earned a full academic scholarship to Columbia University in New York. She gazed at the photos lining her fireplace mantel and the ones mounted to the walls. With very little effort, she relived events from her son's birth to young adulthood: first day of kindergarten, first communion, confirmation, pee wee football, high school graduation and moving onto Columbia's campus. She blinked away tears. *Has any son ever made a mother prouder?*

June swallowed the lump in her throat. "How are your classes?"

"They're all right." There was an echo behind Noah's voice and muted conversations in the distance. He must be using his cell phone in the hallway again. *Is he getting along with his roommate?*

June arched a brow. "After ten weeks of classes, the best review you could give me is 'all right'? Are you keeping up with your readings?"

"Yes, ma'am. It's hard, but I'm making it work." His sigh stirred all her maternal instincts. *Is he getting enough sleep? Is he eating right? He gave up football. Is he still finding time to exercise?*

June took a breath to ask him all of these questions again, but Noah spoke first.

"How was the Books and Bakery Halloween party?" His tone was too casual.

"It was nice. I had a good time." *Didn't we talk about this yesterday?*

June had attended Books & Bakery's annual Halloween party and children's story time on Saturday, which had been Halloween. Trinity Falls's residents had crowded the bookstore and café. They were dressed as historical figures, or popular characters from comic books, novels, movies and television. June had gone as Florence Nightingale. She'd always admired the historical figure. She still wasn't sure what Benjamin had been. Dressed in jeans, flannel shirt, and a tool belt, he'd claimed to be a handyman. June and Megan McCloud, Books & Bakery's owner and the organizer of the Halloween event, had given him a D for effort.

"Are you sure you had a good time?" Noah persisted.

The virtual lightbulb came on in June's brain. *I'm going to ground him.* "How long have you been using Darius to check up on me?" Silence. "Noah?" She used her best warning tone.

"I didn't ask Darius to spy on you, Mom. I promise. You told me you were going to the party. And Darius told me some people have been giving you a hard time. I was worried something might have happened at the bookstore."

"Noah, I can—"

"Take care of yourself. I know." He sighed and June pictured her eighteen-year-old son taking on the weight of the world. "But just like a mother worries about her son, a son worries about his mother."

June was momentarily speechless. *Look at him, using my words to turn the tables on me.* "Noah, I appreciate your concern, but I need you to remain focused on your future."

"I wouldn't be as worried if you were still living in Sequoia. Sequoia is familiar."

June rose and paced across the room to the fireplace. "Neither of us expected Making an Event would file for bankruptcy the week Darius and I moved you into Columbia."

She should have realized the marketing and event-planning company for which she'd worked for the past fourteen years was getting ready to close its doors forever. But she was a single parent, working a demanding job, and helping her son prepare for college.

"I guess Mayor Lopez offering you the job with Trinity

Falls's community center was like good news, bad news." Noah still sounded troubled.

"It was all good news." She injected even more confidence into her voice. "We must remember to count our blessings instead of our burdens. This job is an exciting change. It's a promotion. The pay's better. I was fortunate to sell our home quickly and for enough money to put a decent down payment on this one."

"I remember what it was like when people in Sequoia rejected you. I don't want you to go through that again." The pain in her child's voice ripped her heart in two.

"It's not the same, Noah." She wasn't a young woman on her own with a baby to protect. She was a much more mature and battle-tested woman who'd single-handedly raised an impressive young man. "I already have friends in Trinity Falls."

"People who aren't that friendly are there, too."

"What can I do to convince you that I'm fine?" June paced back across the room and dropped onto the sofa.

"Tell me if people are giving you a hard time."

"What will you do?"

"I might not be able to do anything, but I at least want to know. Promise me."

Tension drained from June, bringing forth a smile. "Well, if you want to know about the difficult people I'm dealing with, let me tell you about my new boss."

"Is he as bad as Miss Gina?" Noah's voice sounded lighter. She pictured the smile on his handsome, young face.

Gina Carter owned Making an Event. She was a nice person, but her lack of planning had often caused chaos for June and the rest of the staff. At least she could reason with the older woman. Benjamin Brooks was distractingly attractive. But once you got past his good looks—no easy feat—he also was distressingly unreasonable.

"He might be worse." June was only half joking. Or maybe she wasn't joking at all. "But first, tell me about your chemistry professor. Did you meet with her about your class project?"

"Yes, ma'am." Noah launched into an amusing account of his meeting with his professor to get clarification on his chemistry report. Thankfully, the anecdote, which had a happy ending, seemed to distract her son from worrying about her. At least for now.

June listened to Noah with one half of her mind while the other continued to brood over her boss and an idea for their year-end fund-raiser. Ever since Benjamin had shot down her Christmas dance idea that morning, she'd been struggling to come up with a substitute event. But The Iceman wasn't being helpful. He knew what he didn't want, but he had no idea what he wanted.

Was it the event itself or the Christmas theme that he was opposed to? Did he have something against the holiday?

Chapter 2

"These cost and income numbers are based on the center's January anniversary event." June ran the tip of her No. 2 pencil down the Microsoft Excel chart she'd printed for her meeting with Dita Vargas, Guiding Light Community Center's recreation and programs manager. Together they were spending Tuesday morning brainstorming new ideas for a year-end fund-raiser, one that Benjamin "Scrooge" Brooks could approve.

Dita consulted her copy of the chart. She'd worked for the center for two years and had helped with some of the arrangements for the anniversary event. "The figures may be a bit dodgy for this report, but they give us the best comparison to date."

Dodgy. It meant *questionable*. Dita was addicted to BBC America's programming, particularly *Doctor Who*, *The Musketeers*, and *Sherlock*. One of her quirks was infusing her speech with the British slang she picked up from these shows.

"Was *Sherlock* on last night?" June looked up at the younger woman, whom she'd grown fond of during the three months they'd been working together.

Dita wore her thick, ebony hair in a pixie cut. Her warm cream features were made up to emphasize her big, brown eyes and high cheekbones.

"No, dearie." Dita seemed only mildly disappointed. "I borrowed the *Luther* DVDs from the library. They have all three seasons."

June hadn't heard her coworker mention that show before. "What's *Luther*?"

Dita's blush-painted lips parted in surprise. "Two words: Idris. Elba. It's a police procedural that I highly recommend you borrow from the library when I'm done with it."

June didn't do blood and violence. In fact, she missed the days of watching *SpongeBob SquarePants* with Noah. *Teen Titans* was as real as she'd let him get until he'd taken control of the remote.

She smothered a wistful sigh and returned to the budget estimate. "We need an event that will give us the greatest return for a modest investment."

"But something that won't put people to sleep." Dita rested her copy of the budget on her lap. The hem of her chocolate-brown skirt came to her knees.

"This budget is adjusted to account for a lower attendance."

"Why?"

"The year-end event won't have the same turnout as the anniversary party." June raised her eyes to Dita again. "The anniversary took place when TFU faculty, staff, and students were returning from Christmas break. With the timing of the dinner dance, people will be leaving for the holidays."

"A lot of students from Trinity Falls go to college out of town. They'll be coming home for Christmas, dearie."

"That's true." June brightened. "And my Sequoia

connections will give us a wider audience to reach."
Several businesses from her hometown had agreed to
carry brochures about the fund-raiser. It would give
Sequoia residents something safe and affordable to do
for the holidays. "Maybe we could host a dinner dance
without labeling it a holiday event."

Dita was shaking her head before the words were
out of June's mouth. "Trinity Falls residents wouldn't
like that. If you host any event after Thanksgiving,
you'd better call it a Christmas party, complete with
holiday food, decorations, music, and Jesus."

"That's what I thought." June's shoulders rose and
fell with a frustrated sigh. "Ben's from Trinity Falls.
Why doesn't he understand that?"

"So what do you think about our new director?" Dita
grinned. "I think he's dishy."

"Since he's our boss, I hadn't noticed," June lied.

Once sending Noah away to college had become a
reality, June had cautiously tuned back into the dating
pool. She hadn't paid much attention to men in almost
twenty years. Yes, it really had been that long. But it
might not have been if there'd been men like Benjamin Brooks around.

Dishy was one way of describing him. At several
inches over six-feet, he was almost a foot taller than
her. His long, lean limbs would make a clothing de-
signer drool. With his clean-shaven, movie-star looks,
he reminded June of Denzel Washington in the movie
*The Preacher's Wife. Oh, to have been Whitney Houston for
just one scene.*

"He's our boss, but I'm not blind." Dita snorted. "All
of the Brooks brothers look like that. Of course,
Vaughn, the middle brother, is engaged to Benita
Hawkins, so he's off the market. But Ben's divorced

and Zach, the youngest brother, is single." Dita wiggled her eyebrows.

"We should get back to the plans for the dinner dance." June glanced at her black Timex wristwatch for emphasis.

"Sure, dearie." Dita lowered her voice. "I heard Ben filed for divorce because his wife was shagging someone else."

June's eyes widened. She was pretty sure *shagging* meant having sex. Benjamin's ex-wife had been having an affair. June lowered her eyes. She knew something about unfaithful spouses. She'd been the victim of one herself. However, since the sham relationship had blessed her with Noah, she could never regret the experience.

"Dita." June held the younger woman's gaze. "I'm not comfortable gossiping about our boss, and you shouldn't be, either."

June had been the subject of more than her fair share of vicious gossip in the past. Now that she'd moved to Trinity Falls, where most people only knew half-truths about her, she was the target of ugly rumors and innuendos again. She wouldn't participate in behavior that had caused her and Noah so much pain.

"You're right, dearie." Dita scanned the budget sheet again. "The game's afoot."

June smiled at the Sherlock Holmes reference. "Not yet, but hopefully, we'll think of something our new boss could approve of and soon."

"What will we do if we don't come up with something?" Dita looked worried.

"Positive thinking, Dita. We'll think of something." But if they didn't, she'd have to reason with The Iceman. Why did she have the feeling that was easier said than done?

*   *   *

June knocked on Dr. Quincy Spates's open door late Tuesday afternoon. The professor's office was in Butler Hall, Trinity Falls University's administrative building. Named after the university's founder, Clara Butler, it was the oldest building on campus.

"I'm sorry to interrupt." But what was she interrupting? June looked from the ruggedly handsome professor of African American history to his glamorous fiancée, Ramona McCloud.

Ramona was seated on the corner of his desk closest to the professor. Moments ago, the two of them had had eyes only for each other. The atmosphere in the room had been thick with desire.

"Hi, June." Quincy stood to his impressive six-foot-plus height. He'd been a college football running back. In his pale green dress shirt and smoke-gray slacks, he looked like he could still play. "We were expecting you."

I doubt that.

June struggled to hold back a smile as she stepped farther into the office. Ramona stood and took one of the two gray visitor's chairs on the other side of Quincy's desk. June took the other. She lowered her purse and briefcase to the floor beside her chair.

Her gaze lifted to the display of framed photos on the shelf above Quincy's computer monitor. Among what appeared to be photos of his family and Ramona were pictures of him with Ean and Darius. One photo in particular caught her attention. It seemed to be a picture of them in their high school football uniforms hoisting a trophy after a game. In the photo, Darius looked so much like Noah, June did a double take. It wasn't surprising, though. Her son was Darius Knight's half brother.

She brought her attention back to the meeting. June had spoken with Quincy on the phone that morning. She'd held her breath as she'd extended a formal invitation for him to present the history and meaning of Kwanzaa at the Guiding Light Community Center. When he'd agreed—with definite enthusiasm—June had done a spontaneous little chair dance.

"I'll try not to take too much of your time." June pulled a folder from her briefcase, sending Ramona an apologetic smile. "When we discussed meeting before lunch today, I hadn't realized you had plans."

"Take your time." Ramona crossed her long dancer's legs. "I'm the one who's interrupting. Quincy didn't know I was coming."

"It's good to see you." June relaxed.

"Same here." Ramona's smile revealed perfect white teeth. Of course.

The other woman was stunning in a figure-hugging scarlet sweater dress. Her glossy, raven tresses framed her diamond-shaped face. Her perfect café au lait features needed very little makeup. Her wide ebony eyes were bright and friendly under expertly arched eyebrows. In the three months that June had lived in Trinity Falls, she'd found Ramona to be as kind as she was beautiful. All of Darius's friends were.

June turned back to Quincy. "I was hoping to schedule the discussion for two o'clock, Saturday, November twenty-first. I realize today is November third, which gives you less than three weeks but—"

Quincy held up a hand to stop her. "You'd asked me about doing this months ago. I've done Kwanzaa presentations before. It won't take me long to refresh my past notes."

"Wonderful." *So far so good.* "Regarding your speaker's fee, we'd like to offer—"

Again, Quincy stopped her. "That's not necessary, June. I'm happy to offer this presentation for the center."

Taken aback, June glanced at Ramona, then again at Quincy. "Our budget is modest but we want to pay you for your time and trouble. It's only fair."

"In that case, I'll donate my speaker fee to the center." Quincy leaned forward, folding his hands on his desk. "The community center was a valuable resource to me when I was growing up. I should have given back to it sooner."

Quincy's generosity touched June. Ramona was looking at her fiancé as though he'd presented her with roses. June felt the same way.

"Thank you, Quincy." June slipped a sheet of paper across his desk. "This is our event goal sheet. It states the date and time of the event as we discussed. It also has information that you should know as our presenter, like our promotion plan."

Quincy and June reviewed additional details, including the length of the event, before she prepared to leave. Ramona offered specific suggestions for setting up the community room with an emphasis on the space's feng shui.

"Thank you again for agreeing to be our guest speaker." June tucked her project folder back into her briefcase. "Your credentials and positive reputation in the community make you a big draw for us."

"Speaking of the community, how are you settling in?" Ramona tilted her head, causing her long raven tresses to swing behind her shoulders.

"Fine." June nodded for emphasis, hoping Ramona wouldn't press the issue. Her hopes were in vain.

"Really?" The former town mayor's eyebrows knitted. "I heard Nessa, Ethel and a couple of our other more judgmental residents were giving you a hard time."

"I can understand Ethel's resentment. I expected it." June shrugged. "I'd probably feel the same way if the situation were reversed. But I needed a job and this offer was too good to pass up."

"I'm glad you feel that way." Ramona nodded. "Just remember there are plenty more people who are happy you're here. You're a great asset to the center and a wonderful addition to our community."

"I agree," Quincy added.

"Thank you." She'd really needed to hear that. June turned away, taking her time collecting her briefcase as she blinked back emotions. "I'll let you get to your lunch. I'm getting pretty hungry myself."

Ramona stood with her. "Just remember, June, other people's opinions of you don't matter."

"You're right." June glanced at Quincy, who'd also gotten to his feet. "I'll be in touch. Let me know if you have any questions in the meantime." With a final good-bye, June left the office.

How often had she given Noah the same advice, other people's opinions don't matter? It was true, but their opinions could still hurt. How long would it take for Trinity Falls to forget her past and judge her on her actions today?

Books & Bakery's inviting atmosphere reflected its owner and the store's staff. June stepped farther into the store Wednesday afternoon and drew a deep breath.

She caught the scent of fresh baked pastries and hot soup. Underneath it all was the hint of lemon wood polish.

Thanksgiving imagery and colors had replaced the Halloween decorations. The heels of her sensible pumps tapped against the dark hardwood flooring as she walked past overstuffed red velvet armchairs on her way to the café. Tabletop displays and rows of bookcases made from the same dark wood tried to draw her off course. They tempted her with the lure of new releases and perennial bestsellers, glossy magazines and fantastic comic books. Somehow June found the will to resist. Her growling stomach kept her moving toward the café in the back of the bookstore. She hesitated only briefly at the genre fiction sections: mystery, romance, science fiction, and fantasy. Noah would love it here.

It wasn't quite noon. Still June counted eight people in the café's lunch line. The line moved quickly, though. Doreen Lopez—formerly Doreen Fever—the town's mayor and café manager, worked the register while an older man and woman filled the orders.

June hesitated when she realized the last person in the line was Ethel Knight. Trinity Falls was a small town at a population of only fifteen hundred and Books & Bakery was a very popular location. They were bound to cross paths often.

Before joining the line, June took a steadying breath, picking up the scents of confectioners' sugar, cinnamon, and chocolate as well as baking bread, seasonings, and fresh vegetables. "Good afternoon, Ethel."

The other woman stiffened. Ethel turned toward her, dark eyes wide as though outraged that June would address her. Ethel opened her mouth once, twice. No sound emerged. Instead she marched out of the line and out of the store. June's skin burned with mortification. She kept her head high, her back straight, and her eyes forward. In a little while, the slights wouldn't hurt so much.

Minutes later, Doreen greeted her at the front of the line. "Hi, June. What can I get for you?"

June returned Doreen's smile as the café manager's kind brown eyes eased her discomfort. "Hi, Doreen. May I have a bowl of your turkey and wild rice soup, please?"

After completing her lunch request, including her beverage, June accepted her change and order receipt, then found a bar stool at the counter. Darius and Ean were already there. The two men had been friends since childhood and now were as close as brothers.

Darius gave her a concerned look. "Are you okay?"

"Of course. Why wouldn't I be?" June settled onto the bar stool.

"You looked upset when Ethel walked out." Darius nodded toward the customer line.

"I'm fine." The uncomfortable knot had returned to her stomach. "And please don't mention this to Noah. He needs to focus on his schoolwork rather than getting reports from you spying on me."

"I don't spy." Darius's look of hurt surprise was obviously feigned. "I'm a reporter. I report."

June snorted. "You're not a reporter anymore. You're the *Monitor*'s managing editor."

"Once a reporter, always a reporter." Darius shrugged. "Which is how I can tell something's bothering you. What is it?"

"What's what?" Doreen appeared, carrying a tray with June's soup, an apple, and a glass of ice water.

"Thank you." June glanced at Doreen, then looked toward the cash register, where a young woman had taken the café manager's place.

"D thinks something's bothering June." Ean lifted his glass of iced tea with one hand while slapping away Darius's reach for his dill pickle with the other.

Doreen gave June a sympathetic look. "Don't worry about Ethel. In time, she'll realize you were as much a victim of Simon's lies as she was."

Had everyone seen Ethel turn away from her and walk out of Books & Bakery? "She has a right to be upset."

Doreen tilted her head, looking at June. "If that's not what's bothering you, then what *is* on your mind?"

"Ben shot down my idea for the Christmas fundraiser and I'm having trouble coming up with another one." June swallowed some of her turkey and wild rice soup. The seasonings caused her taste buds to dance.

"What was your idea?" Ean licked the dill pickle, then put it back on his plate as he sent Darius a smug look.

"A Christmas dinner and dance." It had been such a wonderful idea. June scowled into her soup bowl.

"That should work." Doreen refilled Ean's and Darius's iced teas. "The anniversary dinner and dance was even more successful than we'd hoped it would be."

"That's what I thought." June took a deep drink of her ice water. "I'd hoped to establish the Christmas dinner dance as an annual event and celebrate the center's January anniversary as an annual online day of giving."

"That's a great idea." Megan joined the group. She stood behind the counter with Doreen. "I've read about days of giving. With an online campaign, you have a much wider reach on a much smaller budget."

"Exactly." June's smile was enthusiastic. "It's also motivation to update our website."

"Then why did Ben turn down the Christmas dinner dance idea?" Ean asked.

June sobered at the memory of Benjamin's unequivocal rejection of her plan. "He didn't give a reason. He just doesn't want a dinner dance."

"What does he want?" Darius asked.

"He didn't have any suggestions. He knows what he doesn't want but not what he wants." June tried to moderate her voice but still let slip a trace of resentment.

"Well, you're running out of time." Doreen offered Darius a dill pickle. "Go ahead with your dinner dance idea. It's brilliant."

June sipped more water. "My boss doesn't think so."

"But his boss does." Doreen topped off her water. "As mayor, he reports to me. I'll call him this afternoon."

Panic. The thought of Doreen fighting her battle with Benjamin for her turned her blood to ice. She had enough people giving her the cold shoulder in Trinity Falls. She didn't want to invite more resentment.

June lifted a hand, palm out. "I don't know if that would be such a good idea."

Doreen frowned. "I was the one who hired you for this job even before Ben interviewed for the director's position. Fund-raising for the center is vitally important to this town."

June nodded. "I understand that."

Doreen crossed her arms. "If Ben doesn't have a better idea, we have to go with yours."

This couldn't end well. "Maybe I should speak with him first."

Darius chuckled. "What will you say?"

I have no idea. "I'll think of something."

Chapter 3

The knock on Benjamin's office door was a welcome distraction from his efforts to review the Guiding Light Community Center's budget Wednesday afternoon. How had it remained open for as long as it had?

"Do you have a moment?" June stood at his office doorway.

Her wavy black hair swung around her delicate, heart-shaped face. Her pale green sweater flowed over her torso like a pure stream. Her narrow dark green skirt hugged her slim hips and ended at mid-calf.

"What's up?" Benjamin saved the budget Excel file on his computer, then spun his executive chair to face June. The seat made a protesting squeal. He had to fix that.

June walked into his office. Her black pumps drew his attention to her shapely legs. Benjamin forced his gaze up to her eyes. He didn't want to court a lawsuit. He was trying to rebuild his life not send it farther into the crapper.

"It's really cold in here. You need a space heater." June sat on one of the guest chairs in front of his desk.

"You're right." He'd add that to his growing list of

things he needed: lubricant for his desk chair, space heater, new furniture. But the center's limited funds had other priorities.

"It's been two days." June crossed her legs, adjusting her skirt over her right knee. "Have you had any additional thoughts about a year-end fund-raising event?"

I didn't know I was supposed to. "I was leaving those plans to you."

"Thank you." June nodded. Her hair swung around her shoulders. Near her left shoulder, she'd pinned a small pewter broach. It looked like a reindeer in flight. "Since I haven't come up with a better idea than the Christmas dinner dance, I'll move ahead with those plans."

"I'm not in favor of that event." *Didn't I make that clear?*

"You haven't come up with anything better and neither have I."

"We'll come up with something." Benjamin spread his hands, ignoring his rising agitation. "Give it more time."

"Time's running out. As it is, we'll have to scramble to pull something together in a month."

Benjamin held her tawny gaze. There was determination in her eyes. He was determined as well. "Maybe we should skip the year-end event."

June was shaking her head even while Benjamin was speaking. "That's not an option, Ben."

The sound of his name on her soft, smooth voice sent a thrill down his spine. His thoughts scattered. "Why not?"

"Right now, the community center has momentum in raising its visibility in the community." June leaned forward, adding emphasis to her words. "There was the January fund-raiser, then six months later, Vaughn's summer play. We would benefit from that momentum by hosting a year-end event."

"What difference does it make if the events are six months apart or eight?" Benjamin struggled to hold on to his patience. "Why does it have to be a Christmas event? Why can't we do a Valentine's Day dinner dance in February?"

"Why are you opposed to the Christmas theme?" June's gaze narrowed on his face as though she was trying to read his mind.

Benjamin stiffened. "I told you. There are too many holiday celebrations."

"There's only one communitywide Christmas event. That's Books and Bakery's, which doesn't offer dinner or dancing."

"People have a lot of other expenses at Christmas time. We can't expect them to want another bill."

"The dinner dance registration cost will be a tax deductible donation. They can write it off, just like the January birthday bash."

Benjamin rubbed the back of his neck. Why was June fixated on Christmas? What was the big deal? He rose from his seat to buy time while he considered a new line of debate. The chair squeaked again.

He circled his desk and paced toward the window. "If attendees could write off the event tickets in December, they could write them off in February as well."

June was silent for several beats. Benjamin was beginning to think he'd won this round. Then her question took the wind from his sails. "What's your real objection, Ben? Is it the event or Christmas itself?"

Benjamin stiffened, then faced her. "Why would I be opposed to Christmas?"

"I have no idea." June shrugged. "Personally, I love everything about Christmas: the spirit of the season, the lights, the carols, the traditions. I can't imagine any Christian not enjoying the season."

June's eyes shone with lights that dazzled as she talked about the holiday. Her features softened, becoming even more beautiful. He could feel her passion for Christmas from across the room. It pulled at him, weakening his resistance. Had he ever been as enthusiastic about Christmas? Probably. But he definitely hadn't been in the holiday spirit last Christmas and odds were against his excitement this year.

"I don't dislike Christmas." *Then why did I have to force those words from my mouth?*

"What are your plans for the holiday?" June closed the gap between them.

"It's two months away."

"Are you going to wait two months to decide what you're doing?" She shamed him with a look.

"I just don't think there's a rush."

June came to a stop an arm's length from where Benjamin stood beside his window. "That doesn't sound like someone who likes Christmas very much."

"Well, you're wrong. I do like Christmas." Benjamin was beginning to feel hunted. "I'm going to spend it with my children while they're on winter break."

"They're in college?" Her wide eyes found the framed photographs of his son and daughter beside his computer.

Benjamin followed her gaze. "Those photos are a little old." By about ten years.

"Those are the most recent pictures you have of your children?" When he nodded, June shook her head. "You need to rectify that."

"I will."

"And you need to prove that you like Christmas."

"What? How?"

"Help me throw the biggest and best Christmas party Trinity Falls has ever seen." June's amazing eyes twinkled at him. Every light in the heavens seemed to be in them.

Benjamin felt the force of her personality pulling at him with undeniable strength. Somehow Benjamin resisted her magic. He walked past June and back to his desk. "If you want the center to host a Christmas dinner dance, so be it. Go ahead and plan it. But I won't do anything to support it."

"Duly noted." June inclined her head.

Benjamin watched her leave his office. Her straight green skirt seemed to twitch with displeasure with every step she took toward his door. Her back was straight and her head was held high. She'd won this contest. He didn't know how. He hadn't even realized there had been a contest. So be it. He'd win the next one.

Nessa strode into June's office Thursday afternoon. Crushed ice tumbled into June's stomach. She didn't harbor any illusions that the town council president was here to ask after her welfare. That only meant one thing: another round of this Town Isn't Big Enough for the Both of Us.

June lowered the pencil she was using to mark revisions for the center's ad in *The Trinity Falls Monitor*. "May I help you, Nessa?"

"I hear you're planning a Christmas fund-raiser." Nessa sounded like she was commenting about something on the bottom of her shoe. It took June a moment to realize she was talking about the dinner dance.

"Yes, it's scheduled for Saturday, December nine-teenth." June wrapped her hands around her mug of coffee. She was drinking it not because she needed more caffeine but because she was cold. She could feel the chilled air blowing through her office. Or was that Nessa?

"A week before Christmas." Nessa took the chair in front of June's desk.

I guess she's planning on staying awhile. June stifled a sigh. "We're getting a late start. It's closer to Christmas than we'd like, but we need the extra time. Next year, we'll plan to host it earlier."

Nessa's pencil-thin eyebrows lifted up her broad, brown forehead. "Do you plan to still be living in Trinity Falls next year?"

"Yes, I do." June settled back on her chair, crossing her legs.

It seemed as though Nessa was preparing to remove her gloves. Good. She'd been enduring the other woman's implied digs and insults for the past three months. It was time they got to the point. *Bring it on.*

The town council president sighed. "I've tried to be subtle, but perhaps subtlety is lost on you."

"I'm well aware that you don't want me in Trinity Falls, Nessa." June straightened on her seat. "I believe you're the one who gets lost in subtlety because you don't seem to realize I'm not leaving."

"You're not wanted here," Nessa snapped.

"That's not completely true." June shrugged. "Doreen asked me to apply for this job. She also helped me find a place to live."

"Doreen doesn't represent the entire town."

"Neither do you."

Anger flashed in Nessa's eyes. "What about Simon Knight?"

June frowned. "What about him?"

"Do you intend to rekindle your relationship with him?"

June clenched her teeth to keep her jaw from dropping. "How does that concern you?"

Nessa's oval lips tightened. "As a duly elected representative of this community, everything that affects its residents is my concern."

June managed to keep her voice even. "My personal life doesn't affect the fifteen hundred residents of this town."

Nessa's eyes narrowed in a glare. "What about Ethel Knight?"

"I'm not Ethel Knight's enemy. I'm not here to cause her or anyone else harm."

"You mean any *more* harm, don't you?"

June's pulse was galloping in her throat. "I'm here to work and to live. That's all."

Nessa spoke over her. "How do you think Ethel feels, having you—the woman who destroyed her marriage and tore apart her family—in her hometown? Every day wondering whether she's going to come face-to-face with you around the next corner?"

June's temper grew with every word out of Nessa's mouth. "What does any of this have to do with you?"

"As the town council president, the health of this town is my responsibility. And you, June Cale, are a cancer on this community."

June's body heated with temper. It had been almost two decades since she'd been treated with so much blatant disrespect and discourtesy. Back then, she'd been frightened and naïve. Today, she was mature. And although she didn't consider herself to be courageous, she was much more confident. She didn't have to take this crap.

She rose to her feet and locked her knees. "I want you to leave my office."

Nessa stood, pulling her purse onto her shoulder. "And *I* want *you* to leave Trinity Falls."

"Do the residents of Trinity Falls realize they elected a megalomaniac?"

"You're not welcome here." Nessa gritted the words.

June settled her hands on her hips. "Do you really expect me to run home and pack my bags?"

"Ethel Knight has lived in Trinity Falls her entire life." Nessa crossed her arms. "You just moved here. Who do you think I'm going to protect?"

"Ethel doesn't need protection." June recalled Ethel's snub at Books & Bakery yesterday. "She can take care of herself."

"The people here already are unhappy with having a home wrecker in their town. There's more than one way to convince you to leave. For example, I wouldn't put much effort into planning that Christmas fundraiser if I were you."

June's blood chilled. "And why's that?"

"Because I'm going to make sure it fails." Vicious satisfaction hardened Nessa's voice. "All I have to do is say the word and no one will attend. No one."

June fisted her hands in anger and frustration. Did the town council president actually have that much clout in Trinity Falls? Could she really convince people to withhold support of the community center by staying away from the Christmas dinner dance? Could June risk ignoring the other woman's threat? Her mind raced for a solution when another voice expressed himself.

"What word would that be, Nessa?" The deep voice came from her office doorway.

June's gaze shifted to find Benjamin leaning a broad shoulder against her doorjamb. His attention was centered on Nessa. His muscled arms were crossed over his broad chest, which was wrapped in a nickel-gray shirt. June's eyes closed briefly in despair. Nessa would give him yet another reason to oppose her idea of the Christmas dinner dance. Her mind scrambled to mount a defense against their joint forces. She came up with . . . nothing. June folded her arms and prepared to wait them out.

"Hello, Ben." Nessa spun to face the center's director. She appeared startled that they'd acquired an audience.

"Are you threatening to disrupt our fund-raiser?" He sounded amused.

June scowled. There was nothing humorous about this situation.

Nessa sent her a scathing look over her shoulder before turning back to Benjamin. "If that's what it takes to convince June that Trinity Falls isn't the right home for her."

Benjamin glanced at June, who was standing behind her desk. Her bright white sweater emphasized the red flush in her copper cheeks. He couldn't read her expression. But he didn't need a psychic to guess she was ready to explode. He looked again to Nessa.

"Do you really think you have that much influence in this town?" Benjamin would have found the idea amusing if he weren't furious over the argument he'd overheard.

"You've been gone a long time, Ben." Nessa tried to look down her nose at him, which wasn't easy for her with

Benjamin slouching against June's doorway. "Things have changed in Trinity Falls."

"Have people become more judgmental?" Benjamin shook his head. "That's a shame. How did you get elected?"

"Excuse me?" Nessa's back became ramrod straight.

"Did the town overlook your divorce? But then, you didn't remain single for long, did you?" Benjamin forced a smile. "What's that called, a whirlwind romance?"

"How dare you?" Nessa's face flamed.

"Those who live in glass houses shouldn't throw stones, Nessa." Benjamin straightened from the doorway. He allowed Nessa to see the anger he was restraining. "You're not the only one with connections in this town. I'd recommend you not use the community center as a weapon in your petty squabbles."

"Petty squabbles?" Nessa pointed a finger behind her toward June. "Do you have any idea of her past?"

"No and, apparently, neither do you." Benjamin kept his eyes on the council president. "Now if you'll excuse us, we have a lot of work to do."

"You're siding with her against the people of your hometown?" Nessa dropped her arm.

"Stop being so melodramatic, Nessa." Benjamin stepped back, encouraging Nessa to leave. "June is a resident of Trinity Falls and she works for me."

"She's a negative influence on this town *and* its residents." Nessa seemed to be shaking with anger. "Ethel isn't comfortable with her here."

"That's for Ethel and June to deal with." Benjamin extended his hand toward the hallway. "Good-bye, Nessa."

The council president sent one last glare in June's direction before marching through the doorway.

Benjamin made sure she'd disappeared down the hall before he entered June's office.

He still couldn't read her expression. "Are you all right?"

"I'm fine." Her movements were stiff and jerky as she reclaimed her seat. "Is there something you needed?"

Benjamin considered the tightness around June's Cupid's-bow lips and the strain beside her wide, overly bright eyes. She wasn't fine. Nessa's hate-filled words had shaken her. When Benjamin had heard the council president's accusations and insults as he approached June's office, he'd been overwhelmed by a wave of protectiveness for his deputy director and fund-raising manager. It had made him oblivious to everything else around him. All he could think about was getting to June's side and deflecting Nessa's attack.

Now that he'd banished the council president, what should he do? He seemed to have two choices: talk or touch. The fact that his preference was to wrap her in his arms and ease the agitation in her eyes surprised him. Except for what he'd always feel for his children, he'd thought his experience with Aliyah had stripped all of the softer emotions from his heart.

Benjamin approached June's desk. "Do you want to talk about what just happened?"

A silent breath lifted June's chest and shoulders. "I'd rather not."

"Why does Nessa want you out of town?"

"You should have asked her before you told her to leave." June inclined her head. "Thank you for that, by the way."

Benjamin spent a moment or two fantasizing about June confiding in him. But it was only a fantasy. The stubborn angle of her chin warned him June had said everything she'd planned to say. He wasn't getting anything more from her, at least not this afternoon.

"I wanted to ask about Dita." Benjamin nodded in the general direction of the recreation and program manager's office.

"What about her?"

Faced with the moment of truth, Benjamin didn't know how to articulate his concern. He massaged the back of his neck with his right hand as he scanned June's office. It was surprisingly small. There wasn't any room to pace. Benjamin noticed the scent of cinnamon and apples. His searching eyes landed on the unlit candle beside her computer.

With nowhere to go, he sank onto her guest chair. "This is the second time she's called me 'dearie.' Should I be concerned?"

June's soft, seductive laugh warmed the muscles in his lower abdomen. Tension drained from her full lips. Teasing lights replaced the strain in her tawny eyes. He'd done that somehow. The realization made him proud.

"Dita's not flirting with you, if that's what you're asking." June propped her forearms on her desk and leaned forward. "She loves British television, particularly *Sherlock* and *Doctor Who*. She's always quoting from those shows."

The laughter in her eyes once again mesmerized him. Benjamin was reluctant to leave her now. "Thanks for clearing that up. Is there anything else I should know about the staff?"

June cocked her head as though considering his question and how she should respond. "Well, unless you have something nice to say about Cleveland's football team, don't mention them to Krista."

"A diehard fan, huh?" Benjamin pictured Krista Li, the childcare manager.

"Oh, yes." June grinned, taking more of Benjamin's breath away.

"So am I."

"Then the two of you could commiserate."

Benjamin winced. The truth hurt. "Anything else?"

"Howard Atwell is a conspiracy theorist but really great at his job. I recommend you just smile and nod if you get trapped with him in the middle of one of his rants."

Benjamin frowned. "He's our kitchen manager. Can we trust him to handle our food?"

"Absolutely." June waved away the concern. "He doesn't think anyone is out to get him. Howard just believes the government is lying about the existence of aliens."

"That's a relief." Benjamin noticed the suppressed laughter in her eyes. A few chuckles escaped him. "I appreciate the insight."

"You're welcome." June shared his laughter. "We all have our quirks. But the important thing is that they're all warm, wonderful people. And they're all exceptional at their jobs. They're the reason the center's been able to stay open so long."

"They've been very welcoming to me." Benjamin cocked his head. "What about you? Any quirks I should know about?"

The shift was subtle, but Benjamin sensed a virtual wall going up between them. *Why?*

June shook her head. Her smile never wavered. "I'm pretty boring."

"I find that hard to believe." Benjamin stood. "Thanks again."

"Wait a minute. I have something for you." June

turned to the file cabinet beside her desk and pulled a large metal can from a drawer. "Take this. It's lubricant for your chair. The squeaking must be driving you crazy."

"It is." Benjamin met her eyes. "Thank you."

"Thanks again for defending me to Nessa." June stood. "I know you're not completely sold on the idea of the Christmas dinner dance."

"We're a team."

A light flashed across June's bright eyes. "I like that."

So do I. Too much.

Benjamin inclined his head, then tore himself free of June's spell before he was tempted to stay longer.

What was it that drew him to her like the proverbial moth to a flame? He'd never before felt this irresistible pull to another person. Why now? He was just getting over the painful end of a long marriage. Why June? She worked for him. More importantly, could he still trust his instincts? Benjamin rubbed a hand over his face. He honestly didn't know. He'd been with his ex-wife for twenty years, but her betrayal had caught him off guard. After that experience, could he ever trust anyone again, even himself?

Chapter 4

"Thanks again for coming to my office for this interview." Darius sat with Benjamin at his conversation table in his office at *The Trinity Falls Monitor*'s building Friday morning.

Benjamin squinted at the notes Darius continued to scrawl across his writing tablet. It was for the feature Darius wanted to do on him as the Guiding Light Community Center's new director.

It was a good thing the newspaper man had recorded their question-and-answer session. He didn't think anyone—including Darius—would be able to read the reporter's handwriting. Benjamin glanced at the recorder perched precariously on a stack of newspapers.

"No problem. I wanted to see your new digs." Benjamin looked around the spacious room that made his office look like a very large Jacuzzi.

The walls were covered with special issue schedules and framed news clips. Competitor newspapers stood in stacks on the conversation table and personal photographs were arranged on his shelves. There were pictures of Peyton, Darius's girlfriend, near Wishing

Lake on Trinity Falls University's campus; another of young Darius, Ean, and Quincy mugging for the camera after their high school football state championship win. Next to it was a photo of a young man who looked a lot like Darius posing with June. Was that June's son? In another picture taken at the same event, Darius, Noah, and June stood with their arms around each other's shoulders. They looked like a family. Benjamin felt a sting of envy. And perhaps jealousy?

"The digs aren't that new." Darius leaned back on his chair and folded his arms behind his head. "I've been managing editor of the *Monitor* for more than ten months now."

"Do you like the new position?" Benjamin propped his right ankle onto his left knee.

"I do." Darius paused. "I miss the hard news. But I still have time to write personality profiles like this one I'm doing on you. Now, tell me, why are you really here?"

Benjamin should have known Darius would see right through him. His childhood friend had always been good at reading people. He took a deep breath. The office smelled like newsprint and coffee. He preferred the cinnamon and apples that lingered in June's office.

"What can you tell me about June Cale?" He tried to appear nonchalant. But the truth was, as his attraction to his small-but-mighty deputy director grew, so did his need to know everything about her—and her relationship with Darius.

Darius frowned. "What do you want to know?"

"What was she doing in Sequoia before she moved to Trinity Falls?"

"Don't you have a copy of her resume?"

"Why does Nessa have it out for her?"

"You'll have to ask Nessa."

Benjamin frowned. This was trickier than he'd considered. "Why did she decide to move to Trinity Falls rather than looking for a new job in Sequoia?"

Darius looked amused. "These are all questions for June. Why are you asking me?"

He tried another tactic. "You usually have some insight on situations like these."

"Are you trying to butter me up?"

"Is it working?"

"No." Darius leaned back on his chair. It didn't squeak.

Benjamin's gaze drifted back to the picture of Darius, June, and Noah. "What's your relationship with her?"

Darius arched a brow. "We're very good friends, Ben. Nothing more, nothing less. I'm with Peyton, remember?"

Benjamin had the distinct impression that Darius was laughing at him. "As her friend, aren't you concerned about the way Nessa, Simon, and Ethel have been treating her?"

"Of course. But June's tough. She's had to be. She's also very attractive." There was a message in his childhood friend's dark gaze.

Benjamin acknowledged the look, then inclined his head toward the photo of June and a young man that stood on the shelf above Darius's desk. "Is that Noah, Simon's son?"

"Yes, that's my little brother." Darius's expression softened.

"Not so little. And he looks just like you." The Knight genes were strong.

"He's not the only one who'd be upset if someone hurt June."

Benjamin nodded. Message sent and received, again. But was it necessary? "I'm not looking for a relationship, D. I just ended a twenty-year marriage."

"We don't have to be looking for a relationship to find one." Darius gave him the wry look of a man who'd been blindsided by love.

"I think Cupid knows better than to take any potshots at me." He'd make the little guy choke on his arrow. Benjamin stood. "Thanks for your time. Your insight was helpful."

"You're welcome." Darius rose. "Good luck with Nessa. And be careful with June."

"There's no need to worry." Benjamin turned to leave.

If anything, Darius should ask June to be careful with him. Something about his fearless deputy director was breathing life into the pile of ashes that had once been his heart. What would she do with it if it ever fully healed?

Simon cornered June the moment she stepped into Books & Bakery Friday afternoon.

"We need to talk." It was as though he'd been waiting for her. He took her arm and tugged her toward the nonfiction section of the store, which lay in the opposite direction from the crowded café.

June shrugged off his hold. "Please don't manhandle me. Just tell me what you want."

"I want you to leave." Simon hissed the words.

Didn't anyone have a more original request for me? First Nessa, now Simon; Ethel hadn't said as much, but her killer glares were strong cues.

"That's not going to happen." June started to leave.

Simon caught her arm again. She shifted her gaze

from his hold on her elbow to his almost desperate expression.

Simon dropped his hand. "I was on the verge of reconciling with Ethel before you showed up. Your being here is bringing . . . it . . . all back."

June crossed her arms. "I've never been married, but I'd think that cheating on your wife would fall under the heading of 'problems to work through' not 'things to forget.'"

"As you said, you've never been married." Simon's still-handsome features twisted into a scowl. "Why should I take advice from you?"

"I'm not leaving Trinity Falls." And the more people who told her to, the more determined she became to plant roots. Very deep ones.

"How am I supposed to get my life back when you're around as a constant reminder of why Ethel left me?" Simon threw up his arms.

June looked around. Was it her imagination or were people moving closer, as though trying to better hear what she and Simon were talking about? She jerked her head toward the front of the shop and led Simon to the exit. The bell above the door chimed and a chill mid-November wind stole June's breath as she led him away from Books & Bakery's entrance.

"Has Ethel actually forgiven you?" June stopped and faced Simon.

He shrugged deeper into his army-green parka. "Not in so many words."

Translation: No. And June had a strong suspicion Ethel never would.

"You should have a candid conversation with Ethel about whether the two of you can fix your marriage." June held the collar of her wool winter coat closer to her neck. "You lied to me. And you lied to Ethel."

"I didn't . . . I couldn't . . ."

"Now, instead of taking responsibility for your lies, you're still pretending that none of this happened."

"I haven't . . . I wouldn't . . ."

"I don't harbor any ill will toward you." Amazingly. "Because of you I have a wonderful son. But I understand why Ethel hates us. And I don't blame her."

"Then leave." Simon sounded as though he'd come to the end of his rope. "Stop giving me useless advice about my marriage and just leave."

June shook her head. "I'm not running. And you should stop hiding. Talk with your wife, Simon."

She left Simon on the sidewalk to stew in his frustration. As June re-entered the bookstore, patrons averted their eyes. How many of them had tried to get a glimpse of her and Simon outside? What did the good residents of Trinity Falls think they'd been talking about? June didn't want to speculate. She couldn't control their thoughts. She could only control her reaction, which would be no reaction at all. She squared her shoulders, raised her chin, and strode to the café.

Minutes later, Doreen brought June's lunch request: chicken vegetable soup, an apple, and ice water. "You seem tense. Is everything all right?"

June found comfort in the other woman's concern. "It will be, once Simon realizes I'm not leaving Trinity Falls. And, even if I did, he still couldn't save his marriage."

Doreen poured herself a glass of ice water. "It would take a miracle to save Simon and Ethel's marriage. Don't waste your energy worrying about it. Simon has never known what he's wanted."

"That's a good point." June put her apple in her purse before digging into her soup.

"You have much more important things to think about." Doreen took another sip of water. "How's Noah settling in at Columbia?"

"He's keeping up with his coursework." June felt a new burst of pride. The next half hour was spent talking about children, careers, and their town.

"I meant what I said about ignoring Simon, Ethel, and Nessa's behavior." Doreen refilled June's water glass as she brought the conversation back to June's antagonists. "You may have detractors. But you have admirers, too."

"I appreciate the warm welcome you and your friends have given me." June smiled her thanks. "The dinner party you hosted to welcome me to Trinity Falls was wonderful. And I can't thank you and your friends enough for helping me move all of my belongings."

After she and Darius had moved Noah into his residence hall at Columbia University, June hadn't thought she would have the energy to relocate her home to Trinity Falls. But the next weekend, Darius and Doreen had shown up with Alonzo, Peyton, Ean, Megan, Quincy, Ramona, Jackson, and Audra. They'd helped her pack and clean her house for the new owners. Then they'd loaded their cars and her moving truck for the two-hour drive to Trinity Falls.

"Your friendship is thanks enough." Doreen reached forward to squeeze June's forearm. "But I wasn't talking about us."

"Then who?" June frowned her surprise

Doreen straightened from the counter. Her lips curved into a smile. "Ben Brooks."

My boss? How could he be an admirer? There must be some mistake.

June sipped more water, already dismissing Doreen's theory. "What makes you think Ben admires me?"

"He asked me a lot of questions about you." Doreen leaned against the counter, nodding for emphasis.

June felt a thread of unease. She shook it off. "He's probably trying to get to know his staff. You and Ron hired me a month before Ben became the center's director. And Dita, Howard, and Krista have worked there for years."

Ronald Kendal, the previous director, had worked for the center since its doors had opened. He must have been in his seventies when he'd finally retired in September.

Doreen shook her head. "He wasn't asking about Dita, Krista, or Howard. He only wanted to know about you."

June's unease increased. "What did he ask you?"

"They were fairly personal questions. How long have I known you? How did I convince you to leave Sequoia? What were you like?"

June froze. Those *were* personal questions. "What did you say?"

"That I like and admire you, and that you're an asset to this town. That's all I said. I told him that if he wanted to know anything more about you, he needed to ask you himself."

June breathed more easily. "Thank you."

"He said Darius had told him the same thing."

"He's asked Darius about me, too?" June's eyes stretched wide. "I can't believe he's fishing for gossip about me." Especially since she'd told Dita not to fuel rumors and innuendos about their boss. She was sick with disappointment.

"He wasn't looking for gossip, June. He never asked me about Simon. I think he wants to get to know you better."

"Then all he has to do is ask me." June drained her water. "In fact, I'll tell him that now."

"Your mother's worried about you." Benjamin sat at his office desk, using his cellular phone to check in with his son. He hadn't been able to reach his daughter.

At nineteen, Terrence was his oldest child. His daughter, Zora, was a year younger. He and his children used to be so close, speaking several times a week about everything. The divorce had changed that. Now their conversations were stilted on the occasions Terrence and Zora returned his calls.

"Oh, yeah?" Terrence didn't sound impressed. Although it was difficult to hear his son's voice with Pit Bull's latest hip-hop release blaring in the background.

"Would you turn down your stereo, please?"

"Yeah." Despite Terrence's agreement, the volume didn't sound appreciably lower.

Benjamin's gaze sought and found a recent photo of Terrence and Zora taken outside of their house in Chicago. It stood on the bookcase across from his desk beside a photo of him with his kids. Both pictures had been taken before he and Aliyah had told them about their pending divorce.

"What are you and Zora doing for Thanksgiving?" He was glad Terrence and Zora had both chosen The Ohio State University. They could look out for each other. And now that he was back in northeastern Ohio, he was less than four hours from them.

"What do you mean? Are we supposed to choose between you?" A door slammed in the background. The music had stopped. Had Terrence moved to another room in his residence hall suite? Benjamin could see the layout in his mind's eye.

"Terry, I know this—"

"What are *you* doing for Thanksgiving, Dad?"

He knew where this was going, and he didn't like it. "I'll probably spend it with my brothers. Although you and Zora are welcome to spend it with me."

Terrence snorted. "So it's either Mom's house or Dad's house. Are we supposed to choose between the two of you again when Christmas comes around?"

"We're still trying to figure out the holidays." He'd never imagined he'd be saying that about his family— at least not until his kids were married with children of their own.

"This. *Really*. Sucks." Terrence's voice was muffled as though he'd rubbed his hand over his face as he spoke.

Tell me about it. "I know, Terry. I'm sorry."

"If you're sorry, why don't you do something about it?"

The angry accusation caught him off guard. "What do you want me to do?"

"I don't know. *Something*. But Zora and I agree that you and Mom have destroyed this family."

That accusation hurt even more. "We're still a family, Terry."

"How?" Anger shook his young voice. "We're not even celebrating the holidays together. How are we a *family*?"

Benjamin rubbed his forehead with the tips of his thumb and three fingers. "I never intended for this to happen. This isn't something I wanted. I'm trying to figure it out as I go."

His son was silent for several long, torturous moments. "Why didn't you tell us why you and Mom were getting a divorce? Instead, when we asked you, you didn't say anything."

"It wasn't my place to tell you." Benjamin swallowed the bitterness. "Your mother had to tell you when she was ready."

"You let us think that the two of you had drifted apart. But the truth is Mom had an affair. With your boss."

"Your mother's affair was a sign that we'd drifted apart." It had just taken him two years to realize it.

"Even if that's true, she should have realized her actions would hurt us, too." Terrence's tension traveled down the phone line, and straight into Benjamin.

"I know. And I'm sorry about that." Sorrier than he could ever express.

They sat in silence for a while. Benjamin heard muffled voices and a television in the background.

"How are you doing, Dad?" Terrence sounded drained of energy.

Again, his son's question took him by surprise. "I'm all right."

"If you say so." Terrence snorted his disbelief. "Can you forgive her?"

The questions were getting harder. "I don't know, Terry."

"I can't." Terrence's tone was bitter.

Benjamin hesitated. He could use this opportunity to usurp his son's loyalty. He could capitalize on Terrence's resentment toward Aliyah and convince him and his sister to spend Thanksgiving in Trinity Falls with him. He was tempted. So tempted.

"Terry, I'd really appreciate it if you'd try to forgive her." He forced the words.

"Why?" His son sounded sincerely confused. "You said you're not going to forgive her."

"I said I didn't know if I could." Benjamin was growing impatient. "But she's your mother. And she's been a great one. She loves you and Zora very much."

"If she loved us, she wouldn't have cheated on you and torn our family apart."

His son had a point. Because of that, every time he pleaded for leniency for her, a part of him died. "That's something for your mother and me to figure out."

"How can you say that? What she did has affected all of us." Terrence didn't seem big on leniency. "I don't know if Zora will ever be able to speak to her again. Or if I will."

Benjamin drew his gaze from the photos of happier family times. The images were beginning to hurt.

"Terry, don't let your sister go any longer without talking with her mother." He couldn't believe he was pleading with his children to give his ex-wife clemency when he didn't think he could forgive her. "She's your mother. She knows what she did was wrong, and she's sorry she hurt you."

Terrence's sigh seemed to come from deep within him. "I'll think about it, Dad."

"Thanks, son." That would have to be good enough for now. "What about Thanksgiving?"

"I'll talk with Zora. We'll think about it."

"Okay." Benjamin sat up, preparing to end the call. "Good luck with your classes. Call me if you need me."

"Will do." Terrence sounded like his son again.

They ended their call. Benjamin's marriage was over. He'd accepted that. But he couldn't lose his children. Perhaps all they needed was more time. The thought lifted the burden he'd been carrying in his heart since his divorce.

He set his cell phone on his desk and stood. His mood was lighter as he opened his office door. June's appearance in his doorway startled him. Her hand was raised as though he'd caught her about to knock.

Benjamin stepped back, smiling. "This is a surprise."

She didn't look amused. "We need to talk."

Chapter 5

Benjamin stood back to let June into his office Friday afternoon. "What can I do for you?" He closed his door. Benjamin had a feeling they would need some privacy to discuss whatever it was that had put that look of anger in June's eyes.

June faced him. "You can ask *me* any questions you might have about my personal life. My professional life for that matter, too."

Busted. Who'd told June he'd been asking about her, Darius, Doreen, or Ramona?

Benjamin released his doorknob and shoved his hands into the front pockets of his black pants. He could only hope the heat rising into his face wasn't a blush. "I apologize if I gave the impression that I was gossiping about you. I promise that I wasn't."

She didn't appear convinced. "Then what were you doing?"

I still don't know. But he needed to come up with something.

Benjamin paced forward, careful to keep a certain amount of space between him and the petite powder keg in his office. "You don't talk about yourself. But the people who are smearing your reputation around town won't stop talking."

"I can't help that." June crossed her arms.

Benjamin pulled his attention from her trim figure dressed in an emerald knit sweater and mid-calf length black skirt. An angel brooch was pinned to her sweater. "You're well-liked by all of the people I respect. I wanted their perspective on the kind of person you are."

"Shouldn't you make your own decisions?" Her tawny eyes haunted him. She wasn't showing him any mercy. But he wanted her to. He wanted her mercy and more.

Benjamin freed his hands from his pockets and stepped forward. "I need information to make those decisions. You weren't giving me any."

"Our relationship isn't personal. It's professional. You seem to have forgotten that."

"I want to know who I'm working with."

"Read my resume."

He observed the stubborn tilt of her rounded chin, the irritated scowl knitting her slashed eyebrows, and he had to bite back a smile. "Your resume is one of the driest reports I've ever read."

"I'm not here for your entertainment." Somehow she'd found a way to look down her nose at him despite the fact he stood at least ten inches above her.

"I know that." Benjamin turned away before she noticed the smile twitching around his lips. What was it about her that was dragging his body and mind out of the cold storage he'd packed them into when he'd discovered Aliyah's betrayal? Part of him wanted to run from June. But another part—the more dominate part—wanted to feel again. Desperately.

"Then why are you snooping around my life? What do you want from me?" Her words sucker punched him.

What did he want from her? The answer struck him like an energy bolt. He wanted . . . her. The woman who challenged him, defied him, wouldn't take no for an answer. The woman who was forcing him to feel again.

Benjamin turned to her. "I want to get to know you."

"Why?" June took a step toward him—and Benjamin's restraint collapsed.

He lowered his head to hers and trapped the gasp that puffed from her mouth. Her lips were soft and full. Benjamin watched her eyes drift shut. It was one of the most erotic sights he'd ever witnessed. His pulse stuttered, then rocketed forward. He inhaled and captured her scent: powder and wildflowers. Like the first day of spring after a brutal winter. He drew closer. Hips to hips. Chest to breasts. Her warmth soaked his muscles, stirring imaginings that had been dormant for months. Did she taste as good as she felt? His tongue slid over her lower lip. The muscles of his abdomen tightened. Good Lord, she was better than he'd imagined. More than he could have dreamed of. His arms remained at his sides. He didn't trust himself to hold her. If he did, could he ever let her go?

But then June lifted her arms to his shoulders and twined them around his neck. Her soft palms cupped the back of his head, drawing him even nearer. Her mouth moved against his. Seeking, exploring, demanding greater access. When her lips parted for him, Benjamin eagerly accepted her welcome. His tongue swept inside her, hungry for a deeper taste. He teased hers with touches and licks. Then he drew it deeper into his mouth and suckled her. June moaned at the intimate caress. The sound startled them apart. Her eyes flew open.

Benjamin searched her wide, bright gaze. "I'm sorry." Not for kissing her—for not asking permission first.

June blinked. "Why did we do that?"

We? Tension drained from Benjamin's shoulders. He stepped back before he kissed her again. "I've wanted to do that for a while. Why did you kiss me back?"

"It felt good." June brought her fingertips to her lips.

Heat rushed through him. "Yes, it did."

"We can't do that again." June stepped back. "We work together. I have enough complications in my life without adding an office affair to the list."

"I understand." Or at least he was trying to.

"I'm sorry." June backed toward his door.

"So am I." He watched her disappear from his office and then returned to his desk.

Nessa, Ethel, Simon, and their associates' efforts to force June out of Trinity Falls would be enough stress for anyone. But what if he could convince the town bullies to leave her alone? Would she share more kisses with him then?

"I asked Terry and Zora to forgive Aliyah. But I know I never will." Benjamin shoved aside his now empty plate and looked across the honey wood café table at his two younger brothers.

They'd just finished brunch at Books & Bakery. The lunch crowd was moving in. Early Saturday afternoon sun spilled into the café from the window beside them. It looked deceptively warm for the first week of November.

"Did you tell them you couldn't forgive Aliyah?" His youngest brother—Dr. Vaughn Brooks, the music professor at Trinity Falls University—ran his right hand over his clean-shaven head.

"I'd never tell my children that." Benjamin sipped his water. "I'd only share that with both of you."

"If I were you, I wouldn't be able to forgive her, either." Outrage roughened Zachariah Brooks's voice. Benjamin's middle brother had returned home to Trinity Falls recently as well. The confirmed bachelor was the new vice president of marketing and communications with Trinity Falls University. "She had an affair—with your boss."

Almost a year had passed since he'd found out his ex-wife and his boss had been lying to him for two years. A rush of anger—sharp and hot—tightened his muscles. How could he *not* have known?

"Her lies changed my life." Benjamin wiped the condensation from his glass of ice water. "For the past eighteen years, I'd celebrated Thanksgiving with a wife and two children. This year, I'm spending it with my two bachelor brothers and I won't even see my kids."

"She has a lot to answer for." Zachariah's ebony eyes, identical to his and Vaughn's, glared into his empty coffee mug.

"I'm sorry this is happening, Ben." Vaughn's compassion eased some of Benjamin's tension. "But it sounds as though Aliyah may not see Terry and Zora, either. They might decide to spend Thanksgiving at Ohio State."

"That would be poetic justice." Benjamin had considered that possibility. It would give him a level of satisfaction if his ex-wife didn't see their children, either.

"I hope they don't do that." Vaughn sat back on his chair, smoothing his goatee in a pensive gesture.

"Why not?" Zachariah's expression said he thought Vaughn had lost his mind.

"Thanksgiving should be spent at home with family." Vaughn frowned at Zachariah, who was seated beside him. The brothers were almost identical with their dark eyes and chiseled features. "I don't want my niece and nephew spending it on some deserted college campus."

Zachariah grunted. "Aliyah should have thought of that before she betrayed your brother."

Benjamin looked from Zachariah to Vaughn. "If they stayed in Ohio, I could bring them to Trinity Falls for Thanksgiving."

"True." Vaughn nodded. "But you said you wanted Terry and Zora to forgive Aliyah."

Benjamin clenched his fist on the table. "Why should she have a normal Thanksgiving while I'm here with you? No offense intended."

"None taken." Zachariah sipped his coffee. "It's a fair question. You've lost everything: your family, career, home. All because of her."

"I understand Ben's not being able to forgive Aliyah." Vaughn switched his attention from Zachariah to Benjamin. "But don't use your kids as a weapon."

"I won't." Benjamin rubbed his face with both hands. "But where they spend Thanksgiving is their choice. If they decide to stay in Columbus, I won't try to change their minds."

"Fair enough." Zachariah inclined his head.

Vaughn arched a brow. "As long as we bring them back to Trinity Falls to spend the holiday with us."

"Agreed." Benjamin relaxed back onto his seat. Confiding in his brothers helped him feel marginally better.

"So what are we doing for Thanksgiving?" Zachariah interrupted the heavy silence.

"Benita and I want to host it at our house." Vaughn offered a smile. "We'd like the two of you and Ms. Helen to join us."

"I'm in," Zachariah responded quickly.

"Thanks, V. And thank Benita for us." Benjamin was grateful for his brother's generous invitation even as he regretted the unexpected turn his life had taken.

"Does Doreen still host her Thanksgiving open house?" Zachariah looked in the direction of the café counter, where a display of Doreen's fresh pastries stood.

"Yes, she does, every Thanksgiving evening." Vaughn's confirmation brought happy childhood memories.

"It's good to be home." Zachariah grabbed his empty coffee mug and started to rise from his seat. "Anyone want a refill?"

"Excuse me." A female voice interrupted their conversation.

Benjamin looked over his shoulder to find a tall, beautiful woman standing beside their table. Her small, slim hands gripped a bakery bag. He rose, noting in his peripheral vision that his brothers had stood as well.

A soft pink blush accented her high cheekbones. "Vaughn, I'm sorry to interrupt. I saw you sitting here and just wanted to say hello."

"It's good to see you, Olivia. Let me introduce you to my brothers." Vaughn gestured between the two men. "Ben and Zach, this is Dr. Olivia Stark. She's one of our biology professors at TFU."

Even in casual dress—a thin tan sweater and brown slacks under a calf-length, blue fall coat—the biology professor looked neat and professional. Her straight brown hair was cut in an attractive bob that framed her delicate face.

Olivia offered Benjamin a shy smile and her hand. It was small and delicate in his. "I understand you've both recently returned to Trinity Falls."

"That's right." Benjamin released her hand.

"Welcome home." Olivia turned to Zachariah.

"Thank you." Zachariah held on to Olivia's hand.

"You're the university's new vice president of marketing, aren't you?" Olivia pinned Zachariah with her dark eyes.

"Yes, I started Monday." He finally released her hand.

"Welcome to TFU." Olivia managed to pull her attention from Zachariah and glanced again at Benjamin. "It's a pleasure to meet you both. Enjoy the rest of your weekend."

Olivia inclined her head, then took her leave.

Zachariah watched her walk away. "I think she undressed me with her eyes."

Vaughn snorted. "Give it a rest, Zach."

"I'm not saying that I mind." Zachariah turned back to them. "More coffee?"

"I'll take a refill." Vaughn passed Zachariah his empty mug and resumed his seat.

Benjamin stilled when June emerged from behind the comic book stands. Her petite figure was clothed in a pale green sweater and dark gray denim. Even from here, he could see she'd pinned one of her festive brochures to her shoulder. His smile faded when Nessa left her table to intercept June.

"I'm fine. Excuse me." Benjamin left his brothers to cross the café. What was Nessa up to now?

June had timed her trip to Books & Bakery to miss the Saturday afternoon crush. She adjusted her hold on her bag of recently purchased contemporary romances and retrieved her wallet from her purse. She was going to buy a Trinity Falls Fudge Walnut Brownie, then go home to curl up with it and one of her new purchases. *Heaven.*

"I see you're moving forward with your fund-raiser." Nessa's snide tone dimmed June's bright glow of anticipation.

She braced herself before looking up from her wallet. "Good afternoon, Nessa. How are you today?"

Nessa's dark eyes narrowed. "I don't make empty threats. You should know that."

"And you should know that you can't threaten us." Benjamin's tone was inflexible.

Startled, June turned to find him beside her. *When had he arrived?* His large hand was warm on the small of her back. All of her senses had now converged onto that one spot.

Nessa switched her glare to him. "Why don't you walk away, Ben? This doesn't concern you."

Benjamin's tension communicated itself through the hand on June's back. "June *is* my concern, as are all of the people who work for me."

June's eyes widened. Was Benjamin defending her? Again? In her entire life, no one had ever defended her. Now he'd done so twice in the span of a week. It was an incredible feeling not to have to fight her battles alone.

Still, a part of her shrunk inside as she noticed the attention they were drawing. She looked up at her knight-in-sweater-and-khakis.

"Ben, it's all right." She melted in the fire in his eyes. That fiercely protective expression was for her. June couldn't look away.

"No, it's not." He returned his attention to Nessa. "I won't allow you to bully anyone on my staff."

"It looks like you're letting your attraction to June Cale cloud your judgment, Ben." Nessa smirked.

"What's clouding your judgment, Nessa?" Benjamin lowered his voice.

June shivered at his dangerous tone. She didn't want to be the afternoon's performance. She cringed inwardly, certain this encounter would be repeated in a variety of tales across town.

"You're worried about one woman." Nessa gestured toward June. "I'm concerned about the moral fabric of an entire town."

Zachariah added his voice to the scene. "Those who live in glass houses shouldn't cast stones, Nessa."

June looked around to find the Brooks brothers now flanked her. The situation had taken on a life of its own. "Gentlemen, I—"

"What's that supposed to mean?" Nessa's voice rose to a near shriek.

Vaughn responded. "Your Christian charity has been missing for a long time now. What does the Bible say about treating others as you would be treated?"

Nessa stabbed a finger toward the music professor. "My behavior is beyond reproach."

"I disagree." From out of nowhere, Megan appeared.

"Nessa, I won't tolerate hostility in my place of business. Either return to your table or leave."

Doreen carried a small pastry bag. "As mayor, I'll ask you again not to interfere in Guiding Light's fund-raising efforts. You know as well as I do how critical the center's services are to this community."

June was shaking. Was it relief, shock, gratitude? It was all too overwhelming, having so many people rally around her. Benjamin's arm slipped around her waist, pulling her close against his side. She felt his gaze burning through the top of her head. She didn't have the emotional stamina to face him. But she was grateful for his support. Without it, she would have collapsed like a boneless mass to the floor.

Nessa sniffed. "I'm well aware of that, which is the reason I believe they should be entrusted to someone with greater moral fiber."

Doreen arched a brow. She lowered her voice. "Should we put your moral fiber to a vote?"

Nessa's gaze wavered under Doreen's direct stare. She turned to give June a silent glare, then flounced from the store.

June looked at the people surrounding her: Megan, Doreen, Benjamin, Zachariah, and Vaughn. "I don't know what to say." Her voice was a whisper.

"Say good-bye. I'm taking you home." Benjamin pulled currency from his wallet, then gestured toward the small paper bag in Doreen's hand. "Is that for June?"

"It's a brownie." Doreen gave the bag to Benjamin but declined his money. "That's not necessary."

Does anyone notice me standing here? If it wasn't for Benjamin's arm around her waist, June would have thought she'd become invisible.

"Thanks." Benjamin returned his wallet to his pocket

as he escorted June to the front doors. Outside, he paused on the sidewalk and extended his free hand. "May I have your car keys? I think I should drive."

She looked around the parking lot. "What about your car?"

"Vaughn drove." His expression was determined.

June hesitated. "I owe you money for the brownie."

"No, you don't. Doreen didn't charge us. Now let me take you home."

June shook her head. "I can drive myself home."

"You could. But I think we'd both feel more comfortable if you didn't."

Benjamin had a point. As much as she may want to deny it, she wasn't feeling completely steady. She was used to taking care of herself. This afternoon, for the first time, she didn't have to. June fumbled in her purse, then handed her keys to Benjamin before taking him to her orange Toyota Corolla.

Benjamin handed her onto the passenger seat. He gave her the pastry bag to hold with her newly purchased books before closing her car door. He then circled the trunk to the driver's side. June watched him fold himself awkwardly onto the driver's seat as he adjusted the chair for his longer legs. She would have found the sight amusing if she weren't still disquieted by the scene in the café.

After Nessa's tirade, what would people think and say about her? She hadn't realized she'd still be defending her moral fiber nineteen years later. And to drag Benjamin into this . . .

June gripped the Books & Bakery pastry bag. "Thank you for driving me home."

Benjamin glanced at her as he adjusted her mirrors. "You're welcome. I don't think you should be alone right now."

"You'll want to take a right out of the parking lot." June's eyes traced Benjamin's profile: high forehead, long nose, and square chin. He really was a very handsome man. She could look at his face all day.

Benjamin turned over the engine and reversed out of the parking space, guiding her car to the Trinity Falls Town Center's parking lot exit. He checked the traffic on Main Street before merging into the near lane. "I felt you trembling. The confrontation with Nessa affected you more than you thought it would."

He was right. June sat back and looked out her side window. It was unusually sunny for autumn in Ohio. The sky was a brilliant cerulean blue that made the autumn colors appear even more brilliant. "I don't like to make a scene. Turn left on Town."

"You weren't making a scene. Nessa was." Benjamin stopped at a stop sign, then eased through the intersection. They were still several blocks from Town Street.

"I didn't want any part of that." She was getting agitated again. June took a deep breath to calm herself.

"Just because you don't want something doesn't mean it won't find you anyway."

What was behind the wealth of bitterness in Benjamin's voice? Did it have anything to do with his divorce? June studied his profile. His eyes seemed harder. His mouth had thinned.

"You sound like you're speaking from experience." She posed the question tentatively.

"I am." Benjamin didn't offer anything more and June didn't push.

With the exception of her directions, they finished the drive in silence. She didn't mind. It allowed her to settle her nerves and to wonder. "How are you getting home?"

Chapter 6

"I was hoping you'd take me home after you'd had a chance to relax." Benjamin pulled her car onto her driveway.

He studied her two-story, red-brick-and-cement colonial home through the windshield. It suited her. It was attractive, charming, and dependable. He'd had an attractive home in Chicago. Now he lived in an ugly townhouse.

"Of course." June unbuckled her belt.

Benjamin climbed out of the Toyota, intending to open the passenger door for June. He smiled, shaking his head, when he saw her already mounting the stairs to her front door.

He hurried to catch up with her. "Do you need your keys?"

"That would help." June met his eyes over her shoulder. Her smile seemed unsteady. "Would you like some tea?"

"That would be great." Not really. However, if tea would make her feel better, he'd drink a cup with her.

Benjamin followed June into her home. It had the

same cinnamon-and-apples fragrance he smelled every time he walked into her office. The white-and-silver tile in the entry gave way to thick emerald carpeting that led him across the living room. Her furnishings created a home. A fluffy cream-and-silver matching loveseat and sofa dominated the family room. Tall, thin sterling silver lamps topped the two Maplewood corner tables on either side of the sofa. A centerpiece rested on an emerald green doily on the Maplewood coffee table. Benjamin lingered in front of the glass-and-sterling-silver entertainment center with its large, black flat-screen television. He used to have one like it.

He silently trailed June through her dining room and into her kitchen.

She carried the kettle to the sink to fill it with water. "Have a seat." June gestured toward the honey wood circular kitchen table. "Would you like chai, lemon, or green tea?"

The choices confused him. He wasn't much of a tea drinker. "I'll have what you're having."

"Then we're having chai." She returned the kettle to the stove, then turned up the burner under it. "Would you like to split the brownie?"

"No, thank you. I just finished brunch."

"I'm not hungry, either." She put the brownie in a sandwich bag, then stored it in the refrigerator.

A comfortable quiet settled over the kitchen as Benjamin watched June prepare their tea. It was like watching a modern dance performance. Benjamin enjoyed the silence and the show. Her movements were graceful as she glided from cupboards to drawers collecting tea bags, sweeteners, mugs, and teaspoons.

June ended the silence. Had it made her uncomfortable? They talked about the weather until the water boiled. She arranged the mugs of tea, a bowl of sugar, and the teaspoons on a tray and carried it to the table.

"Thank you." Benjamin searched her delicate features. "How are you feeling?"

"I'm not used to people standing up for me." June settled onto the chair to Benjamin's left.

"If you don't stop Nessa, she'll continue to attack you." Benjamin added sugar to his tea. "That's what bullies do."

"My experience has been that bullies will be bullies regardless of whether you fight back." She stirred sweetener into her tea. "I had a feeling this would happen, but I'd hoped it wouldn't."

"I'm glad you're here. Don't get me wrong. But, if you knew people in Trinity Falls would give you a hard time, why did you move here?" Benjamin sipped his chai tea. It must be an acquired taste.

"I needed a job."

"You have an impressive resume. You could've found another job in Sequoia."

"Once my son left for college, I was going to be alone. I didn't want that." June seemed mesmerized by the steam rising from her mug. "You're never alone in Trinity Falls, even if you want to be. That's something I noticed the few times I've visited."

"But you knew there'd be people who wouldn't want you here."

"And I knew some people would welcome me. Those were the ones I wanted to be with." June leaned back on her seat, bringing her mug of tea with her. "Darius and his friends have made me feel like a part of a really big family."

Exactly what was Darius's relationship with June?

"But Darius's parents are the two people who are most vocal against your being here." Benjamin tried more tea. It still had a bitter taste. He added another half teaspoon of sugar.

"I understand their feelings. I remind them of their failed marriage." June rose from the table and took a lemon from the refrigerator. She placed it on a small blue plate and cut it into four wedges before carrying the slices back with her. "Squeeze one into your tea."

Benjamin tried that. It couldn't hurt. "Simon's the reminder of their failed marriage. He's the one who cheated on his wife."

"But I'm the one he cheated with." June resumed her seat. She squeezed one of the wedges into her tea and stirred it in.

"Can I ask you something?"

June sipped her tea. "You want to know how I got involved with Simon."

"I'm curious." Benjamin tried more tea. The lemon had made a big difference.

"We met on campus in the student center when I was a junior at TFU."

"What was he doing there?"

"He used to be a postal carrier before he retired, remember?" June shrugged. "I think the university was on his route."

"What did you see in him? He's a lot older than you." If Benjamin's calculations were correct, Simon Knight was old enough to be June's father.

"Simon was handsome and charming, and I thought we'd made a connection. I also thought he was single." June made a face. "He never talked about a wife and he didn't wear a ring."

Benjamin nodded. "That would all add up to make you think he was single."

"I didn't learn the truth until I told him I was pregnant."

"That's when he told you about Ethel?"

"I was horrified. I was a home wrecker and I hadn't even known it." June rubbed her upper arms as though the memory still chilled her.

Benjamin wanted to hold her to offer her comfort, but he sensed she didn't want to be touched yet. "It wasn't your fault."

"He wasn't going to divorce his wife." June continued as though she hadn't heard him. "And I wouldn't have wanted him to. It was never my intention to break up a family. Instead, he told me to . . . get rid of my baby. I couldn't do that."

Benjamin's skin burned with anger. "What about your parents? Did they help you?"

June was silent for so long, Benjamin didn't think she was going to answer him. He started to repeat the question when June spoke.

"My parents had never wanted me to go to college." Her shrug was restless, uncomfortable. "I defied them to attend TFU. I think they were afraid something like this would happen."

"But did they help you?"

June shook her head. "They threw me out of their house and told me not to come back. I haven't seen them since."

The knowledge stole Benjamin's breath. "I'm so sorry."

"So am I. But I'm also grateful. With God's help, I managed. I'm raising my son. I also earned my degree and built a career."

"After all that's happened, why aren't you furious with Simon? *I'd* be." Thinking about how the older man had ruined a young woman's life, all for his own selfish desires, made Benjamin want to pummel him.

"I was furious at first. Furious, ashamed, and afraid. He'd made a fool of me. But if it weren't for Simon, I wouldn't have my son." June's face brightened at the thought of her child. Her smile was almost ethereal. "And for that blessing, I could almost thank him. I won't forget what he did. But in my heart, I've forgiven him for Noah."

June amazed him. She'd been through so much. Simon had lied to her. Her parents had disowned her. She'd had to raise her child when she was young, single, and alone. But despite all of those hardships, she didn't seem angry or bitter.

"How can you forgive someone who ruined your life?" Benjamin needed to know.

June blinked at him. "But don't you understand? I'm sorry for the way it happened. But if it hadn't happened, I wouldn't have Noah. How could I remain angry with anyone for that?"

June had a point. How could one hold a grudge against the person who'd give them their children?

"Do you know anything about the six-foot Christmas tree in . . . ?" Benjamin's voice dwindled when he took in the changes to June's office two weeks later.

"The lobby?" June completed his thought. "Yes, it's lovely."

And how would she describe her office? To Benjamin, it looked like Christmas on steroids. Gold tinsel hung in loops across her walls. Bows of red ribbons held tightly to her file cabinet drawer handles. Silver paper snowflakes clung to the window beside her desk. A carol—"Little Drummer Boy"?—played softly from an unseen source. The scent of cinnamons and apples seemed even stronger—or was that his imagination?

Benjamin snapped out of his surprise. "You've redecorated."

"Just getting ready for the season." June glowed with satisfaction as she gazed around her festive office.

"Is that what you're doing with the tree in the lobby?" Benjamin scowled as he brought the conversation back to his original topic.

"That's right." Today's brooch was a gold-and-silver Christmas tree pinned to her warm gold sweater.

The muscles in Benjamin's neck and shoulders tightened as he spotted the mini Christmas tree on her windowsill beside a tiny Nativity scene. He'd been so disturbed by the new addition to their lobby this Friday morning that he'd come straight to her office. He hadn't stopped to shed his parka.

"Shouldn't you have discussed it with me first?" Benjamin's grip tightened on his briefcase.

"What's to discuss?" June shrugged her slender shoulders. "Christmas is as inevitable as my coming to work every day. Do I discuss that with you before getting out of bed?"

Benjamin had an immediate and inappropriate image of June in his bed, wearing sexy lingerie. With an effort, he banished the picture from his mind. "How did you even pay for that display?"

"You mean the tree and its decorations?" June smiled with complacency. "The money came from the Christmas budget."

Benjamin's frown deepened. "We don't have a Christmas budget."

"Of course we do."

His confusion cleared. "Did you pay for it?"

June's response was a smile.

Was there anything that would curb her Christmas frenzy? "Who helped you decorate the tree?"

"Elves."

"Were their names Dita, Krista, and Howard?"

Another silent smile. But Benjamin didn't need her confirmation. His staff had left their fingerprints all over the tree. Benjamin had noticed a miniature spaceship, the logo of the Cleveland football team, and a *Sherlock* figurine among the ornaments.

"It's too early to put up a Christmas tree." Benjamin rubbed the back of his neck. "It's not even Thanksgiving yet."

"I realize that." June grew serious. "But we have a great opportunity to promote our Christmas dinner dance with Quincy's Kwanzaa presentation tomorrow. We should have more than a hundred people here. I thought a fully decorated Christmas tree would help promote our event."

He couldn't argue with her logic. He just wasn't ready to celebrate the season. "Next time, please let me know before you redecorate the center."

"Fair enough."

Satisfied—or at least as satisfied as he'd ever be after negotiating with June—Benjamin left her office. Between the dinner dance event and the hulking evergreen with the explosion of decorations in the lobby, June was determined to surround him with Christmas. How could he make her stop?

"Do you need a hand?"

June looked up from her event preparation checklist at the sound of Benjamin's voice later Friday afternoon. Her heart stopped, then galloped, as he walked toward her from the other end of the community room. His loose-limbed grace brought to mind a panther on the prowl. The jacket of his dark brown suit hung open over his cream shirt. June's fingers twitched to loosen his black tie. Her palms itched to remove his jacket. June fisted her hands to restrain her impulse.

"Excuse me?" She gave herself a mental shake. What had Benjamin said?

She'd been having these mental lapses for the past two weeks, ever since he'd stood up for her to Nessa at Books & Bakery. He must think she was losing her hearing.

"I asked if you needed a hand with anything." Benjamin stopped an arm's length in front of her. The twinkle in his eye made her wonder if he knew the real reason for her hearing problem. "Everyone else is gone."

Surprised, June checked her black Timex wristwatch. It was almost six-thirty. "I hadn't realized it was so late. I should be done in a few minutes."

"Do you really think we'll fill this room on a Saturday afternoon?" Benjamin looked around.

June's eyes were drawn to his strong neck. She took a step back to prevent herself from closing the gap between them, then followed his gaze. She'd rented one hundred seats. But with Dita, Krista, and Howard's help, she had set up only ninety of them, three sections each with five rows of six seats.

"Actually, I'm concerned we may not have enough chairs." June set her hands on her hips. "We have about one hundred registrants. But since the event is free, not everyone would have signed up. And not everyone who registered will show."

Benjamin took the presentation program off a

nearby chair. "I just hope we didn't waste a lot of money on an event that won't be well attended."

June stripped the program from Benjamin's hand and put it back on the chair. "You aren't into the holiday season, are you?"

His quizzical expression was far too sexy. "What makes you say that?"

What is Benjamin doing to me with his voice, his eyes, his scent?

June put her hands on her hips. "You're questioning the draw of the Kwanzaa presentation and you were irrationally opposed to the Christmas dinner dance."

"I wasn't irrationally opposed to it." Benjamin closed the distance between them. "My reasons for not originally supporting it were very logical."

"Give me some credit, Ben." June crossed to the makeshift stage to mask the fact she was once again putting space between her and her attractive boss. "Why are you opposed to the holiday season?"

"Holidays are for families. I've lost mine."

The pain in his voice cut at her heart. June turned to face him. He looked lost, vulnerable, confused.

She hurt for him. "May I ask—?"

"What happened to my marriage? It's only fair, considering the personal questions I've asked you." He dumped his gray winter coat on a chair and shoved his hands in his front pockets. "My wife of twenty years had been having an affair for the last two."

That was what Dita had told her. But Benjamin's confirmation was still shocking. "I'm so sorry."

"So am I." His voice was grim. "I found out the day before Christmas Eve. She'd been sleeping with my boss."

June's eyes widened with surprise. "Did she tell you?"

"No, I got home early from a business trip and walked in on them as they were undressing."

Oh, my word. "What did you do?"

"I threw them out of my house." Benjamin paced away from the stage as though propelled by residual anger. "They'd been having sex *in my bed* for years."

Watching him prowl the community room in pain and anger brought back uncomfortable memories of the day Ethel had learned of her and Simon. June forced those images away and focused on Benjamin. What could she say to comfort him?

"I'm so sorry, Ben."

He spun toward her. Benjamin's expression changed as speculation entered his dark eyes. He paced back to her. "I haven't gotten the female perspective. Tell me, why would a woman have a two-year affair instead of just divorcing her husband?"

At a loss, June shook her head. "I'm still trying to—" *Oh, my.*

"To what?"

She swallowed to ease the dryness in her throat. "To figure out how any woman married to you would want to sleep with someone else."

A flash of heat shot from Benjamin's eyes and into June's bloodstream. He took her in his arms and lowered his head to hers. June gasped as he pressed his hard, muscled body against her.

Oh, my!

Benjamin swept his tongue into her mouth. This wasn't the gentle, searching caress they'd shared in his office three weeks earlier. Yes, June remembered the date and time of that sensual exchange. This kiss was a demand, a possession. With his lips and tongue, Benjamin showed June what he wanted and what he was willing to give her in return. June trembled in his arms. As far as experience, he was light years ahead of her. She didn't know whether she could give him all he asked for. But, oh, she was desperate to try.

She twined her arms around his neck and rose to her toes to mold her body to his. Tentatively, she touched his tongue with hers.

Was that his moan or mine?

She didn't care. She could kiss Benjamin for hours, for days. She loved the feel of him, hot and smooth. The taste of him, spicy and intoxicating. The way he smelled, of cedar and shaving cream.

June stroked the length of Benjamin's tongue, drawing him farther into her mouth. His moan was more of a growl deep in his throat, reverberating to the core of her. Her nipples tightened. Benjamin's hands lowered from her waist and gripped her hips. June felt his arousal press hard against the juncture of her thighs. Her eyes popped open and she met his hard, hot gaze. Benjamin dropped his hands and June stepped back.

"I'm sorry." They spoke at the same time.

"I don't know what came over me." Benjamin rubbed the back of his neck.

June knew what had come over her: lust. But what had such feelings gotten her in the past? Could she risk that it would be any different this time? Should she listen to her mind or follow her feelings? "I should get going. I'll see you tomorrow for Quincy's presentation."

"Are you all right?"

"Yes, I'm fine." Just confused and embarrassed. "You?"

"No." His voice compelled her to face him.

She did. The same turmoil twisting her into knots clouded his gaze. "I don't mean to mislead you. I'm just not sure if what we want is the right thing to do."

"Neither am I." Benjamin took his coat off the chair. "Like you said, things are complicated enough."

"We're both starting over. We should give ourselves some time." But how much time?

"You're right." Benjamin nodded toward the door. "Are you ready to leave?"

"Almost." June gestured toward the stage. "I'll see you in the morning."

Benjamin hesitated. "Don't stay too late. Good night."

"Good night." June watched him leave.

Benjamin was caring, compassionate, handsome, and sexy as hell. As much as she wanted to throw caution to the winds with him, was it worth the risk? And what would she be risking?

"The name Kwanzaa comes from the Swahili phrase *matunda ya kwanza*, which means first fruits." Three weeks later, on Saturday, November twenty-first, Quincy addressed attendees in the Guiding Light Community Center's packed community room.

Adults, teenagers, children, and seniors—familiar faces and new attendees—had crowded into the room this afternoon for the African American history professor's seminar on the roots, meaning, and tradition of Kwanzaa.

Attendance was even greater than June had hoped for, which was good and bad. Good in that the center had correctly guessed the community's interest in this topic; bad because they'd run out of chairs. They'd pulled chairs from other rooms and offices, but still a score or more people were standing and a dozen children were sitting on the floor. Success had its drawbacks.

"Kwanzaa is a cultural holiday rather than a religious one," Quincy continued. "It reflects the need to preserve, revitalize, and promote African American culture."

June looked around at the rapt expressions on the faces of Quincy's audience. She caught Benjamin's eye from across the room. She smiled and he nodded, albeit grudgingly.

"Kwanzaa is observed annually between December twenty-sixth and January first," Quincy explained. "At the center of Kwanzaa are the seven principles, the *Nguzo Saba*: *Umoja*, which is unity; *Kujichagulia*, self-determination; *Ujima*, collective work and responsibility; *Ujamaa*, cooperative economics; *Nia*, purpose; *Kuumba*, creativity, and *Imani*, faith."

With the help of a slide presentation, Quincy showed examples of Kwanzaa's symbols and decorations, including the *kinara*, the candleholder that holds the seven black, red, and green candles that represent the *Nguzo Saba*.

Once Quincy wrapped up his presentation, which took less than an hour, June returned to the stage to moderate the question-and-answer session.

She smiled at Ramona, who was seated in the front row. "Thank you, Dr. Spates. I'm certain everyone enjoyed your presentation at least as much as I did. And we're especially appreciative because you've donated your time to the center." June paused for the audience applause. She used the opportunity to send Benjamin another smug look. "If you have any questions about Kwanzaa, please step up to the mic. We have one in each aisle."

There were very few questions, probably because Quincy's presentation was so thorough. But Quincy addressed each of the participants who wanted to ask questions or share observations with patience and humor.

Benjamin joined June and Quincy on stage to end the afternoon. "Dr. Spates, thank you again for your time. Your presentation was both informative and entertaining." He paused for the enthusiastic applause and sent June a wry smile. "Before we close, I'd like to remind everyone of our upcoming Christmas dinner dance on December nineteenth. Proceeds will benefit the community center so that we can continue to provide events like this one. And remember, your tickets are tax deductible. Have a good afternoon, everyone."

As with most Trinity Falls events, many of the attendees lingered afterward to catch up with friends. After thanking Quincy and Ramona privately, June and Benjamin waited near the exit to the parking lot to wish their attendees a pleasant afternoon and a safe trip home.

During a lull in the activities, June slid Benjamin a look. "Pretty good turnout."

Benjamin gave her the wicked grin that made her toes curl in her shoes. "You want me to tell you that you were right."

"Yes, yes, I do." June folded her hands in front of her, tucking the manila envelope between her arms and her torso.

"June, you were right." He gave her a slight bow. "Congratulations."

"What good does it do?" Nessa appeared beside her. "This event was free. You didn't even raise any money for the center. Isn't that supposed to be your job?"

"Hello, Nessa." June told herself to be cordial. "Did you have a pleasant time?"

Nessa clutched her purse to her side. Her fur-trimmed

woolen coat was buttoned to her neck. "Isn't your job to raise money for the center?"

"Yes, and we already have more than fifty paid registrations for the Christmas dinner dance." June waved the envelope in her hand. She was using it to keep the forms and checks together and secure.

Nessa's eyes moved from June to the envelope and back. She sniffed. "You're wasting your time."

June felt Benjamin standing behind her. She looked around the lobby and saw her new friends gathered in groups talking. Darius held hands with Peyton. Ean had an arm around Megan's waist. Jackson and Audra had their arms around each other. Benita had one hand on Vaughn's shoulder and another on Ms. Helen's elbow. Sheriff Alonzo Lopez stood behind his wife, Doreen, with his arms wrapped around her. Zachariah stood talking with Dr. Olivia Stark. Connections. That's what she saw all around her. That was what she was looking for as well.

June met Nessa's gaze. "I'm afraid you're the one who's wasting her time. I'm not leaving Trinity Falls."

Nessa's eyes flared. She opened her mouth, then closed it again. Without a word, the council president turned and stomped off.

"I'm proud of you." Benjamin's voice came from behind her.

June turned. "For what?"

"For standing up to Nessa and telling her once and for all that you're not leaving Trinity Falls." Benjamin took her hand.

June looked at their joined palms. Connections. That was what she was hoping for. Was that what she'd found?

Chapter 7

"You're not the first guy to check my mother out."
Noah Cale's statement caused Benjamin a moment's
panic before he faced June's son.

"I'm sure I'm not. Your mother's a very beautiful
woman."

June had introduced them shortly after Benjamin
and his brothers had arrived at Doreen's Thanksgiving
after-dinner open house. The gathering had been a
popular way to spend Thanksgiving evening in Trinity
Falls for decades. It offered great company and even
better desserts.

The air around him was rich with the scent of chocolate, baked fruit, confectioner's sugar, cinnamon, and
other spices. Neighbors gathered in various rooms on
the main floor, filling Doreen and Alonzo's home with
spirited conversations and boisterous laughter. Shouts
of approval or groans of disappointment rose periodi-
cally in response to the professional football games
being viewed on multiple television sets.

Benjamin tuned it all out to focus on June's teenage
son. The resemblance between Noah and his older half
brother, Darius, was disconcerting: they both had

piercing dark eyes; tall, lean builds; and chiseled good looks.

Noah scowled. "Don't patronize me. I'm eighteen not eight."

"Is that the way you've spoken to your mother's previous bosses?" Benjamin wasn't offended. He was just curious.

"Her other bosses never checked her out."

We're back to that again. "Is this the part where you ask my intentions toward your mother?"

"I don't know. Is it?"

"Your brother and I have been friends for decades. He can vouch for me."

"Does he need to?" A satisfied gotcha expression settled over Noah's thin young face. Benjamin had seen the same look on Darius.

Benjamin shrugged. "Only if it makes you feel better."

"If you hurt her, you won't only have me to deal with. There are a lot of people here who care about my mother." The knowledge seemed to please Noah. He looked over to the next room, where June laughed and conversed with Doreen, Alonzo, Megan, and Ean. "She didn't have this many friends in Sequoia. She didn't even have her parents. They disowned her when she defied them to go to college."

So that's how June had explained the absence of his grandparents in their lives. It wasn't really a lie. But Benjamin was certain that, if Noah was aware June's being pregnant with him was the reason his grandparents had disowned his mother, the knowledge would destroy him. Instead, June had shaded the truth with the goal of helping her son grow into a confident, capable, and secure man. Who could fault her for that?

Benjamin held Noah's eyes. "I'm glad your mother defied them. It worked out well for her and for you."

"I'm proud of my mom. And I love her very much. Treat her well." Noah's *or else* was implied.

"I promise." Benjamin returned his attention to June.

She was beautiful. Her copper features glowed with happiness as she laughed at something Megan had said. Her parents had been fools. Wherever they were, he hoped they realized that.

"I want to get your mother something for Christmas." Benjamin's eyes widened. *I do?* Where had those words come from?

"Oh, yeah?" Noah eyed him quizzically. "Like what?"

"I don't have any idea." Benjamin shook his head. "But I've never met anyone who's as enthusiastic about Christmas as your mother."

"When I was a kid, I thought she was all into it because of me." Noah chuckled. "You know, making sure I did well in school and helped out around the house so that Santa would bring me something. As I got older, I realized she was just *really* into Christmas."

Benjamin smiled at the images Noah's memories brought to mind. "What do you suggest I get her?"

"Mom's big on giving people gifts from the heart. It doesn't have to be fancy or expensive, just something that reflects your relationship with the person." Noah gave Benjamin a narrow-eyed stare. "What do you know about my mother?"

Benjamin didn't have to consider his answer. "She's determined, stubborn, very smart. She's fearless. She has a big heart and she loves Christmas."

"Then get her something that reflects those things."

Benjamin shook his head. "You sound like Darius."

Noah's response was a smile reminiscent of his older half brother. He took in Benjamin's dark green mock-neck Calvin Klein sweater and his black ECCO boots. "There's this one thing you can get her. But it might cost you. And, if you're serious, you gotta start looking for it now."

"What is it?"

Noah's secretive smile gave him several moments of unease.

Benjamin knocked twice on June's open office door Friday afternoon. It was more than a week after Thanksgiving. Mariah Carey's "O, Holy Night" played in the background. "Do you have plans for the weekend?"

"That depends." June spun her chair to face him. A sterling silver snowflake brooch was pinned to her white sweater. "Why are you asking?"

Benjamin massaged the back of his neck. "My kids are spending Christmas with me. They arrive next Saturday. I should probably put up a tree."

June's winged eyebrows jumped up her forehead. "Considering tomorrow is December fifth, I'd agree with you."

"I'm a little out of practice." Benjamin shrugged uncomfortably. "It's been about fifteen years since I helped put up a tree."

"You haven't decorated a tree in almost two decades?" June looked as if she was going to cry.

"Aliyah and the kids usually took care of it. They said I got in the way." Benjamin allowed his memories to carry him back to Christmases past. "I'd watch, if I was home."

His ex-wife was pretty particular about her Christmas

decorations. He couldn't imagine her allowing a sport team's logo, a TV series poster, or a spaceship on her tree.

"They should have let you help." June sounded outraged on his behalf.

"I didn't mind." Benjamin shrugged again. "Will you help me decorate my tree?"

"I'd be happy to. What time should I arrive?"

Benjamin was more than relieved. He gave June directions to his townhome again and they discussed the specifics of their project: types and quantities of decorations, how long it would take, what to put on the top of the tree.

"Thanks again for agreeing to help." Benjamin returned to his office with a spring in his step. Was it the idea of decorating his tree or of decorating it with June?

Saturday afternoon, June arrived at Benjamin's townhome with enthusiasm and a fistful of compact discs featuring a few of her favorite Christmas carols.

"There are rules to Christmas tree decorating," she explained.

"I hadn't realized that." Benjamin let her in, then locked his front door.

"Don't worry." June pressed her free hand to her chest. "I'm happy to educate you. Rule Number One: Have fun."

"That seems easy enough." Benjamin escorted June to his living room, where he'd built his Christmas tree in front of his window.

"Oh, my word." June stopped in her tracks. The cold fist of horror clutched her heart. "Rule Number Two: Only real Christmas trees."

"What's wrong with this one?" Benjamin gestured toward the abomination near his window.

"*Everything.*" June gaped at the nightmare in his living room.

It stood about three feet tall and two feet wide. There were more gaps than branches. And the few branches it did offer pointed in every conceivable direction. Her heart broke just looking at the not-so-merry mistake.

"It'll look fine once we put some ornaments on it." Benjamin's confidence was misplaced.

"I'm not decorating that." June faced him. "We're going to get a real tree. Right now."

"Why?" Benjamin stared at her in surprise.

"This does not say 'Christmas.'" June waved a hand toward the monstrosity behind her.

Benjamin arched a brow. "You do realize there aren't evergreens in Bethlehem?"

June gave him a pointed look. "I'm not sanctioning this Christmas mistake. Period."

Less than an hour later, they returned with the perfect tree for Benjamin's cozy townhouse. The tree was full and fragrant, and five feet tall. This time, it had been Benjamin who'd put his foot down, when she'd innocently wandered over to the six-foot trees.

June happily moved the Charlie Brown–reject tree aside before helping Benjamin place the miracle tree in front of the window.

She stepped back with a deep sigh of pleasure. "Now this is a Christmas tree."

"I still don't understand why we had to get more ornaments." Benjamin unpacked their recent purchases.

"You can't have too many ornaments." June bent over to examine Benjamin's stereo system. "How does this thing work?"

June looked over her shoulder when Benjamin remained silent. There was a sexy glint in his eyes as he walked toward her. It made her pulse trip. June straightened and stepped out of his way.

"Let me." He loaded the five-disc player with her CDs, then pressed play. Benjamin's townhome filled with NSYNC's "Merry Christmas, Happy Holidays." He gave her a questioning look. "You're kidding, right?"

"Lighten up!" June playfully tapped his shoulders, then danced away. His muscles were hard and hot to the touch through his garnet knit sweater. June's fingertips tingled even after she moved away to assess the tree.

"Where do we start?" His deep voice seduced her from behind.

June's hips swung to the music of their own accord. She studied the tree as she tried to ignore the effect Benjamin was having on her senses and her body. She still felt his shoulders against her fingertips. "First the tinsel, then the ornaments and the lights, I think." She glanced back at him. "Okay?"

"You're the boss." Benjamin's voice was light. He reached for the bag of tinsel. "Silver or gold?"

June covered her eyes with her hands. "Surprise me."

His low laughter vibrated deep inside her. "Open your eyes."

He stood in front of her with the silver tinsel. June nodded in satisfaction. "Perfect."

Benjamin tried to ignore June's gyrating hips. It wasn't easy. Her bright red sweater was oversized, cloaking her figure. But her black jeans hugged the curves of her long, lean legs.

She gave one end of the tinsel to Benjamin and directed him to dance around the tree. He chose to walk. But he enjoyed watching her bounce, wiggle and hop around the evergreen. They followed the same process with the gold tinsel, using rhythm and harmony to wrap his tree in silver and gold. Their conversation was light, playful, perhaps even flirtatious, as they added the lights and ornaments to the tree. Their laughter competed with the Christmas carols in the background. His townhouse finally felt like a home.

Much later, after the sun had set, Benjamin stood beside June as they assessed their work. "I've never had so much fun decorating a Christmas tree. Thank you."

"My pleasure."

"It looks pretty good." Benjamin was surprised.

"Of course it does." June gave him a brilliant smile

Benjamin didn't stop to think. He followed impulse. He bowed to desire. He answered a need and pressed his lips to hers.

His body shook when he tasted June's answering passion. She closed her eyes and lifted her arms to his shoulders. He hadn't expected her immediate response. Had she realized as he had that their attraction was too much to deny? He drew her closer as relief eased the tension he hadn't realized was holding him back.

In the background, "Angels We Have Heard on High" ended and the opening strains of "Baby, It's Cold Outside" played on his stereo. Benjamin deepened their kiss. June parted her lips and kissed him back. Her tentative caresses stirred an even hotter flame deep inside him. The block of ice around his heart was melting. Rapidly.

His palms moved down her back, tracing her firm, toned torso beneath her deep red knit sweater. His hands shaped her tight waist, moving lower to cup her taut hips. Her body was slight but strong. Her curves

were soft and full. She was all woman and every inch of
her set a fire burning inside him.

Benjamin slipped his hands beneath June's loose-
fitting sweater. He broke their kiss to lift it up and off
of her. He stepped back—and froze. Her breasts filled
a barely there, scandalous red demi-cup bra. The sight
of her nipples pressing against the sheer lace almost
drove him to his knees.

"Did you wear that for me?" His voice was as hoarse
as that of a teenager with his first love.

"No." June's lips curved in seduction. She slipped
out of her skinny black jeans to reveal matching underwear. The skimpy lace piece rode low on her slender
curves. "I wear these for me."

Have mercy! The knowledge that she wore under-
garments like these would make it hard to concentrate
around her. Benjamin groaned low in his throat. "Lady,
you should come with a warning label."

Wicked lights danced in June's tawny eyes. She gestured toward him. "What do you have for me?"

"I'm afraid my boxers are going to sorely disappoint
you." He stripped off his garnet sweater.

June's eyes widened, seemingly glued to his naked
chest. Her reaction went a long way toward healing the
scars left by his ex-wife's betrayal. He shed his faded
blue jeans and kicked them away from his feet.

Her gaze slid down his body like a caress and landed
on his black boxer briefs. "Never a disappointment."
Her voice was low, husky.

Blood rushed to Benjamin's lower body. His heart
pounded against his chest. He lifted his right arm, offering June his hand. "This is us and this is now. But
only if you want it."

She accepted his hand without hesitation. Benjamin's

relief was almost overwhelming. He drew her into his embrace. Her smooth skin was soft and warm against him. He lowered his head and kissed her deeply, softly at first. Then with increasing urgency as she responded, showing her his need.

Benjamin walked backward to his couch, continuing their kiss. He drew her down beside him on the cushions. Instantly, June pulled away. She stood, backing away from the sofa.

Startled, Benjamin looked up at her. "What is it?" *Please, God, don't let her have changed her mind.*

"What in the world?" June reached forward to press her hand against the cushion beside him. She straightened and pointed at the furniture piece. "You spent money on that?"

Benjamin chuckled, part relief, part humor. "You have a point." He rose, sweeping her up into his arms to carry her to the stairs. He laughed again when she gasped in surprise. "Whatever my lady requires."

"I require that I not be crushed to dust on that torture couch." She wrapped her arms around his neck, suddenly shy. "I've never had a man carry me up the stairs before. This is very romantic."

His heart softened. Benjamin paused to give her a quick kiss before continuing up the steps. Once in his bedroom, he lowered her to his mattress.

June smiled up at him. "This is much better."

"I'm glad you approve." Benjamin lay beside her.

He raised his torso above her to cover her mouth with his. Benjamin's hands searched her body as she explored his. He followed her dips and curves. Her silky skin and soft breasts. Her toned arms and long legs. June seemed to welcome his bold touch even as her caresses were more hesitant. She was so responsive to his kisses and caresses. His body was torn between making their loving last and giving in to the urgent swelling in his briefs.

Benjamin slid his hand behind June's back to free her bra. Drawing it away from her body, he lifted his head to see her. June's eyes widened in surprise. She brought her hands up, almost in reflex, to cover her breasts.

He pulled her hands away and pressed them to his chest. "You're beautiful. More perfect than I could have imagined."

He held fast to her hands as he lowered his head and drew her nipple into his mouth. June gasped. Her body stiffened. Her reaction excited him. Benjamin suckled and licked her. He pulled her even deeper as her nipple pebbled in his mouth. He moved to her other breast to give it the same attention. June cupped the back of his head, holding him closer to her.

Benjamin moved lower down her body, licking a trail from her breasts, down her flat stomach, in and around her navel to the juncture at her thighs. He came up on his knees and stripped the flimsy underwear from her. His heart pounded against his chest at the sight of her naked on his bed. Reality was better than any fantasy. Benjamin settled between her legs. He drew his fingertips over her nest of curls.

"Ben, I don't know . . ." June's body shook harder.

"Shhh . . . let me." Benjamin pressed a finger inside of her. She was wet and ready for him. Her core was hot and pulsing.

"But I'm not sure . . ." Her voice faded away.

Why was she so shy? Benjamin kissed her curls. June flinched as though she'd never been touched like that.

"Do you want me to stop?" He didn't want to. But if she wasn't comfortable, he would never pressure her.

June took a shuttering breath. "No."

Benjamin smiled. He kissed first her right inner thigh, then her left. He cupped her hips, raised them to his mouth, then kissed her spot. June let out a shocked gasp. Her hips bucked, pressing even harder against him. He kissed her deeply, stroking her with his tongue, teasing her with his lips. June rocked herself against him. Her gasps and moans were testaments to her pleasure. Benjamin loved her more, deeper, harder. Until suddenly, June stilled. Her body stiffened. She shrieked as her muscles shook in his hands. The sound seemed to come from deep inside her. Her body tossed and turned as her voice swirled around them. After a time, she quieted. Then Benjamin lowered her to the mattress.

He stood from the bed and took off his briefs. From the drawer in his nightstand, he pulled out a condom.

"How long have you had those?" June ran her fingertips over his back.

Benjamin looked at her over his shoulder. "I bought them about a week before Thanksgiving. I hoped you'd decide we were worth the risk."

June let her hand drop back to the bed. "Ben, there's something I should tell you."

"What is it?" He shifted to face her.

June held his gaze. "I haven't had sex in nineteen years."

Chapter 8

Benjamin's breath left him. His thoughts tumbled over each other in confusion. More things made sense now: the contradiction between June's sexy lingerie and her shy touches. Her passionate kisses and bashful reactions.

Doubts took hold of his mind. He wanted June so badly, he hurt. But this was a lot of pressure. She'd been celibate for nineteen years. His year of abstinence now seemed like a moment's hesitation. What were her expectations, either consciously or subconsciously? His wife had found her satisfaction with another man. Could he please June?

Benjamin searched her worried features. "Why were you abstinent for so long?"

June crossed her arms over her breasts. "It wasn't exactly a choice. I had other priorities."

Benjamin rubbed a hand over his face. He breathed in her scent where it lingered on his skin. His body hardened. "I don't know what to say."

"Why do you have to say anything?" June sighed. "I'm not telling you to make you uncomfortable. I just thought you should know."

"I'm not uncomfortable." Benjamin turned back to her. "Are you sure this is what you want?"

"Absolutely."

Benjamin hesitated, then offered her the condom. "Help me with this."

June looked from Benjamin's sexy smile to the condom in his hand. She rose up on her knees and lowered her arm to accept the packet. He was introducing her to a lot of new things tonight. She'd never handled a rubber. The thought of touching him so intimately caused her pulse to quicken. She rolled the condom over his erection, taking her time as she went up his length. Then she stroked him, marveling at his size and thickness. And at his response to her touch. She'd made him do that.

"I think you've got it." There was humor and desire in Benjamin's voice.

He climbed onto the mattress, crowding her back. June laid down as Benjamin came over her. He positioned himself between her legs and balanced his weight on his forearms. He held her gaze as though searching for something in her eyes.

"I want you." June rested her hands on his shoulders.

"I'm beginning to think that I need you." He pressed his mouth to hers.

Benjamin entered her with one long, deep thrust. Then he held still. June gasped, stunned at the sensation. He was stretching her. Oh, man. When was she going to catch her breath?

"All right?" Benjamin whispered in her ear.

June shivered as his breath blew against her neck. "I think so."

Benjamin nibbled her neck. "Are you sure?"

June moaned. "I'm sure."

Benjamin moved in her. He awoke an intense feeling

in her core that radiated throughout her entire body, her legs, her toes, her stomach, her breasts. Her eyes flew open in shock. She'd never felt this way before. Benjamin was above her. His chiseled features were sharp with desire. His ebony eyes were dark and shone with a hunger that made her feel beautiful, powerful, strong.

She pulled him closer, straining to meet his thrusts. He pushed harder, faster. She matched his movements, pumping her hips to take him. Benjamin lowered his mouth and claimed her breast. June cried out as a sharp jolt of pleasure shot to her core. Desire flowed between her legs.

Benjamin shifted his hips to stroke her spot. She bit her lip. Oh, he felt so good. Pleasure flooded her body. Her breath came in short, sharp pants. She wrapped her legs around his hips and held on tight. Benjamin groaned into her ear. June arched up into him. He pressed deeper inside her. She felt his every inch. Her muscles strained. Her core clenched. Blood rushed through her veins. Her pulse drummed in her ears. Then her body shattered again. Her climax rolled over her in pounding waves. June grabbed on to Benjamin, holding him close. He tucked her against him, shaking as he followed her in his release. He pulsed into her. June was shaking apart, spinning around. Her body soared up, then drifted down to rest.

Sometime later, June felt the chill air against her bare shoulders. Benjamin tucked her closer against his side.

She kissed his neck. "That was worth waiting for." Her voice was soft and dreamy.

"Yes, it was." His chuckle was low and sexy in the dark room. He kissed the top of her head. "It's getting late. I'll make dinner."

June lifted her head to focus on the digital clock on Benjamin's side of the bed. It was almost six o'clock in the evening. "I'll help."

They cleaned up. Benjamin loaned June a navy-blue sweat suit. She rolled up the legs and sleeves, but she was still swimming in the outfit.

She joined Benjamin in his kitchen. "What are you making?"

"My specialty, spaghetti." He looked at her over his shoulder. "You're beautiful. But I prefer the matching lingerie."

"This is much warmer." June laughed. "Is there anything I can do to help?"

"You can keep me company."

June took a chair at Benjamin's bleached wood kitchen table. They talked about the center, the better-than-expected registration for the Christmas dinner dance, their plans for when their children were on Christmas break and Trinity Falls in general. The conversation topics carried them through dinner. Afterward, June helped Benjamin clear the table and clean the kitchen.

This had been the best day Benjamin had had in almost a year. He didn't want it to end. "Since we're going to spend Christmas Day with our kids, do you want to exchange our gifts on Christmas Eve?" He escorted June into the living room.

"You bought me a gift?" She paused, looking up at him in surprise.

"Am I presuming too much about the gift exchange?"

"No, I have something for you as well."

What a relief. "Great—"

June's cell phone rang. It was in her purse, which sat on his coffee table. "Excuse me." She found her phone. "Hi, Darius. What's up?"

Darius? Why is he calling June on a Saturday night?

Benjamin considered June's body language as she spoke with the other man. From her end of the conversation, it sounded as though they were making plans to get together. Soon. Jealousy and suspicion sank their fingers into his skin.

"Okay. I'll call you when I have more information." June ended the call.

"Does Darius call you often?" The words were out of his mouth before he could stop them.

June dropped her phone back into her purse before facing him. "You sound jealous."

"Just curious."

June considered him in silence. "Good, because you have no reason to be jealous. I'm not Aliyah."

Benjamin flinched. "I never said that."

"You didn't have to. Your good friend, who has a girlfriend, called to ask about his brother, my son. You can't convince me that your suspicion about my phone call doesn't have anything to do with Aliyah's infidelity."

Benjamin straightened from the wall and paced farther into the living room, past June. "Maybe it does. I'm sorry."

"You don't have to apologize. But, Ben, try to forgive Aliyah."

"How can I?" Benjamin massaged the growing tension from his neck.

June crossed to him and put her warm hand on his back between his shoulder blades. "Because she's the mother of your children."

Benjamin scowled. "She should have remembered that before she destroyed our family."

"I agree." June moved her hand in a circular motion on his back. "What she did was ugly. She hurt you and she hurt your children. But if you don't try to forgive her, your anger will only hurt yourself. Look at how suspicious it's making you."

Benjamin expelled a deep sigh. "You're asking a lot."

"I know. But you're a caring, compassionate person. You can handle it." There was a smile in June's voice.

No pressure. But June had a point. He didn't like being in a constant state of anger, with his heart on ice and hating the holidays. He didn't want to be that person any longer. Besides, forgiving Aliyah didn't mean he'd forget what she did.

He dropped his hands and faced June. This was still the best day he'd had in a year. And he still didn't want it to end. "Can you stay the night?"

Interest flashed hot and bright in her tawny eyes. "I'd like that."

He took her into his arms and kissed her. At this rate, tomorrow would also be the best day he'd had all year.

Aliyah's phone number showed on Benjamin's cellular phone caller identification Thursday morning. He considered letting her roll into his voice mail. But then he heard June's voice asking him to forgive her.

Benjamin saved the electronic file he was updating and answered the call. "Hello, Aliyah. What can I do for you?"

"I want to spend Christmas with the children." She had his full attention.

"You were with them at Thanksgiving." Benjamin turned away from his computer and stared blindly across his community center office.

"I know. But this is Christmas." She sounded wistful.

He'd never imagined he'd have to negotiate which

holidays he spent with his children. Now his ex-wife wanted to renegotiate them. Unbelievable. "It's too late to change plans. Terry and Zora are driving to Trinity Falls tomorrow."

"I know. But tomorrow's only December eleventh." Aliyah sounded excited. "They could spend that next week with you, then fly to Chicago Christmas Eve."

"You can't have both holidays." Benjamin felt a spurt of anger. "We told Terry and Zora that you'd have Thanksgiving and I'd have Christmas this year. Next year, we'll switch."

"But they always celebrated Christmas in this house."

Benjamin frowned. "Are you actually going to use the fact that I let you keep the house against me?"

"Please, Ben, I don't want to spend Christmas alone." She used the wheedling voice that had always annoyed him.

"Then spend it with your parents." Benjamin was ready to end the call.

"That's another thing." Aliyah seized on a new argument. "If they spend Christmas in Chicago, they'll be able to see their grandparents."

"They saw your parents over Thanksgiving." Benjamin drummed his fingers on his desk. "They'll spend Christmas with my brothers."

He wasn't giving in. They'd made the holiday agreement at the beginning of the year. He'd been looking forward to celebrating Christmas with his children. He'd even put up a tree. Thinking of his tree reminded him of spending last weekend with June. It had been the best weekend he'd had in a year, despite her lecture on forgiveness.

Aliyah's voice broke into his thoughts. "I'd really like to see them, Ben."

"So would I, Aliyah." Benjamin stopped drumming

his fingers. He sat back on his chair. "Maybe we could come to a compromise."

"What?"

He glanced at the calendar on the wall across from his desk. "Christmas is on a Friday this year. You're welcome to spend the weekend with us at my place."

"I thought you had a townhouse."

"I do." Benjamin leaned into his desk. "It has two bedrooms. You and Zora can share the guest room. Terry can use my room. I'll sleep on the couch."

"It sounds kind of crowded." Aliyah sounded skeptical.

"It's only for the weekend. That's your choice, Aliyah. Take it or leave it." Part of him hoped she'd decline.

"I'll take it. Thank you, Ben."

"Don't thank me. Thank our children." Or more accurately, she should thank June. "Let me know when you'll be arriving." Benjamin ended the call.

He wanted to forgive the mother of his children. But why did he feel as though he was making a mistake?

Chapter 9

June grabbed the gift bag from the passenger seat before getting out of her car Christmas Eve. There was a spring in her step as she approached Benjamin's door. She was still riding the wave of triumph after the community center's successful Christmas dinner dance. She'd enjoyed delivering I-told-you-sos to Benjamin in a variety of fun and creative ways, like the chocolate chip cookie cake with *I Told You So* written in frosting. Luckily, he was a really great sport.

She pressed the doorbell and waited for Benjamin to answer. June was twitchy with excitement, anticipating his reaction to her gift. She was certain his children hadn't given away the secret. She also was curious as to what he was giving her—a Dancing Santa, perhaps?

"May I help you?" The woman who answered Benjamin's door was a stranger.

Am I at the wrong address? June looked around. The other townhomes had Christmas decorations on their doors, in their windows, and/or on their front lawns. This was the only unit that wasn't decked out for the season. No, she was definitely at the right place. *Then who was this woman?*

June glanced at the stranger's black yoga pants and formfitting, low-cut, black sweater. "I'm looking for Ben Brooks."

"He's not here right now." The other woman smiled. "I'm his wife."

His wife. His wife.

June pressed her hand against her stomach as a wave of nausea rolled over her. Her ears were ringing.

His wife. He'd said he was divorced. He'd said his ex-wife lived in Chicago. How could this be happening again?

June backed away from the door. "It's nice to meet you." She forced the socially acceptable greeting from her numbed lips.

"Who are you?" Benjamin's wife regarded her with open curiosity.

"Oh, I work with Ben. I just came by, but since he's not here, I'll just go."

"Do you want to leave a message?"

"No, no, I'll just see him at the office Monday." June turned away. She had to get to her car. "Just . . . have a merry Christmas."

"You, too."

June jumped onto her driver's seat and locked the doors. She turned the key in the ignition, then immediately threw her car into gear. She reversed out of the parking lot and maneuvered out of the townhome complex. But once she was around the corner, she pulled her little Toyota over. The tears were coming too quickly. She could barely see to drive. June put her car in park, turned off the engine, laid her head on her steering wheel, then succumbed to sobs of hurt and pain.

His wife. His wife. His wife.

What was wrong with her? Why did this keep happening?

Her parents' judgment came back to her, screaming in her ears when she'd told them she was pregnant. *Whore, harlot, sinner.* She'd known better than to become romantically involved with Benjamin Brooks. But her affair with him hadn't been a weakness of the flesh. It had been a yearning of the heart.

Sometime later, June drew a deep, shuttering breath. She sat up and pulled a tissue from a small packet in her purse. She used it to dry her eyes, wipe her cheeks, and blow her nose. June took another deep breath before starting her car again.

She couldn't keep going through this. The first time, she'd been lucky and had Noah. This time, all she had was a broken heart.

June's expression was cool when she looked up at Benjamin from the threshold of her front door Thursday afternoon. But her tawny eyes were pink and puffy. Her nose was red. Benjamin's heart sank. He knew he was late. *Am I too late?*

When he'd told his brothers Aliyah was staying with him and the kids this Christmas weekend, they'd been shocked. They'd called him every kind of an idiot under the sun. Ignoring the pain in his back brought on by one night on the torture couch, Benjamin had rushed home, hoping to intercept June before she met Aliyah. When Aliyah told him June already had left, he'd called himself several other choice names. Ignoring his protesting back again, Benjamin had rushed to June's house.

Would she hear him out or banish him to the cold for good? "May I come in?"

She stepped back, pulling the door open wider. Still she never said a word. The cold grip of fear grew tighter.

Benjamin entered her home. "Is Noah here?"

"He's visiting friends." June seemed to take her time locking her front door. "He'll be home for dinner."

Benjamin unzipped his parka. "It's Christmas Eve. I thought we were going to exchange gifts." *Please don't freeze me out. I need you.*

Finally, June met his eyes. "I think I may have gotten mine. Thank you."

His shaky smile faded at the flash of pain that crossed June's delicate features. "Aliyah's not my gift to you."

"Oh. Was she your gift to you?" Anger shoved aside the hurt in her eyes. June propelled herself away from the door and into the living room.

"Of course not. She's not a gift for anyone." No, she certainly wasn't. Why had he agreed to let his ex-wife spend Christmas with him and their kids? *Stupid. Stupid. Stupid.*

"Here. You want your gift? Take it." June snatched a wrapped box from her coffee table and shoved it into his stomach. The air left Benjamin's lungs in a whoosh. Pain burned down his back.

Whatever she'd gotten for him was really hard. He caught his breath. "I have a gift for you."

"I don't want it." June pushed the words through her clenched teeth. "I don't want *anything* from you."

"June, I know you're angry." Benjamin set his gift back on the coffee table and straightened painfully. "But you're mistaken about why Aliyah's here."

"Am I?" June marched to the fireplace, putting the distance of the living room between them. "Your ex-wife is in your *two*-bedroom townhouse with you and your two adult children for the holidays. Where is she sleeping?"

"In my bedroom but—"

"In your room?" Her copper cheeks flushed scarlet. She threw her hands up as she spun away from him. "How can I possibly be misunderstanding that?"

"I'm sleeping on the sofa."

"Oh, sure you are."

Benjamin narrowed his gaze on her slender back. "You don't believe me."

June turned to face him. "You expect me to believe you're sleeping on that block of cement you call a sofa for the entire weekend?"

"Yes, and I have the back pain to prove it."

June angled her chin. Her eyes were cold as ice as they held each other's gazes in silence. She marched across the living room, stopping a hairsbreadth in front of him. Before he could blink, she'd pulled back her fist and punched him in the arm with all her might. Benjamin rocked back on his heels. Pain shot from his shoulder, then radiated across his back. Once again, he lost his breath as his muscles seized up and down his spine. Stars spun in front of him. He squeezed his eyes shut as he struggled to control the pain.

"Oh, my God, Ben. I'm so sorry." June's voice was a thin gasp of horror. She took his arm.

"No, don't touch me," he begged.

"Let me help you to sit down."

"I can't move yet."

"Okay. Then just wait right here." June sprinted past him and up the stairs.

That was the problem. He couldn't move. Although he was getting his breath back. Benjamin attempted to relax his muscles, one by one. First his neck, then his shoulders.

June came charging back down the stairs. Benjamin envied her mobility.

"I'm going to help you take off your coat and sweater." She stopped beside him.

"Why?" How much pain was she going to inflict on him before she forgave him—if she ever did?

"So I can rub this onto your back." June showed him an open jar of some nasty-smelling muscle ointment.

"I don't think that's a good idea." It had been hard enough getting his clothes on this morning.

"I do." June set the ointment on the coffee table beside his much beleaguered gift. "This stuff worked miracles for Noah after his football games."

Benjamin snorted. "I bet Noah snaps to attention when you use that tone on him."

"Yes, he does." June gave him a teasing grin. "And one day, so will you."

Her bright eyes and playful smile were melting the ice around his heart.

June's movements were slow and gentle as she helped him remove his dark gray down parka and his dark red knit sweater. Once he'd striped down from the waist up, she helped him to lie down on her sofa. The cushions were as soft as pillows. The good kind. He sighed. June applied the ointment to his aching muscles with a firm, circular motion. She pressed her fingertips into his back to massage as well as administer. They were silent as she worked to improve his abused back. Her touch was having an effect on other parts of his body as well.

"You're really good at this." The salve was warming

his muscles and easing their knots. "Did you know there are several brands that have odorless versions?"

"You're welcome." Her response held humor as well as sarcasm. "I'm sorry I didn't believe you," she added softly.

"For a little person, you pack quite a punch." His lips curved in an involuntary smile. "Your apology is accepted for as long as you massage my back. This is heaven."

"Then I'm going to have to learn to live without your forgiveness because my fingers are growing numb." June's soft laughter poured heat into Benjamin's lower abdomen.

"Could you help me up?"

June was careful with him as Benjamin adjusted into a seated position on her sofa. She sat beside him. Her fascination with his bare chest melted more of the ice from his heart. Benjamin captured her left hand. He raised it to press his lips against her knuckles. Her hands were moist with the ointment that masked her usual powder and wildflowers scent.

He lowered her hand but kept it trapped in his. "I'm sorry for my poor judgment. Aliyah and I both wanted to spend Christmas with Terry and Zora. Since they'd had Thanksgiving together in Chicago, I thought it was only fair that I got Christmas with them in Trinity Falls."

"I understand. And I do trust you." June's gaze was on their joined hands. She laced her fingers together with his. "I just had an uncomfortable flashback when I saw your ex-wife looking so cozy in your home."

"She won't be for much longer." Benjamin followed his impulse and kissed June's temple. There he found the fragrance he'd been searching for, wildflowers and soft powder.

June lifted her gaze to his. "What do you mean?"

"My brothers opened my eyes to just how stupid I'd been to invite Aliyah to stay in my townhouse." Why hadn't he realized his mistake himself? *How could I have been so stupid?* "Vaughn's going to let her stay with him and Benita. She'll spend Christmas Day with us but sleep at their house."

"That was nice of Vaughn and Benita." June freed her hand from Benjamin's. She rose from the sofa and crossed the room. "How do you feel about those arrangements?"

Benjamin stood with much less pain. "I want our children to see that Aliyah and I are making an effort to get along. I don't want them to feel as though they have to take sides."

"You're right."

"And you were right when you said I should forgive her." Benjamin took a step closer to June. "She's the mother of my children."

"Yes, she is."

Another step and they were an arm's length apart. "But I want to spend my Christmases with my kids, Noah, and you."

June spun to face him. Her bright eyes were wide. Her full lips were parted. "You do?"

"I'm falling in love with you, June. And I'm loving every minute of it." Benjamin's heart was pounding against his chest. His breaths were coming way too fast. "I hadn't realized how numb I'd become until you came into my life. You make me happier than I've been in a very long time."

June's smile was soft and shaky. She stepped into him, placing her hand on his chest above his thundering heart. "I'm falling in love with you, too."

Benjamin closed his eyes as a wave of joy crashed

over him, shattering every speck of ice. He pulled June into his arms and pressed his mouth to hers. With his lips and tongue, he expressed all the love for her that was flooding his heart. And he drank all the love that she shared with him. With her in his arms, he could again believe in Christmas, the joy, the love, and the grace.

June broke their kiss. She rested her head against his chest and sighed. "I want to give you your present now."

"I have everything I need."

She kissed his chest, then stepped back. "But there's something I want to give you."

Benjamin arched a brow. "Really?"

"I don't think your back could handle me right now."

"You're probably right." Benjamin sighed. "Could you help me with my sweater?"

Her gaze caressed his chest. "If I must."

Benjamin kissed away her pout. Together they managed to get his sweater on with a minimum of discomfort. His back was much better. It was an interesting feeling having her putting his clothes on him rather than taking them off.

"Merry Christmas." June handed him his gift.

"Thank you." He kissed her again.

He tore the wrapping paper from the large, flat object although he'd much rather be holding June in his arms. But when he turned the package over, surprise and pleasure washed over him. He was staring at an eight-and-a-half-by-eleven framed photograph of Terrence and Zora, posing on the campus of The Ohio State University.

"How did you get this?" He stared at her in disbelief.

"I drove down to OSU and they let me take their

picture." She gestured toward the gift. "It was time you had a more recent photograph of them."

"This is perfect. Thank you." Benjamin pulled her into his embrace. He couldn't think of a better Christmas gift. He released June to lay the framed photograph gently on the coffee table. He found his parka and pulled a package from its inside pocket. "Merry Christmas."

"Thank you." June carefully unwrapped the paper.

"You're not going to reuse the paper." His anxiety already was at a breaking point and she was taking too long.

"Be patient, Ben." June gave him a scolding look. She pulled the wrapping paper aside—and gasped. She stared at the compact disc as though expecting it to disappear. "How did you know?"

Benjamin grinned his satisfaction. "Noah told me about it."

He tapped the cover of the disc. The words *Diaspora's Christmas Sounds* appeared on the red, green and black background.

Her tears moved him. June dashed them away. "I can't believe you found it. I've been looking for a copy for years."

"That's what Noah told me." Benjamin slipped an arm around her waist. "I was lucky to find it."

"These songs have so many wonderful memories for me."

"Now, you'll have them to play for Christmas."

"Thank you so much." June wrapped her arms around him. She kissed his lips, then smiled into his eyes. "With you, every day is Christmas."

His Christmas Gifts

❦❦❦❦❦

DEBORAH FLETCHER MELLO

Chapter 1

"Unbelievable!" Bianca Torres exclaimed, rushing into the office of her best friend and confidante, Priscilla "Cilla" Jameson. She practically slammed the office door closed behind her.

Cilla sat staring as Bianca moved to the glass wall that bordered the reception and secretarial areas and closed the blinds. Her actions felt clandestine, as if the young woman didn't want anyone to see or hear what she had to share.

"What's wrong?"

"My mother broke her knee!"

"Oh, no!" Cilla exclaimed, concern washing over her expression. "Is she okay? What happened?"

Bianca tossed up her hands in frustration, her tone reflecting her exasperation. "She fell out of a tree. Now she has to have surgery."

Cilla pursed her lips together. Amusement danced in her eyes and she struggled not to laugh. "Why was your mother in a tree?" she asked.

Bianca tossed her friend a look, not finding anything funny. "We're talking about *my* mother," she answered, her eyes expressing that no further explanation was needed.

Cilla's eyes blinked rapidly as she got a visual of seventy-five-year-old Sharon Torres climbing a tree and then falling from it. As she imagined the woman's requisite African-print robes billowing around her petite frame, her snow-white dreadlocks trailing down her back, she suddenly laughed out loud. Seconds later, Bianca was laughing with her.

"Oh, I'm sorry," Cilla gasped, trying to catch her breath. Tears misted her eyes. "I know that's not funny, but I can only imagine what your mother had to be doing in that tree."

"Right?" Bianca shook her head, swiping the tears from her own eyes. "Daddy says she crushed her knee completely and fractured her tibia. She's having surgery tomorrow and then she's in a wheelchair for the next four to six months."

"Oh, your poor mother!"

"No, poor me! I have to go to Boone now. You know how much I hate going to the boonies. It's like being stuck in small-town hell on steroids!"

Cilla laughed. "Now you know it is not that bad. Boone is a beautiful city."

"For long weekends and very short visits. I'm going to be stuck there for the entire month of December. That's all my vacation time and sick days I've accumulated for this year and next! *And* I have to cancel my Christmas cruise!"

"Who goes on a cruise for Christmas anyway, Bianca?"

"Smart people who don't want the family drama."

Cilla shook her head. "How much drama can your family have? Your parents are the coolest, you're an only child, and you haven't been in a relationship with a man during the holidays since forever. There's never any drama with the Torres family."

"Exactly, and that's because I don't spend my holidays with my crazy parents." Bianca shifted in her seat. "So what are you doing for Christmas?"

"Nothing special. I'll probably spend the day in Charlotte with my folks, then I'll spend the rest of the holiday home with a good book."

"Well, Christmas Day I wanted to be floating in an infinity pool, with a drink in my hand and a half-naked stranger sucking on my toes. But no, instead I have to go be the dutiful daughter and make Grandma Jean's Christmas pudding because my almost eighty-year-old mother thought climbing a spruce tree in the rain to check a bird's nest was a smart thing to do."

"You're such a good daughter!"

"I'm only a good daughter because my daddy said he'd reimburse my cruise money and send me on another after the New Year."

"But you'd get a refund anyway, right?"

Bianca narrowed her gaze. "A credit for another cruise. But for sticking me in the boonies, no one needs to know that. Next year I'll get to go on two cruises."

"You're killing me," Cilla said, shaking her head.

Bianca laughed. "Well, I just came to tell you that I won't be able to make the company Christmas party next week because I have to leave for Boone, North Carolina, tomorrow morning."

"You're not driving, are you? I don't think you should drive, Bianca! You and snow are not friends."

"Well, thank you for that vote of confidence. And you call yourself my friend." Bianca rolled her eyes skyward. "No, I'm not driving. I'm taking the train."

"That's good. Make sure you call me and let me know how your mother is doing."

"Just send a fruit basket."

"We'll do drinks and exchange gifts when you get back," Cilla said. "Or I might even come up to Boone to check on you."

"Yes!" Bianca exclaimed, her eyes pleading. "You should do that. Come to Boone and save me from the misery."

"I said I might."

Cilla rose from her seat and rounded her desk. The two women exchanged a quick hug. The duo were life-long friends, having met in grade school. They'd been best buddies since Miss Rayner's third-grade class at Pinewood Elementary School. In high school, they'd been cheerleaders together. After graduation, Bianca had left the state of North Carolina, drawn to the big city lights of New York. Cilla had moved to Chapel Hill, the college town just enough of a city for her.

When Bianca's parents had moved from their Charlotte home to Boone, North Carolina, she had come back to the state, settling herself in Raleigh, and the two women had picked up their friendship as if they'd never been apart. For a time, they'd shared an apartment; then Bianca had bought a fixer-upper in the historic Oakwood neighborhood near downtown Raleigh. Cilla had preferred the newness of her Brier Creek townhome. Their working together at the pharmaceutical company that employed them had been a fluke and a blessing that neither had ever taken for granted.

Cilla tossed her friend a look. "Try to have some fun, please! It is Christmas."

"I've got your Christmas!" Bianca said with a wry laugh.

"Ho, ho, ho to you too!"

* * *

"Excuse you!" Bianca snapped, grabbing her right foot and the suede boot she wore. She had just boarded the Amtrak train headed from Raleigh to Boone, North Carolina's city center.

The young man who'd stepped on her toes turned around, contrition painting his expression. "I am so sorry," he said. He eased his hand out to help her brush the dust from her foot. "I am really sorry," he repeated, his apology genuine. "I wasn't paying atten-tion. I'll pay for your shoes if I ruined them."

Annoyance painted Bianca's face. "Whatever. Just forget it," she said, her tone just shy of being dismissive. She dropped into the pleather seat, adjusting her carry-on bag in the seat beside her. Digging in her handbag, she pulled out her iPad.

The young man dropped into the seat across from her. "Hi, I'm Jarrod."

Bianca lifted her gaze to stare. He was nice looking, mid-twenties with a boyish air. His complexion re-minded her of her mother's chocolate pudding, warm and sweet, and he had kind eyes. There was something about his demeanor that let her know he was one of the good guys.

"Jarrod Christmas," he said, still trying to engage her in conversation.

She nodded. "It's nice to meet you," she said, her gaze still inquisitive. "Is Christmas your real name?"

He nodded. "Please, spare me the bad jokes. I've heard them all."

She shrugged. "I didn't have any jokes. I was just curious."

"I really am sorry about stepping on your foot," he said, pointing toward the floor and her suede boot. "I was talking on the phone with my boyfriend and not paying attention. I'm not usually so inconsiderate."

"You have a boyfriend?" Her brow lifted, her curiosity piqued even more.

Jarrod smiled. "Yes, I do. Is that a problem for you?"

Bianca shrugged. "No, not at all."

"It's an issue for some people," he said with a deep sigh.

"As long as you're happy, do you really care what other people think?" Bianca asked, folding her hands together in her lap.

A slight smile pulled at his mouth. "No, I don't."

"So what do you do for a living, Jarrod Christmas?"

"I'm a doctor. I'm doing my residency at Mt. Sinai Medical Center in New York. My boyfriend's a pediatric surgeon there."

"A doctor. That's impressive. So what in hell are you doing down here in North Cackalacky?"

Jarrod laughed. "Visiting my father for the holidays. It's actually the first time I've been home in a few years."

"Awww! That's exciting. I bet your dad will be glad to see you."

Jarrod nodded. "Yeah, I've missed the old guy. It'll be nice to spend some time with him."

"Will your boyfriend be joining you?"

There was an awkward moment of silence. Bianca lifted her eyebrows in his direction. "Yes? No? Maybe?"

A wave of tension washed over his expression. A nervous titter spilled past his lips. "Not this time. My father doesn't know about us."

"And that's because . . . ?"

"My father doesn't know I'm gay."

Bianca nodded, a smile pulling at her thin lips.

"Well, there's nothing like some good drama for the holidays!"

"That's what I'm trying to avoid."

"Just a little friendly advice, but secrets always have a way of coming back to bite you in the ass at the most inopportune times. Like over the family dinner table during Christmas dinner, Mr. Christmas!"

Jarrod sighed. "Are you really going to curse me like that?"

"I'm not trying to start anything up. I'm just stating fact, my friend."

The young man smiled. "So what about you? You still haven't told me your name."

She smiled back. "Bianca. Bianca Torres."

"Well, it's nice to meet you, Bianca Torres. So what brings you to Boone, North Carolina?"

"My old people. My mother broke her knee yesterday and I have to go help her and my father."

"Sounds like you might have your own holiday drama going on."

"You don't know the half of it!"

Laughter ensued as Bianca and Jarrod continued their conversation for the rest of the train ride. The two were having a great time with each other, and when the train stopped at their final destination, neither was excited to see their good time come to an end.

"Do you have a ride?" Jarrod asked as he pulled his luggage from under his seat.

Bianca nodded. "My father is picking me up."

Her new friend laughed. "That's a coincidence. So is mine!"

Exiting the train, the two followed the other travelers to the arrival platform. The mid-afternoon temperature was crisp, with a definite chill in the air. Bianca

pulled her jacket tight around her torso, wishing she'd
worn a heavier coat. She blew a long sigh, her breath
a fine mist in front of her face.

Jarrod turned to give her a hug. The embrace was
warm and endearing. "You have my number. Please
keep in touch, Bianca."

"I will. In fact, don't be surprised if I call you soon.
I may really need a friend if my old people start driving
me crazy."

"I've got your back, girl!"

She pointed her index finger at him. "And do not
be surprised if I hold you to that!"

Jarrod grinned. "There's my father," he said as he
pointed to a black BMW that had pulled up to the
curve. "Are you sure you don't need a ride?"

Bianca nodded. "There's my dad," she said, pointing
to a crimson-red Buick Enclave parked in the handi-
capped parking spot.

Jarrod smiled. "Merry Christmas, Bianca!"

"Merry Christmas, Jarrod!"

As his son made his way to the car, Ethan Christmas
exited the vehicle, unable to contain his excitement.
The young man stood almost as tall as him with a
slimmer build. There was no mistaking the family resemblance as his mirror image stepped toward him.
Ethan's smile was a mile wide.

For a brief moment, his gaze followed the beautiful
woman who had been standing in wait with his son,
watching as she rushed to catch up with her own ride.
He was suddenly curious about her, wondering if she
was someone close to the young man, since the two
seemed very friendly with each other. He had a host of
questions, but for the moment he was content to just

stand there and stare, eyeing her until she slipped into the waiting vehicle and pulled away. His son calling his name pulled him back to the moment.

"Hey, Dad!"

"Welcome home, son!" he said as he threw his arms around the young man's shoulders and hugged him tightly.

Jarrod took a deep breath inhaling the cool mountain air. "It's good to be back."

Ethan reached for his son's luggage, tossing it into the trunk of his car. "So, who was your friend?" he asked, gesturing toward the vehicle that was pulling out of the lot.

"Her name's Bianca. Bianca Torres. We met on the train."

"Miguel and Sharon's daughter?"

"You know her?"

"I know her folks. They talk about her all the time. I didn't know she was coming home for the holidays."

"That's some small-town stuff, right? Knowing everyone's business?" Jarrod teased, a deep chuckle easing past his lips.

His father laughed with him. "I guess it is."

Jarrod shook his head. "Well, her mother broke her leg. She's down and out for a few weeks, and Bianca's come to give her a hand."

Ethan rounded his car and slid back into the driver's seat. Beside him, Jarrod was already securing his seat belt.

"I guess Boone's not that small," Ethan said. "That news hasn't spread here yet!"

Bianca cringed as her mother called her name for the umpteenth time. Since her arrival it had been one command after another, *Bianca, do this. Bianca, do that.* She was past the point of being ready to pull her hair out as she screamed at the top of her lungs. She took a sip of the coffee that she was trying to enjoy.

Her father was seated at the kitchen table and he smiled. "If you didn't ignore her, Bianca, she wouldn't call you every ten minutes."

"I'm not ignoring her, Papi. I'm preparing myself to do whatever needs to be done next."

The man laughed. "Go see what your mother wants, please."

Bianca blew a heavy sigh as she moved onto her feet and headed out of the kitchen, into the home's family room. Sharon Torres sat in an oversized recliner, a fresh cast wrapped around her broken leg. The appendage was propped up on the ottoman, a kente-patterned sleeve pulled over the stark white wrapping.

"Yes, Mother?" Bianca's eyebrows were raised slightly, her eyes wide. Bianca had been her mother's change-of-life baby, an unexpected surprise after years of thinking she really didn't want children. The matriarch had been forty-two years old and would have sworn she was menopausal until God had a good laugh at her expense.

Sharon laughed, waving her child toward her. "Don't give me that look, Bianca! Come sit with me."

Bianca blew a loud sigh as she eased her thin frame into the seat beside the matriarch. She leaned her head on the older woman's shoulder as Sharon wrapped her arms around her daughter's torso.

"How's the leg?" Bianca asked facetiously.

"Annoying. This couldn't have happened at a worse time. That's why I'm glad you're here," Sharon said as she swept her palm over her daughter's brow, brushing her dark curls out of her face.

"You know I was going on a cruise, don't you?"

"Daughter, who goes on a cruise for Christmas?"

"I do. You know how I am."

"I know that it's way past time that you actually came and spent time with your family during the holidays. It's good to finally have you home!"

"If Uncle Barber pinches my behind or cracks one joke about my hips, I'm on the next train down off this mountain."

"Your Uncle Barber is harmless, and he fancies himself something of a comedian."

"Uncle Barber is a pervert, and one day someone is going to put him out of his misery."

"Just keep him away from the eggnog and he'll be fine."

"You still spike the eggnog?"

"Of course I spike the eggnog."

"Thank goodness for something."

Sharon laughed as she pulled her hand through the length of her gray dreadlocks. She twisted the lengthy strands into a bun atop her head.

Bianca shifted forward in her seat. "So what's on my agenda today?"

"Shopping. I need you to pick up everything I'm going to need for my baking. We have a ton of cookies to make this week. Then, next week, you can pick up the last of my Christmas dinner shopping."

"Why can't I just get it all at one time?"

Her mother tossed her a look as if the question was out of turn.

"What? I was just asking. I don't see why we need to make any unnecessary trips to the market if I can get it all done in one trip. I'm just saying!"

"Well, don't. Just do things the way I need, Bianca. I left your list on the table."

Frustration creased Bianca's brow. She nodded, throwing in an eye roll to punctuate the emotion.

Her mother changed the subject. "Your father tells me you rode the train with Jarrod Christmas."

"I did. He was very sweet."

"His father, Ethan, is a good friend of ours. He and your daddy play golf practically every week during the summer months. We had dinner with him last week. He was very excited about Jarrod coming home. Had I known this was going to happen," she said, gesturing down to her leg, "I would have bragged about you coming home too!"

Bianca shook her head, her eyes rolling skyward. "Well, I'm sure you'll get another chance sometime soon," she said glibly. "Maybe you'll break an arm next year."

"Don't be flippant, Bianca. Your father and I are very proud of you. We like to share your accomplishments with our friends and neighbors."

"It was just a joke, Mother. I wasn't . . ." Bianca started, her tone defensive.

Her mother continued. "You can't begrudge us bragging about you. It's bad enough that you rarely grace us with your presence. Truth be told, most people think your father and I are only imagining that we have a daughter. No one we know has ever met you."

"Now you're just being overly dramatic."

"No, I'm not. We don't see you nearly enough, so sharing tales of your exploits is all we have, and now you want to take issue with that."

Their conversation was interrupted by the doorbell ringing. "I'll get it!" Bianca chimed, quietly grateful for the save. She slid her buttocks up and across the chair's arm, easing out of the seat. Muttering under her breath, she raced toward the front of the home. She passed her father, throwing him a look as he grinned at her, his head shaking from side to side. She tossed her hands up in frustration, her brow creased with emotion.

The man laughed. "Give your mother a break, Bianca," he said, his voice a low whisper. "You know she loves you."

She rolled her eyes once again. "What's love got to do with it?"

The doorbell rang a second time. As the patriarch moved to his feet, Bianca waved him aside. "I'll get it," she repeated as she continued toward the front door.

Her father called her name. "I don't think that's a good idea."

"Really, Dad," she muttered, her tone dismissive. "I can answer the door."

Without giving it a second thought, she pulled the door open, suddenly startled to see Jarrod Christmas and an older version of the young man standing on the other side.

Jarrod grinned, his eyes widening. "Hey, Bianca, is this a bad time?"

"Jarrod, hey!" she exclaimed, her gaze flitting from one man to the other. "Not at all. It's good to see you again."

"Are you sure? Because we can always come back later?"

"Really, it's not a problem."

Jarrod gestured over his shoulder. "This is my father. Ethan Christmas, meet Bianca Torres. Bianca, my father, Ethan."

Bianca's gaze rested on the man, and she was suddenly standing like a deer in headlights. She'd expected that Ethan Christmas would be as handsome as his son, but she hadn't anticipated him being such a tall, delectable drink of chocolate. He stood a few inches taller than Jarrod, who was easily tipping six feet. He wore a Carolina blue polo shirt, a navy wool trench coat, and tan slacks, and his solid build filled the garments nicely. His hair was closely cropped and there was just the faintest hint of gray to his edges. His features were chiseled and his eyes were large pools of black water. The man had a distinguished air about him that Bianca found breathtaking. Her eyes were wide as she struggled not to salivate, her mouth open in awe.

Jarrod cleared his throat, pulling at her attention. A wide grin filled his face from ear to ear.

She blinked rapidly, shaking the sudden fog from her head. "Mr. Christmas, it's nice to meet you," she said politely. "Please, come in." She opened the door wider to allow them inside.

Ethan was staring at her as intently, a look of bemusement painting his expression. "Please, call me Ethan. It's a pleasure to meet you as well. Your parents speak quite highly of you." His gaze skated the length of her body and back, the man visibly struggling to keep his eyes focused on her face.

Bianca tossed him a quick smile, her own eyes dancing eagerly across his dark complexion. "So what brings you two here?" she asked.

Ethan answered, gesturing with a bouquet of flowers in his hand. "We wanted to stop by and see how your mother was faring. We were sorry to hear about her accident."

Before Bianca could respond, her father came from the family breakfast room. "Ethan, good morning!" he exclaimed, moving to shake the man's hand. "And this must be your son."

Bianca took a step to the side as the three men traded pleasantries. She continued to cut her eyes toward the senior Christmas until she realized Jarrod was watching her intently out of the corner of his own eyes. The two exchanged a look as she eyed him with a raised brow. Jarrod grinned at her, shrugging his shoulders, amusement seeping past his stare.

Her father gestured toward the back of the home. "Sharon's taken up residence in the family room. Come on in and say hello," Miguel said, leading the way.

Bianca blew a low gust of air past her thin lips. She moved to close the front door, and as she turned she caught a glimpse of her reflection in the antique mirror that adorned the foyer wall.

Her mouth dropped open as shock washed over her. Her eyes were wide and heat flushed her face, tinting her complexion a deep shade of red beneath the mud-colored clay mask spread across her cheeks and forehead. Her hair was a matted, tangled mess of curls pulled into an awkward ponytail that peeked from a scruffy satin cap. To add insult to injury, she was wearing an old ratty T-shirt that had been her father's and a pair of oversized track shorts that hung awkwardly beneath the top's hem, along with striped knee-length socks. She looked like a hot mess.

Chapter 2

The scream that echoed from the home's front foyer was piercing. In the other room Sharon's eyes widened as her head snapped with concern. She met her husband's eyes with a questioning stare. "What in the world . . . ?"

The matriarch turned just as Bianca raced past the family room's entrance toward the guest bedroom at the end of the hall. She was ranting as the door slammed harshly behind her, and it was only then that her mother realized her predicament. She laughed heartily, tossing her head back against her thin neck.

Miguel chuckled with her as the other two men struggled to contain their own laughter. "That's your daughter," he said, his head waving from side to side.

Sharon nodded, mirth still bubbling past her wide smile. She gestured for Ethan and his son to take a seat. "You'll have to forgive our baby girl," she said, looking from one to the other. "Bianca can be quite a challenge!"

In the other room, Bianca was pacing like a mad woman. She paused to take another look at her reflection in the full-length mirror. She screamed again, her tightened fists shaking at her sides. How could her parents have let her meet the most beautiful man that she had ever laid eyes on looking like she'd been dragged out of a gutter? Because Ethan Christmas was some serious eye candy and she wasn't looking like anything sweet. She shook her head from side to side as she snatched off her head scarf, rubbing at the facial mask with the corner of the satin fabric.

The hint of laughter could be heard in the distance and Bianca could only imagine the snarky comments coming from her mother. She blew a low sigh, dropping her body down against the bed.

Bianca knew that she gave her mother little credit. The dynamics of their relationship always had one or the other teetering on that line between love and hate. Her mother loving her choices one minute and hating them the next. Neither had mastered the skill of biting her tongue, each sometimes too quick to share her thoughts. But they shared a unique bond, and Bianca would not have traded the matriarch for anything else in the whole wide world. Plus, it was like her father often said: the two were exactly alike, which was why they bumped heads more times than not.

A knock on the bedroom door pulled at her attention. "What?" she snapped, still miffed by the circumstances that had her there still looking like death warmed over when she should have been in the home's family room being cute while she flirted shamelessly.

"Who is it?" she said when the knock came a second time.

Jarrod pushed the door open, hesitating as he peeked his head inside. "May I come in?" he asked, his expression smug.

Bianca cut her eyes in his direction, tossing him a look. Then they both burst out laughing.

"You do know that this is not the norm for me, don't you?" Bianca said.

Jarrod shrugged as he moved into the room and took a seat beside her. "I just know it's not a pretty look," he said.

"Well, tell me something I don't know!"

"Hey, I'm just being honest with you."

"What did your father say?"

"He didn't say anything. But if he did, he would have told you that you looked good. He would have lied to spare your feelings. I'm your friend. I don't care about your feelings. I'm obligated to tell you the truth."

Bianca narrowed her gaze until her eyes were thin slits.

Jarrod laughed heartily. "I told your mom I'd check on you. Apparently you're supposed to be going to the grocery store."

"So why are you here again?"

"My father wanted to come check on your mother. She's sweet, by the way. I like her."

"You would."

"What's that supposed to mean?"

"I bet you're a mama's boy, right? Where is your mother, by the way? Does she live here in Boone? Are she and your father still married?"

Jarrod shook his head. "They've been divorced since I was eight. She lives on the West Coast with her third, or maybe it's her fourth, husband. I'm not sure which."

The comment took her by surprise and she eyed him intently.

He met her stare and smiled. "Mama was the rolling stone in their relationship. We were all happier once they got divorced. Dad raised me and Mom took me on fantastic vacations. She and I are good friends."

"So you *are* a mama's boy."

He grinned. "She's my best girl and the only woman who will ever have my heart like that."

Bianca nodded her understanding. "So why didn't you tell me your father was so cute?"

He tossed her a look. "Really? He's my father. Why would I think he's cute?"

She shrugged, amusement painting her expression.

Jarrod winced. "Ewww! Please do not tell me that you're interested in my father. He's old, and well . . . he's old!"

"He's not that old."

"He's old enough to be *your* father. That makes him *too* old for you."

"Maybe, but that doesn't mean I can't appreciate his good looks."

Jarrod shook his head. "On that note, I'm leaving. I think I smell bacon."

Bianca smiled. "I guess I need to finish getting dressed. How long are you staying? Will you and your father still be here?"

"Your dad invited us to join him for breakfast," Jarrod said, moving toward the door. "Besides, we wouldn't want to miss your miraculous transformation."

"Oh, so now you have jokes!"

He laughed heartily.

"By the way," Bianca called after him.

"Yes," he said, pausing with his hand on the knob.

"Does your father have a girlfriend?"

* * *

Ethan said little when his son returned to the family room and rejoined the conversation. He was still curious about the relationship between his only child and the woman who'd greeted them at the door. Questions furrowed his brow as Jarrod met his probing stare with a wry smile.

"So," Sharon said, interrupting his thoughts, "will she be joining us?"

Ethan shifted his gaze in the woman's direction, noting her raised brow. Sharon gave him a warm smile, her own eyes moving back to his son.

Jarrod nodded. "Yes, ma'am. She's fine. She's changing and said she'd be right out."

"I'm so glad you two are so comfortable with each other," Sharon quipped. "We won't have to work quite so hard trying to fix the two of you up! Will we, Ethan?"

She winked an eye at her friend.

Ethan smiled, neither agreeing nor disagreeing. His gaze shifted toward his son, who was suddenly blushing profusely. He leaned forward in his seat, clasping his hands together in front of himself. "The old people used to say that if you want to know what a woman will look like when she gets old that you only have to look at her mother. Clearly, there's hope for her, son."

Sharon and Miguel both laughed heartily.

Bianca's voice echoed from the entranceway. "I see the whole family has jokes. Now I know where you get it from," she said as she moved to Jarrod's side, her arms crossed over chest. Her gaze was locked with Ethan's, the two studying each other intently.

Jarrod shook his head. He lifted his hands as if surrendering. "Leave me out of this," he said.

Ethan blushed as profusely as his son, suddenly choking on the words he'd just spoken. Gone was the disheveled woman who'd opened the door on their arrival. Bianca Torres cleaned up nicely, the woman having captured his full and undivided attention. He felt himself grinning like a Cheshire cat, his lips pulled wide and full, his eyes like two large saucers.

Bianca had slipped into denim leggings that she'd paired with thigh-high black suede boots and a black turtleneck sweater. Her attire fit like a glove, the form-fitting garment wrapped like paint around her petite figure. She'd swept her thick, lush curls into a casual updo that complemented her delicate features. Just a hint of blush and lipstick in a warm shade of chocolate adorned her face, accentuating her warm mocha complexion. She was stunning.

"No more cute comments?" Bianca said, her words harboring a hint of challenge. Her eyes were narrowed as her gaze swept over him.

Ethan laughed, his head shaking. "I'm still trying to swallow the foot stuck in my mouth," he said.

Bianca's lips pulled into a slight smile, amusement dancing in her eyes.

Her mother interrupted the moment. "Bianca, why don't you and Jarrod go set the table? Daddy was just waiting for you to come out so he can scramble the eggs."

Tearing her eyes from Ethan's, she tossed her mother a look. The matriarch didn't seem to notice, resuming her conversation about the town's city council and their decision to execute an agricultural lease for twelve acres of land at Azalea Park. Bianca opened her mouth to comment, but Jarrod gave her a gentle shove toward the dining room, stalling her words.

"Let it go," Jarrod whispered under his breath. "You like to start a mess with your mother."

"My mother likes to start a mess with me," Bianca hissed back. "Why do we need to set the table together?"

"Because our parents are playing matchmaker. They want to fix us up with each other. I'm sure they think this is a great opportunity for us to talk."

Bianca laughed out loud. "You're kidding me, right?"

"I don't kid. I'm very serious. They seem to think you and I would make a wonderful couple."

Bianca chuckled again. "I guess we're the only ones who know that they've got some seriously bad intel," she said.

Jarrod blew a low sigh. "I'm starting to think that coming home might not have been a good idea."

"I told you about secrets coming to bite you in the ass," she said as she reached for a stack of dishes in her mother's china cabinet.

Jarrod blew another sigh. Their conversation was interrupted by her father.

"Good," Miguel said. "You're setting the table. I'm just about to pull the biscuits out of the oven."

"Daddy, you need to talk to Mommy," Bianca said, moving around the dining room table. "Jarrod and I don't need to be fixed up."

Miguel laughed. "Figured it out, did you?"

Bianca rolled her eyes skyward. "Please, make her stop."

Her father shook his head. "Nope. It gives her something to focus on while you're home. You'll be gone after the New Year and then it won't make much difference. If you two remain friends, all well and good. If sparks fly, even better. It'll make your mother happy."

"There will be no sparks," Bianca said emphatically.

Jarrod nodded in agreement. "But we are good

friends," he added. "We're definitely more like brother and sister though," he concluded with a nervous chuckle.

Miguel laughed, too. "Well, just wait until Labor Day to tell your mother. She'll be heartbroken. She was hoping to have you married and pregnant with our first grandbaby by Valentine's Day."

Bianca and Jarrod exchanged a look. "I told you," she said. "My mother is certifiably crazy!"

Minutes later, they were joined by Ethan and Sharon, Bianca's mother rolling her way in a wheelchair. Despite his offer to push her to her destination, Ethan had been relegated to the other side of the room, the woman adamant that none of them get in her way. Once they were all seated and the food served, the conversation turned to the holiday.

"Ethan, do you and Jarrod have plans for Christmas?" Sharon asked. She looked from one man to the other before taking a bite of her husband's infamous sausage casserole.

Ethan swallowed the mouthful of food he'd been chewing. He reached for his water glass and took a sip. "We were just going to enjoy a quiet dinner together at home, Sharon. Nothing elaborate."

Sharon fanned a hand in his direction. "I'll not have it. You two will have dinner here with us."

"We wouldn't want to intrude . . ." Jarrod started.

"Baby, please! Don't be ridiculous. We'll have more food than we'll ever know what to do with. I'm sure your daddy has told you that we have an open-door policy in this house. Everyone's welcome at any time. In fact, I think you should both plan on helping us trim the tree this weekend. That's our Saturday project. Bianca's making baked spaghetti for dinner."

"I am?" Bianca's head snapped as she turned to face her mother. "When did I start cooking?"

Sharon ignored her outburst. "It's my recipe and Bianca is going to execute it. It'll be a great time!"

Ethan smiled. "Well, thank you. We appreciate both invitations and look forward to it."

Bianca's gaze shifted back in his direction. There was a slight smirk on the man's face as he met her stare. His eyes were dark and intense, something decadent simmering beneath his gaze. The look he gave her was lingering, and she felt a wave of heat waft slowly across her spine. She found herself sliding into the moment when there was an unexpected slam to the side of her leg. The motion was swift and abrupt, and when she realized Jarrod had kicked her under the table, she resisted the urge to cuss out loud. She turned to give her new friend a look, confusion washing over her expression.

Her father's voice broke through the fog. "Bianca, did you hear me, baby girl? Pass the casserole, please!"

The two men sat at a stop sign at the intersection of Inglewood and Windsor Roads, just minutes from their Asheville Avenue home. Jarrod was berating his father, miffed that he'd played into Mrs. Torres's delusions of grandeur.

Ethan laughed. "She wants her daughter to meet a nice guy. You're a nice guy. What else was I supposed to do?"

"You could have *not* given her the impression that I was interested in being fixed up with her daughter."

"But you like her daughter."

"I do like her daughter. We're friends. But I'm not

interested in a love connection with her. She's not my type."

Ethan smirked. "She's beautiful. How can she not be your type?"

Jarrod cut an eye at his father, his jaw tight, his lips pursed into a tight line. "She's just not," he muttered.

"So what is your type, son? What turns you on?"

Jarrod shrugged. There was a moment of hesitation before he answered. "I like them blond and blue-eyed," he finally said, thoughts of his best friend and partner easing into his mind.

He and Stefan Hunter had met his first week of residency at Mt. Sinai. Their attraction had been instantaneous, and he'd been drawn to the other man's strong Nordic features. Stefan was blond, his hair a messy mass of thick curls, and blue-eyed, their color reminiscent of ocean water. With his warm vanilla complexion and lean muscular frame, it had been love at first sight. Jarrod was suddenly uncomfortable when he looked over to see his father eyeing him intently.

There was a look of surprise on Ethan's face. "I don't know why, son, but I never figured you for dating white women."

Jarrod chuckled nervously, color heating his face. "Me neither," he muttered.

"Well, are you dating anyone special in New York?" Ethan asked as he turned into the driveway of his home and shut down his car engine. He turned in his seat to face his son.

Jarrod cut his eyes in the man's direction. "There is someone but . . ." he started, his voice trailing off. He took a deep breath. "It's nothing serious," he finally concluded, desperate to change the subject. "I don't even know why we're having this conversation."

Ethan squeezed his son's shoulder. "Okay, I'll stop being nosy about your private life," he said. "Just know that I want you to be happy."

Jarrod took a deep breath. "I am happy, Dad, which is why I don't need you and your bingo buddies trying to hook me up."

Ethan laughed. "Bingo buddies! That's cute."

Jarrod finally broke into his own smile. "Isn't that what you old people do when you retire? Hang out and play bingo?"

"I've never played bingo a day in my life. And I'm not that old, thank you!"

Jarrod shrugged. "Whatever you say. Just know that Bianca and I are friends, but we will never be anything more. Besides, you had her interest more than I did."

"Me?" Ethan's eyes widened. "Did she say something?"

"Yeah." Jarrod laughed. "She said you were cute and she wanted to know if you had a girlfriend."

Something like astonishment washed over Ethan's expression. His eyes skated back and forth as he replayed every conversation between them over in his head. Jarrod interrupted his thoughts.

"Yeah, that was how I felt about it. Kind of makes your skin crawl. She's my age, for heaven's sake!"

"Oh, yeah," Ethan said, still lost in thought. "She's definitely too young."

Jarrod's deep chortle was gut deep, his head shaking from side to side. "Y'all are too funny," he said. "You're just as bad as she was."

"What?" Ethan said, his eyes shifting in Jarrod's direction. "What'd we do?"

Jarrod motioned to exit the car. "You'll figure it out," he said. "I'm going inside. It's cold out here."

Ethan nodded, thoughts of Bianca still fluttering in his head.

"And, Dad?"

"Yes, son?"

"A word of warning. Bianca Torres is way out of your league! She will eat you alive and spit you out before you can blink! You might want to tread cautiously!"

Chapter 3

Bianca blew a heavy sigh as she studied the lengthy list of groceries her mother had requested. Shopping that should only have taken some ten minutes was already taking an hour longer than necessary. The neighborhood market should have been sufficient, but her mother had insisted she shop at Earthfare, the organic supermarket on the other side of town. Her parents, who used to eat anything and everything, were suddenly on a health food kick, insisting that everything they consumed be GMO and preservative free. It was enough to have Bianca pulling her hair out as she stood in the aisle trying to figure out which brand of flaxseed would garner the least amount of complaints from the family matriarch. She was just about to give up when a familiar voice sounded beside her.

"Bianca?" Ethan Christmas's deep baritone voice resounded like warm honey, smooth and seductive. "What a surprise!"

She turned, a smile creeping across her face. "Ethan, imagine running into you again."

He smiled back, the bend to his lips pulling at her

attention. He had a beautiful mouth, full lips like lush pillows that begged to be kissed.

"I frequent their juice bar. I just dropped in to get a shot of wheatgrass and one of their fruit smoothies."

Bianca grimaced. "Sounds like a waste of a shot to me. Wheatgrass?"

"Don't knock it until you try it. It's good for you."

Her smile widened. "Is it like some organic aphrodisiac?"

Ethan laughed as a faint blush teased his cheeks. "I don't know about all that, but it's a good energy booster."

Amused that she could make him blush so easily, Bianca laughed with him. But she was hardly convinced about the wheatgrass and she said so.

"Two ounces of wheatgrass juice has the nutritional equivalent of five pounds of the best raw organic vegetable," Ethan said with a nod. "It has twice the amount of vitamin A as carrots and is higher in Vitamin C than oranges! The stuff contains the full spectrum of B vitamins, as well as calcium, phosphorus, magnesium, sodium, and potassium. It's also a complete source of protein and essential amino acids," he concluded, sounding like a walking advertisement for some health institute.

Bianca stared, her eyes blinking rapidly. She shook her head. "I'll stick to shots of tequila. That's more my speed," she said, turning back to the display of dry goods.

Ethan suddenly felt awkward, his son's comments about Bianca being out of his league ringing in his thoughts. But his eyes danced the length of her body, admiring the round of her backside. Her buttocks were high and tight, sitting like two lush melons in her denim leggings. There was no denying that the beautiful woman had him sweating, and he was suddenly self-conscious, feeling out of sorts with the deviant thoughts that had crossed his mind.

He suddenly needed a swift retreat, unable to explain why he was feeling like a twelve-year-old trying to get the attention of the popular girl. He couldn't remember the last time any woman had him feeling so intimidated. But Bianca Torres had him feeling some kind of way.

"Well," he said, "it was good to see you again."

She turned back toward him, two bags of flaxseed in her hands.

"I believe your mother buys that brand," he said, pointing at the bag in her left hand, and with another endearing smile, he turned and disappeared down the aisle.

Bianca blew another heavy sigh, a warm breath blowing past her lips. Dropping the recommended product into her grocery cart she pushed it in the direction he'd headed, catching a glimpse of him as he moved toward the registers.

There was something about Ethan Christmas that teased her sensibilities. The man was blessed with good looks, a banging body, and a maturity that was lacking in most of the men who usually wined and dined her. She wished she could will him back to her side and she was annoyed with herself for not thinking to invite him to sit down for a cup of coffee or juice and one of the store's famed vegan cookies. She would have even been willing to try that nasty-sounding wheatgrass for a few more minutes of his attention.

As she reached the checkout, she spied him at the

store's entrance in conversation with a woman who was a tad touchy-feely. He was laughing as the stranger's hands danced over his chest and down the length of his arms, an occasional finger gliding along his profile. Bianca felt herself bristle, something like jealousy flooding her spirit. The emotion was disturbing and it surprised her. She took a breath and then two, inhaling and exhaling deeply before making her own exit.

As she made her way to her car, she tossed him a wave of her hand. "It was good to see you again, Ethan!" she called out before sliding into the front seat of her mother's Camry, pulling out of the parking space, and heading in the direction of home. She meant every word.

Wheatgrass. He'd given her a whole dissertation on wheatgrass, as if there'd been nothing else for the two of them to talk about. Ethan could only imagine what Bianca had to be thinking about him. If she was even thinking about him at all. And why was he even concerned? As his son had repeatedly reminded him, Bianca Torres was young enough to be his daughter.

Ethan shook his head suddenly aware that he was still sitting in his car in the supermarket's parking lot. Their chance meeting hadn't been by chance at all. He'd overheard the young woman's conversation with her mother and, knowing the organic venue would be the only place Sharon Torres would send anyone shopping for her, he'd come purposely hoping to run into her. Now he was feeling slightly foolish.

It also hadn't helped that he'd run into Vanessa Langston, the widow of former Mayor John Langston. The woman had made it quite obvious that she was in want of a new husband and he was high on her list.

Ethan had been running from her advances for over a
year, having no interest at all. He hated that Bianca had
seen the two of them together, with Vanessa's hands
practically down the front of his pants.

His cell phone suddenly chimed for his attention, a
text message noted on the screen. He read the message
quickly and a bright smile filled his face. Sharon Torres
needing help had suddenly given him an opportunity
to redeem himself with her daughter. Her timing
couldn't have been better.

Bianca found herself humming along with her
parents, the couple both singing Christmas carols at
the top of their voices. She couldn't help but smile at
the absurdity. She had texted her buddy Cilla to complain, and Cilla had texted back that if she couldn't
beat 'em that she should join 'em. Bianca had taken
the advice to heart, and she'd actually been having a
great time in the kitchen with her mother.

The whole house smelled of vanilla and cinnamon
and as she pulled the last pan of cookies from the oven,
Bianca had to admit that she was starting to enjoy
being home with her parents for the holiday.

She suddenly began to sing out loud, joining them
in a rendition of "Gloria in Excelsis."

Her mother clapped her hands excitedly.

Bianca rolled her eyes skyward as her parents both
chuckled warmly. Her mother suddenly gasped out
loud.

"What's wrong?" Bianca exclaimed, eyeing the
woman with concern.

"I forgot to have you pick up some extra trays from
the dollar store. I want to send cookies to the EMS boys

that came to get me up off the lawn and the nurses at the hospital who supported me right after my surgery."

"I can go back out now if you want," Bianca said with a nod.

"Do you mind, baby? I would really appreciate it."

"No, ma'am! I don't mind at all. Let me grab my coat."

A few short minutes later, Bianca was bundled warmly. She moved back into the room with her parents. Her mother was on the phone, deep in conversation. She waved her index finger in Bianca's direction.

"I really appreciate that," Sharon said into the phone's receiver. "Bianca is headed to the store for me now. She should be there in a few minutes."

There was a momentary pause in the conversation, and Bianca suddenly sensed her good mood turning. She was curious to know whom her mother was speaking with and what it had to do with her running what was only supposed to be one quick errand.

Sharon finally disconnected the call. "That was Ethan Christmas. He picked up the poinsettias for the church, but he won't be able to drop them off at the bishop's office before he has to go to practice. Jarrod is going to meet you in the shopping center, if you would please just collect them for me. Your father will make sure they get delivered to the church when you get back."

"Why can't Jarrod just take them to the church himself? Wouldn't that make more sense?" Bianca asked.

Annoyance washed over her mother's face. "It would, but he's doing something at the hospital and that's in the other direction. Why are you being so difficult?"

"I just asked a question!"

"Well, don't," Sharon admonished. "You'll be doing all of us a service."

"And it will give you and that nice Jarrod boy a chance to see each other again," her father added, a smug look on his face as he struggled not to laugh out loud.

Bianca threw her hands up in frustration. "I'll be back," she snapped, grabbing her mother's car keys.

"Thank you!" Sharon chimed. "And you might want to think about asking Jarrod out for coffee or something. He's such a nice young man," her mother called after her.

As Bianca reached the front door Sharon tossed in one last comment. "And you two are so cute together!"

Bianca had pushed the speed-dial number on her cell phone before she pulled out of the driveway. She waited for her call to connect as the phone engaged with the car's Bluetooth system.

Jarrod picked up on the third ring. "Hello?"

Bianca screamed, a loud, ear-piercing shriek intended to wake the dead.

Jarrod laughed. "Is it that bad?"

"It's worse than bad," she said. "If one more person makes one more crack about you and me being a perfect couple I'm going to commit bloody murder!"

Jarrod laughed again. "Sorry about that."

"It's not your fault. I'd be a perfect partner for any man. I've got it like that!"

His deep chortle made her smile. "So how long before you get to the shopping center?" she asked.

There was a moment of silence and Bianca could almost see the confusion on his face. "You don't know what I'm talking about, do you?"

"Sorry. Should I?"

"My mother said you were bringing poinsettias for the church. That I'm supposed to pick them up from you."

"I don't know anything about that," Jarrod said. "However my father did just leave the house. He might be on his way with them."

Bianca reflected on the comment for a brief moment, her mind spinning a mile a minute. "You don't have something to do at the hospital here?"

Jarrod shook his head into the receiver. "No. I don't have privileges at any hospital here in N.C. Besides, I'm on vacation, remember? Why would you think that I would be working at the hospital?"

"Something my mother said," she finally answered. "I guess I misunderstood."

"Well, I was actually about to go meet some old friends from high school for drinks. Do you want to come along?"

"I appreciate the invite, but I'm going to pass. I have a feeling I'm going to find something more interesting to do," she said with a low chuckle.

"Then I'll see you Saturday for that baked spaghetti dinner you're making."

Bianca laughed. "Bring booze. You're going to need it."

"Oh," Jarrod said before disconnecting the call, "tell my father I'm giving him a curfew. He needs to be home before midnight. And Bianca?"

"Yes?"

"Go easy on the old guy! I don't think he has a clue what he's getting himself into."

Minutes later, Bianca was still laughing heartily.

* * *

Ethan was standing in the parking lot when Bianca pulled into an empty space beside his car. He looked slightly nervous, and that made her smile. Putting two and two together, she'd peeped his hold card and was amused that he'd gone out of his way to see her.

Since their earlier encounter, he'd changed his clothes. He sported black slacks, a black turtleneck, a black wool blazer, and black leather Timberland boots. The ensemble was classic and casual, and as he stood with his hands pushed deep into the pockets of his pants, he looked like a *GQ* cover model. The man was breathtaking.

"Hi!" she exclaimed brightly. "What are you doing here?"

Ethan tossed her an easy smile. "Your mother is expecting these," he said, gesturing toward a multitude of poinsettia plants that rested in the cargo space of his SUV.

"Oh, I thought Jarrod was bringing them," she commented, her eyes meeting his evenly.

Ethan smiled again. "Something came up so I said I would bring them."

"Oh, really?" Bianca said.

Ethan laughed. "Don't sound so disappointed."

"I'm not disappointed. I'm not disappointed at all. In fact," she said as she leaned back against her own vehicle and crossed her arms over her chest, "I'm glad you came instead."

Ethan shifted his stance, his gaze still locked with hers. "Does that mean I might be able to convince you to come have a cup of coffee with me? Maybe dinner?"

Bianca barely hesitated before responding. "Dinner sounds like a plan. But I'm thinking we might want to drop those plants off at the bishop's office before we do. I wouldn't want to be you if anything happened to the church's poinsettias. I can't save you from my mother," she said as she walked around to the passenger side of his vehicle and climbed inside.

Two stops later, the two were seated across from each other at the Southern Kitchen and Bar. Bianca's mother had been overly excited to hear that Bianca wasn't coming right back home, stopping to spend time with Mr. Christmas. Bianca hadn't bothered to clarify which Mr. Christmas. She felt only a little guilty allowing her mother to assume that she was hanging out with Jarrod, but the little white lie was well worth being able to spend time with his father.

He'd ordered the lobster mac and cheese for her and a beef Manhattan sandwich for himself. They were both enjoying one of the restaurant's signature coffees, the BFK, a mix of Bailey's Irish Cream liqueur, Kahlua, and a locally roasted gourmet coffee.

"So what do you do in Raleigh?" Ethan asked, swiping at his lips with a cloth napkin.

"I'm a pharmaceutical scientist for Merck. I spend most of my time in a laboratory discovering how different compounds interact with disease-causing cells and organisms. Then I investigate how those compounds interact with the human body to ultimately determine if they can become new drugs."

"So you're a geek!"

She smiled. "I have my moments. How about you. What do you do in this retirement village?"

Ethan laughed. "Well, I'm hardly retired. I dabble in real estate investments."

"Dabble?"

He shrugged his shoulders slightly. "I own a number of properties, and properties with a certain cache."

"So where do you fall in the ranks with moguls like Trump, Steve Wynn, and the Rockefellers?" She leaned forward, resting her chin atop her hands and her elbows on the table.

Ethan smiled, then chuckled softly. "I like to think I'd make the list. If there was a list, of course."

"Is that your arrogance speaking?"

"That's nothing but confidence."

Bianca gave him a bright smile. "I think I like you, Ethan Christmas. I think I like you a lot."

"Would you still like me if I was a plumber?"

"Would you like me if I was a waitress?"

He nodded. "Yes, I would. I definitely would."

"I'm impressed by your confidence, sir, not your career of choice."

There was a slight bob to his head as he reflected on her comment.

Bianca grinned. "So tell me something interesting about you, Mr. Christmas?"

"Only if you promise to stop calling me Mr. Christmas. It makes me feel old and I'm only fifty-three."

"Fifty-three? That's ancient!"

"Says you. And exactly how young are you anyway?"

"I'm twenty-eight."

"Almost thirty."

She laughed. "Cute! I'm *almost* nothing. I *just* turned twenty-eight."

"Jarrod says you're too young for me."

"Your son doesn't want to see you get your feelings hurt."

"Are you going to hurt my feelings?"

"I'm twenty-eight, not eighteen. And I'm not looking for a sugar daddy. I think you're safe in my hands."

"So what are you looking for, Bianca Torres?"

Their gazes locked and held, something heated wafting thick and full between them. It was comforting and safe, and satisfied a yearning neither had known existed.

Bianca took a deep breath and held it until her lungs burned. Ethan shifted his head slightly, the gesture seeming to repeat his question.

"I'm not sure," she finally answered. "But I have a feeling I've already found it."

The grandfather clock in his foyer had just struck twelve when Ethan secured the lock on his front door. He had just closed the hall closet after hanging up his winter coat when the lights clicked on in the family room. Jarrod sat upright in one of the leather recliners. A rerun of *Criminal Minds* was playing on the big screen television, the volume barely audible.

"What's up?" Ethan said, moving to take a seat on the upholstered sofa.

Jarrod grinned. "I should be asking you that. I see that you got my message," he said as he stole a quick glance at his Seiko watch.

Ethan's gaze narrowed curiously. "What message?"

"I told Bianca to tell you that you had a midnight curfew."

"You talked to Bianca?"

His son nodded. "She called me earlier. Something about some poinsettias for the church?"

Ethan laughed out loud realizing that Bianca had caught him red-handed.

"Did you have a good time?" Jarrod asked.

His father nodded. "I did. I had a really great time. We—"

Jarrod held up his hand, an open palm waving at his father. "Please, spare me the details. Bianca is my friend, and if whatever is going on with you two goes south, I want her to still be my friend."

Ethan nodded, sighing deeply. "She's an amazing woman. I really like her," he said. "But I guess you already figured that out."

Jarrod nodded, his brow knitted. "It's too weird for me, Dad. It's like you're trolling the school yard."

"I take offense at that."

"The high school yard, not preschool," Jarrod clarified.

"And that makes it better?"

"Not really. It's still weird having my father chase a teenybopper."

"First, I'm not chasing anyone. Second, I don't think Bianca would appreciate your assessment. She'd be offended, too."

Jarrod chuckled warmly. "I can't wait to give her a hard time."

"You two seem very close."

"We've become good friends. She has great energy."

"Does it bother you that I like her?"

Jarrod shifted forward in his seat. He shook his head. "Not really. I can appreciate what you see in Bianca. She's a very special woman and you deserve someone like that in your life. But don't get yourself twisted if it doesn't work out. I don't think dating Bianca is an easy thing for any man to do. She'll tell you she's high maintenance and demanding. She isn't going to make it easy for you."

"Well, we're not that serious, son. We just enjoy each other's company."

Jarrod laughed. "If you really believe that, I've got a bridge I'd like to sell you."

"I'm serious! We're just getting to know each other, that's all."

"The next time you two are in a room together look in a mirror. If you see what I see, you won't tell that lie." The young man moved onto his feet. "It's all good, Dad. Don't let it bother you. I'm headed up to bed. I'll see you in the morning."

"Sleep well, son," Ethan said, and the two men bumped fists.

Ethan watched as Jarrod took the steps two at a time. When he heard his room door close, he leaned back in his seat, swinging his legs up onto the sofa. He extended his body lengthwise, drawing both of his hands behind his head as he stared at the television screen, watching a late-night infomercial hawking the latest and greatest Chia pet.

He was still reeling from his good time with Bianca. The beautiful woman challenged him, and he liked how that felt. Their conversation had been easy— light-hearted banter about everything and about nothing. Then there had been those moments when they had caught each other's eye or laughed as they instinctively finished the other's thoughts when he'd felt something simmering deep in his core. The emotion had caught him off guard and he'd found himself fearing it and craving it at the same time.

He had hated for the night to end. The ride back to her car had been fraught with sexual tension and it hadn't helped that Bianca was a tease to the nth degree. The innuendo and not-so-subtle banter had left him hard and wanting, his condition fodder for her amusement. She'd left him with a friendly kiss on the cheek, but her lips had languished a second longer than necessary, a warm palm resting high on his thigh. The tips of her fingers had been heated and teasing, and then she'd eased from his car into her own and had disappeared out of the parking lot.

Ethan took a deep breath and then another, blowing them out loudly. He should have been tired but he wasn't. He couldn't help but wonder if he was making a mistake, thinking about his friends and neighbors and what they might think of him. And then he realized he really didn't care. Being alone and being lonely had taught him much about himself over the years, and what he knew best was that life was short. He wasn't promised tomorrow, and he didn't take his blessings lightly. He lived a good life, and what he wanted most for himself was someone to share that with. He wasn't going to let an opportunity for happiness pass him by.

Kicking off his shoes, Ethan adjusted a pillow beneath his head. He couldn't stop thinking about her. Bianca Torres haunted his thoughts as he imagined where the next few days might take them. Like a fast-growing fungus, she'd gotten under his skin and there was nothing that was going to make her go away. Ethan smiled, a bright smile filling his face. He suddenly imagined that if Santa were really watching, he'd be straddling that fine line between his naughty and nice lists. Heaving another deep sigh, he closed his eyes and eventually drifted off to sleep, the memory of Bianca dancing sweetly through his dreams.

Bianca had been able to sneak into the family home without disturbing either of her parents. Her father had fallen asleep in his favorite chair, snoring loudly as the late-night news watched him from the TV set. Peeking into her parents' bedroom, she was happy to find her mother in her own deep slumber, the heavy exhalations of her breathing echoing through the room.

After cutting off the light that they'd left on in the kitchen, Bianca took a quick shower before sliding beneath the cool sheets of her queen-sized bed. As she pulled the covers up and over her pajama-clad body, she wondered if Ethan was in his own bed. And she wondered if he was thinking about her the way she was thinking about him. Because she was thinking about Ethan Christmas.

She slid her palm across her stomach, then clenched her hand into a tight fist. She had enjoyed everything about their evening together. It had been a great time. Spending time with Ethan was easy and it was comfortable. Something about the man was like the sweetest balm.

She rolled onto her side, wrapping her body around an oversized pillow. She couldn't remember the last time she'd laughed so easily with a man. But Ethan made her laugh. He had a sense of humor equal to her own and his energy ignited something voluminous within her. He excited her and she loved how that felt. It would have been nothing to spread herself open to him, and had their circumstances been different, she wouldn't have hesitated. As Bianca bit down against her bottom lip, she heaved a deep sigh. Sleep was elusive, but when it finally came, she drifted off thinking about Ethan and nothing else.

Chapter 4

Bianca was giggling into her cell phone when her mother slammed abruptly through her bedroom door. Her eyes widened in surprise at the intrusion. "Hold on," she muttered just before clamping her hand over the receiver.

"Are you okay?"

Sharon was still fighting with her wheelchair, trying to maneuver it to her bidding. "I'm fine. I need you to . . ." she started, pausing midsentence. "Are you on the phone?"

"I was," Bianca said with a slow eye roll.

"I'm sorry. I guess I should have knocked. Who are you talking to?" Sharon asked, eyeing her curiously.

Bianca shook her head, returning to her call. "I'll have to call you back," she said into the receiver.

Ethan laughed. "Your mom, huh?"

"This is so not working for me."

He chuckled warmly. "It's not a problem. I was thinking about you and I just wanted to call to say hello."

"That was very sweet of you," Bianca said, her voice

dropping to a whisper. She turned her back on her mother, mindful of the woman's watchful eye.

"I guess I'll see you in a few hours."

"Definitely," Bianca responded.

He called her name.

"Yes?"

"Tell me you miss me as much as I'm missing you."

She felt herself grinning foolishly. "You are so not funny!"

Ethan made kissing sounds into his cell phone. "Blow one back to me."

"Thank you for calling," she answered.

"Just pucker up and blow me one kiss. I dare you."

Bianca laughed, a warm blush flooding her face as she disconnected the call, not bothering to respond. Her mother was still eyeing her curiously.

"So what can I help you with?" Bianca asked, avoiding the look her mother was giving her.

Sharon paused, eyeing her intently. "Why are you blushing? Was that Jarrod?"

"It was a friend."

"It was Jarrod!" Sharon clapped her hands excitedly.

"You're going to drive me crazy," Bianca said, lifting herself from the bedside.

Sharon laughed. "Don't be embarrassed. I'm glad you two are enjoying your time with each other."

"So what was it you needed?" Bianca asked a second time.

"All the ornaments are downstairs in the storage room behind your father's man cave. I need you to bring up all the red plastic containers."

"All of them? You have like fifty red boxes down there."

"It's not that many, but I need them all."

"We don't even have a tree yet. Is Daddy ready to go get the tree yet? I can go with him to pick one out."

"It's been taken care of. Ethan and his son volunteered to bring it when they come. Ethan has an old pickup truck so it won't be too much of a problem. Your father went down and paid for it earlier this morning so we're all set."

"Isn't that special," Bianca muttered.

Sharon ignored the comment. "Bring up the boxes please, and then we need to get started on dinner."

Bianca layered the last cup of grated cheddar cheese atop a baking dish of spaghetti and crushed tomatoes.

"When you're done with that, Bianca, dot it with a few pats of butter," her mother ordered, "then it will be ready to cook. It needs to bake at three hundred and fifty degrees for an hour so we probably need to go ahead and get it in the oven."

Bianca nodded. "What are we serving with it?"

"You need to make a tossed salad, and I have some garlic toast in the big freezer in the washroom."

Bianca wasn't willing to admit it out loud, but she really was enjoying her time with her mother. Taking orders as her mother held court at the kitchen table was teaching her the mechanics of old family recipes that she'd not eaten in a long while. She was actually looking forward to replicating them on her own once she went back home to Raleigh.

An hour later, the table was set for five, the baked spaghetti was almost out of the oven, and the rest of the meal was ready to be served. When the doorbell rang, Bianca could barely contain her excitement.

"I'll get it," she exclaimed. Her eyes were wide as she

swiped her hands on a kitchen towel, snatched off her apron, and adjusted her blouse.

She moved hurriedly toward the front door just as her father pulled it open, tossing her a look over his shoulder.

"I've got it," he said, amusement teasing his words.

Her mother had wheeled herself to Bianca's side just as her father pulled the door open. On the other side Ethan and Jarrod were both grinning as they peeked from behind an oversized tree. The Fraser fir stood close to eight feet tall. It was lush and full, a deep, rich green, and it smelled like Christmas. As the two men and her father dragged it inside, Bianca's holiday spirit increased tenfold.

"Thank you," Sharon exclaimed. "You two don't know how much Miguel and I appreciate this."

"It was our pleasure," Ethan said, tossing Bianca a quick look.

"We will work for food," Jarrod added with a warm laugh.

Her mother smiled. "Jarrod, did you and Bianca have a good time together the other night? She never tells me anything."

Bianca's eyes widened as she rushed to Jarrod's side, grabbing his hand. "Do not answer that! There will be no interrogations going on here," she said, her gaze meeting her mother's. She pulled Jarrod toward the back of the home, meeting Ethan's nervous stare with one of her own.

Behind them, her mother laughed. "Young love!" she exclaimed, chuckling heartily. "Ethan, make yourself comfortable. I'm sure our children will be back as soon as Bianca tells Jarrod what he can and cannot say. She's bossy like that!"

Jarrod was smiling brightly as Bianca closed her

room door behind them. "This is really starting to get interesting," he said, crossing his arms over his broad chest. "You didn't tell your parents that you had dinner with my father?"

"No, and you're not going to tell them either."

"And my father is okay with this?"

"He doesn't have a choice. I don't want the drama."

"Weren't you the one lecturing me about secrets coming to bite you in the ass?"

"This is different. Now, I'm keeping your secret so you have to keep mine. You cannot tell! Promise me!"

Jarrod shook his head. "We're both headed straight to hell. This is going to blow up on both of us and it's off to Hades for me and you."

"We'll cross that bridge when we get to it."

"So what am I supposed to do if your mother asks me any more questions?"

"Say nothing. I'll call her off, but if she keeps coming after you, I'll handle her."

"You hope."

Bianca reached up to kiss his cheek. "Thank you. I owe you one."

"You owe me more than one."

She laughed. "Your father will pay it."

They were still laughing as they returned to the other room. The festivities were already under way as Ethan and her father secured the tree in the tree stand, her mother conducting its position in the corner of their family space. Ethan turned to stare at them and Bianca gave him a bright smile.

"How can I help?" she asked, cutting her eyes in her mother's direction.

"The lights are in that box on the table. They need to go on first," Sharon said.

Moving to where her mother pointed, Bianca lifted the lid on the container and peered inside. She laughed as she examined its contents. "My mother is so OCD!" she exclaimed, pulling the first set of lights from inside. The strand was pristinely wound around a plastic tube and wrapped neatly in plastic.

"You'll appreciate my OCD when you see how easy it is to hang those lights," she said with a slight giggle.

Bianca shook her head as she moved to Ethan's side. Her gaze danced easily with his and he grinned brightly. She passed one end of the lights into his hands. "Mr. Christmas, do you mind?"

"Not at all," he said, his expression smug.

Jarrod laughed. "I want to help too!" he said, his tone teasing.

Bianca rolled her eyes as he stepped to her side to give them both a hand. In no time at all, the lights were strung, the ornaments hung, and they were all tossing strands of silver garland at the branches. Laughter filled the room as they all shared anecdotes and stories, enjoying the fellowship.

Ethan reached for the large star, passing it to Bianca. The two exchanged a look before she turned and moved to her father's side. "Ready, Daddy?"

Miguel nodded as he wrapped an arm around his daughter's shoulders and hugged her warmly. He gestured for her to step onto the foot stool and he extended his arm to help her prop the star atop the tree. Her smile was full and bright and she couldn't help but think about all the past Christmases when her father had lifted her in his arms to put the last trimming on their holiday tree. The memories brought a tear to her eyes and as she stepped back down she wrapped her arms around his neck and hugged him back.

Ethan's voice suddenly rang out from where he was standing, the man breaking into a chorus of "Oh, Christmas Tree."

He was a tenor and his tone was smooth, like rich velvet. As he sang, Sharon shut off the lights in the room, allowing the bright glow of the lit tree to illuminate the space. Bianca stared, completely awed, still holding her father's hand. When his song was finished, Ethan suddenly looked embarrassed, color rising to his cheeks.

"That was beautiful!" Bianca exclaimed. "I didn't know you could sing."

Ethan laughed. "I do a little every now and then."

Her mother chimed in. "Don't let him fool you, Bianca. Ethan is quite the talent. Every year he leads the annual Messiah Open Sing at the United Methodist Church. It's always spectacular!"

Bianca's gaze shifted back to Ethan. "Handel's 'Messiah'?"

He nodded. "Jarrod will be singing with me this year. Won't you, son?"

Jarrod shook his head. "Only because you're forcing me."

"That's wonderful! I'm sure Bianca would love to hear you both sing, wouldn't you, Bianca?" Her mother grinned.

Bianca looked from one to the other. "Oh, I wouldn't miss that for anything in the world," she said, her gaze finally resting on Ethan.

"It's a date then," her mother mused. "Bianca will be there to represent the family this year. Miguel, you should go with her, honey."

Bianca's father shook his head from side to side. "That sing thing is just a little too dull for me. I'm sure there has to be a basketball game playing that night that I can't miss. I'm almost positive."

They all laughed.

"Something smells really good," Jarrod said, breaking the reverie. "Really good."

"The food's ready if you two are," Bianca quipped.

"I didn't know you could cook, Bianca," Ethan quipped back.

She tossed him a look, a wry smile blooming full across her face. Heading in the direction of the kitchen, she muttered under her breath as she passed him, her voice a low whisper for his ears only, "There's a lot you don't know about me, Ethan Christmas!"

Bianca stood at the kitchen sink rinsing the last of the dishes before placing them in the dishwasher. In the other room, her mother was regaling their company with stories of her activism and social service. She'd been a die-hard hippie back in her heyday and still possessed that carefree spirit of a flower child. Bianca had heard the stories of their protest marches and sit-ins since she'd been a little girl and was almost able to quote the tales verbatim. She found herself smiling and appreciated how Ethan and Jarrod both appeared interested even though she suspected it was all polite pretending.

"Can I be of any help?" Ethan asked, moving into the kitchen and standing beside her.

Surprised, Bianca felt herself grinning. "Now you offer to help, after I'm almost done?"

He grinned with her, shrugging his shoulders. "Better late than never," he said as he bumped the side of her body with his own.

"That's just like a man."

He laughed. "Jarrod's enjoying your mother. She and your father have had a fascinating history."

"I thought they might be boring you two to death."

"Not at all. Jarrod's a history buff and he's always taken advantage of any opportunity to talk to seniors about their experiences."

"I like Jarrod. He's a good guy."

"He is. I hope he finds a good woman one day. I'd like to have grandchildren."

Bianca eyed him for a moment before commenting. "What about children? Have you thought about having any more?"

Ethan paused in reflection. "I'll be honest. I really hadn't given it any thought. Once my ex-wife and I separated and Jarrod left home, I put all that behind me. What about you? Do you want children?"

Bianca took a deep breath. Her mother had been talking about grandchildren since Bianca first learned how babies were made. But she'd truly had no interest, thinking that one day, with the right man, her biological clock would chime, she'd answer the ringer, and the matter would be settled one way or the other. Bianca had never imagined herself just deciding one day that she wanted to be a mother. But, if it happened, she would roll with the flow and move Sharon Torres close by to babysit.

She shrugged her shoulders. "I have more interest in practicing *how* babies are made than actually having a baby," she said with a slight smirk.

Ethan laughed. "Nothing wrong with that, I guess."

There was a moment of awkward silence that wafted between them. Ethan looked around the room nervously, pushing his hands deep into the pockets of his slacks. "Well, I guess I should go back and rejoin the festivities."

Bianca nodded. "That's probably a good idea. We wouldn't want you to be missed."

He was just about to make an exit when Bianca grabbed his arm. Tossing a look over her shoulder to ensure no one was watching them, she turned, backing him against the refrigerator door. She leaned her body against him, her pelvis locked tight to his. Ethan's gaze flickered with heat as he tossed his own cautionary glance toward the room's entrance.

The two locked gazes and held the connection, allowing a wave of heat to flood them both with emotion. Bianca bit down against her bottom lip, gliding her hips in a slow shimmy against the front of his slacks. Ethan gasped, sucking in a swift breath of air. His body stiffened, fighting the rise of nature that threatened to expose his growing desire. He crossed his arms over his chest, tucking his fists beneath his armpits. Despite his best efforts, he couldn't ignore the effect she was having on him. He wanted nothing more than to wrap his body around hers and let his fingertips dance against the warm caramel tones of her skin.

Bianca took an abrupt step back, her seductive mouth lifting into a teasing smile. Ethan found himself panting ever so slightly, disheartened by the cool air that suddenly blew between them. The moment had been too heated and it had left him yearning. He looked nervously toward the door as he swiped a hand across his brow. "You are bad," he whispered, the words coming with warm breath.

Her laugh was low and seductive as she turned from him and moved to the other side of the room. She tossed him a look, her dark eyes shimmering with mischief. "I beg to differ. I'm just that good!" she said before making an about-face and exiting the room.

Chapter 5

Bianca slid into a booth at the High Five Coffee Bar. After ordering a large espresso, she ticked items off the long list her mother had sent her out the door with earlier that morning. It had taken most of the day, but she'd finally whittled down the lengthy to-dos and only had one more errand to run before she could call it a day.

Outside the weather was beginning to turn and the temperature was dropping rapidly. Bianca felt chilled through to the bone and she was excited for that cup of coffee. As she sat studying the menu, trying to decide on a BLT or a pastry, she didn't notice Ethan enter the coffee spot. But he'd seen her, having spotted her mother's car parked out on Broad Street.

Sliding into the booth beside her, he flashed her a bright smile before gesturing for the waitress.

"Mr. Christmas, how are you, sir?" the young woman asked, eyeing them both curiously.

"I'm doing well, Ms. Barker. How are your parents?"

"They're good. Will you have your usual, sir?"

"I will."

The girl nodded, her gaze shifting toward Bianca. "Ma'am, have you decided on what you want to eat?"

Bianca nodded. "I'll have the BLT on whole wheat, please. And one of those chocolate croissants."

"That actually sounds good," Ethan interjected. "I'll have the same."

The girl nodded with a warm smile. "Coming right up. Will this be on separate checks?" She looked at Ethan, then at Bianca and back.

"No, one check and Ms. Torres is buying today."

The young woman named Ms. Barker nodded and, with a flip of her blond curls, headed back toward the front counter.

"You have some nerve!" Bianca said, turning in her seat to eye him head-on.

He shrugged, his broad shoulders filling a wool argyle sweater nicely. "I do, but then any man worth his weight would when it comes to you."

"Sounds like you still have a little attitude."

"You left me in a precarious position the other night. It wasn't pretty."

She laughed heartily. "I don't know what you're talking about, Mr. Christmas."

"Like hell you don't," he said, chuckling with her. "How was your day?"

"It's been busy. My mother is keeping me on my toes."

"Speaking of, I don't like lying to your parents." His expression had changed, an air of seriousness flooding his face.

"Have you lied to them?"

"By omission."

"That's really not like lying. Trust me. I've not told them thousands of things. It's kept the peace between us."

"That's not how I operate, Bianca. You pretending that it's Jarrod you're interested in, it isn't fair to him. And it's not fair to me."

Bianca blew a heavy sigh. "You are seriously starting to ruin my good mood."

"Tough. So what are we going to do?"

She reached for her coffee cup and took a sip as she reflected on his words. She turned back to face him. "You know my parents well. How do you think they're going to react to you lusting after their daughter?"

"Who says I'm lusting?"

Her gaze narrowed. "Then what are you doing?"

"I'm getting to know a woman who has captured my full attention. I find her desirable and I'm not ashamed to let people know that. I'm interested in seeing how far she and I can take our growing relationship."

Bianca blew a low sigh. "You're killing me, Ethan. This was only supposed to be a holiday fling if it amounted to anything at all. And we are nowhere near the fling part yet. Why are you making it so serious?"

"Is that what I'm doing? Because I don't remember ever saying I was interested in just having a fling, holiday or otherwise."

"I . . ."

He cut her words off, his voice raising an octave. "Are you telling me that you're not feeling what I'm feeling?"

"I'm telling you that this is not the time or the place for this conversation," she hissed between clenched teeth as she tossed an anxious look around the room.

Ethan slid his body closer to hers, cornering her in the booth. He slid a large hand around the curve of her neck, his fingers easing into the thick of her hair to cup the back of her head. His other hand clasped the side of her waist, the tips of his fingers heated as he pulled her body against his own. His face was millimeters from hers, his warm breath teasing. Her mouth parted slightly, her lips moist with anticipation. Heat had risen with a vengeance, almost combustible. It took her breath away.

And then, just as quickly, he let her go and he slid himself from her, moving himself out of the booth to the other side of the table. Bianca inhaled swiftly, gasping for air as she fought to catch her breath.

"You feel it," Ethan said matter-of-factly. "And we can talk about it when and where you want. But I wouldn't wait too long if I were you because, if it comes down to it, I have no problem having the conversation with your parents first."

Bianca's eyes widened. Before she could comment, the waitress returned with their orders, leaving them with one last smile.

Bianca watched as Ethan took a bite of his sandwich, chewing it slowly. "Are you challenging me, Ethan Christmas?"

He met her stare. "Do you feel challenged?"

In that moment, something like joy filled Bianca's spirit. For the first time in forever, she finally felt as if she'd met her match. Ethan was clearly a cut above all the other men she'd ever dated. He had no problem calling her on her crap and didn't think twice about pushing her buttons. She liked everything about him. And she hated to admit that he was right. If they were going to take their newfound friendship any further, they would have to come out to her family. She blew another sigh.

"You really should have kissed me, Ethan Christmas!"

He grinned, his eyebrows raised. As she continued, he took another bite of his sandwich.

"You should have taken full advantage of my weak moment and kissed me."

"So I did make you weak?"

Ignoring his question, she rolled her eyes skyward. "If you had kissed me I would know if going public with you is worth it."

Ethan chuckled. "Woman, please. You didn't need a kiss to know the answer to that."

"Maybe not, but it sure would have been nice."

"Do you want me to come over there and kiss you now?"

"No. You blew it."

Ethan laughed. "I'll get another chance."

"You are so sure of yourself, aren't you?"

Ethan reached for her hand, entwining his fingers between hers. "I'm sure of you, and you, my dear, are definitely sure of me."

The ride home found Ethan deep in thought. Every time he found himself in Bianca's company, he wanted to spend more time with her. Bianca hadn't been ready for the conversation they'd needed to have, but he'd known it was necessary. He'd known it when he'd found himself driving by her family home hoping to run into her.

Over coffee and multiple refills, they'd talked for a good long while, and despite all her efforts to avoid discussing her parents, they'd still come to an agreement of sorts. Ethan had agreed to be persistent, and Bianca had agreed to not fight him on the issue, even if she didn't agree. The absurdity made him smile. Everything about Bianca made him smile. She was stubborn and defiant, engaging and funny, and he had never met any woman who moved him in the way that she did.

As he maneuvered his way home, he turned on the car radio and cranked up the volume. He allowed himself to drift into the music, the jazz station playing Ramsey Lewis's version of "Here Comes Santa Claus." A master of the saxophone, Lewis had transformed the holiday favorite into a soulful blues improvisation. It made Ethan smile.

He took a deep breath. He had a long list of things he needed to do, but he couldn't focus. He was just days from the holiday concert. He still needed to do his own holiday shopping. Plus, the weather center was predicting heavy snow and he had property in the mountains that he needed to check and secure. With Christmas coming sooner than later he needed to get himself together but he couldn't stop thinking about Bianca, and about him and Bianca together. He blew out the breath he'd been holding.

As he sat at a stoplight, traffic beginning to back up in the center of town, he engaged his Bluetooth and dialed her number. Bianca answered on the second ring.

"Hello?"

"I knew you were missing me so I thought I'd call."

"And how did you know that?" she responded, the hint of a smile in her tone.

"Because I'm missing you."

There was a moment of pause before she spoke again. "You're quite the romantic, Ethan. I never would have taken you to be so starry-eyed."

Ethan laughed. "Starry-eyed? Really?"

She laughed with him. "It was a compliment."

"Even if it was a little backhanded, right?"

"The only kind I do."

He chuckled heartily. "Have you made it home, yet?"

"Not yet. I had to stop and pick up clothes from the cleaners."

"Can I see you later?" Ethan asked. His tone was teasing, but he was dead serious.

"What would I tell my mother?"

"The truth."

"I keep telling you, the truth can be overrated."

"Then lie. Because I really want to see you."

Bianca laughed again. "Ethan Christmas, did you really just tell me to lie? After all that sanctimonious posturing you did about our moral obligation to be open and honest with my family, you are now telling me to lie?"

"Damn right. I want to see you so if it's going to take a lie, so be it. I'll apologize and make amends for it later. What do you say?"

Bianca blew a low sigh. "Seven-thirty. Meet me at the mall. I'll be in Victoria's Secret," she said.

Ethan grinned. "I'll be there with bells on!"

It actually took Ethan twenty minutes to find a parking spot at the mall. He was in awe of the volume of holiday traffic that was moving into and out of the shopping center. By the time he'd parked and made his way to Victoria's Secret, he was a good thirty minutes late.

He rushed into the store, his gaze sweeping up one side of the store and down the other. Moving farther inside the establishment he passed the checkout corner, easing past the displays of bras and panties. Bianca was nowhere to be found.

"Can I help you?"

Ethan turned to see a tall, leggy redhead eyeing him curiously. He nodded. "I was actually looking for someone. She's about this tall," he said, gesturing with his hand. "Dark curls . . ."

"Oh, yes, your wife said to tell you she's in the dressing room," the woman said, pointing him toward the back of the store.

"My wife?"

"You are Mr. Christmas, aren't you? Cool name, by the way!"

"I am," he said with a nod of his head. "And thank you."

"Mrs. Christmas said you'd be looking for her." She pointed again toward the back of the store.

Ethan smiled his appreciation as he turned, easing past a table of silk thongs. Outside the dressing room doors, he called her name. "Bianca?"

A hand appeared over the top of the end cubicle. She waved him in her direction, unlocking the door and pulling him inside when he reached her.

"What took you so long?" Bianca asked.

Ethan found himself tongue-tied as he stood staring at her. Barely dressed in anything at all, Bianca wore a bright red mesh and lace teddy with side cutouts, sexy crisscross straps at the open back and a racy thong bottom. The neckline plunged deeply, the lace was see-through and the garment fit her like a second skin. With a pair of gold pumps and her curls loose about her shoulders, she was mesmerizing.

Like a deer caught in headlights, Ethan stared. An erection had pulled full and taut in his slacks and he sat down abruptly, crossing one leg over the other. Still unable to speak he forced himself to shift his eyes from her body to her face. His gaze kissed hers. The smile on her face was teasing, flaunting the temptation that painted her expression. She lowered her stare, peeking at him from narrowed eyes.

"Cat got your tongue?"

Ethan took a deep breath. "Woman, are you purposely trying to give me a heart attack?"

Bianca laughed, feigning innocence. "What? What did I do?"

He gestured with both hands, fanning them up and then down. "My God, are you beautiful!" he exclaimed, no other words coming to his mind in that moment.

Her smile widened. "Thank you. I wasn't sure about this one, but if you like it . . ."

"Like it? Hell, I'll buy you one in every color if you want me to!"

Bianca laughed heartily. She moved forward, easing her body over his. As she straddled one leg to his left and the other to his right, Ethan felt like he might combust, every nerve ending on the verge of explosion. She wrapped one arm around his neck as the other teased the buttons on his oxford shirt.

Eye to eye with him, she shifted against him, her pelvis pressed tight against his hardened member. The touch was intoxicating, both consumed with desire so intense that it was palpable. She leaned in close, brushing her check against his, skin teasing skin. Ethan's breath came in a low pant as he bit down against his bottom lip.

Just as Bianca leaned in as though she intended to kiss his mouth, there was a knock on the dressing room door. The harsh rap startled them both, Bianca sliding off his lap and taking a step back.

The redhead's voice echoed from the other side. "Excuse me, ma'am, but only one person is allowed in a dressing room at a time. Your husband will have to wait out here."

Bianca tossed her head back against her shoulders,

shaking it slowly from side to side. "Thank you," she called out. "Sorry about that."

Ethan stood up. He took a deep breath, his hand pressed at his crotch as he adjusted himself. As he stepped past her, he drew his hand across her breast, his fingers lightly caressing the round of lush tissue. Bianca's eyes widened, air catching in her chest. Her smile widened.

He leaned to whisper in her ear, his lips pressed to the side of her face. "I'll be outside, *Mrs.* Christmas."

When Bianca exited the dressing room Ethan was still beet red, his cheeks heated with color. He held his jacket folded over his arms, hanging low in front of himself. The redhead was chatting him up in conversation, but it was obvious that he wasn't paying her an ounce of attention, his thoughts still focused on their earlier encounter.

"How did everything fit?" the woman asked, turning her attention to Bianca.

"Perfect. I'll take everything," she said.

Ethan nodded. "Excuse me, but do you have that red one in any other colors?"

The woman turned. "It does come in black."

"She'll take it in black, too," he said.

Bianca laughed.

Minutes later, the redhead wished them both a happy holiday as she left them and their selections at the counter. The young woman at the register gave them a bright smile.

"Did you find everything you were looking for?" she asked as she began to ring up Bianca's purchases.

Bianca nodded. "I did. Thank you."

Ethan reached over the counter and passed the young woman his credit card.

Bianca tossed him a look. "That's not necessary."

"Oh, it's definitely necessary. Consider it an early Christmas present."

Bianca smiled. "Thank you. That's so sweet."

As the salesclerk passed him his card and receipt, she tossed Bianca a smile. "You're lucky. I don't think my father would ever buy lingerie for me," she said.

Ethan's eyes widened, his mouth falling open with shock. Bianca burst out laughing, slapping her hand over her mouth. She was still laughing when he snatched the shopping bag from the counter and headed toward the door. The salesclerk eyed them both nervously.

"He's not my father," Bianca said as she turned to follow him out.

Behind them, she could hear the two saleswomen talking, the redhead correcting the other woman's mistake. "That's her husband!" the young woman whispered loudly.

At the door, Bianca caught up with Ethan, who looked like he'd been slapped twice. He cut his eyes at her. "That wasn't funny!"

"That was really funny."

"I do not look *that* old."

"No, you don't. You actually look very good for your age."

"I don't find that mess funny."

Bianca's smile was miles wide and she giggled. "It was funny."

He stood staring at her. The light in her eyes was electrifying and her laugh was engaging. Joy filled her face and flooded her spirit. He found everything about her intoxicating. He took a deep breath.

"So maybe it was a little funny," he finally said. "I can't help it if you don't look that mature. You still look like a teenager."

She slapped him playfully in the chest. "Oh, don't

get it twisted. This isn't about how I look!" She took a step toward him, her arms slipping around his waist. "Besides, when we were in that dressing room I'm *sure* I looked *very* mature!"

With his head tilted slightly back and his eyes lifted toward the ceiling, Ethan thought back to that moment. Heat rushed through his southern quadrant with a vengeance. He dropped his gaze back to her face, her expression speaking volumes. He nodded. "Yes, you did," he said. "You looked amazing!"

"I thought I'd give you something to think about when you go to sleep tonight."

"You made sure that thinking about you will keep me up all night, is what you did."

She smiled. "Mission accomplished. When a man as honorable as you are is willing to lie to see you, you have to give him something special."

They were holding hands as they walked the mall's perimeter, maneuvering past holiday shoppers and peering into the windows to admire the seasonal displays. The level of comfort they shared was exceeded only by the sexual tension that danced its own dance between them. Conversation came easily, expounded by the subtle innuendo and overt teasing that kept the duo laughing warmly. Hours later, Bianca was grateful that she'd come to meet him, loving that he'd wanted to enjoy her company as much as she was enjoying his.

Ethan walked her to her car, his hand resting on the open driver's side door. "Thank you," he said.

"For what?"

"For a great night. I had a lot of fun. Shopping with you is definitely an experience."

She giggled. "But you did finish all of your shopping."

"Yes, I did. And I think Jarrod will really like the present you helped me pick out."

Bianca took a quick glance down to her wristwatch. "I should probably be going. I'm sure my mother is chomping at the bit wondering where I disappeared to."

Ethan nodded as he stared into her eyes. She had beautiful eyes, and he found it easy to lose himself in their depths.

"I really should be going," she whispered softly.

Ethan shook his head. "What are we doing, Bianca? Is this a game?"

She inhaled deeply. "The only time I do games well, Ethan, is when I have a willing partner."

He nodded. "So you're not going to break my heart?"

The smile she gave him was sweet and endearing. "Your heart is safe with me, Ethan. You can trust that," she whispered softly.

As he smiled back, Bianca reached up to give him a gentle kiss on the cheek. Then she slid into the driver's seat of her car, waved good-bye, and headed home.

Chapter 6

The Christmas oratorio was being performed in the sanctuary of the Biltmore United Methodist Church. The place was packed, with seating by voice type on the main floor, surrounding the small orchestra, and with a few onlookers in the balcony. There was a slew of soloists of mixed quality who occupied the front pews. In the orchestra there was a harpsichordist, an organist, a cellist, the concertmaster, and a trumpet player. The rest of the orchestra was populated by some of the region's leading freelancers, many of whom had years of experience with the music, and other artists at varying stages of musical and technical development. It was a motley crew of performers who came to sing and play from their heart, moved by the spirit of the season.

Ethan looked particularly dashing in a black tuxedo. He was polished and pretty, and as she sat waiting for the evening's performance to begin, Bianca found herself fantasizing about the two of them together, the thoughts deviously decadent.

Meeting the look she was giving him, Ethan tossed his hand up shyly, waving in her direction. He'd noticed her the minute she'd arrived, taken aback by her stunning appearance. The dress she wore was red velvet and formfitting, complemented by four-inch love-me pumps that accentuated her toned legs. She'd pulled the length of her hair back in a slick ponytail that was braided down her back. Her makeup was tasteful, and simple diamond drop earrings pierced her lobes. She was intoxicatingly beautiful, and as he stole glances in her direction he was suddenly fearful of being too distracted to sing. He took a deep breath and tore his eyes away.

He turned abruptly, almost slamming directly into his son. Jarrod looked distressed.

"Yo! Sorry about that. I didn't see you standing there," Ethan said. "Are you all right, son?"

"Just a little nervous. It's been a long time since I've sung in public."

His father smiled. "You'll be just fine. I don't think you realize just how talented you are."

He shrugged his shoulders, not overly convinced. "How soon before this thing starts? I need to make a phone call."

Ethan tossed a quick glance around the room and down to his watch. "You've got a good ten minutes. People are still coming, and we advertised that we'd begin promptly at seven."

Jarrod slapped his father warmly against his arm. "It shouldn't take that long. I'll be right back."

Ethan nodded.

"Hey, did you see Bianca?" Jarrod asked, pointing in her direction.

Ethan's head continued to bob up and down against his thick neck. "Yes, I did."

"She looks great, doesn't she?"

Ethan was still nodding, his gaze having shifted back

to Bianca. "She's absolutely gorgeous," he said, his tone wistful.

His son laughed. "Down, boy! You do need to focus."

Ethan laughed with him. "I'm trying, son. Believe me, I'm really trying."

The two men hugged before Jarrod turned and headed out the sanctuary doors, his cell phone in hand as he exited the room.

Ethan heaved another deep breath. His own cell phone suddenly vibrated in his breast pocket. Reaching for the device he pulled it to his ear. "Hello?"

"You look good, Mr. Christmas!"

He grinned as he turned his eyes back to Bianca. "Thank you. And you are stunning. Red is a beautiful color on you."

"I figured we should both look pretty when you take me to dinner after this sing-ding thing."

He chuckled softly and his voice dropped to a low whisper. "You don't know how badly I want to come up there and kiss you right now."

"Come on." Her tone was teasing. "We could give this small town something to talk about in case someone sings off-key tonight or the tuba player down there blows a wrong note and ruins the performance."

Ethan laughed. "There is no tuba player. That's a trumpet."

"Same difference. He blows wind and it's loud."

"I see we're going to have to work on your musical appreciation."

"I'm sure I can find a few things you can help me work on, Mr. Christmas."

The lights overhead suddenly flickered on and off, indicating it was time for the show to begin.

"Break a leg, handsome," Bianca said.

He was still staring as she blew him a kiss and winked her eye.

As they disconnected the call and Ethan turned his attention to the orchestra, Jarrod came back through the door. His face was reddened and he was obviously flustered. He tossed Bianca a wide-eyed look, his gaze sweeping between her and the back of his father's head as he tossed up his hands in frustration.

Uneasiness washed over Bianca's face. Her gaze narrowed as she mouthed her concern, a silent *Are you okay?* blowing past her lips.

Jarrod shook his head no as he began to type a text message. He'd just pushed the send button when his father gestured for his attention and Mrs. Florence Peacock, the ceremony mistress, signaled for the opening of the show.

Ethan's voice was pure silk. His tone was full and rich as it echoed out of the microphone and around the room. He stood there, tall and magnanimous, his eyes closed as he belted out a pitch-perfect concerto. Bianca had never heard anything as beautiful. The repertoire of music was full of passion and drama, the works of music inspiring. She was filled with such awe and reverie that tears misted her eyes. The entire room overflowed with holiday spirit against the backdrop of twinkling white lights and the aroma of sweet pine that wafted through the room.

She was so distracted by the sheer magnitude of the evening, it wasn't until the room stood for the "Hallelujah Chorus" that Bianca remembered the incoming text message on her phone. Staring down at the device, she read the message Jarrod had sent. Then she read it a second time, a smile pulling at her lips as amusement danced in her eyes. Jarrod's boyfriend was coming for Christmas!

* * *

Both Bianca and Jarrod watched as Ethan strolled the length of the restaurant, heading in the direction of the men's restroom. When he was out of sight, Jarrod's head snapped in her direction.

"What am I going to do, Bianca?"

She leaned back in her seat. "I told you, secrets always come back to bite you. Just tell your father the truth. I'm sure it'll just be fine."

"You don't know my father like I do."

"I know your father loves you. I also know that he is a very kind and generous man with a compassionate spirit. He's also open-minded and non-judgmental. I don't see that you'll have a problem."

"My father is a card-carrying, Bible-thumping Christian. He subscribes to the biblical teachings that he was raised on, and he is not going to just accept that he has a gay son."

Bianca shook her head. "I think you're wrong. I'm willing to bet that your father's love for you will transcend any other feelings that he might have about your sexuality."

Jarrod heaved a deep breath, tears burning hot behind his eyelids. "I'm not ready for this, Bianca." He suddenly thought back to the conversation he'd had earlier with his partner. Dr. Stefan Hunter had called to say that he was coming to Boone to be with Jarrod for Christmas. An unexpected schedule change had given him a whole week off. There had been no changing his mind.

"Then tell him not to come," Bianca said. "If your boyfriend loves you, he'll understand."

Jarrod shook his head. "Do you know I've met Stefan's entire family? I call his parents Mom and Dad.

His twin sister will text me every day. Her children call me Uncle Jarrod. I cannot tell him that I'm afraid to introduce him to my father. I don't want him to know that I'm scared to death that my father is going to reject him, and me."

Bianca reached across the table and dropped her hand atop his. Her touch was soothing, and Jarrod clasped her fingers tightly between his own.

"Ethan is not going to reject you. Tell your father, but don't wait until Stefan is standing on your doorstep. Tell him now."

Before either could say another word, Ethan was re-crossing the room toward the table. Bianca gave Jarrod one last look, her eyebrows raised. She pulled her hand back into her lap, the gesture catching Ethan's eye.

Ethan looked from one to the other as he returned to his seat. The air was thick with tension, giving him reason to pause. "What's going on?" he asked, looking first at Jarrod and then Bianca. "You two okay?"

Bianca nodded. "We're good. Jarrod was just saying . . ."

"I was telling Bianca how much we appreciated her coming out to support us tonight," Jarrod said, interrupting. He gave her a quick look before shifting his eyes toward his father.

Ethan nodded. "I hope you had a good time," he said, turning to give her a smile.

She nodded. "I really did. You both sang beautifully. My mother actually got this one right. I had such a good time."

"Jarrod doesn't appreciate just how good he is," Ethan noted, paternal pride gleaming from his eyes.

His son rolled his eyes skyward as he lifted his wine-glass to take a sip.

She smiled. "You're quite the crooner yourself!"

Ethan brushed the backs of his fingers against the lapels of his tuxedo jacket. "I try," he said, grinning broadly.

A round of laughter rang across the table.

"So, who's having dessert?" Ethan asked.

"I'm going to pass," Jarrod said, shifting his chair back from the table. "I'm actually going to turn in early. It's been a long day."

"Don't rush off!" Bianca exclaimed. "The evening is still young."

"Are you sure, son? Bianca said she was going to take us dancing after this. It should be quite entertaining since you know I don't dance."

Jarrod laughed. "Don't believe that, Bianca. He can dance almost as well as he can sing."

"I'm not bad, but I'm definitely no Fred Astaire," Ethan chuckled.

Bianca's brow furrowed slightly. "Who's Fred Astaire?" she asked, her tone teasing.

Jarrod laughed. "Before our time, Bianca. Before our time."

"No, you didn't!" Ethan exclaimed, the trio laughing heartily.

"I did," Jarrod said as he leaned to kiss his father's cheek. The two men hugged warmly. "I'll see you in the morning, Dad. You and Bianca have fun tonight."

Jarrod leaned to give Bianca a kiss on her cheek. The two exchanged a look between them. Promising to give her a call, Jarrod waved good-bye to them both and headed for the exit.

After Jarrod was gone, an awkward lull fell over the table. Ethan and Bianca sat staring at each other, neither saying a word. The moment was interrupted when their waiter stepped forward with the dessert menu. After ordering two slices of New York–style cheesecake, both sat savoring the decadent dessert accompanied by freshly poured coffee steaming in oversized mugs.

"This is really good!" Bianca purred. "I really like this place."

"Me, too. It's one of my favorite restaurants," Ethan said.

She reached her fork across the table, lifting one of the strawberries from his plate. Pulling it to her mouth, she teased it with her tongue before allowing it to slip past her lips. Amused, Ethan watched as she chewed it slowly, her eyes locked with his.

"So you're eating my cake," he said when she reached for a second bite.

She shrugged her shoulders slightly. "I know what my cake tastes like. I just thought I'd try yours."

"I think you just get a kick out of teasing me."

"That I do," she responded, a seductive smirk pulling at her lips.

He nodded. "Not to dampen the mood," he started as he laid his own fork against the plate, "but did Jarrod seem out of sorts to you? I got the feeling something's going on with him."

Her eyes flitted from side to side as she pondered how to answer his question. "I think he has a lot on his mind," she said finally, lifting her gaze back to his. "You should talk to him."

"Did he say something to you?"

"He said he had a lot on his mind." She smiled.

"You two are quite comfortable with each other, aren't you?"

"Are you jealous?"

"Should I be?"

"I hope not. I think that would be a little weird."

"Me, too."

That blanket of silence dropped back between them.

Ethan broke the silence. "I know I told you this earlier, but you look absolutely stunning tonight, Bianca," he said, his voice a loud whisper. "You're the most beautiful woman in the room."

Bianca smiled, a hint of blush warming her cheeks. "Thank you."

Ethan twisted his cloth napkin nervously between his two hands. "You really have me feeling some kind of way."

She grinned, leaning forward in her seat. She dropped a warm palm against his knee. She gestured with her other hand, a crooked finger motioning for him to come closer. When he leaned in, mere inches separating them, Bianca gave him a wink of her eye, that index finger caressing the profile of his face.

"You're not feeling anything yet! Just wait until I get you on the dance floor, Ethan Christmas!"

Hearing the front door close, Sharon Torres called her daughter's name. Bianca stood in the front foyer with her high heels in her hand. She blew a heavy sigh, having no interest in dealing with her mother at this late hour. When her mother called a second time, she moved into the family room, finding the matriarch waiting in her wheelchair, a hardcover book in her hands. In the corner the Christmas tree flickered softly, the bright white lights illuminating the space with a warm glow.

"Hey, why are you still up?" Bianca asked, dropping onto the loveseat.

"I was waiting to hear how your evening went. Did you have a good time?"

Bianca nodded. "I really did. The Messiah Open

Sing was spectacular. Ethan was brilliant! He and
Jarrod both have magnificent voices! Then we went to
Limones for dinner. After that, we went to Tressa's.
They had a live jazz band tonight."

Her mother clapped excitedly. "That's great! I'm
glad you had a good time."

"I did. I'm glad you made me go."

"So things with you and Jarrod are good?"

Bianca smiled. She blew another low sigh. "Things
with Jarrod and I are fine, Mom. We're friends and
that's as far as our relationship is going."

"It probably just takes a little more effort from you,
Bianca. He's a doctor!"

Bianca laughed. "He could be a plumber and it
wouldn't make any difference. He's not interested in
me like that, and I'm very comfortable just being his
friend. Neither one of us needs you playing matchmaker."

"That's not what I was doing, Bianca."

"Yes, you were, and you need to stop. I really don't
have any problems finding a man, Mom. I'm just not
ready for a serious relationship right now."

"So when are you going to be ready, Bianca? You're
not getting any younger, daughter."

Bianca laughed again. "Good night, Mom!" she said
as she moved back onto her feet and headed in the
direction of her room.

"I'm still talking to you, Bianca."

"We can talk in the morning, Mom. I'm exhausted.
Take your meds and go to sleep. Please."

When Bianca closed and locked her bedroom door,
her mother was still calling her name. Stripping out
of her clothes she crawled into bed, her mind muddled.
Thoughts of Ethan consumed her and she hadn't
wanted her mother's dramatics to crush the decadent

thoughts she was having of him and her together. It had been a very good night and all Bianca wanted was to fall asleep fantasizing about Ethan and how their being together could get even better.

When Ethan finally found his way home, Jarrod was sleeping soundly, having passed out on the living room sofa. He snored loudly, his body clearly craving a good night's rest. After tossing a warm blanket over his only child, Ethan cut off the lights that blazed brightly in the room and headed up to his own bed.

After a quick shower, he lay himself down, pulling the blankets up beneath his chin. He was anxious for sleep himself, his body in a state of complete chaos. Being with Bianca had left him in turmoil, his muscles knotted so tight that every joint was cramped.

They'd danced cheek to cheek, every inch of her cradled against him as if they were one body instead of two. She'd fit in his arms as if she'd been born to be there, and he'd held on to her, unwilling to let go. The music had been slow and seductive. They'd done a dirty shimmy, pelvis to pelvis, the rich bass guiding them across the dance floor. As they closed down the club, it had taken every ounce of his fortitude not to take her right there. He'd wanted nothing more than to make the sweetest love to her.

He blew a sigh as he rolled against the mattress, his hand palming his hardened member. He stroked himself gently, wishing it was Bianca's hand wrapped around his manhood. As the tension began to finally subside, he rolled onto his stomach and drifted off to sleep.

Chapter 7

Ethan buttered two slices of whole wheat toast, adding them to a plate of eggs he'd just scrambled. He sat down with a cup of hot coffee, slowly savoring his breakfast. He lifted his hand in greeting as Jarrod entered the room.

"Good morning, son," he said. "How'd you sleep?"

"I really slept well once I got off the couch and got in my bed."

"I don't know why you keep falling asleep on the sofa. You've done that since you were in high school."

Jarrod shrugged as he poured his own cup of coffee and sat down at the table with his father. "So what's on your agenda today?"

"I have some shopping I need to get done, but that's all."

Jarrod nodded. "I'm done with my shopping and I have no desire to deal with the crowds. You have fun with that!"

Ethan smiled. "It's not that bad. I think it adds to the holiday fun."

"If you say so."

Ethan took a sip of his drink, slightly slurping the hot beverage. "Do you have any plans?"

"I'm going to spend some time at the children's cancer clinic this afternoon. I don't know if you remember my friend Tyler, but he's the admission's director there and he invited me to visit. Dr. Malcolm Prince leads their medical team."

"Dr. Prince was one of your professors at Johns Hopkins, wasn't he?" his father said, the name vaguely familiar.

Jarrod nodded his head. "He was. He was a great mentor and I'm looking forward to seeing him again."

Ethan took a bite of his toast and eggs before continuing. "Tomorrow I need to go check on the cabins. They say we have some bad weather coming in. Do you feel like driving up with me?"

Jarrod hesitated. "Actually I have a friend coming into town. I promised I'd pick him up from the train station. I was actually going to talk to you about him spending Christmas with us. I hope it's not a problem."

"Of course not! You know any friend of yours is always welcome here."

His son smiled. "I know, but there's still some things I'd like to speak with you about before he gets here. Maybe we can do dinner tonight? I can grab a couple of steaks and we can grill."

"Definitely! Let's plan on it."

"Thanks, Dad!"

Ethan nodded. He glanced down to his wristwatch. "I need to get out of here," he said, rising from his seat. "You have a good time today," he said as he slapped his son on the shoulder.

Jarrod smiled. "You, too, Dad! You, too!"

* * *

Bianca stood in line at the Belk department store, waiting for her last gift to be wrapped. It cost extra for the service. Her mother would consider it to be a waste, but it saved Bianca a few hours of much-needed time.

As she watched the salesclerk select a box and then tear off a length of silver wrapping paper, she was oblivious to Ethan moving to stand behind her. His hands eased around her waist, his fingers resting gingerly atop her belly button. He pressed his lips to the back of her neck, inhaling the sweet scent of her perfume.

"Do I know you?" she quipped, a sly smile pulling at her lips.

Ethan chuckled softly into her ear. "Probably not. I thought you were my wife."

"Your wife must be a very lucky woman," Bianca purred.

She tilted her head slightly, allowing him better access to her neck. His touch was heated, a delicate caress that burned hot with anticipation. Biting down against her bottom lip, she didn't miss the curious look the saleswoman was shooting in her direction.

"I missed you," Ethan finally whispered in her ear before taking two steps back to allow a waft of cool air to billow between them.

Bianca smiled. "So what brings you here?" she said, spinning around to face him.

"Last-minute Christmas shopping."

"You and me both. I can't believe Christmas is just a few days away."

"It came fast, and I still have work I need to get done."

"What work do you have to do, Ethan?"

"I need to check on some property before the weather turns. They're predicting some major snow,

and I need to make sure my investments are secure."
He changed the subject. "So, what did you buy me?"

Bianca laughed warmly. "I actually found the perfect
present for my best friend. Cilla has an impressive
collection of blue glass and they had a beautiful platter
that will be a nice addition to the other pieces she has."

"I can't wait to meet your friends," Ethan said, earn-
ing him a wide smile from her.

She nodded. "How's Jarrod?"

"He's good. He's visiting at the hospital today. I was
hoping he'd ride up the mountain with me, but he says
he has plans. Some friend of his is coming into town. I
swear the boy comes home and everyone else sees him
more than I do."

Bianca's head shook from side to side. "I'll ride
shotgun if you want some company," she said.

Ethan grinned. "Are you sure? I know your mother's
been keeping you busy."

"I'm positive. My uncle and his wife get in tonight.
She'll have more than enough help."

"Great! I can pick you up in the morning."

"I'll meet you at your house. It'll be much less complicated."

"You need to tell them, Bianca!" he exclaimed.

Bianca didn't respond, just smiled and turned to the
woman who gestured that her package was ready.

The two women were laughing heartily together.

"So you and this man have been hanging out together since you got there and you haven't gotten one
kiss yet? I find that really hard to believe." Cilla Jameson
laughed again.

"I know, right! It's absolutely crazy, but there's something really special about him, Cilla."

"Is that because he's old enough to be your father? Or because he's old enough to be your father? I never pegged you for having daddy issues, Bianca. You've always had a great relationship with your father."

"That's the thing. I'm never reminded of his age when we're together. He's just a good time and we have fun together. And he's sexy as hell! The man is *foine*!"

"Obviously he's not that good of a time since you two are still in the hand-holding stage. Especially since patience isn't one of your strong suits. Or is that him being old-fashioned about sex?"

"Ethan's quite the gentleman, but there's nothing prudish about him, if that's what you're asking. I think when it happens it'll just be that the moment is right and we're both ready. There's nothing wrong with us taking things slow."

"Where's Bianca Torres? What have you done with my best friend?"

"You're making fun of me when I'm being serious."

"I'm serious, too. You have always been the queen of hit it and quit it. Being in the moment and getting yours. Now you're talking about perfect moments and the timing being right. You sound like a romance novel and my friend Bianca has never been interested in romance!"

"I have, too!"

"Do you remember Dante?"

"Who?"

"Dante Pierce, the short little cutie that used to dance at Club Solas?"

Bianca winced. "Don't go there."

"I'm going there. Brother had it so bad for you that he would have washed your dirty drawers. He had your wedding planned, knew how many babies the two of you were going to raise and what you were going to be doing in retirement and you had only known each other for three hours!"

Bianca laughed. "It was not that bad."

"Yes, it was. You were three sheets to the wind when you and some random guy got your groove on in the parking lot of Waffle House while Dante was bumrushing everyone inside the club trying to find you. Dante was pure romance the way that man fawned all over you, and you wouldn't give him a hint of a chance."

"Dante was just a momentary distraction. You remember him better than I do."

"My point, Bianca, is that you have always been impulsive, slightly obsessive, and extremely crazy. You've never been afraid to just do you. That's the Bianca I know."

"Well, you need to give a girl a break. Obviously, I've had some moments that I'm not proud of, but I'm trying to change my wanton ways. When you know better, you do better."

Cilla chuckled softly. "Bianca Torres! What is that I hear in your voice?"

"What?"

"You sound quite responsible. There's an air of maturity there. Have you," Cilla gasped with exaggeration, "dare I say it? Have you fallen in love?"

There was a moment of silence that filtered over the phone line between them.

"There's just something about him, Cilla," Bianca repeated, her voice dropping an octave.

Excitement rang in Cilla's tone. "You've fallen in love!"

"Girl, hush your mouth! You know we do not use

that four-letter word. If I were there, I'd wash your mouth out with soap and water!"

"Bianca's in love! Bianca's in love! Bianca's in love," Cilla chanted.

Bianca shook her head. "I thought you were my friend. I'm not talking to you anymore." She laughed, her cheeks warm.

The laughter between them continued, the wealth of it abundant and easy.

"Bianca?" Cilla called her friend's name one last time.

"What?"

"I'm happy for you, girl, so please don't blow it. From everything you told me, he really does sound like a great guy."

Bianca smiled into the receiver. "I know, right!"

Jarrod dialed his father's number, making another attempt to reach the man. This time, Ethan answered on the second ring.

"Hey, son!"

"Hey, Dad."

"What time are you coming home?"

"That's why I was calling. I tried to reach you earlier to see if we could reschedule dinner. I'm still here at the hospital."

"Not a problem. I got stuck in a meeting myself and missed your first two calls. Did you want to do a late dinner?"

"I'm actually headed to dinner with Dr. Prince and Tyler. They have a fascinating program here and I'm learning a lot from them."

"It's no problem. I don't feel abandoned at all."

Jarrod chuckled. "Okay, make me feel guilty. I promise I'll make it up to you. Maybe we can do breakfast before you leave in the morning. I really do need to talk to you."

"Is everything okay, Jarrod?" Concern suddenly rang in Ethan's voice. "I know something's been on your mind for a few days now."

"Fine. Everything's fine. It's nothing serious," Jarrod answered with a heavy sigh, the little white lie feeling like a lead weight hanging over his spirit. "I just need . . . I just need some advice about my career is all."

There was a momentary pause between them before Ethan finally responded.

"Depending on what time you get in tonight, we can do hot chocolate and popcorn, like the old days. If it's too late, then we can do breakfast."

"Thanks, Dad!"

"Stay safe, son. I love you!"

"I love you, too!"

"Don't you want to help me sneak out?" Bianca asked, shifting her cell phone from one ear to the other. She settled her back against the mound of pillows that decorated the bed in her room.

Ethan laughed. "Are you planning to crawl out the window or something?"

"Or something! If I don't, I'm going to go crazy."

"It can't be that bad, Bianca!"

"You haven't met my uncle Barber yet, have you?"

"Actually, we have met. He and your aunt were visiting over the summer. He played golf with me and your father. He seems like a nice guy."

"When he's not discussing my child-bearing hips and tapping me on my ass, he's a really great guy!"

Ethan laughed. "Oh, he's that kind of uncle!"

"Exactly! Which is why I might need a safe haven to run to."

"Well, you can always count on me to come to your rescue."

"Can I really?"

"Without fail. And I come with a red cape and tights for your rescuing pleasure."

Bianca laughed warmly. "Tights, too! Now I'm excited!"

"I've got a slight hard-on myself!"

Bianca gasped. "Ethan Christmas!"

He shook his head. "That was slightly crass. I apologize."

She was still giggling. "Apology accepted. But now you have me intrigued! Tell me more!"

It was late when the two finished talking and wished each other a good night. They'd talked into the wee hours of the morning, their conversation branching in a million different directions. From cartoons to politics, no subject had been off limits, a few sometimes moving him, her, or both to blush profusely. Once or twice, Bianca found herself giggling with glee, feeling as if she'd gotten the attention of her celebrity crush. She'd been excited and emotional and completely out of control as Ethan had pushed her out of her comfort zone and she'd pushed back. For everything they didn't have in common, every subject that had been debated vigorously, there were as many likes that they did share. The only thing that could have made the time better was if they'd been in the same room, side by side, relishing each other's company as they traded easy caresses back and forth.

Saying good night and disconnecting their call had come with much hesitation. But with a plan in place to spend the next day together, they wished each other well, excited for the night to end and the new day's sun that would see them together again.

Chapter 8

A cold front promising ice and snow was inching in their direction. Although Boone was known for getting much snow in the nearby mountainous ski resorts, the downtown area was usually sheltered from the worst winter temperatures. Its elevation variance seemed to insulate the small town, with typical snowfalls fleeting but spectacular. This storm was going to be different, however; the local weathermen were issuing all kinds of warnings to prepare residents and visitors for the blizzard that was about to pummel them.

Bianca noted the drastic change in temperature, that the air was cold and heavy with moisture. Gone was the temperate that had her in a wool blazer the day before and now in her mother's down-filled, insulated parka. She inhaled, filling her lungs with the cold air.

Ethan laughed at her. "You look like Nanook of the North," he said teasingly. He eyed her from head to toe. Her denim jeans were tucked into UGG Adirondack boots and a black turtleneck peeked out of the collar of her practical, hip-length, winter coat. Her curls were trapped beneath a black, faux-fur trapper hat that completely covered her head, sitting low on her forehead with flaps that draped over her ears. A red wool scarf was knotted around her neck, completing her winter ensemble.

"I feel like a polar bear. This is absolutely ridiculous!" She rolled her eyes, her arms wrapped tightly around her torso, her glove-covered hands tucked beneath her armpits. "I hate the cold!"

"It's just cold," he said. "But I warmed the car especially for you."

"Good," she said as she moved in the direction of his SUV. "And I hope you pumped the temperature to super high!"

Behind her, Ethan was still laughing. He reached for the passenger door, pulling it open. As she slid inside, he tapped her backside, giving her a wink of his eye.

"What was that for?" She grinned, eyeing him sheepishly as she palmed the spot he'd just slapped.

"I didn't want Uncle Barber to be the only one admiring my woman's backside," he said.

"Your woman?" Bianca laughed, a loud chortle that spilled from somewhere deep in her gut.

"Damn right!" Ethan said as he laughed with her. He closed the car door and sauntered to the other side of the vehicle, sliding in behind the steering wheel. With a bright smile, he dropped a warm palm against her upper thigh and gave it a quick squeeze before starting the ignition.

"You couldn't change Jarrod's mind about coming?" she asked as he checked his rearview mirror and backed out of the driveway.

He shook his head. "I don't know what time he came in last night, but he is knocked out cold. I tried to wake him twice. He'd said he wanted to talk about something, but I guess it'll have to wait."

She nodded. "Did he say what?"

"No, just that it had something to do with his career. I think he might be considering moving back here and working at the children's cancer clinic. One of their doctors is someone he admires, and I suspect that he's been thinking about working with the man."

Bianca's gaze shifted out the window. She hated knowing Jarrod's secret and not being able to tell his father. She found herself feeling out of sorts about keeping things from Ethan. She liked that they were so open and honest with each other, and she wanted to keep it that way. She blew a soft sigh.

"So what did you tell your mother?" Ethan asked, cutting his eyes in her direction.

"I told her that I was spending the day with a friend."

"But you didn't tell her that friend was me, right?"

"Not outright."

"So she probably assumes you're spending the day with my son?"

Bianca shrugged her narrow shoulders. "Are you going to ruin the start of our trip by making me feel bad? Because what my mother thinks really isn't important. What is important is that I'm spending my day with you. My mother is not going to miss me. She's too busy catching up with my aunt and uncle."

He sighed. "There isn't going to be an argument. I want us to have a good time and I don't want to ruin the holiday. But the day after Christmas I'm telling both of your parents. We can't keep lying to them, Bianca."

Bianca's head snapped in his direction. Her mouth opened and then closed, once twice, and then a third time, making her look like a fish out of water gasping for air. She finally turned back to stare out the window, having no words to convince him otherwise. She hated to admit it, but she knew he was right. There was nothing she could say.

"So, where are we actually going?" she asked, finally breaking the silence that had dropped between them.

He tossed her a quick glance. "I own one hundred acres of mountain land adjoining the Blue Ridge strip of North Carolina's Appalachian Mountains and the Mountains-to-Sea Trail. And on that acreage I have twenty-five private, luxury mountain cabins, a fully stocked trout pond, and some natural waterfalls. Usually those cabins are rented out through the year, and most of them are rented out now for the holidays. But I have two of them that are vacant and my property manager left for the Virgin Islands yesterday. With the inclement weather coming, I need to make sure those two homes are secure."

Taking it all in, Bianca sat staring at him, her eyes blinking rapidly. A hundred acres, twenty-five cabins, and a pond with some fish. She was both awed and confused, a ton of questions flooding her thoughts.

Ethan tossed her a look, amused by the expression on her face. He laughed out loud. "What's wrong? You look like you want to say something."

She bit back her first thought to ask her second. "You don't need to check the other twenty-three properties?" she said, her gaze still locked on the side of his face.

He shook his head no. "Everyone up there is a repeat renter. They know what to do."

"Just how much property do you actually own?" she asked, her third thought slipping past her lips.

He laughed again. "Where? Here in Boone?"

"You have property in other places, too?"

He nodded. "New York, Miami, Dallas, Los Angeles,

Chicago, and internationally I own buildings in London, Italy, Germany, Switzerland, and Morocco."

"Morocco?"

"Have you ever been?"

"No, but it's on my bucket list of places to visit before I'm fifty."

"Then I'll have to take you. Before you're fifty, of course."

There was an amused smirk on her face, but she didn't bother to respond.

"So what else is on your pre-fifty bucket list?" Ethan asked as he flipped on his windshield wipers, the falling precipitation beginning to get heavier.

She grinned, her smile wide and bright. "I want to visit Morocco, Mozambique, and do an African safari in Maasai territory. I also want to learn how to make pasta with Chef Mario Batali, take golf lessons from Tiger Woods, and ride in a race car with Bill Lester."

Ethan laughed, thoroughly amused. He nodded his head. "I'd love to make all of that happen," he said. "We can call Bill as soon as we get back."

Bianca laughed with him. "You don't know Bill Lester."

"Yes, I do. He and I are old friends."

"Prove it."

"Grab my cell phone," he said. "You'll find his name in my contact list."

Bianca reached for his cell phone and began to scroll through his lengthy list of contacts. Sure enough, the name Bill Lester was listed between Laurie Landry and Thomas Lions.

She pushed the dial button, pulling the phone to her ear. Ethan shook his head.

"Yes, Bill Lester, please," she asked when the line

was answered on the other end. "Mr. Ethan Christmas calling."

Her eyes were suddenly wide as she clamped her hand over the device. Her grin was miles wide. "He says he'll speak to you."

Ethan laughed as he pushed the button for his Bluetooth, engaging the phone through his car so that it was on speaker. "Hey, Bill, Merry Christmas!"

"It's good to hear from you, Ethan. How are things?"

"I can't complain. How's the family?"

"The boys are good and Cheryl is happy."

"Glad to hear it. And business, how's that going? You still driving?"

"You know it. I'm thinking about buying a race track. I might need some investors! Men like you with deep pockets!"

Ethan laughed. "I'll be down in Florida in a few weeks and I hope we can catch up with each other when I get there. You can tell me then how deep I'm going to have to dig into these pockets."

"Let's plan on it. I think you still owe me a drink anyway. You lost a bet if I remember correctly."

Ethan laughed again. "I don't remember that."

"I think her name was Lucy or Lacey or something like that."

"Say no more. Memory jogged," Ethan responded with a nervous chuckle. "I definitely owe you."

"It's a date. By the way, when did you get a secretary?"

Ethan tossed a look in Bianca's direction. "I didn't. I got a new girlfriend."

His friend named Bill laughed. "Say no more. Completely understood. I can't wait to meet her!"

"Kiss your wife for me and you have a great holiday!"

Disconnecting the call, Ethan reached for his phone, pulling it from her hands. "Do we need to call Mario now?"

"You know Mario, too?"

"He catered my fiftieth birthday party."

"I'm done with you, Ethan Christmas!" She tossed up her hands, her face gleaming with joy.

"What?" he said with a deep chuckle. "I don't know Tiger personally, but I'm sure I know someone who knows someone who knows him. I figure we can knock out that bucket list before you're forty, and then you'll have to think of some other things to do before you're fifty."

Amusement danced across her face, the joy teasing. "You are truly special, Ethan!" she said teasingly.

He tossed her another quick look and a smile, then refocused his eyes back on the road. Outside, it looked like a winter wonderland run amuck. Thick snow blanketed the grass and trees, covering everything that was standing still. They were climbing steadily upward, the journey to the mountaintop suddenly feeling precarious. Since leaving the city limits, Bianca had been able to count on one hand the number of cars they shared the road with, and for the first time since they'd departed, the trip was making her uneasy.

"It's getting nasty out there," she said as Ethan slowed his speed substantially.

He nodded in agreement. "There's a layer of ice on the road, too. It's slicker than I expected."

"Should we turn around?"

"No, we're not too far from the first house," he said. "I think we'll be okay."

Minutes later, he turned onto a private road. He shifted his vehicle into four-wheel drive as he navigated the narrow passage. Almost two miles down the road, a large log home came into view. Against the snowy backdrop, the home was spectacular, its rustic appearance like something off the cover of *Architectural Digest* magazine.

Bianca shifted forward in her seat to get a better view. "It's beautiful!" she exclaimed, her eyes flitting back and forth to take it all in.

"The views are magnificent all year round. It's one of my favorite places. The next house actually sits right on the pond. It's the one house I don't usually rent out. I keep it for my personal use. Jarrod and I used to spend weeks up here in the summer fishing and hiking. We have a lot of good memories from here."

"You two have a beautiful relationship. He has great respect for you."

"I'm very proud of my son. He has been a joy and a blessing to me."

"How old was he when you and his mother divorced?"

Ethan tossed her a quick look as he shifted the car into park, leaving it to idle. He took a deep breath, blowing it slowly past his full lips. "He was only eight, maybe nine. His mother and I had joint custody, but she moved around a lot so he spent the majority of his time with me."

"Did you ever think about remarrying?"

"Never found a woman who was able to capture my heart like that."

Bianca nodded.

"Until you," he said, turning to stare directly at her.

Bianca smiled, the feelings sweeping through her warm and fuzzy.

He turned to stare back out the window. "I'm going to leave the car running. This is going to take all of two minutes. I just need to check the thermostats so that the house stays warm enough to keep the water pipes from freezing."

Bianca nodded and, just as Ethan had said, minutes later they were headed back down the drive toward the main road. The ten-minute ride to the next property took almost an hour. There was no denying that the weather was problematic; so much so that Ethan and Bianca both were beginning to question if it was even safe to attempt to head back down the mountain.

"This is not cool!" Bianca exclaimed, one hand clutching the door, the other braced against the dashboard.

Ethan was proceeding slowly, his body tensed as he struggled to keep the car from slipping and sliding about. "No, it's not," he said. "I don't think they expected this storm to come in so fast. From all the reports I listened to, I thought tomorrow was going to bring the worst of it."

"Are we going to be able to make it back to town?" she asked.

There was a momentary pause before Ethan answered. "We'll just take it slow," he said, his tone unconvincing.

He turned off the main road, down another long drive. The roadway was steeper than the last and he revved the engine, shifting gears to keep them moving forward. As they reached the top of the hill, something large stood in the road in their path. Bianca suddenly screamed and she grabbed Ethan's arm, her nails digging into the padding of his winter coat. Startled, Ethan turned the steering wheel abruptly, then over-corrected, losing control of his car as it careened toward the trees. He had barely missed slamming into a large black bear that had reared up on its hind legs.

For a split second, it was as if everything were

moving in slow motion. Snow rushed past the windows, cascading skyward. And then the vehicle slammed forward into a ravine and up against a line of pine trees. The stop was harsh, propelling them both forward, and then just like that there was nothing but silence and the sound of them breathing. Each breath came in short, quick gasps.

"Bianca? Are you okay?" Ethan asked, concern registering in the pitch of his voice.

She was shaking, anxiety sweeping through her body. Her head bobbed up and down as if it were unhinged. "I think so," she said as she pulled at her seat belt, the device having tightened around her torso. "Yeah, I'm okay."

Ethan's gaze swept from one side of the car to the other as he assessed their situation. He turned the ignition to off, shutting down the engine. He reached for his cell phone.

Bianca eyed him anxiously. "Can't you just back up?" she asked, looking about as well.

He shook his head. "No. The tires aren't doing anything but spinning. We're going to have to walk the rest of the way to the house. I don't have any cell phone service so we're going to have to call for help there."

"Walk?" Her look was incredulous, her eyes wide. "Did you not see that bear? It's not safe out there!"

"It's not safe here, baby. This snow is coming down fast. We definitely don't want to get buried under it."

Bianca tossed up her hands, her tone terse. "You have lost your mind! I am not walking anywhere. And I'm definitely not walking out there where a bear can get to me. You better figure out how to send up a smoke signal or something."

"Please, don't be difficult, Bianca."

"Difficult? I'm being smart!"

"Not really, baby."

"Not really, what?"

"Sweetheart, you're not being smart. Because we can't just sit here. There is no one who's coming to get us any time soon. So we really need to get moving."

Bianca bristled, indignation across her face. "Don't call me sweetheart," she hissed between clenched teeth. "And you're not about to make me bait for some crazed animal! I'm *smart* enough to know that! It was a bear, for goodness sake!"

Ethan sighed. He pushed against the door, but it wouldn't budge, the car wedged deep in the snow drifts. "Try your door," he said, shooting her a look.

She met the look he was giving her, but she didn't move, showing no sense of urgency to do anything at all.

He asked her a second time. "Please," he added.

She took a deep breath, then pushed against the door. She pushed once and then twice, throwing her whole body into the effort. A wave of panic suddenly washed over her, the wealth of it furrowing her brow.

Ethan reached a hand out, drawing his palm across her thigh. "Relax," he said. "It's going to be okay."

"It's not going to be okay," she shouted, fear flooding her words. "We're stuck, and if we don't freeze to death, we'll probably be eaten by wolves."

"Which is why we're going to get out of the car and get to the house before it gets dark," Ethan said. "We can handle the bear. We might not be able to handle a pack of wolves."

"Oh, my God!" Bianca muttered, suddenly imagining everything that could go wrong.

Ethan turned the ignition back on, then rolled down the driver's-side window. Bianca watched as he twisted his body about until he could pull himself out of the car. When he was finally standing upright, he walked the perimeter of the vehicle, assessing the extent of the damage. Snow was still falling and in no time at all his head and shoulders were covered in thick, white flakes. He moved back to the window and leaned low, peering inside.

"You're going to have to come out on this side," he said. "I'll help you."

Bianca shook her head. She took a deep breath, then began to crawl over the center console into the driver's seat. Ethan reached his arms out to help her climb out through the window. When she was standing, adjusting to the deep snow beneath her feet, she tightened the hold she had around his waist, hugging him tightly. Ethan hugged her back, the two briefly clinging to each other.

She tilted her face upwards to peer into his. "I'm not good in situations like this," she said, her voice low and soft. "So I'm going to apologize now for my bad behavior."

He nodded. "It's all good. Just stay close. The house is about a mile up the road so we've got a bit of a hike and it's not going to be easy. This snow is heavy and the visibility it bad. It's going to be hard to see."

"What about the bear? What do we do if it comes back?"

"It's not going to come back."

"But what if . . . ?"

Ethan stalled her words by pressing his index finger against her lips. He shook his head. A silent exchange passed between them, no words needed to share what the other was feeling. They hugged again, and then he clasped her hand in his, gently pulling her along beside him.

Although it sat only a few short yards from them, Bianca couldn't fully appreciate the beauty of Ethan's mountainside home. The luxurious log cabin was truly a sight to behold. The timber-framed masterpiece showcased rustic, hand-peeled logs, expansive windows, and exquisite stone work. But Bianca was frozen and exhausted by the time they made their way to the front door.

Inside, Ethan rushed to find blankets to wrap her in, then lit a fire in the stone fireplace. Within minutes, it was raging, the heat abundant as it began to seep into the room. As he moved about checking windows and doors and turning up the thermostats, she watched him, completely enamored. Her teeth were still chattering when he moved to her side, a steaming cup of coffee in hand.

"There's not a whole lot here, but we won't starve," he said. "I hope you like chicken soup and canned spaghetti."

She smiled. "I'm sure we won't be here that long. Will we?"

He sighed, a harsh gust of air blowing past his lips. "The phone service is down and I still can't get a signal on my cell phone. And with the snow they're predicting it might take a day or two for them to get to us."

"Let me check mine," Bianca said as she reached into her pocket for her phone.

"Anything?"

She tossed the device onto the coffee table. "My battery's dead."

Ethan shook his head. "And we don't have a charger."

"So no one knows where we are."

"Well, Jarrod knows, but it might take him a minute to realize something's wrong and come looking for us. But his getting here might be a whole other issue if this storm doesn't let up. Like I said, we might be snowed in something good."

"Well, if we had to be stranded someplace for Christmas Eve," Bianca said, "at least we're stranded someplace pretty."

Ethan smiled, and both of them turned to stare out the massive glass windows. The outside landscape was a pretty postcard in the making.

"I need to get out of these wet clothes," Bianca said, her teeth still chattering. "Please tell me you have hot running water here."

He chuckled. "As much as you need. I can toss your clothes into the dryer while you shower and I'm sure I have a bathrobe around here someplace that you can use until they're dry." He pointed her in the direction of the master bathroom.

She paused in the doorway, throwing him a look over her shoulder. "And I'll have the chicken soup," she said. "I *hate* canned spaghetti!"

In spite of the inclement weather Flight 5271 out of Charlotte arrived on time, landing just before the flight board at the regional airport lit up with cancellations. Jarrod stood nervously in the arrival waiting area, both anxious and excited as he waited for Stefan to disembark. He missed his partner, but despite his excitement at seeing the man again, he was nervous about how his dad would receive his friend.

He'd missed the opportunity to talk with his father and Jarrod was still concerned with how the patriarch

would react once he discovered Jarrod was gay and in
a relationship with another man, but there was no
turning back. Stefan was there in Asheville to spend
Christmas.

Jarrod took another deep breath and dialed his
father's number. He'd been trying to connect with him
for most of the afternoon with no luck. Bianca wasn't
answering her phone either. Jarrod had been glued to
the television set before heading out to the airport and
he knew the snow was hampering travel statewide, with
blizzard conditions at the higher altitudes. Familiar
with how hazardous the snow could be in the mountains near their cabin home, he suspected his father
had sought shelter for the two of them and imagined
he'd hear from one or the other in due time.

Just to be safe though, if he didn't hear from them
and they weren't back by morning, Jarrod made a
mental note to contact the local sheriff near the cabin
home to do a wellness check, knowing it would be
easier for an officer on snowmobile to get up the
narrow trails. After leaving one more voice mail message that he was worried, he turned up the volume on
his ringer and dropped his phone back into his pocket.

The first passengers had begun to make their way
down the carpeted aisle toward the luggage carousels.
Jarrod's heart was beating like a steel drum in his chest.
His palms were moist and his knees were actually quiv-
ering anxiously. He saw Stefan before Stefan saw him,
and a smile blossomed full and wide across his face.
Stefan was his best friend, and he'd missed him more
than he'd realized.

With his blond locks looking windblown and the hint
of a tan to his pale complexion, courtesy of their local
tanning booth, Stefan looked like he should have been
headed to a beach resort and not a winter haven. He

was dressed from head to toe in Armani: black wool pants, a double-breasted cashmere pea coat, and black leather penny loafers. His New York style made him stand out, garnering much attention. But the curiosity didn't faze the man at all. Jarrod envied his boyfriend's confidence and his lackadaisical attitude. It was those qualities that he loved most about him.

Stefan waved excitedly, the two men locking gazes. Both were grinning from ear to ear. Jarrod stepped into Stefan's open arms, hugging him warmly. The embrace was met with curious looks and stares, but neither noticed.

Stefan kissed his lips. "I missed you!"

Jarrod nodded. "I missed you more! How was your flight?"

"I was afraid they were going to cancel it at the last minute. They say this storm is a real bear!"

"You made it. That's all that matters," Jarrod said, his hand gently caressing the man's back.

Stefan looked around. "Is your dad at the house?" he asked.

Jarrod took a deep breath. "I think he's stranded up in the mountains. I haven't been able to reach him or his girlfriend."

"Your father has a girlfriend?"

"It's a long story," Jarrod said. "Let's get your bags and I'll tell you all about it."

Chapter 9

Sharon Torres slammed the phone receiver back onto the cradle, her face twisted with emotion. Her husband eyed her curiously.

"What's wrong? Did Ethan know where the kids are?"

"I didn't speak to Ethan. I spoke to Jarrod."

"Jarrod? I thought he was with Bianca?"

"Well, he's not. He's home. He thinks his father and Bianca are stuck up in the mountains at his father's cabin."

"Why is Bianca up in the mountains with Ethan?"

"That's what I want to know. Seems that our daughter hasn't been seeing Jarrod at all."

There was a moment of silence during which Bianca's parents both drifted off in thought.

"Then who has she been seeing?" her father suddenly asked.

Sharon tossed the man an annoyed look. "Really, Miguel? Do you really have to ask?"

Confusion washed over his expression. He shrugged his shoulders, still unable to put two and two together.

Sharon shook her head, her eyes rolling skyward.

She tossed both her hands up in frustration. "Your daughter has been dating your good buddy," she said finally. "She's been seeing Ethan."

Miguel blinked rapidly as he reflected on her comment. He suddenly burst out laughing, his head shaking from side to side.

"There is nothing funny about this, Miguel!"

"Oh, yes, there is," he said, wiping tears from his eyes.

"Well, I'm not amused. Bianca should know better."

"You can't be mad. Bianca has always done things her own way. You've got to love her! Our little girl has always been a handful!"

"Oh, I can *be* mad, Miguel Torres. I can be *very* mad."

He shrugged, still chuckling. "It could be worse. She could be dating someone like her Uncle Barber."

Sharon bit back a response, fighting not to laugh out loud. She tossed a look into the family room, eyeing her brother, who was asleep in her favorite chair, the television remote in his hand, his feet perched on the coffee table. Barber was family, but he definitely wasn't a good catch for any woman. The family often asked what his wife saw in him, believing that she could have easily done better.

She blew a low sigh. Her husband had a valid point. The real estate mogul was prime property on the marriage market. His philanthropic ventures continually kept people talking and he'd been called one of the area's most eligible bachelors. Ethan Christmas was definitely a good catch, even if he was too old for her baby girl.

When Bianca woke, it took her a quick minute to remember where she was. She lay very still listening

for the two dogs that lived in the house adjacent to
her Raleigh home. There were no familiar yips and
squeaks. Then she listened for her parents' voices, half-
expecting her mother to be talking loudly about
whatever was playing on the morning news. But that
recognizable cackle was nowhere to be heard. It had
been some time since she'd last woken in a house
that was so quiet. But, as she lay in the king-sized bed,
listening for a hint of movement, there was none. The
silence was slightly unnerving.

Sitting upright, Bianca rubbed the remnants of
sleep from her eyes and then remembered where she
was and why she was there. From where she rested, she
had a full view of the rear yard, the expanse of windows
allowing in a wealth of natural light. The outside was
bright and white, snow blanketing everything that it
had landed on. And it was still falling, slower and not
as thick, but coming down as if it had no intention of
ever stopping.

Lying back down against the pillows, she rolled and
pulled her knees to her chest. She'd slept unexpectedly
well. After her hot shower, she'd sat down against the
bedside to catch her breath, and before she'd been
able to even think about counting to ten, she'd been
out like a light, snuggled under a mountain of warm
blankets. Not even the promise of chicken soup had
been enough to keep her awake.

Although Bianca considered herself somewhat ath-
letic and in fairly decent shape, she had never expected
that hiking a mile in a snow storm would have been as
brutal as it had been. But that short walk had completely wiped her out, and she imagined that it had
done the same to Ethan. A smile pulled full across her
face as she thought about him.

Ethan had been her personal superhero. Even when

she had become surly and angry, her frustrations turning her into a snarling, fire-breathing witch, he hadn't blinked an eye. His tone had been soothing, his touch patient, and he'd gone out of his way to make her feel safe and secure. The man was more than she could have ever anticipated and he definitely topped her to-be-stranded-with list.

As she lay there thinking about the two of them together, she realized that there was something brewing between them that actually frightened her. She had never felt for any man what she found herself feeling for Ethan. He had her feeling some kind of way, and despite her efforts to resist the growing emotion, she was completely beguiled. There was a word for the emotion consuming her, but it wasn't one Bianca used readily, the mere mention of the four-letter sentiment enough to send her running. She blew a low sigh, hugging her arms tighter around the pillows she was cradled against.

She suddenly thought about her parents. She could just imagine what her old people had to be thinking. She didn't want them to worry, but she knew there would be much going through their minds, especially when they discovered that she'd stolen off with Ethan and not his son. She anticipated the Christmas fireworks that would ensue would surely outdo any Fourth of July display that she could imagine. Her mother would be ballistic when everything came to light, and Bianca knew it wasn't going to be pretty. With any luck, she'd get most of it out of her system before she and Ethan made it back to civilization.

Sitting up, she took a deep breath and then a second. She tossed her legs off the side of the bed and stood. Tightening the plush terry bathrobe tighter around her naked body, she moved toward the door, headed to search out Ethan.

In the other room, Ethan lay stretched out across the oversized sofa. One leg was hanging over the side and both of his arms were pulled up over his head. A wool blanket was pulled up between his large thighs and over his chest. She stood staring, her eyes dancing over his rugged features. Despite their predicament, he looked comfortable, an air of peace blessing his expression.

The fire was still burning nicely in the fireplace. Moving on tiptoe through the space, Bianca paused in the kitchen, noting the canned soup, ceramic bowls, and empty pot that rested on the counter. He hadn't eaten either and she felt bad. The kitchen was striking with an oversized center island, and gourmet stainless steel appliances. Bianca moved to the pantry, peering inside. The shelves were lined from floor to ceiling with canned goods. The freezer was well stocked too, with an assortment of meats and frozen vegetables inside. She was actually surprised by the various selections. Moving to the refrigerator, she found it practically bare, housing a couple of cans of soda, a bottle of ketchup, and an opened box of baking soda.

Minutes later, the aroma of sausage sizzling pulled Ethan from a deep sleep. He sat upright, rubbing the sleep from his eyes. Tossing off the blanket, he moved onto his feet, stretching his body upright. He took a deep breath and then a second, the savory aroma teasing his senses. He moved to the kitchen door.

"Good morning."

Bianca met his stare, smiling brightly. "Hey! Did I wake you?"

"I needed to get up anyway," he said with a nod. "It smells good in here. What are you cooking?"

Bianca flipped the sausage patties over, then shifted her gaze back toward him. "Sausage and instant grits."

He nodded as he moved to the kitchen's counter and took a seat on one of the bar stools. "Sounds like a meal to me," he said, giving her his own bright smile. "Are you okay this morning?" A quiet concern danced in his eyes.

She nodded, twisting the belt that closed her terry bathrobe. "I'm good. How about you?"

"I followed your lead and took a hot shower," he said. "Then I passed out. Did you come back out to get something to eat last night?"

"No, I fell asleep too."

"We needed the rest."

She tossed him another easy smile as she stirred the pot of hot grits. "You're well stocked. Why do you have so much food?" she asked, curiosity seeping from her gaze.

He shrugged. "I actually spend a lot of time up here. I try to keep the pantry and the freezer stocked. Then, when I come up, all I have to worry about is bringing perishables. Unfortunately, this trip I wasn't planning on needing milk and eggs."

"I found frozen orange juice," Bianca continued, "and there's instant coffee, but I couldn't find any sugar. I didn't know if you drank your coffee black or not."

He pointed to a corner cabinet. "There's a large

red tin on the top shelf. There should be some sugar there."

"Oh, good," Bianca said, clapping her hands together excitedly. "Now we can make snow cream!"

"Snow cream? What's that?"

"You've never had snow cream?"

He shook his head, shifting in his seat as she sat a plate of food down in front of him. He took his first bite as Bianca eased into the seat beside him.

"Snow cream is ice cream made with snow. It's the best!"

Ethan chuckled softly. "That sounds . . . interesting . . . sort of . . . maybe not . . ."

She laughed with him. "It'll be fun. And since it looks like we're stuck with each other, and it's Christmas Eve, we should at least have fun!"

Ethan eyed her, a slight smirk pulling at his full lips. The robe she was wearing had fallen open slightly, the thin belt barely holding the garment closed. Her bare legs were crossed teasingly, and there was just enough cleavage showing to hold his attention.

He licked his lips as he shrugged again, just the slightest shift to his shoulders. Realizing where his eyes were focused, Bianca grabbed the front of the robe and pulled it tighter.

"That is not the kind of fun I had in mind, Mr. Christmas!" She giggled, color flushing her face.

Ethan laughed heartily. "You can't blame a man for hoping, Ms. Torres."

She shook her head. "Eat up! Then we need to get ready."

"Ready? For what?"

"For Christmas. We have to find a tree, make the snow cream, figure out what we're gifting each other."

He laughed again. "I bought you a present, but it's back home."

"I bought you one, too, but since we don't have them, we have to make each other something. We can't wake up Christmas morning without a present for each other."

He grinned. "Make?"

She nodded. "You have to be creative, Ethan."

He smiled, completely smitten with her enthusiasm. "So what do we need to do first?" he asked.

Bianca swallowed the last bite of her breakfast. "First, we need to get dressed so you can stop stealing looks at my boobs," she started. Ethan laughed, and Bianca gave him a look, amusement dancing over her face. "Then we need to find us a Christmas tree!"

Chapter 10

Ethan and Bianca sat together in the living room, winding down from their full day. The fire that burned in the fireplace was raging as the crackling flames illuminated the space. She leaned into his side, her arm looped through his, their legs extended up on a shared ottoman. Soft jazz played in the background, and a full moon outside reflected brightly off the white snow that painted the landscape.

After breakfast, they'd bundled up and gone back out in the weather. There had been a distinctive chill in the air, the atmosphere thick enough to cut like pie. It was eerily quiet, everything hauntingly still. Bianca had been standing in the midst of it, taking it in, when Ethan suddenly pummeled her with snowballs.

The first had hit her backside, and when she'd turned in surprise, the second had landed just beneath her chin. The snow was soft and wet and cold, and then the battle began as she grabbed handfuls of snow and began to pelt him back. They'd laughed, playing like children, ducking behind trees and dodging the clumps of snow that were being thrown.

Play had come to an abrupt end when Ethan had

suddenly tackled her, spilling her down into the damp pile of snow. Lying there with Ethan above her had left her breathless, her eyes locked with his, intense emotions sweeping between them. Fighting the rise of passion, Bianca had twisted awkwardly in his arms, accidently kneeing him in the groin. As he lay beside her, his knees pulled to his chest, excruciating pain had twisted his expression. Eyes wide, Bianca had apologized profusely as she'd helped him to his feet, still laughing at the absurdity.

Once Ethan had recovered from the low blow, they'd searched out the natural setting for their Christmas decorations. A branch now sat in the center of the coffee table, propped in a narrow wineglass. It was a Charlie Brown tree strewn with the pearls that Bianca had worn and two ornate silver tea balls that she had found in a kitchen drawer. A red cloth napkin encircled it like a tree skirt.

Back inside they'd warmed the canned soup, enjoying their afternoon meal with a pack of stale Ritz crackers. Then both had retreated into their own areas to create the gifts Bianca had insisted on. Her excitement was infectious. She'd run from one room to the other, shouting out encouragement and teasing him unmercifully about hers being better than his.

When the presents were done and hidden from sight, they'd gone back to the kitchen and she'd watched as Ethan had prepared dinner. He'd grilled two rib-eye steaks on the stovetop grill and had steamed vegetables in the microwave oven. The meal had been tasty and filling, complemented by a bottle of merlot from his wine collection. Then she'd taught him the intricacies of making snow cream.

"I had to be five, maybe six years old the first time

my mother made me snow cream," Bianca had said, the memories bringing a smile to her face.

They'd gone back outside to collect the perfect snow, enough clean, white, untouched, icy goodness to fill an oversized bowl. She'd poured a can of condensed milk sweetened with extra sugar over the top and stirred in vanilla extract. When the consistency met with her approval, she'd passed him a spoon.

"So how often do you make snow cream?" Ethan had asked.

"Actually, it's been a few years. Mommy would make it all the time when I was younger and it snowed. It was always a lot of fun."

"So why do you give your mother a hard time now? It sounds like you two had a great relationship when you were growing up."

Bianca had paused at the question, a spoonful of sugared ice melting against her tongue.

"It just got too hard to be my mother's daughter. Her expectations didn't mesh with my dreams for myself. I think I distanced myself so I wouldn't be a disappointment." She paused, then spoke again. "I sometimes felt like a disappointment so I think I distanced myself so that I couldn't see it in her eyes." She'd blown a low sigh.

"I don't think your mother has ever been disappointed with you, Bianca. She loves you, and the way she talks about you, she couldn't be prouder."

"Trust me, she'd be happier if I was married with two kids."

"And that's not what you want?"

Bianca's eyes had locked with Ethan's, the two sharing a moment as she reflected on his question.

She'd finally given him a smile, her expression smug

as she pulled another spoonful of creamy goodness into her mouth. "I don't have an issue with being married, Mr. Christmas, but you are too old to be having children."

Ethan had laughed, her comment surprising him. "I beg your pardon!"

"You're in your fifties. If we had children now, you'd be close to seventy when they graduated high school. People would think you're their grandfather."

He'd shaken his head, reaching for her hand. "That shouldn't stop us if that's what you want. I might be close to seventy, but I'm going to be a good-looking seventy, I assure you. Now the question is whether or not you're going to be able to keep up or if I'm going to have to replace you."

"There you go! Already planning to troll the school yard again!" she'd said with a giggle.

"You and Jarrod must be trading notes. He said the same thing."

She'd laughed. "We had a good laugh about it."

The moment had been interrupted by a loud knock on the front door. The two had eyed each other with surprise as Ethan slid off the bar stool and hurried to the front entrance. A uniformed sheriff had stood on the other side, holding a ski helmet in his hand. His snowmobile had been parked behind him.

"Hey, Jack!" Ethan had exclaimed.

"Ethan, good to see you," the man named Jack had said, shaking Ethan's hand eagerly. "Your son called the office and asked us to do a wellness check. I saw your car in the ditch at the end of the road and wanted to make sure everything was okay."

Ethan had nodded. "I appreciate that." He gestured in Bianca's direction and she tossed the man an easy wave of her hand. "We got stranded and the phones are down. I figured it was going to be a day or two before we'd be able to get out of here. But we're good."

"No problems with the power?"

"No, you know all my lines were run underground. Best investment I could have made. Plus, I have the generator if anything does happen."

"Well, I'll call your son back and tell him you're okay. It'll probably be sometime after Christmas before we can get the roads clear enough for someone to get in here to get you. Do you need me to bring you anything?"

Ethan had shaken his head. "No, I think we're okay, but if you'd please tell Jarrod to call Bianca's parents to let them know she's safe, I'd appreciate that."

"No problem," Jack had said.

"Do you want to come in? We can make you a cup of coffee."

"I appreciate the offer, but I need to get back. I need to check on the Johnsons over on highway nine. I know they lost power. Then I need to get home and put together a Barbie playhouse for my baby girl. Santa duties, you know?"

"I understand completely."

"Merry Christmas to you, and I'll come check on you again in a day or two."

"Thanks again and Merry Christmas to you, too!" Ethan had said, standing in the doorway until the man was down the road and out of sight.

As he'd closed the door, Bianca had retreated back into the kitchen, intent on washing and drying the dishes.

Now they sat together in front of the fireplace, enjoying the company and the conversation, sharing their second bottle of wine. It had been a perfect day. Bianca couldn't remember being so overwhelmingly happy. They'd had fun together, enjoying each other as if they hadn't a care in the world. And now, being so close to him had her heated, the intensity of it having nothing to do with the warmth of the room or the fire in the fireplace. Ethan's touch was teasing, his hands gently kneading, his fingertips surging with energy.

"It's almost midnight," Ethan said softly, his hand caressing her forearm. "Another few minutes, and it'll be Christmas."

Bianca snuggled closer against him. "Did you write Santa a letter this year?" she asked, her smile teasing.

He nodded. "I did. I asked him to bring me the prettiest girl in the whole wide world."

She laughed, her expression smug. "Looks like you made Santa's good list this year. Your present came early."

He sat up and looked around the room. "Really? I don't see . . ."

Bianca laughed with him, punching him lightly in the forearm. "Be careful what you wish for Mr. Christmas!"

He wrapped his arms around her shoulders and hugged her close. "Santa done good this year. I have no complaints."

Bianca nodded. "Well, I have a complaint. A big one!"

"Really? What's wrong?"

"I'm still trying to figure out why you haven't kissed me yet, Mr. Christmas. You've seen me in lingerie, you've sung to me, I've cooked you breakfast, and I haven't gotten one toe-curdling, smoldering kiss from you yet."

Ethan laughed, throwing back his head. "I've wanted to kiss you, but you've been keeping me at arm's length. I've just been waiting for permission to make my move."

Her expression was smug. "So you need permission?"

"I'm old fashioned," he responded. "These young boys just dive right in and hope they get it right. But you've got to know a woman wants you there before you take that leap."

She nodded. "So I need to let you know that I want you?"

"That and I need to make sure the timing and the setting are absolutely perfect. It takes a lot to make sure everything's in place so that you get toe-curdling and mind-blowing. Especially with a woman like you, Bianca Torres. You make a man work for it!"

She laughed. "Do I really?"

He turned to face her shifting back in his seat. "Yes, you do. You know you do!" he said emphatically.

"Interesting," she said, her eyes skating.

He leaned toward her. "So, do you want me, Bianca?"

She stared at him, scrutinizing every line in his face. His dimpled smile was engaging, the look in his eyes mesmerizing. She felt her head nodding, a slow up and down. Her answer shimmered in the dark depths of her eyes. Her voice was low, the words a whisper blowing past her lips.

"Yes," she said. "Yes, I want you!"

Ethan's grin widened as he reached for his glass and took one last sip of his drink. He trailed his hand across her profile, the pads of his fingers teasing her nose, her lips down to the curve of her chin. He suddenly stood up, moving to the plush rug that decorated the floor in front of the fireplace. Turning back in her direction, he crooked his index finger at her, beckoning her to him.

Bianca took a deep breath. She hesitated for a brief moment as she stared at him. The man was magnanimous and in that moment everything about the two of them together was sheer perfection. She stood up slowly, easing her way to his side. Standing before him, she gasped as he eased an arm around her waist and drew her to him, his body heated as it connected with hers. His other hand snaked across her back, to the back of her head, his fingers tangling in her hair. She suddenly felt weak, her hands clutching the front of the sweatshirt he wore.

"What time is it?" Ethan asked as he caressed her cheek with his own, his breath warm against her ear.

Bianca blinked, the question pulling her from the stupor she'd been falling into. "Time? What?"

"What time is it?" he whispered again, his hand dancing across her back, teasing the round of her buttocks.

She took a deep breath, her gaze shifting to the grandfather clock. "Almost midnight," she whispered back, distracted back to his touch.

Ethan muttered something incomprehensible, his words muddled in the decadent thoughts that were sweeping through her. He pulled her closer, his face nuzzled in her neck, his lips grazing her flesh as he licked a slow trail from one ear to the other. She panted, her breath coming in stilted gusts. His touch was intoxicating and she was drunk with an unfathomable desire.

The grandfather clock suddenly chimed, the bells ringing for the midnight hour. Ethan clasped his hand against the side of her face. She opened her eyes, shifting her gaze to meet his. His own breath was heavy, his hardened muscles twitching eagerly for attention. He licked his lips slowly, his gaze piercing.

"Merry Christmas, Bianca," he whispered.

She smiled, lifting her lips into the sweetest bend. "Merry Christmas, Ethan!"

And then he kissed her, his mouth connecting with hers in the sweetest kiss imaginable.

The anticipation had been overwhelming, but with that first touch, his lips meeting hers for the first time, Bianca melted. The emotion that had been building and growing between them took on new life, rising like a phoenix to dispel the doubt and reservation that had previously had them both questioning the direction the relationship was headed.

His mouth danced against hers, his lips like plush pillows, and he tasted sweet like sugared grapes and mint. His tongue was teasing, searching, searing. He drew her in, seducing her until she had no other choice but to comply, her desire raging. The intensity between them was overwhelming. Clothes were flung with abandon, and before either could say mistletoe, they were sprawled naked atop the rug in front of the fireplace. Skin kissed skin, touch was met with touch, and the kisses were abundant and sweeping.

There was something exquisite about his touch as he teased and taunted her sensibilities. His mouth followed where his fingers led. Warm breath blew in slow, heated gusts as his tongue twirled and lapped simultaneously. The intensity of each pass of his hand was mesmerizing as he stroked and cupped her breasts, her buttocks and thighs. His caresses were slow and easy as if she were fragile, then intense, him kneading and palming every square inch of bare flesh as if he were kneading life into the sinewy muscles.

He parted her legs easily, Bianca opening herself to him with complete abandon. There were no words to describe the intense sensations sweeping through her limbs. Her body rippled with pleasure, convulsions tensing each muscle as perspiration beaded across her brow. And then he touched her sweet spot, his fingers dancing between the delicate folds of her most precious place. Moans rang loudly through the early morning air, the sound of his breath and hers coming in perfect syncopation.

Ethan paused, murmuring her name against her skin as he called for her to open her eyes and look at him. When she did, the reflection in his dark stare quickened her breath and had her panting heavily. She clutched his broad back, her nails digging into the dark flesh as she pulled him in, willing her body to his as if they were one and the same. She stared, every ounce of emotion shimmering in her gaze and then he entered her, his hardened lines melding easily against her soft cushion.

He made love to her slowly, their connection the sweetest thing either had ever known. Their dance was lyrical, the perfect syncopation of low and high notes as he played her body like a finely tuned instrument. They made beautiful music together, their connection an exquisitely choreographed ballet.

They made love until the flaming logs were nothing but slivered embers. The air in the room had cooled, but neither noticed, their bodies nicely heated. Their loving moved from the carpeted floor to the sofa, across the kitchen counter, against the stained logs that lined the hallway, and into the bedroom, where they finally fell into the bed. The sun was just beginning its ascent in a bright sky. As they finally closed their eyes, their bodies were cradled one against the other. Both smiled as they drifted off to sleep knowing that Christmas had become their new favorite holiday.

Chapter 11

"Aargh!" Bianca screamed, shaking her clenched fists in the air. The tow truck driver looked from her to Ethan and back.

"This is not going to be an argument, Bianca," Ethan said, his tone even.

She stomped her foot, her candy-colored mouth pushed into a petulant pout, and then screamed a second time. "But, Ethan . . . !"

Ethan shook his head, giving the driver a raised eyebrow. He grabbed Bianca's hand and pulled her off to the side, the two of them out of the other man's earshot. "It's not going to happen. I'm not sending you home and catching up with you later. I have spent the last three days making love to you. It was like pulling teeth to get you to agree on a game plan for us moving forward as a couple. So I *will* walk you to your door and have a conversation with your parents and my good friends about our relationship." He took a deep breath.

"Now, you are going to get in that truck before I take you back in the house and spank that delectable behind of yours."

Bianca rolled her eyes and blew a loud sigh. "Promises, promises," she muttered, making an about-face, her arms crossed over her chest.

Ethan smacked her backside, the sting of his palm surprising her. He laughed as she spun back to stare at him, her eyes wide. Her smile pulled slowly across her face.

She shook her index finger at him. "You don't know me that well, Ethan. You better watch yourself."

He laughed heartily. "I know everything I need to know about you, Bianca! I know that I'm never letting you go and I want your family to know that," he said as he leaned to kiss her lips, his tongue slipping past the line of her teeth.

When he broke the connection, she stood with her eyes closed, relishing the tingle of electricity that coursed down her spine. When the sensation passed, she lifted her gaze to meet his. "It's your funeral. I was just trying to save you from the wrath of Sharon Torres," she said.

Ethan laughed as they made their way to the tow truck, on which his car was anchored, and climbed inside.

The driver gave them both a look. "So are we good to go?" the old man asked.

"We're great!" Bianca said as she leaned into Ethan's side. And she meant it. It had been a perfect three days. Making love to Ethan had become the sweetest addiction that she had no intention of ever curing. He'd spent every waking moment teasing her sensibilities and making her feel special. Their time together had been priceless, the memories etched deep in her heart.

As the driver pulled out onto the main road, Bianca tossed one quick glance to the landscape behind them, then settled her eyes on the bracelet that circled her wrist. Ethan's homemade present had been an intricate twisting of old shoelaces, recycled ribbons and a pipe cleaner that he'd braided and knotted into a delicate arm piece. As she twisted it in a circle around her thin wrist, she knew she would cherish it for the rest of her days.

Ethan pressed a warm kiss to her forehead, tightening his arm around her torso. The embrace was endearing, and she suddenly fought the urge to cry. They were a few short minutes from the Asheville city limits, and her perfect holiday would quickly come to a close.

Jarrod and Stefan were in the kitchen when Bianca and Ethan finally found their way back to his home. Both men were sitting in T-shirts and boxers enjoying an afternoon meal of roast beef sandwiches, crinkled potato chips, and chilled bottles of dark beer. Jarrod jumped nervously as the duo made their way into the home, his eyes wide.

"Merry Christmas!" Ethan chimed, Bianca echoing the sentiment. He gave his son a quick hug then extended his hand in Stefan's direction. "It's a pleasure to finally meet you, Dr. Hunter! I hope you've been enjoying your stay."

Stefan shook his hand excitedly. "Stefan, please, and it's a pleasure to meet you, sir. Jarrod's told me so much about you."

Jarrod still stood nervously, twisting a dish rag in his hand. Bianca shot him a look, her head moving from side to side as she introduced herself. Stefan stood to give her a hug. "It's nice to finally meet you, too, Bianca," he said.

"So, did you two have a good Christmas?" Jarrod asked, finally sitting back in his seat.

His father nodded. "We really did. We had an amazing time actually." He gave Bianca a quick wink.

Bianca smiled. "Did you get to my mother's for dinner?" she asked, shifting her attention back to her friend.

Jarrod nodded as he and Stefan exchanged a look. "It was . . . interesting," he said, laughing.

Stefan laughed with him. "Your mother is quite the character," he said "She was very entertaining."

Bianca smiled. "Has she calmed down yet?"

Jarrod shrugged his shoulders. "You're not off the hook, if that's what you want to know." He tossed his father a look. "You're in the dog house too!"

Ethan took a deep breath. "I was afraid of that. I guess we should just go get it over with." He shifted his gaze to his son's friend. "Stefan, will you be here for New Year's? Bianca and I thought we might have a dinner party here to celebrate and exchange gifts since we weren't around to do it Christmas Day." He looked toward Jarrod. "What do you think, son?"

Jarrod nodded as he and Stefan exchanged a look. Stefan's eyebrows were raised, his gaze piercing. Jarrod took a deep breath. "Dad, there's something . . ." he started.

Ethan interrupted. "Maybe you could invite some of your friends. That Madison girl you used to date is home. I'm sure she has a girlfriend that she'd love to introduce to Stefan."

Stefan swiped a napkin across his thin lips and dropped it against his plate. His stare spoke volumes as he turned and focused his gaze on Jarrod.

"Dad, there's something I need to tell you," Jarrod said.

Ethan nodded. "What's up?"

Jarrod's gaze shifted in Bianca's direction, her expression encouraging. He took another deep breath.

"I wouldn't invite Madison or any of her friends. Stefan is already in a relationship."

Ethan cut his eyes to one and then the other. He looked confused. "Okay? That's fine. You say that like there's a problem?"

Jarrod sucked in a second gust of oxygen. He held it briefly before blowing it back out. "Dad, I'm gay and Stefan is my boyfriend. He and I are in a relationship with each other."

The silence that dropped over the space was suddenly palpable, the air so thick you could have sliced and diced it.

Stefan interjected. "I really love your son, Mr. Christmas. Jarrod is my best friend and we're really happy together. And since we've been living together . . ."

Ethan suddenly snapped. "Living together? You two live together?" His tone was harsh, his voice rising slightly. The venom in his tone surprised them all.

"Ethan, it's okay," Bianca said.

His head snapped in her direction. "No, it's not okay!" His eyes swept back to Jarrod. "That's not how I raised you! I raised you to be a man!"

"It doesn't have anything to do with how I was raised, Dad. And I am a man. I just happen to be homosexual. It's just who I am, Dad."

Ethan shook his head from side to side. He turned abruptly. "We have to go see Bianca's parents," he snapped as he headed for the exit, leaving them all standing in shock. He turned back, his eyes on Stefan.

"Be out of my house when I get back. Please." And then just like that he was out the door.

"Well, that didn't go well at all, did it?" Jarrod said, a quiver of hurt in his voice.

Stefan shook his head. "He needed to know. How long have I been telling you that you needed to talk with him?" He tossed his hands up, frustration creasing his brow. "I need to go pack," he said, rising from his seat.

Jarrod suddenly looked frantic. "Where are you going?"

"To a hotel. Your father made it very clear that he doesn't want me here," he said as he headed out the room in the other direction.

Jarrod turned his eyes toward Bianca. "What now?"

Bianca moved to his side and wrapped her arms around him. "Give your father some time. You've known most of your life that you were gay. You expect him to find out and be accepting of it in ten minutes, and that's not going to happen. But he loves you. He'll come around."

Jarrod shook his head, tears suddenly burning behind his eyelids. "I want to believe that, but I'm not so sure."

Ethan sat alone in the car, emotion flooding his spirit. He couldn't believe what he'd just heard, and he wasn't sure how to handle how he was feeling. He had always imagined his only son married with children, a wife and family sharing his adult life. Never in his wildest dreams had he fathomed that Jarrod would ever be in a relationship with another man. But as he sat there thinking about his son and how he was raised, the girls who were always more friend than girlfriend, he had to admit that a small part of him had always wondered. Pushing the thoughts aside, because they hadn't fit the dreams he'd had for his child, had kept him from seeing the truth. He slammed a clenched fist against the dashboard, his brow furrowed with tension.

Bianca suddenly slid into the passenger seat, slamming the door closed. She tossed him a look, her incredulous expression searing. They sat staring at each other for a brief moment, her head shaking from side to side.

"What?" he snapped.

Her torso shifted backward ever so slightly and she eyed him with a raised brow. "Excuse me? I'm not your punching bag so watch your tone."

Ethan blew a heavy sigh. "I don't want to fight with you, Bianca."

"We're not going to fight. But I do have something to say. Your son needs you right now. How could you treat him like that? And you were horribly rude to Stefan."

"Did you know about him and that guy?"

"That guy has a name and yes, I knew. Your son told me."

"So why didn't you say something? How could you let me be blindsided like that?"

"The bigger question is why your son was afraid to be honest with you. That's what you should be asking yourself."

"Don't you think I'm doing that?" Ethan shouted. "Don't you think I'm broken that my son didn't trust me enough to let me help him?"

"Help him? Help him do what? Not be gay? He doesn't need *help* because there's nothing *wrong* with him. He needs to know that you still love and support him. He needs you to at least try and get to know his partner. That's what he needs!" she shouted back. "I cannot believe you're homophobic!"

"I'm not! I just . . . I . . . Jarrod is . . ." he stammered, searching for the right words as he tossed up his hands in frustration.

Bianca shook a finger at him. "Take me home!" she spat. "Now!"

The ride across town was deadly silent. Bianca stared out the window for the entire ride, the radio turned up loud. She was stunned, unable to fathom that Ethan was so closed-minded. The Ethan who had just broken his child's heart was not the Ethan who'd successfully managed to capture hers.

Pulling into the driveway of her family's home, he shifted the car into park, then turned to face her. "Bianca . . ."

"Don't say one word to me," she hissed between clenched teeth. "Not one word!" She jumped out of the vehicle, the door vibrating harshly behind her. He sat watching as she slammed into her parents' home. A full ten minutes passed before he finally pulled himself out of the driver's seat and followed behind her.

Bianca's father met him at the door.

Miguel extended his hand in greeting. "Ethan, come on in," he said warmly. "I just put on a pot of coffee. Would you like a cup or can I get you something stronger?"

"I could really use a scotch," Ethan said as he followed the man into the home's family room.

Miguel chuckled. "Scotch coming up. I guess you've met my daughter's mood swings."

Ethan gave him half a smile. "Something like that."

Sharon sat in her wheelchair, her broken leg extended outward. She waved a hand in Ethan's direction, gesturing for him to take a seat. "Ethan, Merry Christmas!"

"Merry Christmas, Sharon!" He leaned to kiss her cheek. "How was your holiday?"

"Not as eventful as yours, I'm sure."

Ethan nodded. He cast a quick glance around the room.

"She stormed into her room," Sharon said, reading his mind. "Apparently she's not happy with you right now."

He nodded. "I'm not happy with me right now, Sharon. I really . . ."

He paused as Miguel passed him a drink and set a cup of coffee on the table beside his wife.

Sharon crossed her arms over her chest as Miguel took the seat beside her. After taking a quick sip of her beverage, she gestured for Ethan to finish his thought.

"I really want to apologize to you both for not telling you about the relationship that was developing between me and your daughter. Bianca had reservations and I just wasn't thinking. But she's very special to me. I've fallen in love with her and I want to see where we can take this."

Sharon tossed her husband a look before resting her gaze back on Ethan. "Are you sure that's what Bianca wants?"

He blew a deep sigh and shrugged his shoulders. "I'll be honest. I'm not sure about anything anymore, Sharon."

"You're a good man, Ethan. You're also very settled and I couldn't honestly tell you that I think Bianca is ready for the kind of relationship that I think a man like you is looking for. I believe that the age difference between you will prove to be a problem. Bianca has never considered children and by the time she's ready to think about a family you might not want to be bothered. I'm afraid that both of you being in such very different places in your life will prove to be your undoing. If that happens, I don't want to see my daughter hurt."

Ethan nodded. He sat forward, clasping both of his hands together in front of him. He looked from Sharon to Miguel and back. "Make no mistake, I've thought about all of that, and so has Bianca. I've never met a woman like your daughter. She makes me a better man and I like how I am when we're together. I didn't think I could ever be as happy as Bianca makes me. We're not going into this thing blind, trust me. And I promise you I will never do anything to purposely hurt her. Never."

Sharon nodded her head slowly, then suddenly changed the subject. "We had a very nice Christmas dinner. Your son is a sheer delight and we thoroughly enjoyed his friend. Stefan is quite the catch himself!"

Ethan forced himself to smile but said nothing as Sharon continued.

"Ethan, I'm sure you've already discovered that Bianca does what Bianca wants. She's been that way since she was a little girl. Miguel and I have not always agreed with our daughter. Nor have we been accepting of all her choices, but her happiness has always been of utmost importance to us. I'm sure you feel the same way about Jarrod."

Ethan met the look she was giving him, nodding his head slightly.

Sharon continued. "How we react when they do something we don't like will sometimes determine what our children do, but I'm sure you know that as well. Bianca is an adult now. She pays her own bills, owns her own home, and she has never disrespected me or her father. We're very proud of her. And more than anything, we want her happy so if you make her happy then there's not much else we can say."

"Thank you," Ethan said.

Sharon nodded. "As a parent, you know you've done a good job when your child becomes a productive member of society. Miguel and I know that we've done good. And you should know that too. Your son has honored you with his accomplishments. He's made you proud and you love him. But you don't pay his bills and he is standing on his own two feet making us all proud. Just like Bianca, he has a mind of his own and he's bright enough to fight for what makes him happy."

"I may have damaged our relationship."

Sharon shrugged. "It happens. But there's nothing that can't be fixed. Your child loves you and you love him. Y'all will work it out."

With a slight smile, Ethan nodded, reflecting on her comments. "I appreciate that," he said.

Miguel extended his hand. As Ethan shook the appendage, he clasped it tightly. "If you ever call me *dad,* it's going to be on!" he said with a smile.

Ethan laughed, tipping his head.

Sharon rolled her wheelchair backwards, turning to exit the room. "Bianca's mad at you right now. I'm embarrassed to say that she's not very nice when she's mad. Been like that since she was a baby. I suggest you head back home until she cools off. Use the time to make things right with your son. His happiness is just as important as your own," she said as she disappeared down the hall.

Chapter 12

There were tears in her eyes when her mother entered her room, pushing her way through the door without being invited. The two women exchanged a look and Bianca rolled to the other side of her bed, turning her back on the matriarch. "If you came to fuss me out, I'm not in the mood," she said, her tone soft.

Sharon closed the room door. "No, I didn't come to fuss. How was your Christmas?"

Sharon rolled back to look at her mother. She sat upright on the bed. "I thought it was perfect and then we came home."

Her mother smiled. "That sounds about right. Once the honeymoon is over, reality will set in."

"He was horrible to Jarrod!" Bianca cried, repeating what had happened at the Christmas family home. "I can't believe he would be like that."

"Men are funny about their sons. That doesn't mean they don't love them."

"There was nothing loving about what he did to Jarrod. Nothing."

"No one knows that better than Ethan, and trust me when I tell you that he's feeling really bad about it."

"Not bad enough."

Sharon chuckled. "Don't be so hard on that man."

Bianca shook her head. "It shocked me, Mom. I thought I knew him. I trusted him. I didn't expect that he would disappoint me like that."

"You two are still getting to know each other. You might find yourself disappointed a few times. You'll just have to decide how much you're willing to take and if he can redeem himself. It'll be that way with any man."

"I love him. I really love him and he doesn't even know it."

Sharon laughed. "Trust me, he knows. You should have heard him out there begging for our approval."

"He begged?"

Her mother smiled. "Groveled!"

Bianca smiled. "Are you going to give us a hard time?"

Sharon pondered the question for a quick minute. She shook her head from side to side. "Yes!"

Her daughter laughed.

"So does this mean you're moving here to Boone? Will I be able to see you every day?"

Bianca's eyes widened. "Oh, heck no!" she exclaimed. "I'm going back to Raleigh and occasionally I will come up here to visit. And when I can, I'll travel with him on business. We're going to try a semi-long-distance relationship and see where it goes."

"Is that how you young people do it now?"

"He's not young."

"I know that's right!" Her mother laughed. "I'm glad you said it and I didn't have to."

Bianca reached to give her mother a hug and kiss her cheek.

The two women sat talking for another good hour, both catching up on all they'd missed during the three days Bianca had been gone. Hours later, Bianca dialed her phone and waited for Jarrod to answer on the other end.

"Hi, Bianca!"

"Hey! I wanted to check on you. How are you and Stefan doing?"

"We're actually doing really well."

"Did you hear from your father?"

"We just had dinner together. We talked and he actually apologized."

"Your father loves you. It'll work out."

She could sense Jarrod smiling into the receiver.

"He loves you too, so what are you going to do? I think he's really afraid that he's going to lose you."

She smiled. "I'm not going anywhere. Not anytime soon anyway."

Jarrod laughed. "I like you two together. You keep him on his toes."

"He keeps me on mine."

"Why don't we meet up sometime tomorrow and talk about the New Year's party? I still think it would be a good idea."

"I do, too. Let's try to get together for lunch."

"That's a plan. Bring Dad with you."

"You all aren't at the house together?"

"No. Stefan and I thought it would be better if we stayed at the hotel tonight."

Bianca nodded, forgetting that he couldn't see her. Her mind was suddenly racing.

"You still there?" Jarrod asked.

"Yeah, I was just thinking about your father."

On the other end, Jarrod smiled. "I'm sure he's thinking about you, too!"

* * *

The doorbell surprised Ethan. He wasn't expecting company and had just settled down for the night. He sat rereading the homemade present Bianca had surprised him with on Christmas morning. The gift made him smile every time he looked at it. Bianca had cleverly crafted a picture book bound with ribbon. Each page captured a stick-figure representation of him and her and the things Bianca envisioned between them. There was them playing in snow. Them dancing beneath a full moon. Them standing in front of their first home. And, on the last page, the two of them with three little stick-figure babies by their side.

Between rereading the book, thinking of ways to make amends, and missing her, he'd been trying anxiously to reach Bianca, annoyed that she had yet to answer her phone. He was desperate to apologize, to share that he'd reached out to Jarrod and had apologized to Stefan and was willing to admit that he'd been wrong. To say that he was committed to doing better.

Pulling himself out of his bed, he grabbed his bathrobe and hurried to the front door. Throwing on the porch light, he peeked out the side window to see who it was. He took a step back as a smile spread full across his face. Undoing the locks he pulled the door open.

Bianca stood on the other side, bundled in an oversized fur coat with an attached hood. "What took you so long? It's cold out here," she said as she eased past him.

He grinned. "I was in bed."

"Alone?"

He nodded as he relocked the door. "You have to ask?" he said, turning toward her.

"You never know about these things."

"You know there's no one else who would be in my bed." He took a deep breath. "I love you. No one but you."

Bianca smiled. "I do know that. And since I couldn't have you here all by yourself I had to come over. I had something I wanted to give you."

His eyes danced across her face as mischief shimmered in her eyes. She took a step back, moving to the center of the room. Her movements were slow and deliberate as she undid one button of her coat and then the second. When they were all undone, she pulled the garment open and let it drop to the floor. Naked beneath the outer garment, Bianca stood in nothing but a red bow that was wrapped around her waist and thigh-high black suede boots.

"I love you too, Ethan," she whispered, a come-hither expression washing over her face. "Now come get your gift, Mr. Christmas!"

Bianca's Snowcream

Ingredients

1 can of Evaporated Milk
2 teaspoons Vanilla Extract
3 cups Sugar

Directions

Chill a large glass or metal bowl in freezer for fifteen minutes. Mix evaporated milk, sugar and vanilla extract in chilled bowl. Add clean, powdery snow until thick and creamy. Enjoy!

Don't miss Deborah Fletcher Mello's

Playing For Keeps

On sale in November 2015!

Chapter 1

The employees at the Glenwood Avenue Starbucks greeted Malcolm Cobb by name. It was just past five-thirty in the morning and their cheery demeanors always amazed the man. He had finished his morning run ahead of schedule and was one of the first in line to get his coffee to kick off his day.

"Will you be having your usual today?" a young woman named Allison asked.

Malcolm nodded. "I will, Allie."

The girl gave him a bright smile. "One venti caramel macchiato, skim milk and extra caramel, coming right up!"

Malcolm nodded. "Thank you."

"We had a great time at your nightclub this past Saturday," another Starbucks employee chimed in as he blended coffee and cream into an oversized container. "I took my girl and her sister. They're still talking about it!"

"I appreciate that," Malcolm said as he moved from the order lane to the pickup counter. While he waited, he made conversation with the staff and the man in line behind him. The morning chatter was casual and easy as they caught up on their weekend endeavors and mused over the news headlines.

Malcolm looked across the room as the bell chimed over the entrance door, announcing a customer's arrival. His eyes widened as he caught sight of the woman coming through the door. He knew beyond any doubt that the full-figured beauty was a woman who garnered a lot of attention when she came into a room, because she definitely had his.

She had an air of sophistication and glamour that few other women he knew possessed. She was dressed in a formfitting dress that showcased her voluptuous curves and four-inch pumps, and she carried a high-end leather bag across her arm. Her hair was abundant, a healthy mass of natural curls that cascaded past her shoulders. Her makeup was meticulous and flattering to her biracial-brown complexion. She actually took his breath away, and it was only when the Starbucks employee called for his attention that he realized he was staring.

"Mr. Cobb, is there anything else we can get for you?"

Malcolm's head snapped around as he pulled his attention back to the young employee looking at him with a bright smile across her face. He nodded. "Yes, there is something you can do," he said as he leaned over the counter, his voice dropping to a whisper. "Charge my credit card for that woman's order. Whatever she wants."

Allison looked toward the end of the line. "The woman in the blue print dress?" she asked.

Malcolm nodded. "Yes."

The girl smiled. "Not a problem, sir."

Moving out of the line, Malcolm took his macchiato and a cinnamon Danish to a corner table. Settling down in his seat, he watched as the woman placed her order. As she reached into her handbag for her wallet, Allison pointed in his direction. He smiled and waved a slight hand.

Cilla Jameson had noticed him when she'd entered; the handsome stranger had caught the eye of a few women in the room. She'd barely given him a second glance though as her mind had been elsewhere, too many thoughts racing through her head. Foremost was whether or not she had paid her credit card bill and if her card would be accepted when they swiped it to pay for her morning coffee. She was desperate for a good cup of coffee. His generosity was a welcome blessing.

She studied him curiously. She recognized him from somewhere but was having a hard time remembering where. It wasn't often that she couldn't remember a handsome face when she saw one, and the man was definitely handsome. He was tall and dark, his beautiful complexion smooth and clear like black ice. He had a slim build, but he was fit. From his running shoes, shorts, and sweat-stained shirt, she reasoned he'd either just left the gym or finished a long run. His jet-black curls were cropped low and close to his head, the precision cut and meticulously lined edges flattering to his face. There was an abundance of attitude shimmering in his dark eyes and a bad-boy aura that surrounded him. If a stranger picked up the tab for her morning meal, she was thankful he was a good-looking stranger.

Picking up her order, she crossed over to where he sat, a bright smile across her face. "Thank you. That was very kind of you," she said, nodding her head in appreciation.

Malcolm smiled back as he gestured to the empty seat on the other side of the table. "Do you have a minute to join me?"

Cilla hesitated for a brief second before she said, "I

think I do have a minute." She placed her beverage on the table top. She was only slightly surprised when he stood up and moved behind her, pulling out her chair. She tossed him a quick look over her shoulder. "Thank you."

He nodded as he sat back down. "My name's Malcolm. Malcolm Cobb."

"It's a pleasure to meet you, Malcolm. I'm Priscilla Jameson, but everyone calls me Cilla."

"Cilla . . . that's a beautiful name."

She smiled. "I keep thinking that I know you from someplace, but I can't figure out where."

"Did you go to school here in Raleigh?"

She shook her head. "I was born and raised in Charlotte. But I graduated from UNC–Chapel Hill."

"I went to school here. I did my undergrad at Shaw University and my graduate work at NC State. I studied industrial design and engineering."

"I majored in pre-law, but I'm working in pharmaceuticals at the moment."

Malcolm smiled. "I'm not sure how to take that," he said, the hint of laughter in his tone.

"I don't deal drugs if that's what you're implying," Cilla said with a slight roll of her eyes. "I'm a healthcare administrator for a biotech company in Research Park."

"Well, I own a nightclub downtown."

Cilla snapped her fingers. "That's where I know you from. You and your business partner were featured in the *News and Observer*."

Malcolm smiled. Since its grand opening, the nightclub had been featured in the local newspaper a number of times. Most recently, word of their success had reached a national level, The Playground being named a must-stop on things to do in Raleigh, North Carolina.

Co-owned with Romeo Marshall, his best friend and fraternity brother, their night spot was the place to be and both of them, the men to know. The success of The Playground had propelled them right into the spotlight. "It wasn't a good picture," he said. "They didn't get my best side."

Cilla laughed. "So which is your best side?"

"The one they didn't show."

There was a moment of pause as the two sat grinning foolishly at each other.

"So, your club is a jazz and blues bar, right?" Cilla asked.

"It is, with a hint of R and B and soul." He reached into his pocket for his wallet and pulled a business card from inside. "If you have some time, maybe you can stop by," he said as he passed it to her.

She studied it momentarily. "The Playground . . . sounds like it would be a good time."

"It will be," he said, his tone smug. "I'll be there."

She smiled. "You don't know when I'm coming."

He shrugged. "I'm always there, so you can't miss me."

Cilla took a quick glance down to her wristwatch. She took one last sip of her morning brew. "Thank you again for the coffee. I really appreciate it."

He stood up with her. "I'm here every morning, same time," he said. "In case you're interested in another cup."

Cilla laughed, the soft lilt of it stirring a wave of heat through Malcolm's spirit. "Always here, always at the club, doesn't sound like you have any time for much else," she said.

Malcolm's mouth pulled into a seductive grin. "I would make time for you, Cilla Jameson."

GREAT BOOKS, GREAT SAVINGS!

When You Visit Our Website:
www.kensingtonbooks.com
You Can Save Money Off The Retail Price
Of Any Book You Purchase!

- All Your Favorite Kensington Authors
- New Releases & Timeless Classics
- Overnight Shipping Available
- eBooks Available For Many Titles
- All Major Credit Cards Accepted

Visit Us Today To Start Saving!
www.kensingtonbooks.com

All Orders Are Subject To Availability.
Shipping and Handling Charges Apply.
Offers and Prices Subject To Change Without Notice.